D1524332

CONTENTS

THE KING'S SORCERER

By B.T. Narro

Jon Oklar:
Book 1

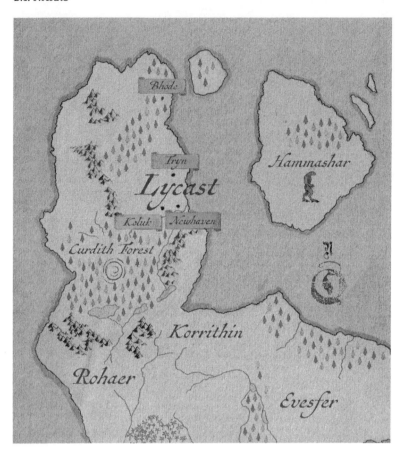

CHAPTER ONE

I'd felt this energy buzzing in my mind since I was twelve years old. It had been six years now, and I couldn't take the mystery anymore. I had to know what it was. I'd come to the city of Tryn a week ago. I had told myself that if I couldn't find someone here who could explain this strange feeling, I was going to travel to the capital next.

It had been a long trip to the city from the small town of Bhode, where I was born. I'd left before winter to ensure the snow didn't stop my horse from completing the three-hundred-mile journey. The only reason I hadn't left sooner was because of news that had reached Bhode just a few months prior. There had been a rebellion against the king.

Apparently he had been preparing for war, but his people had turned against him. Now he was dead and someone else was king. I knew little about it, except that the kingdom was safe for a young man like myself to travel without fear of being swept up in a war.

That was the only benefit to being so far removed from the rest of the kingdom. The small number of us in Bhode were mostly immune to all of the political drama. However, I had no plans to return to the place where I'd lived my whole life. There was nothing left for me there anymore.

I knew little about the woman I was to meet today.

She was a sorcerer named Scarlett, and she would speak to me sometime this evening. I was to wait in this tavern, where I had lingered nervously for the last hour. I had purchased a mug of ale so as not to look suspicious. Now I stood against one wall of the common room, somewhat close to the door, the air filled with joyous chatter.

I knew there was nothing wrong with my curiosity. I had not committed a crime, but discussion of the magical arts in Tryn made people uneasy. It would be foolish for me to think that the lord of this city did not take the investigation of sorcerers seriously.

I still wasn't sure if I had it in me to be one someday, but I had always wanted to find out. I didn't know how much truth there was to the stories of the magical arts. Apparently they could be used to perform many impressive spells, from providing water to dry crops to enchanting swords with some kind of enhanced ability. If this was something I ultimately could be capable of, I had best find out sooner rather than later.

Eventually I saw a woman enter who glanced around as if looking for someone. She located me a moment later. She had her red hair tied back in a tail. There was a twinkle in her green eyes as she looked at me pointedly, as if she had much she wanted to say. She was older than me by at least five years, but there was a youthful beauty to her unblemished face. I lowered my head in a slight bow as she approached.

"You must be Jon Oklar," she said as she offered her hand for a shake.

Her palm was rough to the touch. "And you must be Scarlett." I hadn't been told her surname and didn't think she would give one if I was to ask. There was no reason to even trust that Scarlett was her true name.

I had been asking about the magical arts to anyone who seemed like they might know something, including city guards. I had wanted to show them especially that I had nothing to hide. It wasn't long after that an older man I had not met before approached me in the street and told me to be at this tavern at this time to meet a sorcerer named Scarlett.

I had contemplated skipping the meeting for my own safety, but I figured that if I was to be arrested it would've been done without any clandestine theatrics. Again, I had not broken any laws. Inquiring about sorcery was not illegal.

"You've been stirring up some trouble," Scarlett told me with a wry smile. "I presume you were not born around here."

"I arrived from Bhode just recently."

Her brow furrowed. "I've never heard of it."

"It's a small town far north."

"Why did you leave?" she asked.

I was a little surprised by her sudden question. I wanted to ask her why it mattered, but she had information that I wanted, and I had nothing in return. I was not in control of this conversation.

"I didn't have much reason to stay after my father died," I answered.

"What about your mother?" Scarlett asked, stepping a bit too close for comfort. I figured it was only because of the noise in this tavern and not any romantic interest on her part, given the difference between our ages.

"Tell me about yourself first," I tried. "Are you a sorcerer?"

"Yes. I'm a mage."

"Is that different from a sorcerer?" I asked.

She showed me a little smile that seemed to be forgiving me for what I was beginning to think was a stupid question.

"Who do you work for?" I asked.

She spoke with an exaggerated lilt. "Why the lord of Tryn himself, Byron Lawson."

Even though I had only come here two weeks ago, my father had spoken about Byron Lawson. I felt as though I knew the man well. My father's relationship to the lord of Tryn was one reason I was not as scared about "stirring up trouble," as Scarlett had put it.

"You know him?" Scarlett asked.

I nodded. I was about to answer how, but her mouth dropped open.

"Jon Oklar...as in the son of Gage Oklar?" She let out one loud "ha!" Then she put her hand on my shoulder. "I was beginning to think you were just a simple-minded young man who, with that face, was used to getting what he wanted. But now I'm beginning to see there's much more to you."

I might've been flattered about her comment toward my looks, but someone entered the tavern and looked right at me over Scarlett's shoulder. There was recognition in his gaze, though we had never met. He stomped toward me with burning aggression in his dark eyes.

He was on the taller side, about my height. And although he didn't have the same mass to his shoulders and arms as I did from all the years of sparring in sword and hand combat with my father, I feared him. He had the confidence of a drunken goon looking for a fight but the robes of a rich man, with his fancy blue cloak billowing behind him.

The man stopped behind Scarlett and seemed to be just barely in control of his anger.

Scarlett lost her smile and let out her breath as if sensing him behind her. She slowly turned around.

"Did I not tell you, mage," said the man, "that recruits were to be sent directly to me?"

"I only just met him!"

A sense of alarm shot through me. I looked past the older man at two armored guards entering the tavern. They took their places just behind the man who was now leaning over Scarlett. The place quickly quieted. Soon everyone's gaze was on us, murmurs quickly spreading.

I didn't understand why I was being spoken about as if I belonged to either of them, but the word "recruit" was what put a fire into my legs. The thought of running was short-lived, however. It would be hard enough to get around the four of them in my way. Even if I did, I doubted I could escape one or possibly two sorcerers.

"You can leave now, mage," said the man to Scarlett.

She started toward the door, but then stopped to look back. "Treat him well, Barrett," she said. "You don't want to make another powerful enemy."

The older man swept his gaze across the tavern. Everyone who was looking earlier pretended not to have noticed anything as they returned to their conversations. I waited for the man to speak, but he appeared to be content to move his head around me like a dog trying to pick up the scent.

He had gray hair trimmed short and neat. His wiry

mustache was black, but it faded to gray as it melded into his groomed beard. His dark eyes looked like they held a plethora of secrets, some I probably wanted to know, but many more I probably didn't.

I was beginning to understand something I wish I had known before. Although there was a magical art form that was illegal, this was not the reason that the people of Tryn chose not to speak about these arts. It was probably out of fear that someone like this man would treat them like a recruit. But a recruit for what? That's what I needed to know.

Seemingly content with whatever he sensed around me, the man leaned back and put on a false smile. "My name is Barrett Edgar. I work closely with King Nykal."

So that was the new king's name. Barrett appeared disappointed, presumably because I did not say I was honored to meet a man of such high rank. My father had told me about kings, lords, and noblemen. There were few of them where I came from, and my father said we were better off because of it.

"Tell me what you're doing here," Barrett demanded.

"I just came to learn more about sorcery."

"Because you feel something," he said.

"You heard?"

"No. I can feel it on you as well."

Part of me couldn't believe I was here speaking about this to someone so influential in the kingdom. I had hoped that it would be a moment much less important to my future that would start to reveal sorcery to me, not that I would get the attention of the king's councilman.

My mother didn't make it after childbirth. My father was my closest friend, but he died a little more than a year ago from an illness. We had one healer in our town, a monk who recommended prayer above all else. Before my father passed, I had tried to convince him that we should move to the city where he had spent most of his life. It wasn't the northern cold that bothered me the most. It was what the townspeople lacked.

No one knew a lick of truth about the magical arts, and no one knew about the illness that eventually took my father's life. This ignorance, including my own, had been a source of powerful rage. After a very long year, I left on the anniversary of my father's passing.

My father, Gage Oklar, had been an expert swordsman and was the head guard for the lord of this city until he retired and moved north with my mother. They had me soon after. With the passing of my mother, my father was the one who taught me everything. He often boasted to our neighbors that I absorbed anything and everything I could, but eventually I reached a point in my life when I wanted to find out more than he could teach me. Specifically, I needed to know what this energy was that I could grasp and hold out in front of me. I could feel it buzzing, vibrating. It was like moving a cloud that held a lightning bolt. Through all my willpower, however, I couldn't figure out how to use it.

The stories of sorcery drove me mad. There were many summers in which the whole town of Bhode wished for rain. I witnessed many prayers and rituals in which the people of my town hoped to influence the elements, never with any luck. But there really *was* a way to control the elements, and more. My father had seen sorcery here in Tryn. The magical arts were real, and I knew this energy within me was real as well.

"Can you tell me what it is?" I asked Barrett.

"What do you plan to do after you find out?"

That depended on many things that I wasn't prepared to divulge to this politically, and possibly otherwise, powerful man. I wanted to explore Tryn as well as the capital, Newhaven. I wanted to see the castle at the center of the large city. Then I wanted to enter Curdith Forest and witness for myself if the rumors I'd heard about the huge, twisted trees and exotic and dangerous wildlife were true.

I didn't have much coin left, however, so I needed to find work soon. I had planned to speak to the lord of Tryn about joining the governing force as a constable. I was certain that my surname of Oklar would at least allow me to demonstrate the combat skills my father had taught me. I was young, at eighteen, but I was somewhat tall and very strong. Even if the lord of Tryn didn't need me, I was certain I would find work elsewhere. I had been happy to arrive in Tryn, considering all the options it provided me. I had just wished my father was here with me.

Even a small portion of this was too much to reveal to someone I had just met. I figured Barrett probably already knew about my father and expected I had at least some skill with sword. He could've been lying about this energy he claimed to feel near me, just to get me to sign some contract. There were certain agreements made by a certain type of sorcerer in which you were bound to the contract you signed. You could not ignore it even if you tried. My father had not witnessed anything like this, but he told me they did exist.

When I'd asked how he found out, he'd told me, "The lord Tryn had referred to them many times. Binding contracts, they're called, made with magic."

Not only was sorcery extremely rare, but it was guarded by those who knew about it. Apparently, there was one way of using the magical arts that frightened not just the commoners but even other sorcerers. I still had no idea what it could do or why it was illegal.

"I'm not looking to fight in some war," I said.

"I'm not here to force you."

I wasn't sure I believed him. "I think it's time you tell me what this is." I grabbed the energy with my mind and held it out in front of me. I couldn't see, smell, or hear it, but something told me that it was there. It was part of me.

Barrett looked right at the invisible vibrating thing that wanted to break out of my mind's grasp. Part of me wondered if he might be able to see it, the way his eyes narrowed and a little smile formed with the crinkle of his beard.

"That is called a note of mana, specifically 'Upper F,' or 'uF' for short. It is a very valuable note for many reasons, but you won't be able to cast anything with it without training."

I let it go. It was difficult to hold onto for long, but I always felt it somewhere in my body even after I released it. I couldn't quite pinpoint its exact location. When I focused on it within my chest, it was there. When I focused on it within my mind, it was there as well. It either moved around or it existed everywhere I searched for it. It seemed to be as much a part of me as my blood.

Barrett turned to address the two armored guards behind him. "Prepare the carriage. I will be leaving soon."

One gave a nod before both of them left.

Barrett looked straight at me. "There are many people like you who began to feel a note of mana like this in their early teenage years, but most have forgotten the feeling by the time they're your age. I don't know why it is that you have focused on it and even strengthened it over all this time, but you have."

I went from confused to enthusiastically greedy for more information. I had many questions, but I still wasn't sure he could be trusted. His impatient tone gave me the impression that he was ready to leave without me.

"What does 'Upper F' mean?" I asked.

He gave a resigned sigh. I saw now that the tavern had mostly emptied out. Perhaps I should've run off as well, but I had come this far just to speak to someone like this. I at least had to hear a little more.

"It's part of a language that is used to discuss spell craft. I understand that is something you're very interested in." He leaned forward ever so slightly. "If you come with me, you will learn everything you want to know."

My heart skipped in my chest. I had figured this offer would come, but I still was not prepared for it.

I swallowed the lump in my throat and asked, "And what do I have to give in return?"

"Nothing."

It had to be a lie. "I must be required to perform some service."

"The king is not the kind of man to make the same

mistake as the last king. He would never force his citizens to endanger themselves against their will in some form of military service. It was the current king, Nykal Lennox, who led the rebellion against the late king, Oquin Calloum, because of the danger Oquin brought upon the kingdom of Lycast."

He looked at me as if that should be enough to convince me, but it wasn't.

"Where would we be going?" I asked.

"First, you are to be tested at the castle, Jon Oklar. Depending on the results you achieve, a number of options will be provided to you. This is an opportunity that has only been offered to eight people now, including you, and all others have accepted enthusiastically. They are on their way to the castle right now, where all of you are to meet each other. You will be arriving a little late, because I only recently found out about you, but you will not have missed anything vital."

Barrett sounded eager to leave. Too eager, like he was getting the best part of the deal. And yet, I had offered nothing.

Or perhaps he was ready to give up if I did not agree here and now. I believed him that this was an opportunity, but I knew there had to be more to it than he let on.

"How did you know to find me here?" I asked.

"There are many people who know something about sorcery and are loyal to the king. We received a message from one of them."

"Someone who isn't Scarlett."

"That is correct. She was going to take you down a different path. She cares only about this city and the immediate threats to the people here. I, on the other hand, have the entire kingdom to worry about. If you wish to remain in Tryn for the rest of your foreseeable future and learn from an amateur mage, then you may find her again. But if you wish to be part of something greater, as I sense you do, then you will come with me to the castle and meet the king himself."

I still had many questions, like what Scarlett meant earlier about Barrett making another powerful enemy. There was a lot to take from that single statement, but I wasn't going to lie to myself any longer. I knew I would be following this man to the castle. I could ask more questions on the way.

"I'll pack my things."

"Excellent," he said with a victorious smile.

CHAPTER TWO

Barrett's two guards followed me to the inn where I had been staying. I needed to figure out what I would do after I arrived at the capital. If this didn't turn out to be the opportunity Barrett had made it out to be, then I needed a plan.

There was a more immediate problem, however: my horse. I had purchased my mare from an older gentleman in Bhode. He'd no longer needed the animal after his daughter married and left the town. She'd been the only one who'd taken care of the horse, a quiet woman who was older than me but who I never got to know very well.

There was another young woman who I spent more time with—a few weeks of confusing, kindled romance in the midst of it—though she had a childlike tantrum and even threw a fork at my head when she found out I was leaving for good. I supposed she thought we would marry, and I do know why. She was the only girl around the same age as me. We never got along that well, though, and I had stopped showing any passion for her when my father had started to become ill.

I would've liked to bring my horse with me to Newhaven, but she was quite finicky and unused to the reins of a carriage. When I mentioned her to the guards, I was told that Barrett was already off finding a new home for her. She would be taken care of and given back to me if I wished to return here. I figured that meant he was handing her off to Byron Lawson, the lord of Tryn.

It seemed that Barrett was in a rush when we were about to leave. "Everyone will have already arrived by the time we do," he told me as he opened the door to the carriage for me. "They will be waiting."

I had hoped to speak to Barrett more during the trip, but he closed the door and did not join me in the carriage.

The curtains were already drawn when I entered. I started to open them, but Barrett told me, "Keep them shut and stay quiet." Then I heard him climb into place to drive the carriage.

It would be a full day of travel, with breaks for the horses. Everything I owned was with me. I had a cloak and a warm tunic that had seen me through the harsh winter last year, but most of my other clothing didn't fit as well as it used to years ago. I wanted to replace some of the tighter shirts, but I only had six buckles and five pennies left. It wasn't much. A loaf of day-old bread in Tryn was one penny, and the room at the cheap inn I had chosen cost five a night.

Two possessions of mine that would not change hands anytime soon were my two swords. My father had brought them from Tryn to Bhode when he moved there with my mother. They were finely crafted, managed well by us over the years and actually hardly used, I was realizing, as I now thought about them again. I remembered fighting pretend opponents with my sword more often than actually striking anything, and my father hadn't done much with his.

My father and I had sparred with wooden practice swords instead. They were both worn down worse than some of the old pennies that the townspeople of Bhode traded back and forth. I hadn't seen a reason to bring them with me, so I'd left them behind, along with a few other things I would never see again, like my father's clothes. I knew some people cherished mementos of loved ones, but just about everything reminded me of him already. A shirt wasn't going to change anything. He was still gone.

The hours passed by as I sat alone in the carriage. I was tired of long journeys, even if this one was only going to take a day. I didn't see myself returning to Tryn anytime soon. I had barely explored the city, but it was the capital and the forest near Newhaven that interested me more. Curdith Forest probably wasn't any different than the woods in my backyard, but there was history to the southern forest.

Neighbors of mine in Bhode, an older husband and wife who were Formationists, liked to talk about Basael and the demigods. They often used the gods to answer any question my young mind could come up with about sorcery. I remembered one time sitting in front of the old couple's fireplace, completely entranced, as the man and woman told me story after story about each of the demigods. My father had ridden out of town that day, I can't remember why. But I would never forget how excited I was to tell him everything I had learned.

My father had a thick beard that, when he frowned, crinkled in a way that sapped my gleeful wonder like wrapping me in a wet towel. He'd told me that none of these stories could be taken as fact and that I should forget them. He also made sure to leave me with different neighbors the next time he had to go somewhere alone, which wasn't very often.

I'd spent most of my days beside my father, and I did forget all of the tales about Basael and his demigods, except for one important thing. It was something even my father agreed to be fact.

Very long ago, all elves used to live in Curdith Forest, but something monumental flew down from the stars and struck the middle of the forest. The destruction was so great that it was called the Day of Death. The small number of elves who survived traveled south and made a new home far away, in Evesfer. They still lived there, in a forest city called Dreil, where humans were not welcome.

After the Day of Death, Curdith Forest was destroyed. It's been said that there is still a great crater in the center of the forest, but no one has seen it for lifetimes. These days, the forest was dense with strange trees that could not be found anywhere else on Dorrinthal, but it was really the bloodthirsty beasts of the forest that prevented anyone from making their way to the crater.

It was my father who told me all of this, which led me to believe even now that it had to be true. Gage didn't believe in these types of events unless he had good reason. It was Curdith Forest and the strange things he had seen there that made him and my mother choose to travel away from it and raise me in a place they deemed to be safe. That, and the surge of illegal sorcery. At least that's what he'd told me. Whenever I asked more about this illegal sorcery, he said he didn't know anything about it, only that the people who used it were dangerous. It didn't seem like my father to run from something he didn't understand, but eventually I stopped asking about it.

Their deaths, both of which I believe were preventable at the hands of a good healer, demonstrated to me just how wrong they were about moving for reasons of safety. It is not safer to be so far removed from the rest of the world unless you believe man to be inherently dangerous. It was one subject in which my father and I always disagreed. He told me war was inevitable. If two men with crowns atop their heads wanted to send thousands of soldiers at each other, there was no stopping them.

He didn't live long enough to hear about the rebellion. The people of Lycast had stood up to and even killed their own king when he'd tried to send them off to war. Barrett had mentioned that the current king had led this rebellion to fruition. I wondered if my father had heard of this man, Nykal Lennox.

We rode through the night. I made a pillow out of my clothing and slept through most of it.

I awoke later in the morning as we came to a stop.

"Jon, you may leave the carriage," Barrett announced.

I heard the sound of a river nearby. I opened the carriage door and had to shield my eyes from the morning sun. Winter was coming, and yet there was no sign of it that I could feel. By now in Bhode, there was a chill to the air that the sun could not break. But here, the only thing in the air was the fresh smell of grass, and water, and...horse manure. I wrinkled my nose as I glanced at one of the animals relieving itself.

"You may rinse your face in the river if you wish," Barrett said. "We'll arrive in a few more hours. Your breakfast can be eaten in the cariole, but don't make a mess."

I looked south with my hand over my eyes. The road to Newhaven was clear. Strewn across the land were large farms, where horses and cattle grazed. I thought I could spot Newhaven near the coast, a speck of gray between the rolling hills.

I strolled toward the river with a smile on my face. It was a lovely day. This weather was rare in Bhode during this time of the year.

"Be quick," Barrett called after me.

I knelt down over the stream of clear water and washed up. I was just about done when Barrett started calling to me again.

"Come back. Quickly! Come on!"

With cold water dripping down my face, I hurried back toward the carriage. "What's wrong?"

"Quiet. Get in." He held the door open.

I looked around with worry.

"Get in!" he repeated.

I saw one woman waving to us from no less than a hundred yards away. She had come out of her farmhouse and spotted us.

"What? You're worried about her?"

One of the guards, who still wore much of his steel armor, started to push me into the open carriage.

"All right!" I said. "I'm getting in."

The guard let go and allowed me to step into the cariole on my own. I turned around before they shut the door.

"What are you worried about?"

But Barrett closed the door abruptly, forcing my head back.

"You are not to be seen by anyone," Barrett said

from outside. "It will be explained later."

But plenty of people in Tryn had seen me speaking with Barrett and then leaving in one of his carriages. I supposed it was the people around Newhaven whose gazes he feared more. I didn't understand why, but I had a lot of time to figure it out.

The most dangerous answer was that he planned to do something to me in which witnesses would be a problem. But if something was going to happen it would've been during the night, away from both cities. Barrett didn't mean to harm me.

It was probably what I had assumed from the beginning. He planned to use me somehow, but why could I not be seen if that was the case? Probably because whatever he wanted me to do was not something he wanted people to know about. There was some solace in the idea that there were seven others just like me who I would meet soon. This was an opportunity for all of us, Barrett had said. It might've been foolish to think so, but I believed him, at least for now.

Really, anything was an opportunity compared to living out the rest of my life in Bhode, where I was likely to marry a woman who would throw utensils at me when she became upset.

The ride resumed as I took the cloth napkin off my awaiting breakfast. It was a bowl of beans and thick slices of brown bread. I ate quickly and hungrily, using my recently filled water pouch to wash it down.

When I was done, I shut my eyes and focused on this buzzing energy within my body. It was this that had inspired me to be where I was now—on my way to the capital with nothing to turn back to. "Upper F," Barrett had called it. But that was just the description of it in the language of spells. It meant nothing specific except for one very important thing. It really had to do with the magical arts.

I was tempted to open the curtains when I heard the city sounds of voices and foot patter, but part of me had grown to trust that Barrett knew what he was doing. He had found me in Tryn, after all, and he had come quite far for me. This matter had to be of some importance.

"Councilman," said someone ahead of our stopped carriage.

"Open the gate," Barrett ordered.

I heard iron groaning, and soon we were heading right through the city. I could hear it all around me, curious voices as to who was in the carriage. I could imagine their reaction if they were told the truth. Why, it's the great Jon Oklar of Bhode!

The image of their confused faces lifted a chuckle out of my stomach.

Some people recognized Barrett driving the carriage, the salutation "councilman" ringing out here and there. I imagined busy men and women stopping along the crowded streets to bow. I even heard a group of children.

"Look it's the king's councilman!"

"Councilman Barrett!"

"Hello, young lads."

After we passed, one chirped up, "He spoke to me!"

"No, he was looking at me!"

There was no fear in their voices, a complete contrast to the people of Tryn. There was one similarity between them, however. All denizens reacted to Barrett as if he could alter the course of their lives on a whim. I wondered which city had the more accurate view of him.

I supposed I would find out soon.

CHAPTER THREE

Eventually the carriage stopped. The loud creaking and groaning of something large began moving in front of us. I knew little about castles, but I figured it had to be a drawbridge.

My suspicion was confirmed when it came to rest with a deep thud and our carriage started up once again. But shortly after, we stopped. I waited as I listened to murmured voices.

I heard the drawbridge lifting back up to close behind me. Eventually, I made out Barrett hopping down from the driver's seat. He finally opened the door to the cariole.

The massive walls of the castle on either side of us draped us in shadow. I didn't quite understand where we were. We had crossed over the drawbridge, which now rested in its vertical position and blocked entrance to the castle, but on the other side was just another wall, this one as tall and thick as the outer stone barricade.

It was only after Barrett led me around the carriage that I saw a gate of sorts. It was arched like it could serve as an entrance, but beams of iron crossed over one another, barring any passage. I didn't see how they could be moved.

"This is a portcullis," Barrett explained.

Just then, it began to lift up and disappear into

the arch high above. There must've been a crank and a wheel somewhere.

Marvelous, I thought.

When it had nearly disappeared into the arch of the passageway, I followed him through where I saw a large guard huffing near the wheel I had predicted.

The guard lowered his head before the councilman as Barrett ignored and walked past him. I offered my thanks, though the guard only looked at me curiously, his eyes drifting down to the old sack of my belongings in my hand and my two sheathed swords in my other. Apparently, even this guard within the castle had no idea what someone like me would be doing here.

I found myself walking behind Barrett through a large courtyard. There was a well off to my left side with a decorative statue atop it of what appeared to be a woman in armor. I figured the statue represented someone relevant to the history of Lycast, but I had no clue who it was. The castle keep had to be the tall structure of stone directly across the courtyard. I figured the king spent most of his time in there. I wondered if I might see him through one of the windows, but I didn't catch a glimpse of anyone inside as I followed Barrett toward it.

The inner wall of the castle wrapped all the way around the courtyard, enclosing the keep and a number of buildings built with wood. The largest of them was just left of the keep. I had heard the term great hall before and figured this was the one. It was three stories tall, still shorter than the keep, but it was so long that a hundred people could probably dance on its first floor without fear of bumping into each other. I had no doubt that important visitors to the king would visit, if not sleep in, the great hall.

On the other side of the keep was a more modest structure that resembled a massive inn. It was the third largest building and probably served as apartments for the castle workers. I could not guess what the other structures had within them, and my mind was too preoccupied to wonder. I wanted to figure out why this whole place was strangely quiet.

There was no one else in the courtyard besides me, Barrett, and the guard who'd let us through the portcullis. The two guards who had come with Barrett to collect me from Tryn had stayed back to stow the horses and carriage, most likely storing them somewhere outside the inner wall but within the outer one. I hadn't seen the stables, but this castle in its entirety was huge.

Although it was magnificent, I felt myself growing nervous as I looked around. I had too many questions and curiosities to appreciate the massive size of the buildings or the sheer amount of wealth on display. I had heard that the castle had a dungeon underneath it where prisoners were kept. The keep, out of all the structures in front of me, seemed the most likely to be connected to an underground dungeon because it was the only one made out of stone.

Barrett led me toward the building to the right of the keep, which I had figured was the apartments of the castle workers and possibly the guards. It was two stories tall, with windows of glass that were in common with every structure here. The roof was made of slate tiles, an expensive and sturdy material you'd never see in Bhode and was rare even in Tryn.

There was one entrance to the large apartment building. The inner wall encapsulating the courtyard

seemed to block access to the backside of each structure. The door was shut but not locked. Barrett pushed
it open and walked in first. Then he waited by the door
like a gentleman for me to enter so he could close it
after me. If he was acting polite to alleviate my concerns, then it was working.

We walked into a somewhat confined space within
the lodging house. The hallways were too narrow for
more than three people to fit side by side, and hallways
were all I saw besides the stairs that led forward and
then back to reach the second floor above. Closed doors
most likely marked the rooms of the inhabitants, but
it was quiet here as well. I doubted it was empty, but
nothing I saw or heard made me believe otherwise.

"Where is everyone?" I asked as Barrett led me up
the stairs.

"The castle staff who live here on the first floor are
out. The others who are here for the same reason as you
must be performing a task. You will receive one soon, I
presume."

"From who?" It clearly wasn't going to be from Barrett, and I hoped I wouldn't be meeting the king just
yet. Such a meeting was an honor they would prepare a
man for in advance, right? It had been more than a full
day since I'd bathed if I didn't count the quick rinse of
my face in the river, and it was too warm for me to hide
my shabby clothing with my one good cloak.

"When he is ready, a sorcerer named Leon Purage
will meet you," the councilman replied. "We are likely
to see each other again, but you won't be handling anything for me directly."

From the top of the stairs, we went down one hallway. The closed doors to various rooms had plenty of

space between them, giving me the impression that the quarters were quite large.

"You said I would learn everything I wanted to know if I came here," I reminded Barrett.

"And you will, from Leon, so long as you prove yourself. This is your room." He took out a ring of keys and inserted one into the keyhole. He fiddled with it for a little while before giving up and trying another key. This one worked, the lock sliding to a resting point. He opened the door for me. I was astonished at what I saw.

At the center was a beautiful bed large enough for two to sleep comfortably. It was decorated at the corners with spiraled posts of brown wood that matched the tall headboard, which was shaped like a wide and pointy hat for the end of the bed. There was an assortment of pillows on the mattress, most of them too small to be of use, but there was plenty of space in the room to put them.

There was a white hearth in front of the bed with an open mantle above it. The roof was high and angled, with strong beams of thick wood decorating the open space above me. There was a dresser beside the bed that had been crafted magnificently, with a curvature to it that gave it an elegant design. It was glossy on top, reflecting the sunlight that came in through a large window with open blue curtains.

A brown and green rug with a repeating pattern of squares covered the wooden floor. On the other side of it from the door was a large chest of fine wood. There was even a desk and a chair to match, and a tall mirror on the same far wall.

"The bathhouse for men is on the first floor," Barrett said, "on the western side. There are towels there.

If you would like your clothes cleaned, put them in a laundry bag, which can be found in the chest, there." He pointed across the room. "Just leave the bag outside your room at night and it will be collected in the morning and returned sometime later."

"Why?" I was a little embarrassed at the question that came out, but I hadn't been able to stop myself.

"Excuse me?" Barrett asked.

"Why do all of this for me?" I felt like a beggar who'd just been given a handful of gold creds.

"This is not permanent, Jon. You will have to prove yourself. Think of it as incentive. I recommend you bathe and prepare yourself to meet your instructor. I believe he will send someone to fetch you from your room soon enough."

Barrett started to leave as I asked, "Will I see you again?"

"Yes, but the purpose of our meetings can change depending on how you handle your first task."

"What happens if I fail?"

"Then I will send you back to Tryn, if that's where you wish to go. You will not be able to remain here."

I nodded. He turned on his heels and walked off. I could hear the sounds of his footsteps down the hall and then down each step.

My room was beautiful, but I hated how quiet it was around here. In my house in Bhode, there was always something to listen to. The wind, the animals, the neighbors all made idle noise. Tryn was even louder. There was never a quiet moment except in the dead of night.

I had one clean shirt and pair of pants left, but I didn't want to wear them. There were some things I never got rid of unless a reason provides itself. My shirt was one of these things. It had a few small holes in it, and one big hole at the cuff around my wrist. I hadn't put it on in so long that it was starting to smell like dust.

My backup pants, on the other hand, were only worn while I cleaned my good pair. They were cheaply made, uncomfortably stiff and made me look like one of the many poor laborers one might find walking down most streets in Tryn. I wasn't normally embarrassed by such clothing, but exiting this apartment building with those clothes on would probably elicit laughter or scorn from the sorcerer, who was likely to be very high in rank.

It was a shame I had grown out of most of my other clothing. I had reached my maximum height a year or two ago, but my muscles had continued to develop. I stared at myself in the mirror in an attempt to see what my instructor would see when he or she first laid eyes upon me.

I hadn't had a real look at myself in a good mirror in a very long time, perhaps even since my father had died. I'd figured earlier I was going to shave in the bath-house when I bathed, but now I thought twice about it. My light brown stubble had grown to cover the planes of my defined jaw leading to my sharp chin. I liked how the faint beard gave age to my face, and it seemed to complement the lush brown hair atop my head that I'd let grow out.

My eyes were mostly familiar, but there was something different about them as well. I looked deep into the brown irises before me in the mirror. This man looked stronger than I felt. There was something in those eyes that made me feel that this man could handle any challenge. I had almost forgotten he'd existed. This was the man who'd made his father so proud.

There was a strange mixture of dark and light in my eyes, akin to what I felt in my heart. I tried to practice a smile, but I did not appear friendly. I had always been terrible at forcing an emotion onto my face. Through my shirt, I could see hints of the defined muscles of my shoulders and chest. I wanted to act as strong and capable as I looked.

I left the room feeling like a new man. I knew who I used to be, but I wasn't that person anymore. I looked forward to finding out what kind of person I could become.

The bathing quarters and the baths themselves were quite nice, but I didn't take more than a moment to appreciate the setting. I figured I would the next time, if I was still here. Now I bathed quickly, eager to meet this sorcerer who would give me some kind of task.

I did not consider myself to be naive. I knew the king planned to use me, as well as the seven others like me who Barrett had mentioned. Nonetheless, it would be a relief to finally find out just how I was to be used.

It was like wondering what kind of illness afflicted a loved one. Even if it was to kill my father no matter what we did, I would've given almost anything to at least have known what it was so we could've found out what to expect from it.

CHAPTER FOUR

I waited in my room for the better part of an hour, worried that Leon Purage was waiting for me elsewhere due to some miscommunication. I eventually saw a number of people moving about the courtyard. Most of them were women of various ages, all wearing the same uniform of a gray tunic with white down the front. They moved quickly, busily.

I was beginning to feel hungry as I waited. I thought the councilman should've offered me lunch before making me wait to begin my task, but he was either too busy or too eager to leave me as another man's problem.

I watched two men emerge from the great hall. Both walked briskly toward the door to the apartments, where I was watching from my window above them. It was finally time. I hurried downstairs and opened the door to the building.

"Jon Oklar?" asked the older man, stopping a few yards away. It was difficult to place his age. The downward tilt of his bushy eyebrows gave his expression the appearance of a scowl, but there was not a single line across his face. Perhaps this was his resting countenance.

His blond hair was straight and short at the sides but longer and slightly messy on top. His long mouth, a straight line, rested above a prominent chin. He had bright, green eyes that regarded me as if I had already failed him.

"Yes," I answered. "Leon Purage?"

"That's correct. Where the hell did Barrett find you?"

I didn't understand the point of the question, but I answered without delay. "In Tryn."

Leon tossed his hands outward petulantly and looked at me as if expecting a longer answer.

"I, uh." What did he want?

"What were you doing there?" he asked in a tone as if I was dimwitted.

"I don't see why that's relevant, but I was—"

"It doesn't matter if you see the relevance to my requests or not. You will do them, or you will leave."

Holding back my frustration, I nodded. "I was there looking for a sorcerer."

"What kind of sorcerer?"

"Anyone who could explain the magical arts to me."

Leon rolled his eyes. "Airinold's taint, another useless daisy. At least tell me your family's rich like this one." He gestured at the young man behind him who was looking at me with disappointment.

"No," I answered the instructor.

"You know *nothing* of sorcery?" asked the young man. He had the lilt of nobility.

"Quiet," Leon said as he put his fingers over his eyes. "I need to think."

I didn't want to stare at the other young man, for this was awkward enough already, but he was glaring at me as if my presence was an insult to him.

"I'm sure neither of you are ready for a difficult

task," Leon said. "So the two of you are going to fetch something important, instead. Do either of you daisies know what a vibmtaer looks like?"

"I do," said the other man.

"Are you sure, Reuben?" Leon didn't sound as if he believed him. "I don't want you bringing back a manamtaer or something equally useless to us."

"I've used a vibmtaer many times. I know what it looks like."

"Fine. Don't get it at Dennison's. His 'Magic Shop' is full of overpriced instruments, most of which don't even work."

"But there are no other magic shops in Newhaven." Reuben spoke with confidence.

"This is going to be impossible," Leon muttered to himself, then sighed and looked up at Reuben again. "There's a shop called Enchanted Devices on Exeter Street. It's on the far western side, on the corner of Speedwell. Hopefully you will meet a woman named Pamella, if she's still there. She actually knows what she is selling, unlike Dennison, and she won't rip you off."

"Very well," Reuben said, then stared at Leon expectantly.

"What?" Leon asked.

Reuben cleared his throat and hesitantly extended his open hand.

"Your father owns a quarter of this city and you expect me to hand you coins for a vibmtaer?"

Reuben retracted his hand. "I figured the coin would come from the king."

"The king is none of your concern. I am. And I'm telling you to do something. Most of the others will be back soon, so hurry on up."

Reuben made a sour face. "How much is a vibmtaer?" he asked.

"However much Pamella says it is. Bring four gold just in case."

"Four!?"

"Yes. Now go."

I was alarmed as well. I'd never even *seen* enough coin to equal four gold creds. My six silver buckles and five pennies suddenly felt very light in my coin purse. I expected Reuben to make a quick run to his room to retrieve the coin, but he just started toward the portcullis.

"Come on, Jon!" Reuben roared, no doubt deflecting his anger onto me.

We jogged to the portcullis and then waited for the guard to open it. Reuben looked me up and down.

"What are you, a blacksmith's apprentice who got lucky?"

"I—"

"Who's your father?"

I was hoping he might interrupt again, but I wasn't so lucky.

"He passed away."

Reuben pretended not to hear as he walked through the now open passageway, but soon we were waiting for the drawbridge to be lowered.

"You're too embarrassed to tell the truth," he muttered mostly to himself.

The clanking and grinding of the drawbridge was loud, but I'd heard every word. I waited until we were exiting the castle before I gave my reply.

"I'm not too embarrassed to tell you anything. My

father really did pass away. You can believe me or not. I don't even know why I'm here, to be honest. I just arrived today."

"What do you mean you don't know why you're here?" He made a shooing motion. "And you will walk behind me."

"I mean I haven't been told the reason yet. And I will walk beside you."

Reuben stopped and faced me. "You are clearly far beneath my rank. Don't embarrass me. Stay behind." He started up again, quicker this time. I was too shocked to move at first. My father had told me about men and women who valued their status in society over all else, but I had yet to meet one personally. Until now.

I hurried to catch up to Reuben's side, matching his stride. He walked faster, but so did I. He began to jog, and I matched his speed again. Then he broke into a run. He was quick, but so was I.

We raced down the busy street, zipping around people. A few looked our way in anger, but none said a word. It was probably Reuben's attire that shut their mouths, for he was dressed like a young lord, with his bright clothing, rings on his fingers, and a whipping cloak.

Soon I pulled slightly ahead. I would've liked to think it was because I was faster, but it was most likely because his quality outfit was as thick and heavy as it was expensive. He really was fast, for a snobby boy.

We separated around a crowd. I didn't slow, my competitive nature getting the better of me, but then I reached an intersection and realized I didn't know which way to go. The crowd was dense, many crossing by me every which way as I stopped to look around. I didn't see the rich dolt.

"Reuben!" I yelled. "Where are you?"

My fear was that he was still racing and didn't realize that I had lost him.

"Reuben!" I tried again. Everyone ignored me, even those crossing right in front of me. It was a curious thing. In Bhode, people came out of their homes at the sound of anyone shouting.

I had a loud, deep voice that could pierce the sound of almost anything to reach someone's ears. I was certain Reuben had heard me, wherever he was. I hurried forward in hopes of catching up to him.

I ran all the way to another intersection. I looked both ways, up and down, but I couldn't locate him.

I didn't quite understand his plan in losing me. Did he expect to make me look bad by purchasing the vibmtaer and returning without me? It would cast a shadow onto both of us. We had been given this task together.

I supposed he planned to make up some sort of lie as to why we got separated. He expected no one to believe the poor over the rich if I was to go against his word, and he might be right. I didn't know these people.

But I thought back to what Leon had told Ruben. The shop was called Enchanted Devices. It was on the far western side of Exeter Street, on the same corner as Speedwell, which was probably another street. The only issue was that I had never walked around this city in my life.

I saw I was at the cross between Longwall Street, the main road that ran parallel along the castle's western wall, and a smaller curved road called Edward Street. There was a woman crossing by holding hands with her young child. I met her gaze wearing an expression that made it clear I was lost. When she smiled, I approached.

"Excuse me, madam, can you point me to Exeter Street?"

She looked down at her child, who was kicking some hard dirt up from the road. "Can you help him find Exeter?"

Apparently I had not demonstrated well enough that I was in a hurry.

The shy child shrugged without glancing up.

"Remember?" his mother asked him. "We walked down Exeter just yesterday to visit your grandpa."

The child pointed forward, clearly unsure of himself.

"That's right!" said his mother. She had a proud look as she met my gaze again. "Keep following Longwall across Market. It turns into Exeter North."

Damn, there was more than one Exeter Street? I didn't want to ask this woman anything else in case she might have her child answer again.

"Thank you," I said as I rushed off in the direction the boy had pointed.

Market Street was wide, with hawkers selling their wares, and carriages pulled by horses bustling along each way. I zipped, hopped, and skidded around people and their carriages, and soon I was running down Exeter Street North without having seen an Exeter Street South.

The street became less crowded the farther west I ran. It wasn't long before I spotted the corner ahead. I didn't bother trying to make out the fancy calligraphy of any of the shop names. I looked for Reuben standing within them instead.

I found him inside the last shop on the southern corner. I looked up at the display sign just to make sure: Enchanted Devices. I could see Reuben panting for breath through the large window with its shutters open. He turned and caught my gaze. Then he made a face as he groaned.

I sported a smile as I entered the shop. "Hello again."

He ignored me.

There was a counter with space for someone to stand behind, yet I could hear them in the backroom, a closed door blocking my view. I glanced around at the rest of the shop.

A variety of small and interesting things cluttered the shelves and tables. None of them looked even a little familiar. Sure there were rings and necklaces, but I had never seen the colorful gems attached on them. There was one red stone in the middle of a bracelet that glowed. I put my hand over it and even felt a bit of heat. There were many other bracelets beside it that looked nearly identical except for the color of the stone. One was almost clear except a little cloudy, like a gust of wind picking up some dust, stuck in time. Another was blue and cold like ice. There was another blue one, but lighter in color. Water, I presumed, going off the theme of elements, if the others were fire, wind, and ice.

Although the shop was small, it was clear that most everything in here was too expensive for someone like me to purchase. I was careful as I glanced around, worried I might break something and have to spend the rest of my life paying it off.

"Don't touch anything!" Reuben complained.

"I'm not."

"You lied to me earlier," he accused.

"What? When?"

"You gave me the impression that you had never been to the city. You just arrived, you said."

"That was true. This is the first time I've been in Newhaven."

"You lie. You wouldn't have found this place as quickly as you did if that was true."

"Believe what you want. Is she getting the vibmtaer now?"

"Yes. You will not touch it."

A young woman came out holding what looked to be some sort of instrument for measuring something. There was a small glass panel on the front, but there was nothing showing, no scale of numbers or letters of any kind. The rest of the instrument looked to be designed to gather something possibly from the air. It was round, small enough to be held with one hand, with a tiny rectangular opening at the top. The device seemed to be made of a dark wood, though finely crafted and with a sleek varnish.

The young woman glanced over at me. She had a kind, comely face, but she didn't look older than I was, too young to own a shop. I stepped past Reuben.

"I'm Jon," I said. "Are you Pamella?"

"That's my mother. I'm Greda."

"Nice to meet you." I extended my hand with a warm smile. I planned to return here when I had time, and hopefully more coin, and find out more about everything she sold.

"You as well," she said, setting down the device to put her whole attention into shaking my hand.

She glanced nervously at Reuben as she took her hand back. She looked to be waiting for him to introduce himself. But he took the vibmtaer off the counter and strolled out.

"It had better work," he said without looking back.

"Thank you for the vibmtaer," I told her as I stuck around.

She showed me an agreeable smile. "Do let me know if something's wrong with it."

"If there is, I'll take it back here myself and leave Reuben out of it."

She held her smile. "Thank you," she said quietly as she eyed Reuben. The rich young man was already walking away from the shop, and at a quick pace.

"I'm sure we'll meet again because I plan to come back when I have more time," I told her. "Excuse me, but I have to catch up to him."

"Goodbye, Jon!" she called as I hurried out.

"Goodbye, Greda." I ran to catch up to Reuben. I was glad when he didn't sprint away from me.

I came up on his side as he pocketed the vibmtaer. I waited for him to complain about me in some way, but he pretended I didn't exist. I wasn't sure that was better.

"Now we're not even going to speak?" I tested.

"I don't speak to liars."

"Well I don't usually speak to disrespectful young men, but I'm willing to make an exception for you because it seems like we'll be training together."

He stopped and glared at me.

Reuben had brown hair. It was dense and wavy, looking as if he had combed it over the side of his forehead and it had become disheveled throughout the day.

He had eyes of the same color that showed no hint of hardship. He had possibly the most normal nose and average mouth of any man his age, which matched the not so prominent structure of his subtle chin. With different clothes, he would've blended into the city as easily as any commoner. He was on the taller side for most men, like myself, though it hadn't been something I noticed until now.

"You are the disrespectful one," he said coldly.

He held my eyes in his gaze, his lips tightly pressed. It was as if he expected me to challenge him to a duel. I wasn't about to fight someone here in the street, especially someone who could be training with me.

"Look Reuben, we could bicker and quarrel for as long as we know each other, but that's not what I'd prefer. I've been honest with you about everything. I didn't choose to come here. I was trying to find out more about sorcery in Tryn, and suddenly Barrett Edgar showed up and practically dragged me to the castle. I don't claim to have what you have, money and knowledge about sorcery, but I'm eager to learn. I just won't walk behind you. Leon sent us on the same task, as equals. I am not yours to command. We don't have to be friends, but at least let's not be enemies."

His expression had softened a little by the time I was done. He started moving again.

"Fine, I give you permission to walk beside me."

I guessed that was all I was going to get from him for now. With the tension still thick between us as we walked back, I decided not to ask any of the many questions I had about sorcery that he might've been able to answer.

Instead, I tried one more innocent. "What about

you? What led you to arrive at the castle?"

"I have been training with sword and mana since I was thirteen years old. I received a letter from the king himself asking me to arrive at the castle today. I did so in the morning, but I haven't been told what I would be doing."

"Did you say mana?" I asked.

"You don't even know what *mana* is?"

"I don't."

His expression slowly morphed from bewilderment to anger. "I don't understand why you are here! It is not just."

I decided not to tell him about the energy I had felt which had led me here. Perhaps it was some form of mana, as he had called it, not that the word meant anything to me yet.

"We are *not* equals," he added.

I sighed in frustration. There was no point in arguing.

We didn't speak again.

After a long, awkward walk, we reached the castle. The drawbridge was already down, a couple of guards standing in the way. The portcullis behind them was up as well, and I could see people gathered in the courtyard, mostly young women.

"Looks like the others have returned," I commented.

Reuben took the vibmtaer out of his pocket and rushed forward. I didn't bother to keep at his side the rest of the way into the courtyard, glad to distance myself from him.

CHAPTER FIVE

All eyes were on us as we entered the courtyard. I recognized Leon gesturing for us to hurry up, but there were six others I had not met. They all looked to be around my age. There were two other young men besides Reuben and myself, and four young ladies.

I jogged behind Reuben over to the small crowd. He handed the vibmtaer to Leon. Our blond instructor looked inside the opening on top, then held it away from him and lifted up his hand, most likely for some kind of spell. The glass panel at the front displayed a dull red color.

"Glad to see it works," Leon said. "All of you form a line."

Reuben and I were the last two to get in place on the far end, the boys on one side and the girls on the other.

"All of you are wondering what exactly you'll be doing here," Leon said. "But keep your questions to yourself. All you need to know right now is that you were selected for a reason, but that reason is different for each of you. There's a lot we need to accomplish in a short amount of time. If you listen to what I tell you to do, then you'll get to stay. If you slow us down, then you're gone. Don't piss me off. You'll find out what we're doing *after* you prove yourself. Then *you* can decide if you want to stay."

Leon looked down the line. He shook his head as if

displeased with what he saw.

The sound of the drawbridge closing turned many heads.

"Pay attention to me!" Leon practically shouted. He started to pace as he spoke. "I know a little about each of you, and that's more than I care to know." He pointed at the dark-haired young man standing beside Reuben. "Like you, Michael."

The young man waited for Leon to look away, then shrugged over at Reuben and me to show his offense and confusion. I shrugged back apologetically, while Reuben stared ahead. Leon continued.

"Some of you may have already heard what I'm going to say, but it needs to be said again for the truly stupid of you to really understand it. We will be using the language of sorcery soon enough. All of you specialize in something different. Some of you don't even understand what that is yet."

He gave me a pointed look as if my presence was an irritation. A quick look down the line showed every man and woman staring at me. I was not usually one to blush, but I felt my cheeks redden.

"Soon you're going to find out more than what you specialize in," Leon said. "You're going to find your range of mana. It will determine just what you're capable of and, more importantly, what you are not capable of. You might be disappointed with the results. Tough. When disappointment can't change a damn thing, it's as useless as tits on a shield. Let it go and move on. No one wants to hear you complain, especially not me."

Reuben raised his hand. I regretted even being near the fool as Leon stared daggers at him.

"What is so important, Reuben?"

"I have already been tested. I know my range."

Leon put his hand over his forehead and leaned back as he groaned.

"I'm only trying to save you time," Reuben continued.

"Oh, thank you for that!" Leon said with anger in his fully wide eyes, his sharp green irises bright and honestly a little scary. "So much time you're saving us right now!"

Reuben looked at the dirt.

I wish I could understand Leon's mood, but I couldn't for the life of me figure out why he was *this* pissed off already. Couldn't the king have chosen someone else? Anyone else? I looked over at the keep, hoping the king was watching, but I saw no one through the windows.

"Are you done?" Leon asked.

"Yes," Reuben muttered.

Leon suddenly stared at me. He pointed. "You, come here."

What did I do? I wondered. I quickly left the line.

"Stand here," Leon said as he pointed to his side. I took the position. Then he said, "Tell everyone your name and where you're from."

"I'm Jon Oklar," I said, confused. "I'm from Bhode."

"Bhode?" Leon exclaimed. "Where the hell is that?"

"It's a small town far north." It was more than uncomfortable to stand there with everyone staring but especially with Leon breathing down my neck.

"I was told you were found in Tryn."

"I was there when Barrett found me. I came from Bhode."

"Airinold's taint, fine. I'm the most curious about you, so you're going first. Take this vibmtaer and bring it to Barrett in the great hall. I'll be right behind you. Go."

He plopped the device into my palm, the force of his gesture letting me know that the vibmtaer wasn't quite as delicate as I had first thought.

I ran toward the great hall. Leon began to shout, and I almost stopped at the sound of his voice.

"I'll decide the order for the rest of you! Walk with me."

I was glad to be far from the instructor, even if just for a moment. As I neared the great hall, I wondered what it was about me that made him curious. It had to be the same reason Barrett had come for me, probably this energy. I let go of my frustration toward Leon as I realized I would finally find out exactly what it was, with this vibmtaer somehow the key.

The entrance room of the great hall was magnificent. The wood of the floor, walls, and ceiling glistened with a yellow, almost golden tint. It wasn't a large room, but it was elegant. A red carpet led to a beautiful staircase that split into two curved stairways to the second floor. There were two sets of doors on the ground floor, one pair on each side of the walls. I wished they were open so I could see inside, but all were closed.

There were two incredibly intricate lamps at the base of the stairs, bright with no less than ten candles each. Coming down the stairs was Barrett, but he stopped midway and waved for me to come to him. I didn't know how he could stand within such a magnificent place and scowl, but he found a way.

He started up the stairs again as I closed in, continuing to stay ahead of me even after we reached the second floor. He seemed to be in a rush, probably for the same reason Leon was so impatient with us. Whatever our purpose was here, it seemed urgent.

The second floor wasn't nearly as spectacular. There were a couple intersecting hallways of similar design to the ones in the apartments. Barrett led me down one of them and then another. We came to a door that was already open, a stairway leading up to the third floor.

The room he led me into was another marvel to behold. Plenty of light came through the large, arched windows across the wall that led to a long table with a decorative cloth draped over it. There was a pair of ceramic pots on top with a stick of unlit incense poking out of each one. There were two candles as well, and a large paper with a number of colored squares painted on it.

A guard stood by the table. He was covered in armor from a helmet to boots. There were a number of other items and pieces of furniture around the large room, but most of it seemed decorative. My eyes were on the table as Barrett led me over to it.

He took a seat on one of the two chairs. He didn't gesture for me to join him, and I was glad. I wanted to stand to better appreciate everything.

"The vibmtaer," Barrett said as he held out his hand.

I took it out of my pocket and handed it to him. He set it down with the glass panel facing him. Then he positioned the paper with the squares of many colors in front of him. He had a notebook open as well, with quill and ink beside it.

"You may start now," Barrett said.

"Start what?" I asked.

A vertical line appeared between his eyes. "Didn't Leon explain this?"

The last thing I wanted was to speak ill of my instructor. I held my tongue, figuring Leon would show up soon.

"What did he say to you?" Barrett's tone was as if Leon was a child who often misbehaved.

"He said he was coming right after me."

"Before that."

Leon arrived. Barrett stood to address him. "What did you tell Jon before coming here?"

"What's wrong?" Leon asked.

"He doesn't know what he's supposed to do."

Leon's fierce look made me feel as if I had betrayed him. "How do you not know what to do?" he demanded of me. "I explained this to everyone. All of you need to find out the range of your mana."

"That's the part I don't understand."

Barrett spoke. "He knows nothing, Leon. He doesn't even know what mana is."

"How is that possible?" Leon shouted at me. It was probably loud enough for the others to hear outside the great hall.

"Calm down," Barrett told him.

"You bring me a man who doesn't even know what mana is, and you expect me to teach him anything before it's too late?"

"Yes. Don't you feel what I feel? Or are you not the sorcerer you claim to be?"

"Of course I feel it. That's why I chose him to go

first. I was hoping for some interesting results. But if he knows nothing about mana, then it doesn't matter if he has a natural inclination toward uF. It's not like he can do anything useful with it. You should send him back to Bhode. He'll only slow me down otherwise."

"I'm a fast learner," I interjected. "Just tell me what I need to know to take this test and then let me show you."

"You fool," Leon said. "For you to even take this test, you're going to need weeks of training."

Could that be true? I reminded myself that Barrett had seen something in me. He had taken a risk bringing me here. I gave him a look that showed I was ready for anything.

"You're the one who brought me here," I said. "If you still believe in giving me a chance, I will gladly take it."

"Do you hear him, Leon? He will be your best student soon enough. Just give him a chance to learn."

Leon looked into my eyes. He seemed to find whatever he was looking for, giving a subtle nod before leaning back. "All right," he said. "Let's find out just what kind of man you are. Pay attention, because I'm only going to say this once. This mana—this strange thing to you—that I'm sure you can touch with your mind is vibrating at a certain rate. The rate of its vibration is extremely important. It's what makes the difference from one note to another."

I had heard the word "note" before in regard to music, but I was beginning to understand what it meant for magic. "So this mana..." I held it in front of me with a little shove of my mind. "This is a note called uF?"

"Yes, a note called Upper F," Barrett confirmed as he pointed at the vibmtaer. "Look."

The glass on the front panel had changed color. It was now a very light grayish purple. But it quickly faded away as soon as I let go of the buzzing energy.

"Now look here," Barrett said as he pointed to the paper with the colored squares. "Which one is it?"

"It's either one of these," I said as I used two fingers to gesture at two colors next to each other in a vertical row. They both appeared nearly the same as the light purple-gray I had seen on the vibmtaer. Looking closer, I saw that these colors were labeled as uE and uF. "This one," I said pointing at uF. "But I wouldn't have been able to tell if didn't already know I was making uF. They look too similar."

"That is the issue with a vibmtaer," Barrett explained. "There are only so many colors it can display. When two notes are close to one another in vibration, they look similar on the vibmtaer, especially vibrations of very high or very low frequencies."

"Why is the vibmtaer designed like that?" I asked.

Leon let out his breath in exasperation, but at least Barrett did not appear frustrated as he answered. "The vibmtaer is the only device in the world that can measure a note. It is already exceptionally designed and cannot be improved. There is a metal within it called birlabright that you probably haven't heard of in Bhode because it is rare and can only be found in Curdith Forest. It changes color depending on the vibration of mana nearby. The rest of the vibmtaer acts as a magnet to draw mana in near the birlabright to increase the efficiency. A different metal is used for that. It's called fusemanol."

Leon huffed out a breath. "None of this matters right now," he argued.

"You can't tell what's going to matter and what isn't to someone who knows nothing about the subject. He might find interest in devices later because this conversation stirred something."

It was all overwhelming, but the thing that made me the most nervous was that Leon would be my instructor and not Barrett. Why was Leon chosen for the job if he was this impatient and irritable? There had to be something special about him, but I had yet to see it.

"Can you explain a little bit more about how all this works?" I asked Barrett. "Understanding it will help me take the test."

"Yes. In very general terms, everyone has a range of mana just like a range to their voice. Right now you can cast a single note of mana. It's like making a sound with your voice—you can change the frequency by lowering or raising the pitch of your voice. Your mana is the same—you can lower or raise the frequency of your mana by using your mind."

"That's clear," I said.

"Your natural mana is at the frequency of uF," he continued. "Slowing your natural vibration will lower it below uF while increasing its vibration will raise it above."

"That I understand, but how do you make magic from my mana?"

Leon looked like he wanted to strangle me, but I ignored him.

"A spell is usually composed of multiple notes at the same time," Barrett explained. "The name for this is the same name as a group of musical notes, a chord.

Spells are simple to describe but extremely difficult to perform. They are just a chord of mana—multiple notes of mana used at once. It's the specific notes of mana within the chord that determine what type of spell it will be."

"Oh, sounds simple enough." I spoke with relief. "So my natural mana of uF, or in other words Upper F, is just another note of mana, and it is high range?" I asked.

"High frequency, yes," Barrett slightly corrected me with a proud smile. "Everyone's natural mana is different, but men typically have a lower vibration and women higher."

"What does it mean that mine is very high?"

"It most likely means, unfortunately, that you won't have access to many spells that someone with a more neutral mana will be able to cast."

"There's no benefit?" I asked.

"There is one great benefit you may already be prospering from," Barrett replied.

"It's a curse," Leon spat.

Barrett gave him a disapproving look with his fatherly gaze. He set his dark eyes back on me.

"Variants of F, like Lower F and Upper F, have properties of life in them. There are spells in which uF is the foundation, like forms of healing, but there are other uses as well."

"You're already stronger because of uF," Leon said. "If you're not a complete fool, you might've noticed that you don't have to eat as much as others do. If you do, you'll get fatter than they will unless you work it off."

It was something I'd noticed about my body.

"And you may live longer," Barrett added with

raised eyebrows.

"How much longer?" I asked.

"There is little science behind it."

"Aye," Leon agreed, "which is why I actively try not to use my uF anymore. It's been nothing but a curse, like I said."

"You're the same?" I asked.

He seemed insulted by the question. "Can we get on with this, councilman?"

"Very well."

I had blissfully forgotten that everyone else was waiting for me to finish, but I had so many more questions.

"Pay attention," Leon said. "It's time to prove yourself. You're going to take your note of uF and increase the vibration as high as you can so we can find your maximum frequency."

"How do I do that?"

"Normally? Through hundreds of hours of practice, but we don't have time for that. I'll give you a minute. Go."

A sweat broke out as I took hold of what I now knew to be mana. I muttered a curse under my breath. I still had very little idea about any of this, but I had spent years fooling with my mana. I knew how to alter it. I'd just never been told what that altering was doing.

I could feel it buzzing quicker as I put force into it. The feeling was like trying to hit a high note with my voice. It was something that had become easier over the many years I had toyed with the mana. I felt it shift numerous times. It was just like hearing my voice rise through many pitches, only I sensed my mana without using my ears or my eyes. It was all in my mind, as real as a memory.

"Airinold's taint!" Leon shouted as he stared at the vibmtaer. "Higher! Higher, Jon!"

I pushed and pushed, not realizing until then that I had my hand out as if to grasp the mana that continued to shake faster. Soon it became so unstable that I lost my hold. I collapsed to my knees as I panted for breath.

"Damn fine job!" Leon said as he slapped my back.

Barrett was grinning ear to ear as he was writing something down in his notebook.

I got to my feet for a look at the vibmtaer, but the panel at the front was clear again. "What color did it get to?" I asked, still catching my breath.

Barrett put his finger over uF on the color chart. "You started here on the bottom of the fourth column. But you quickly went through all the colors here on the third column." He moved his finger down each row, traversing all the light colors of pink, orange, yellow, green, blue, and purple. "Most people can't make it to the third column at all, and I thought you would stop there, but you pushed through to the second column." He slowly moved his finger down the second column, listing each one he passed. "uuC, uuDm...and then, finally, uuD."

I could tell from his expression that uuD meant something good, but just how good, I had no idea.

"I've heard of a woman reaching Up-Upper D," Leon said with a laugh. "But never a man."

"So what does it mean?" I asked.

"It means you are probably going to specialize in dvinia," Barrett said warmly. "It's a magical art very high in frequency. We don't know too much about it, but there is one spell that everyone has heard of."

"Everyone who knows a lick about sorcery," Leon said with a huge smile that looked a little silly on him. "Have you heard of it, Jon?"

I shook my head.

"This might not mean anything to you right now but memorize it: uF, uG, uuC, uuD. It's the only spell you're going to practice for a while."

I repeated the four notes twice. Then I asked, "Does the order matter?"

"There is no order. You have to execute each of the four notes at the same time or the spell won't work."

"But I still can't do more than one at a time."

"You will eventually. Hold on a moment; you can't go much lower than uF, right?"

"I think I can," I said, full of pride.

"I doubt so," Leon said. "But let's find out."

I took a few breaths to compose myself. Pulling the mana out of my body was no longer a strange sensation. Akin to spitting, it just took a little concentration. The more concentration I put into it, the more force and volume I could achieve. I didn't bother with a large volume of my mana, because it didn't seem to matter right now. I put all of my focus on altering it once it was hovering there.

Lowering the frequency was harder, but again, it was something I had done many times without knowing what I was doing. I thought of it as trying to calm uF, akin to slowing my heart rate through deep breaths and meditation.

I pushed it as low as I could and felt like I reached my limit almost instantaneously. The mana buzzed quieter in my mind, but I couldn't tell just how slowly it vibrated compared to the natural frequency of my mana at uF. I felt sweat drip down my face as I struggled, incapable of telling if I was changing it at all anymore.

"Can you go any lower?" Barrett asked. The disappointment in his tone made me push harder.

"Did it change?" I asked through the immense strain, my hands shaking.

"Yes." He shared a worried look with Leon.

I stopped before collapsing this time, doubling over as I gasped for breath. Barrett was looking at me as if he was about to inform me that I was deathly sick. But Leon seemed furious.

"What the hell have you been doing to your mana all these years?" Leon yelled.

From his seat, Barrett handed me a cloth to wipe the sweat from my face. He seemed too disappointed to look up at me.

"I don't know," I said. "I fooled around with it a lot."

"That's what your cranny hunter is for! You should've left your mana alone."

"No, he should've had proper training since he first started using his mana. This is not his fault."

"I don't understand," I admitted. "How low did I reach?"

Barrett turned the color chart toward me. "Most male sorcerers can reach as low as here, 1C, or Lower C." He pointed to the top row of the eighth column. "But most of these men usually can't reach a frequency above uD, even after years of training." He pointed to Upper D. It was on the same column as my natural mana, Upper F, but it was three rows before uF. So it wasn't even as high as my natural frequency.

"As you can see," Barrett continued, "you have very peculiar mana. Even most women can't reach higher than uB, but you went well above that. We thought earlier that this would mean that you would specialize in dvinia, which takes place in this range." He moved his hand around the second, third, and fourth columns. "But you pushed your mana to a very low frequency, down here." He pointed at the top of the eighth column. "Lower C. This is what most male sorcerers can reach as their lowest frequency."

I didn't know what any of the individual notes meant or represented, but I did understand they were saying that my lowest frequency was the same as most men, and yet I could reach a much higher frequency than they could...than even most of the women, whose mana was usually higher.

"Isn't that good?" I asked. "I have a wide range."

"You don't want a wide range," Barrett explained.

"That's why we hoped uF was the lowest note you could reach," Leon said. "This is taking too long. I say we just give him an essence of fire and be done with it."

"I'm inclined to agree." Barrett stood as if this was over.

"Wait, what exactly are you both saying?" I had no inclination toward anything to do with fire. Dvinia, now that sounded like something I should pursue, especially considering how excited they'd seemed at the idea.

"We're saying you're not going to specialize in anything without an essence," Leon explained. "Your range is *too* wide."

"But wouldn't a wide range mean I can cast many different spells?"

"Theoretically," Barrett said, "but not practically."

"You can explain it to the young man," Leon said as

he made his exit. "I'll figure out who's next."

I told Barrett with my heart on my sleeve, "I don't want to specialize in fire. There must be something else."

He put up his hands. "It doesn't have to be fire, but you will require an essence."

I had no idea what that was. "Then can't I use an essence of dvinia?"

"There is no essence of dvinia. There are only essences of erto: fire, water, ice, and air."

All of the elements seemed too limited, and it sounded like just about any sorcerer could learn them. "Dvinia is what I want to learn. I know I can with just a little instruction." I had learned everything else that way.

He gave a sigh. "Allow me to explain. Your knowledge of mana right now is like a toddler trying to learn to speak. Imagine this hypothetical scenario for a moment. There is a small boy who can only make a few different sounds. He could say any word that requires these sounds. He could even practice shouting these words, singing them, or holding one part of the word for longer than the other. This little boy would master these sounds quickly. He would speak words with these sounds better than any other toddler trying to say the same words. A small range of mana is like that. This boy won't be able to make words that involve other sounds, but he will excel at a few specific words, while other toddlers will struggle with all words."

He stood up as if he would soon be done with me. "Most spells require a chord of three notes to be cast at the same time. Someone who has a narrow range, like from C to uC, can create spells in that range much easier than someone like yourself, who has a much wider range. It's going to take weeks for you to feel the difference between close notes like uF and uG, and you're likely to get confused between octaves, like uG and G. You'll spend hundreds of hours just learning the difference between most notes. Now imagine you have to accurately cast three notes at the same time, and if even one of them is slightly off, the spell could seriously injure you."

"I can train," I said. "I would just focus on the notes in the range of dvinia."

He chuckled. "You don't even know what dvinia is yet."

"I don't need to. I saw Leon's and your reaction to it."

"There is plenty you can do with erto. There are many people in this world who would give up one of their hands for what you have. You can choose from any of the essences. That is extremely rare even for a sorcerer. Most people can only choose one or two depending on their range, and some of us, like myself, cannot choose an essence at all."

I was not ready to give up on dvinia. It was true that I didn't know what it did, but they had told me that it was something I was capable of using. How could I give up something that excited them that much if I was capable of doing it? I tried to think of some way to argue my point, but first I needed to know more about spells.

"You are a sorcerer, correct?" I asked.

"I am. It's how I was able to tell that your mana was uF."

"What is your range?"

"I have a narrow and low range. I am very good at

ordia because of that. My specific class is called a harbinger. You, too, will work your way up to a class. You will one day be a mage."

"What is the class called of someone who specializes in dvinia?" This would tell me more about what I might be able to accomplish.

"Just like someone who specializes in the other magical arts, there are multiple classes available to them depending on their affinity toward certain notes within and even outside of the general range of their magical art. Enchanters, for example must use ordia and earth to enchant gems, or ordia and mtalia to enchant metal."

"What about someone who just specializes in dvinia?"

He took a slow breath before he answered. "They are wizards."

"That." I pointed. I had heard the word only in myth. "That's what I want to be. A wizard who uses sword, is there a name for that?"

Barrett looked as if he had eaten something that he was just starting to realize was spoiled. "That would be a battlewiz...or a bladedancer."

Yes, that sounded more like me than a mage.

"I will learn dvinia," I assured him. "I promise I will."

He was shaking his head. "Jon, listen to me. The king is not going to house and train you this way."

"Can you help me convince him otherwise?"

He raised his voice. "I would be the one advising him to throw you out of the castle!"

I was stunned. I had thought Barrett was on my side no matter what. He had sacrificed a lot to get me here.

I supposed I didn't have any friends here after all.

"I've had enough of this conversation," Barrett continued, his frown deepening. "You are lucky to be here. If you forget that, you are not going to be happy with the result. Fire and water are important for any capable sorcerer to learn, and they are the easiest at the middle of the spectrum. You are going to start with one of your choosing and then move on to the other. Depending on how quickly you learn to control them, you may be able to learn other spells. But casting without an essence takes even the most exceptional casters months of training. Yet a few months might be all we have."

"Why, what is happening?"

"It will be explained once you and the others can be trusted and have proven yourselves, as you are failing to do right now by showing insubordination. Go back to the courtyard and wait with the others until everyone has been tested. We have already spent long enough on you."

I left as I told myself the four notes Leon had revealed earlier when he thought I could be a wizard: uF, uG, uuC, uuD.

I would find a way to cast this spell soon enough.

CHAPTER SIX

I was rattled as I slowly made my way out of the great hall floor by floor. I passed by Leon leading a young woman the opposite way.

I looked back to find her glancing back as well, our gazes meeting. She quickly looked away as if embarrassed to be found looking back at me.

"Hello," I called out without thinking.

She stopped and turned around to face me fully. "Hi," she said with a nervous smile.

I had seen many kinds of beautiful women in Tryn, but I felt a warmth that spread through my chest when I looked at this one. Her dark eyes were large and striking. She had pouty lips below a nose of a gentle curve and slope, and the thick locks of her dark brown hair cascaded down beyond her shoulders. I had an acute urge to know more about her, but I couldn't get my mouth to move.

"I'm Jon," I forced out suddenly, like a fool.

"I'm Ali," she said.

"Come on, Aliana!" Leon yelled from down the hall. "You can gawk at each other later."

"Oh god," she muttered to herself as she turned and ran after him.

I couldn't help but watch her go. She made it all the way to the end of the hall, but she did turn there to look at me one more time.

I felt embarrassed and disappointed at remembering how I'd practically burped out my name like it was stuck in my throat.

By the time I made it out of the great hall I remembered that there were other, more serious problems I had to deal with now. Six young men and women stared at me, the courtyard destitute of any sound.

I had heard them talking just before I saw them, but now it seemed like they were all waiting for me to speak. They had formed a messy circle that opened as everyone turned toward me.

"What happened up there?" asked the dark-haired young man. Like Reuben and me, he was on the taller side, but the shape of his body was closer to Reuben's than mine. He was a healthy weight and probably decently strong, but he surely hadn't spent the same amount of time and effort with a sword as I had.

I suddenly remembered that this was the person who had shown offense and confusion when Leon had picked on him. Leon had called him by name, "Michael." He and I had shared a look when Leon turned away. He had a warm smile and friendly eyes. His mouth was scrunched in a half-grin as if he was holding in a joke.

"We heard Leon screaming," he said. "And it took a long time, I mean a really long time...like much longer than it should have to take for anyone to have their range checked. Then you come out looking as if you just sprinted a mile." He held the silence for a long while. "Did Leon abuse you?"

A few people chuckled.

"Not exactly," I said, glad for the humor as I felt the tension break.

"I'm Michael, by the way," he said. We shook hands. "We got your name earlier, Jon. But we've been here talking a while and learned each other's names." He glanced at the crowd. "It's only fair you get to know ours as well."

I greatly appreciated Michael welcoming me. I was usually good with names and faces, but my mind was clouded with worries, so I really made myself focus as they introduced themselves one by one. There were three other boys besides myself and three other girls besides Aliana. I felt that all the people here had a certain charm to their appearance, in one way or another, except Reuben, who I disliked too much to find anything notable.

It seemed a bit odd to me for us all to be similar in age, and for there to be an equal number of boys and girls, but I shrugged it off as coincidence.

Reuben was the last one. He folded his arms and said, "We already met."

"All right..." Michael said dismissively. Perhaps he was used to Reuben's seemingly permanent haughty mood. "Will you tell us what happened now, Jon?"

Although I felt welcomed, I still didn't know anyone here well enough to want to divulge my disheartening and somewhat confusing experience with the vibmtaer. But I wasn't about to tell them nothing, either. That would make me look more snobbish than Reuben.

Before I figured out how to begin, however, Aliana came out of the great hall. Our gazes caught for a moment.

She found someone in the crowd. "Charlie, you're next." There was more confidence to her voice now.

"I want to hear from Jon first," Charlie said.

Charlie was of average height, the shortest of the men here. He looked a little younger as well, not that I could be sure of this fact. It was his hair that was his most notable feature. It was a messy mop of dark blond curls and waves that covered his forehead. His blue eyes were somewhat gray, but they were sharp as they looked at me. His gaze did not falter. It was as if the crowd did not exist to him as he awaited my answer.

My experience seemed to be of great importance to him, so much so that he didn't realize that making Leon and the rest of us wait could never be worth the information I could provide to him. He was eerily calm as everyone shifted uncomfortably around him.

"Charlie!" Michael complained. "Get up there before Leon makes all of us suffer."

"All right," he said with some confusion. He ran into the great hall without looking back.

"What is wrong with him?" Reuben asked. His gaze drifted around the crowd but eventually settled on the one woman with blonde hair. Her name, Kataleya, was memorable because she had spoken it with the same lilt of nobility as Reuben. I was glad to see that she chose to shrug rather than make fun of Charlie with Reuben.

"Well," I said to break the silence. I put my hand across the back of my neck as my nerves got the better of me. "I'm not good at speaking in front of people," I warned them. "But if all of you want to know what happened, I could try to explain it." I chose to address Michael mostly, as I felt the most welcomed by him, but I also took sweeping glances across the crowd here and there.

"I had never even heard of mana before now," I admitted. Many people were audibly shocked.

"How did you end up here, then?" Michael asked.

"I didn't know that I had actually been using mana for years now. No one in Bhode knows anything about sorcery, which is why I traveled to Tryn. I had a feeling that this thing, which turned out to be mana, could be something substantial. I was in Tryn trying to find someone who could explain sorcery to me when Barrett Edgar showed up. He explained a little, but not much, and convinced me to come here with him."

I pointed up at the great hall. "In there, however, you're going to find out the same thing as I did. There's a time constraint on whatever we are here to do. A few months, apparently. They didn't tell me what it was exactly. The rest of the time was spent discussing my range of mana."

We heard the footsteps of someone running through the great hall. Charlie emerged, out of breath. "Eden Ledell, you're next," he said as he pointed at her.

Eden was short, with dark hair that was almost black. It was stylishly combed mostly to one side, her flair for fashion quite evident. She had a cute, youthful face. Under her thin eyebrows were deep-set eyes, large and brown, with long lashes. With a button nose and a small but round chin, her pixie face was a contrast to the confidence that emanated from her. She was cute, any man would agree.

She smiled as if excited, then ran into the building nearby without a word.

"Aliana or Charlie," Michael said while mostly looking at Aliana. "Did they tell you what we would be doing here like they did with Jon?"

Charlie answered first. "I wasn't told anything about that. They tested my range. Then I left."

"I wasn't told anything, either," Aliana said. She gazed at me with a question in her eyes.

Reuben asked me, "Why did you take so long? You must have had a problem."

Unfortunately, it was true.

"Apparently my mana has too wide a range for me to specialize in what I want."

"What's your range?" Michael asked.

"1C to uuD."

There was a wide range of reactions. Most everyone seemed to be surprised, but Reuben appeared angry.

"Here you are lying again."

"Wait, I don't think he said it right," Michael said to quiet the crowd. "He just admitted he knew nothing about mana until now."

"That is true," I agreed. "I knew nothing about mana, but I do remember exactly what happened. They tested my upper range first and told me I could specialize in dvinia. I reached uuD, I'm certain of it. It was because of their excitement that I was eager to learn dvinia, even though I know nothing about it. But then they tested my lowest frequency, 1C. I took a while after because I argued with them. They want me to pick an essence and learn from that, and I don't even know what that really means yet. But I know it didn't excite them as much as dvinia."

Murmurs broke out. Aliana looked as if she wanted to ask me something.

"You really knew nothing about mana?" she asked when the noise died down.

"I hadn't even heard the word before."

Her expression was as if she didn't believe me.

I was beginning to understand that everyone here probably knew a lot about mana and sorcery in general. I had to make sure of it, though. It was one thing to think you knew less than everyone, and something much worse to confirm it.

"All of you have been training with mana before coming here?"

There were nods all around. My heart dropped.

"Can someone tell me what dvinia can do?"

The blonde woman with the noble lilt, Kataleya, spoke up. "There isn't much known about dvinia. I've only heard that the energy made by wizards is a strong force."

That sounded pretty good to me. Working with a strong force gave me options, as opposed to controlling fire or water.

Eden returned with a proud smile. "Michael, you're up."

He walked into the great hall.

"Did I hear dvinia?" Eden asked excitedly.

"It's within Jon's range," Kataleya explained.

"What? You?" She gaped at me as if I were about to transform into a mythical creature before her eyes. She put up her hands. "I didn't mean it like that. It's just that...you're a man, and dvinia requires a very, very high frequency."

"He can reach Lower C as well," Aliana said.

Eden's mouth dropped open. "I thought you knew nothing about mana."

"I didn't."

I had been the subject of everyone's focus for far too long. As much as I had many questions about myself that needed answering, they could wait.

"Enough about me. What about the others who have been tested?"

Eden practically sang, "I'm going to be...an enchanter!" She performed a little twirl.

Congratulations poured out, and I quickly learned to join in even though I wasn't sure exactly what that meant for her. I had heard only a little about enchantments, all of it rumors.

Eden said, "Yeah, I have a low range for a girl."

"So, ordia and mtalia?" Charlie asked, but continued before she could answer. "That's my specialty. Mtalia. I already knew before testing. I was a blacksmith's apprentice. I like to build with metal."

He didn't use a cadence as if he was done speaking, so it took everyone a moment to start congratulating him as well.

"I'm in the low range as well," Aliana said. "And my range is very narrow. They say I'll probably be a ranger."

"Well you certainly have the name for it," Eden teased.

Aliana and a few others laughed. "That's true."

I didn't understand the joke, but Eden noticed my confused expression and told me, "Her surname is Forrester."

"Ah."

"I have already been tested many times," Reuben broke in. "I have a normal, low range, which I have been specializing in for years. I will be a sorcerer of order. One day I will be able to enchant as well, Eden, but gems not metal." He spoke as if this was somehow better. "I also hope to learn to be a harbinger."

"What is that?" I asked, ignoring his snooty attitude. "Barrett said he is one."

"Of course he is," Reuben replied with a roll of his eyes. "He is councilman to the king, as I imagine I will be groomed to be as well." He looked at Kataleya as if this should impress her, but she glanced away from him.

I imagined that Reuben was someone who had been given everything he'd ever asked for, except a woman's heart, and now he had no idea how to win one on his own. I didn't know much about women myself, but I did know one thing about Reuben. His personality wasn't doing him any favors.

"I know my range as well," Kataleya told mostly the other girls and without the same enthusiasm as Reuben. "Erto is my specialty, specifically water. In fact, just recently I found out I can cast without an essence."

"That's incredible," Eden said, and Aliana agreed.

There was one person who hadn't spoken yet except to give her name earlier. She looked shy and possibly even felt that she didn't belong, as she stood on the outskirts of the circle. But I was sure she belonged here as much, if not more, than I did.

Eden probably noticed the same thing because she looked at this young woman and said, "What about you, Remi? Do you know your range already?"

Remi looked down and spoke to the ground. "Um, I've never been tested with the vibmtaer, but I have a very narrow range."

"Many of us do," Aliana said to comfort her. "I can barely get my mana above 11B, so I'm pretty limited to earth as much as I'd like to at least reach ice. What about you?"

Was I understanding this right? 11B was lower than

I could reach, but I thought women were supposed to have a higher natural frequency than men. Eden also said she had a low range, so I was beginning to wonder just how true that stereotype was.

"Fire," Remi said meekly.

I was surprised. I would've figured anything besides fire if I had to guess from looking at her. Her pale cheeks blushed red, matching the crimson color of her lips. Remi had light brown hair that was thin and yet somehow still a little wild. It curled and frayed as it tried to stay together in a tail down her back. Her eyes were on the smaller side, dark green, almost brown. There was a twinkle to them as she looked up again. I felt as though they held a secret.

Michael returned. "They are telling me to specialize in wind! Wind!" He sounded upset. "What am I going to do with more wind?"

"More?" Kataleya asked.

"Yeah, I already make plenty of wind without sorcery!"

Eden and I were the only ones who laughed.

"You are disgusting," Reuben complained.

Michael swiped his hand down in Reuben's direction, then promptly ignored him. "What did I miss?" he asked the crowd.

Our conversation continued on like that until all had finished their test. Everyone's company made it easy for me to forget my issue with mana. I had feared that many of these people would turn out to be like Reuben, but I was pleasantly mistaken.

When Leon returned with the last person to be tested, Reuben, there was a quick change to the mood. Everyone quickly closed their mouths and stood with purpose. Leon paced back and forth in front of us. He was shaking his head as if extremely disappointed. It was so exaggerated that I started to wonder if it was an act. But I realized how wrong I was when he opened his mouth.

"I kept hoping, *dreaming*, that one of you would show me some real skill. Kataleya and Reuben are the only ones who were close." He pointed at the rich young man. "You'd better stop smiling right now, Reuben. Ordia? What am I supposed to do with a sorcerer of ordia, hmm?"

"I—"

"At least Kataleya can do something useful with her mana."

Reuben looked to be grinding his teeth as he glanced down.

"And the rest of you." Leon waved his hand dismissively in Aliana and Eden's direction. "I got a *female* ranger and a *female* enchanter. You two and Jon had your cords crossed at birth or something. And you!" He threw both hands out at Charlie. "Mtalia, and that's *it*? You—I have absolutely no idea what I'm going to do with you."

Many of my peers hung their heads, but anger kept mine up. I wanted to say something, but everything I thought of would've just made it worse. This was one of those moments where the faster it was over, the better.

"I'm a good builder," Charlie said. "I can—ow!"

Michael nudged him firmly with his elbow, then Michael put his finger over his lips.

"I'm impressed," Leon said sarcastically in response to Charlie. "I'm actually impressed at how dumb you are."

Charlie joined many others in looking at the ground. I felt like I really had to say something now, but I shouldn't.

"None of you have earned enough trust to be told more about what we're doing," Leon continued. "None of you are even close. You all still need to prove to me that you can actually do some good. If you aren't prepared to work hard to improve yourself, then you might as well leave right now and save us the trouble of putting up with you. Go ahead." He pointed toward the portcullis on the other side of the courtyard. "Go! What are you waiting for?"

No one moved.

"Really, none of you? Not even you, Charlie?"

Michael put his hand on Charlie's shoulder. "He's staying."

Charlie smiled up at Michael, who nodded at him.

"Fine," Leon said. "If none of you are leaving by choice, then I will decide who deserves to stay."

The air held still. I could just about feel everyone's fear of even breathing in Leon's direction.

"I will decide in three days," Leon added, and we collectively let out a sigh of relief.

Did he enjoy scaring us, or was he just a terrible instructor?

I was beginning to realize that he wasn't an instructor at all, so we were not students, either. Whatever was happening here, there was something Leon needed to accomplish, and he needed us to help him.

Why was it that no one was leaving? I knew my reason. I had to at least learn more about sorcery and mana, and then I could make an informed decision about my future. But why did it seem that no one else even pondered the idea of walking out of the castle now?

Perhaps they all felt what I was starting to feel. The king needed Leon, and Leon needed us. It was the only explanation for his crotchety, ill-tempered mood. We were the best he was going to get, and he knew it. We still weren't nearly good enough, but we could damn well try to be better.

CHAPTER SEVEN

As I rushed out of the castle, I had a feeling that everything was going to happen quickly now. It was as if all
of us had been introduced to a dance and would soon
be expected to show it off, only everyone else had been
practicing the dance for years.

I had been intent on learning dvinia no matter the
cost, but my mind was starting to waver. Some of my
peers, like Aliana, had been disappointed at their results. She said the only class she could be was a ranger,
and she didn't seem sure that she would ever be a good
one.

I was still getting used to all of the terminology.
A magical art was something like dvinia or ordia. A
class, like a ranger, mage, or wizard, seemed to be a
specialization within a magical art. For example, I had
come to learn that there were many classes available
for people with a very low frequency of mana, like enchanters, harbingers, and rangers. I wished I could've
spent the rest of the day asking Leon every question I
had, but all of us had gone off to prepare for our first real
test. It could be the last one for me if I failed to show
any progress—another reason I was considering giving
up on dvinia, at least for now.

I felt like a storm was coming and I only had a few
hours to prepare. All of us would spend the next two
and a half days in solitude, and then we needed to re-

port back to Leon. I was looking forward to the time alone as long as I had everything I needed.

The king, through Leon, had given all of us our weekly stipend. Leon had explained that we would continue to be paid each week unless we proved we weren't worth the coin anymore. We had each received a whopping four gold creds in the form of the most used currency: silver buckles. The forty buckles, combined with my six, had made me feel rich until I realized my predicament.

Everyone who needed an essence was to use their coin to purchase the essence they wanted. I still hadn't understood the concept of the essence, so after everyone else had left, I had been forced to stay behind and put up with Leon belittling me during his explanation of it. What's worse was that I was the only one who needed to purchase an essence. Everyone else who needed one already had one. There were other people, like Charlie and Aliana, who couldn't reach a high enough frequency with their mana to match any essence, so there was no point in trying. I didn't know what they would be doing during these days of solitude, or how they were supposed to prove themselves when it came time. All I could do was hope they would make it, because I had my own problems to worry about.

Not only did I have to buy everything I lacked to keep me alive while I was on my own, but I had to use some of my newly acquired forty buckles to pick out an essence. I had hoped to save some money for new clothing, but I didn't know how much I would have left after picking one out. I might just choose the cheapest one when I visited Enchanted Devices again. I was on my way there now as I remembered what Leon had told me about essences.

I found the concept, of how they helped a sorcerer in training, simple to understand, even if Leon wouldn't tell me exactly how an essence worked. He'd said that first I had to understand spells better. A spell was made up of three or four notes, he'd reminded me. Leon then explained that the similarity between mana and music was why magic was written out in the way it was, like uF for Upper F. It was like the high pitch of a musical note, and lC, my lowest range, was like a low note—Lower C, for example. I hadn't even known that musical notes were labeled like F and C. Leon had lectured me as if I'd learned them a while ago and stupidly forgotten. It was pretty much how he spoke about most things, it seemed.

Each note of mana did something on its own. Leon had told me something miraculous after that introduction. I still had trouble believing it.

"You're natural mana, for example, is uF. I sincerely hope you remember that by now, or you're even more hopeless than I think."

"I remember," I'd told him.

"Upper F is a very powerful note of mana. It even has its own name: vtalia. Almost all notes of F work in harmony with each other. There are spells that involve a combination of lF, F, and uF. I might teach you one of them one day, but I'd have to see you greatly improve first or my time would be wasted."

"Can you give me an example of what one of the spells can do?"

"Vtalia can manipulate life itself."

The more I learned, the more questions I had. But

after explaining the essences, Leon had sent me off.

"Take the essence of water, for example," he'd explained. "It is a combination of three notes that are trapped in a moonstone: C, E, G. Together they form a chord, an easy one to reproduce. Most spells require a combination of notes like this."

"So a spell is just a chord?" I asked.

"No, some spells are just one note, like mtalia. But most spells are a chord, yes—a combination of notes."

I reminded myself that a note was just a frequency of mana, like my uF. So a spell was just multiple frequencies of mana used at the same time. However, I still had no idea how to produce more than one frequency at a time, and I had better learn soon.

I'd almost made it to the shop. I figured I would buy food afterward, as it felt like the least important thing right now.

Leon had gone on to explain that an essence was like listening to the right sound for the spell. Imitating the sound was incredibly easy—his words—while forming the sound without any reference was impossible for someone like me.

His advice, and first real instruction, was that the first thing I needed to learn was to feel mana. I was to use my mind to hold my mana carefully in front of me, without exerting myself too hard, until I could recognize the differences between one note and another. After I spent enough time familiarizing myself with specific notes, I would be able to feel the three simultaneous notes emanating from the essence that I was to keep near me during my entire time of solitude. Then it would be up to me to imitate these notes with my own mana.

Leon recommended that I start with one note at a time until I could mimic all three of the essence. Only then should I start attempting to split my mana in half in order to mimic two at a time.

I hadn't appreciated how he'd laughed bitterly as he shook his head in a way that was becoming irritatingly typical. "And only after you can do that," he'd said, "can you hope to split your mana into *three* notes at a time. There's nothing more I can tell you right now. Everyone learns differently. Good luck. You'll need it."

I was hoping I might run into one of my peers at the shop—maybe someone had realized they wanted to purchase something they hadn't thought of before —but none of them were there when I arrived. I was pleased to see Greda still there, though.

"Hi Jon," she said. She had a long, elegant mouth that set her whole face smiling when she flashed her white teeth.

I returned the expression. "I said I would be back."

"You did."

I looked around the small shop as I made my way to the counter. There was so much to see, the shelves packed, everything unfamiliar. But then I spotted the four colorful gems I had seen earlier that I now knew to be essences. I would take a closer look at them in a moment.

"I need a ward of dteria, not that I know what it is," I admitted. I suddenly had the sense that I wasn't supposed to admit to anyone trying to sell me something that I knew nothing about it, but it was too late for that. I felt that I could trust Greda, though, and I usually had a good sense about people.

"You don't know dteria?" she asked.

"Wait, is that the illegal magical art?"

She nodded with wide eyes as if in disbelief that I didn't know this. I was somewhat shocked myself. How had I not pieced it together sooner? All Leon had said was that everyone who didn't have a ward of dteria had to purchase one immediately. Of course I was the only one.

My head was full of so much new information that I could barely pass a thought about any of it. I had a brief moment of panic right there as I saw myself failing to improve in my two days of solitude and then being thrown out of the castle.

"It's all right," she said, reaching out as if to touch my hand resting on the counter but stopping short. "I was only surprised, was all. A dteria ward is eight buckles. It's going to take me about an hour to make. I could begin now if you pay upfront."

I took eight of the small silver coins from my coin purse. "Of course," I said.

"I'll be right back."

She opened the door to the room behind her. I had a small peek at a variety of animal paws, plants, gems, and raw metal on a large table before she entered the room and closed the door.

Greda returned a moment later holding a small polished stone in one hand, white and cloudy, and a single claw as if from a dog in the other. She set both on the counter between us, then went back to shut the door to the back room.

"I'll need to concentrate during this time," Greda said. "Would you like to come back later?"

"You're going to make the ward right here with just that stone and claw?"

"I am."

"How do you do it?"

"Oh, I...you really don't know anything about the magical arts?"

"I just started learning today."

"Why today?" she asked.

I wasn't supposed to tell her about anything I was doing with Leon. "I'm beginning today as the apprentice for a sorcerer," I lied. "He sent me here to pick up a few things."

"What kind of sorcerer?" Greda asked.

"A mage." I leaned closer and spoke softly. "He has quite the temper, so I'd much rather learn from you if you could take a moment to teach me." I gestured at the stone and the claw.

"Of course," she said. "It's actually quite simple." She picked up the small white stone. "This is a moonstone. It's needed to make any ward. All I have to do is enchant it with something, like a claw from any Canidae, and it's done."

"How does the enchantment work?"

"It's a spell that takes a while to set into the stone, but then the effect continues indefinitely. My mother can do it in half the time."

"And that spell is done with which magical art?"

"Ordia is needed for any enchantment, but you also need mtalia to enchant metal or earth to enchant a gem like this one."

"Is earth the same as erto?"

"No. Erto is a broader category for any natural element: earth, ice, water, fire, and wind. Erto is one of the few magical arts that is used more as a description than something a sorcerer chooses to specialize in.

Most sorcerers who choose an element, like fire, focus only on that one because erto itself encompasses too wide a range. On the other hand, ordia is a small range. It's easier to learn if your mana can reach a low enough frequency."

"I was told that women usually have higher natural frequencies. Is this really true?"

"Yes, my mother and I are strange," she said with a slight laugh. "Usually if a sorcerer has an irregular range of mana, they pass it on to their offspring."

I wondered about my father. What if his mana could've reached uF, and he could've done something to help himself through his illness had he known how to use it? I had always figured that he would've survived had he fallen ill in a populated city. Someone would've known how to do something, or at least told me or my father how to help him with our own mana, if my father had some.

That prompted another question.

"Does everyone have mana?" I asked.

"They do, but most people never learn how to use it because it takes too much practice."

A shadow fell over me. I truly believed my father could be alive today.

"Are you all right?" she asked.

I put on a false smile. "I am. Can I browse your shop while you work on the enchantment?"

"My mother's shop. Certainly, but I won't be able to talk much."

"Not a problem."

I went to look at the essences again. Nothing was labeled, no prices listed. I supposed most of the people who came here had some knowledge of sorcery already and had expectations about the cost of everything they might want. They probably haggled. Perhaps I should've tried to convince her to lower the price of the dteria ward. I looked back at her, a line across her forehead as she concentrated over the counter. Too late now.

The dog's claw and the moonstone were pushed close together. Greda held her hand over them, but I didn't see anything happening. I wondered if the claw would change in some way when she was done, perhaps even disintegrate. There was so much more to learn about sorcery. I wish I had begun years ago.

There were only four essences on the shelf, each in the form of a gem fused onto a bracelet. It was easy to assume what each one did. I pretty much had done that when I'd come in here earlier, before I knew a thing about mana. The red one glowed, a little heat emanating from it. Fire. The one without color was a little cloudy. It had to be wind. The last two were both blue, one the color of water and the other the color of ice.

I put my hand over the essence of water and closed my eyes. Ice was a little cold, but not this one.

I was shocked that I felt something. It was neither heat nor cold, nor did I feel it moving, but it was there like a sound I could barely hear. Mana.

I dissected it by pinpointing the invisible hand of my mind on one of its three parts. I could feel the mana. It seemed like I might be able to mimic it, but I didn't know how. It was like trying to remember something that I was certain I knew. How should I begin? It almost seemed like beginning and ending would happen at the same time, and there was nothing in between.

I extended my own mana over the stone, the note

I now knew to be uF. It was a high frequency, buzzing without sound. I held it close to the stone of water as I tried to determine the difference between the mana within the essence and my own mana. I knew mine was supposed to be higher, but I couldn't feel just how much. I tried lowering the frequency of my note to match what I felt, but I couldn't seem to get it, a tension building when I thought I was close.

It didn't take long for me to start breathing hard. I took a break, feeling as tired as if I had just sprinted a medium distance. Using only my mind usually didn't fatigue me physically like this. It had to be my use of mana. That was new.

I experimented with each essence. If I understood Leon's lessons correctly, each of these essences was a spell trapped within a stone. That meant there were three frequencies of mana vibrating within each stone at the same time. I still had to figure out how to split my mana into more than one frequency, but that was pointless unless I learned how to match the different vibrations that a spell required.

I lost track of the time as I experimented. When I took another break, I checked on Greda to find that the dog's claw had lost all its color, now white as snow.

Fascinating. I had spotted many animal parts in the backroom. I hoped they had only come from animals that had died naturally.

I would be alone in the mountains for two days to figure out how to cast a spell, but I was beginning to believe that I would need more time than that. Or perhaps I just needed an advantage of some kind.

A rather disobedient plan came to me.

I looked around the shop and recognized a vibmtaer. Greda or her mother must've made another to replace the one we'd purchased, or it had been in the back. Now this was exactly what I needed.

Leon would have a fit if he knew what I planned to do, but the device was small enough that I should be able to hide it from him when I returned to the castle. We were all to meet one last time before Leon took us to the mountains and left us in solitude.

I brought it to the counter. "How much for another vibmtaer?" I asked.

Her hand continued to hover over the stone and claw. "Two and a half creds," she said, then looked down again.

Damn, it was expensive. "What about for the essences?" I asked.

"Depends on the essence," she answered curtly.

"Which one is the cheapest?"

She looked up at me and didn't bother to hide her irritation. "Fire and water. One cred, one buckle each."

"Thank you," I said and let her be.

I didn't know exactly what dteria did, but I had to assume the ward was necessary. I didn't want to accidentally learn an illegal magical art during my trials and be thrown out of the castle. Or would I be put in the dungeon? Yeah, I had to get the ward. That left me with a little more than three creds worth of buckles.

I had been told that I would have to provide my own food during this time in solitude. I also needed to eat supper in town before I left. I was running out of time. The coin I had was supposed to last a week, and I had no idea what other purchases might be required. It was disappointing, to say the least, that food was not provided to us within the castle.

Would that change after we proved ourselves? The king seemed to need us for something. It didn't seem likely that he would let us starve if we spent our weekly stipend on other things, though he might be a little peeved.

I couldn't afford an essence *and* a vibmtaer unless I used all my coin here, which meant I couldn't buy food or anything else. So I had to decide between one or the other.

I already knew which one I was going to pick. I spent the rest of the time thinking about how much trouble I might be in if it didn't work out as I hoped.

A lot, I realized. *A whole lot.*

I took the vibmtaer to the counter. I already had twenty-five buckles counted out and ready. "Do you have a color chart for this vibmtaer?"

"In the back."

"Could I purchase it with the color chart? I promise this will be the last time I bother you until you are finished." I put the coins down on the counter.

"You want another vibmtaer?" she asked, confused.

"I do," I confirmed.

"All right," she said with a shrug as she collected the silver coins. She started toward the back room but stopped. "If you don't know much about mana, you might want a color chart with ranges."

"Absolutely." I didn't even know there were other color charts. "Whichever chart has the most information on it is best for me."

"Let me see."

Soon she returned with a rolled parchment. She handed it over. "This is as detailed as they come."

"Thank you."

She murmured a sound of agreement as she got back to work on the enchantment.

I was glad the purchase of the chart seemed to be included with the twenty-five buckles. I unrolled it for a look.

Marvelous. It seemed to have everything I had already heard about mana, except for dteria, of course, but it helped tremendously to have it all laid out in front in me.

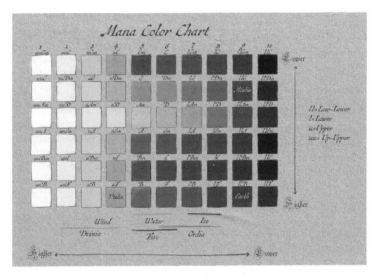

I had just taken it to the other corner of the room for a better look when a city guard stepped into the shop.

"Greda Waxler?"

"Yes?" she said with large eyes.

"Your mother was found on the street, unconscious."

"Oh god!"

"We took her to a healer who needs to be paid for

his service. I think she will be all right. Will you come with me?"

"Yes, of course." She grabbed the moonstone and claw off the counter and rushed over to the guard. He led her out of the shop. Both of them had just begun to run when I had the thought to step out of the shop and shout after her.

"Greda, what about your shop?"

She jerked to a stop, then spun around and ran back. "I have to lock it up. I'm sorry. I have to go."

"I understand."

"Your ward, though." She stopped and looked down at her hand holding the stone and claw. She took my hand with her free one. "Come with me. We'll figure something out."

But the guard pushed out his palm. "Only family."

"And your shop still needs to be locked," I reminded her.

Her head whipped back. "Of course!" Through her panic, she closed the door and inserted and turned a key from her pocket. "I will come back in an hour and give you the ward."

"Are you sure? I'll understand if you can't."

"I can do it."

"All right, I'll meet you back here. Thank you."

"Thank you, I'm sorry. Let's go," she told the guard.

They rushed down the street.

It took a few breaths for me to calm down. I hoped her mother would be all right. I wondered what had happened. I knew I was new in the city, but a guard coming to tell someone their loved one was found unconscious in the street had to be a significantly rare and alarming experience for anyone.

My thoughts started to return, and so did my worries. She wouldn't be back for a while, if at all today. I'd better find a meal, a cheap one, and figure out what to do next.

Fortunately, this area of the city didn't seem as expensive as some of the others I'd passed through to get here. Greda's shop was close to the wall surrounding the city, far from the castle at the center. Most of the places here were on the smaller side. I found the nearest tavern after a short walk and asked about a meal. They were offering salted pork and roasted potatoes for four copper, a good deal where I came from. I gladly paid and used my own water rather than purchase an ale for an extra copper.

I ate quickly, as I often did. Soon my empty plate was taken away and I set down the vibmtaer and color chart in its place. I was very glad to have purchased them before the guard had come.

The tavern was mostly empty, and I was graciously left alone. I looked closer at the ranges displayed on the bottom of the color chart. Fire and water overlapped evenly. They had the same range. Dvinia and wind overlapped as well, but not evenly, as dvinia extended farther toward the higher notes than wind did, requiring a higher frequency than wind.

I was shocked as I noticed something. My range was 1C to uuD, which meant that I had access to not only wind, fire, water, and ice...but to ordia as well. I could learn it after all.

My heart sank as I realized, however, that both earth and mtalia were below my range. That meant I never would be able to use ordia to enchant metal or gems. I didn't know what else I might be able to do with it, create magical contracts perhaps? I wasn't very interested in taking the time to learn how, at least right now.

I was getting ahead of myself. My plan was simple and possibly foolish, but I was determined to make it work. Rather than buying an essence and spending two days trying to mimic it so that I could cast one spell of water or fire, I decided to learn the frequencies of dvinia one by one. Once I mastered them, I should be able to cast the spell easily.

In theory, this would work if I could learn to manipulate my mana as quickly as I learned most other things. Neither Leon nor Barrett had wanted to give me the chance to prove myself, but I knew I could do it. One spell—one spell of dvinia—that's all I had to show Leon after I returned from my time in the mountains. They wouldn't force me to mimic an essence of an element after that, and I could move on to other spells.

Unfortunately, the one spell of dvinia that Leon shared with me required four frequencies, not three. The lowest one was my natural vibration of mana, uF. I didn't have to learn that one. The other three were all higher: uG, uuC, and uuD—the last one being the highest frequency I could reach.

Of these three notes that I had to learn, I soon found that the highest note was actually the easiest one to cast because I just had to exert my mana to its limit. But it was the hardest one to maintain. Everything between my natural mana and the highest I could reach took less of my stamina, but I found it impossible to discern the difference between these notes.

I decided to experiment, a method of learning that usually helped me. I wanted to see how slowly I could push my mana to vibrate faster. It became tense, resistant to my will as I excited it. I watched the color on the vibmtaer's panel shift from purple to pink, and then to orange as I pushed harder. I tried to continue increasing the frequency gradually, but it was strenuous to adjust my mana evenly when it took so much out of me to maintain it at this high frequency. Doing so felt like trying to change the pitch of a shriek. After another little push, the colors on the panel jumped through light green, blue, and purple in a blink, just to land on pale yellow, my limit.

I sighed. I really needed to have better control of mana at high frequency to have any chance of casting this spell, but I didn't know the best way to improve. It wasn't as if I had time to keep failing.

As I practiced longer, I was really starting to see how having a wide range of mana made this more difficult. If the note of my natural mana was right in the middle of dvinia, I could just lower it and raise it subtly to reach the notes I required. But three of the notes I needed were above my natural mana, and there were so many frequencies below that I sometimes slipped into when practicing.

I had nothing to show for my time after a half hour had passed. I figured Greda would probably not be returning to her shop anytime soon, but I needed a short break anyway because I was unusually fatigued. I decided to walk around.

It was a shock when I passed the shop to see Greda inside looking down at the counter as if she'd never left.

I walked inside. She didn't look up. On the counter in front of her was the moonstone, no claw in sight.

"Greda?" I tried. "Is your mother all right?"

She nodded, barely looking up at me. She pushed the moonstone toward me.

I walked over to the counter. "You sure your mother's all right?"

She nodded again, then nudged the moonstone closer to me.

I didn't quite understand her mood. Perhaps her mother hadn't recovered yet but was still alive? I didn't want to push Greda to answer me if she didn't want to speak, but I did need to know about the moonstone.

"You couldn't have finished the enchantment yet, could you?"

She nodded again, clearly incensed now. She picked it up and dropped it into my hand.

"I'm sorry," I said. "But I have to make sure of it. This *is* a finished ward against dteria?"

She finally looked up at me and nodded once more. Then she pointed at the door.

I was confused and irritated, but clearly something had happened involving her mother.

I walked to the door, then turned back. "I hope everything turns out all right. Sorry for the trouble."

She gestured, rather rudely, for me to leave.

I left the shop feeling more bewildered than insulted. I understood that worrying about a loved one could alter anyone's mood severely, but her reaction didn't quite make sense to me. Why not at least say something to clarify the situation? It was as if I was the one who had caused her mother to fall in the street unconscious.

I looked at the moonstone carefully when I was a street away. It was white, opaque. I didn't know what to look for to determine if I had been cheated. I would

show it to Leon when I returned, but first I had to purchase the food I would need for the entire duration
of my solitude. By the time I was done, I probably
wouldn't have more than a few buckles left.

CHAPTER EIGHT

Everyone was waiting by the portcullis when I returned. They all had their packs and bedrolls. Leon was searching through each of their belongings. Was he checking to make sure they had their wards and essences? I would need to avoid the search somehow. He was not to catch me without an essence, or I could be expelled from the group without a chance to prove myself.

It didn't seem as if everyone had been waiting long. No one made any remarks toward me about being late. Nonetheless, I rushed past them to fetch spare clothing from my room.

When I returned, they were already walking out of the castle. I hurried to catch up. I had decided against showing my ward to Leon in fear that he would ask me which essence I had chosen and possibly search my bag for it. What was even more likely was that he might find the ward to be faulty and send me back to purchase another, or worse, exclude me from the trip.

At noticing Michael toward the back of the group, I had a better idea. I came up on his side.

"Hey, Jon," he said. "Glad you made it."

"Thanks. I thought I might see you at the shop for an essence of wind."

"Oh, no, I already knew that wind was my specialty. I've known for a year. I just thought it would be funny to make a jest out of it."

"I see," I said with a chuckle.

"Did you get everything you needed?" he asked.

"Actually, I have a question about that."

"What is it?"

I looked ahead. Leon was at the front, the group of four girls behind him. Reuben was right behind Kataleya, but he didn't seem to be speaking to her. Charlie was behind Reuben, a little space between him and Michael and me at the back.

"I had to buy a ward of dteria, but I'm not sure if it works." I took it out of my pocket and showed it to him.

He took a look at it. "Honestly, I can't tell. I can't even tell you how these things are supposed to work, but I don't blame you for not wanting to ask Leon." He handed the ward back to me. "The man's got a stick up his ass, and I mean deep in there."

I put the ward back in my bag.

"Shouldn't matter much if it doesn't work," Michael said. "Just focus on matching your mana to the essence and you'll be fine. Which did you choose?"

I didn't want to lie to him, but I wasn't prepared to share the truth, either.

Leon was taking us south through the city. I could already spot the tops of the mountains not too far ahead of us. I'd heard something about the capital being close to both mountains and Curdith Forest, but I didn't realize just how close Newhaven was to both until now.

I eventually came to the conclusion that Michael wouldn't want to know what I had done because it would put him in a difficult position.

"Let's pretend you didn't ask," I told him with a

look from the sides of my eyes.

"Oh Jon, you play a dangerous game. I really hope you know what you're doing."

"I hope so as well."

As we followed the group out of the city, Michael and I started to share our first impressions of the castle. It didn't take long for Charlie to slow and listen in. It was a little odd that he didn't say anything but also didn't bother to hide that he was listening. He sometimes turned around and stared directly at whoever was speaking, his mop of blonde hair bouncing and swaying with each step.

We tried to include him a few times by asking him about himself, but he would only shake his head and say, "I just want to listen."

Michael informed me that everyone else had met a half day before Reuben and I showed up. Leon had sent them out to purchase a variety of things after making them promise they wouldn't speak about any of it to anyone. They had suspected since the beginning that they were being tested, but they'd been separated as well. There hadn't been much time for them to discuss their tasks with each other.

Michael had been sent to purchase several moonstones from the same shop I had visited. Afterward, he'd been fed and sent to his room to sleep. In the morning, he was told to fetch hay for the stables. He had begun to fear that the guard who'd brought him here had lied. He'd been told that he would learn the magical arts from the best instructor in the world.

"Imagine my surprise after I met Leon," he said, giving me a chuckle.

Like me, Michael had no guardians anymore. His

father had died only a year ago, just like mine, but his father was killed by a thief during the night, not taken by an illness. And Michael's mother didn't die during childbirth, as mine had.

"She left me and my father when I was a baby," Michael said. "She'd never wanted a child. I don't know where she went, but if she'd stayed in Newhaven my father and I would've run into her at least once. He was a carpenter and worked everywhere."

"How did you learn about the magical arts?" I asked.

"When I was thirteen, my father landed a big job for a sorcerer and found out a few things. He told them to me, and I was hooked like a fish."

"Could your father ever cast anything?"

"He could feel his mana, but he never could do anything with it."

It sounded like my experience, except I had been using my mana without knowing what it was. After I told him my tale, we fell silent for a little while. There was now a large gap between the three of us and the rest of the group, with Reuben still trailing close behind Kataleya and the other women.

"Tell us about your family, Charlie," Michael tried.

"I grew up with a blacksmith," he said without turning around.

Michael and I sped up until the three of us were walking abreast.

"He isn't your father?" I asked.

"I don't think so."

"You don't think so?" Michael said. "Why is that?"

"Because he found me in a barrel when I was a baby. Fathers don't find their sons in barrels." Charlie said it so matter-of-factly that it took a moment for me to realize what an extreme story of negligence it was.

"I'm sorry," I said.

"I don't care. I don't remember. I like Karl. I like the work I do at the blacksmith."

"Wait, you said earlier that you know mtalia?" Michael asked, hinting at something.

"Yes."

Michael slapped my shoulder with the back of his hand. "He's the blacksmith's apprentice I've heard about in Newhaven! Charlie's actually pretty well known."

"Yes, people talk about me." If Charlie had an emotional reaction toward this, he didn't show it.

"What do they say?" I asked.

Michael was silent for a while as Charlie looked at him.

"Well, um…" Michael stammered.

"They don't like me," Charlie admitted. "I'm not good with people. Karl has told me this often. It's why he gave me to the king."

"We like you, Charlie," Michael said. "Don't we, Jon?"

"We do," I said and was glad to see Charlie smile.

"How did your father end up giving you to the king?" I asked.

"A guard came by and told Karl, 'The king wants Charlie. He might be gone a long time, but he will be paid well. Do you accept?'"

Michael and I waited, but Charlie seemed to be done.

"And what did *you* want?" I asked.

He looked at me with shock, as if I didn't understand something. "It is very prestigious to work for the king. Of course I wanted to."

"I didn't know you cared about prestige," I said.

"I do."

Leon shouted from the front, "Get up here and pay attention!"

We hurried toward the rest of the halted group, our packs bouncing on our backs.

"All of you are going to split up now," Leon explained. "There are a few hours of daylight left. Find somewhere among the hills and mountains—your own spot! There are plenty of caves. There are no bears here. Nothing is going to kill you, except me if I find out you wasted this time or spent it with anyone else in the group. You will meet back in the castle the morning after tomorrow. That means you have two full days to teach yourself something new."

Charlie raised his hand. It was a shock when Leon pointed at him without yelling. "What?"

"Why do we have to stay here during this whole time?"

"That is an excellent question. Sometimes I forget how dumb all of you are and I need a reminder, so thank you for that, Charlie."

Charlie lowered his head.

Leon explained, "The southern range of mountains ahead of you are close enough to Curdith Forest for them to give you a little bit of the benefit to your mana that can be found in the forest. But the mountains do not have the same dangers as the forest. In other words, the connection of your mana to your mind is better around here, and you won't be so distracted or endangered to let it go to waste."

I raised my hand. He pointed at me.

"How is it that the forest and these mountains have that effect?"

"No." He shook his head at me. "I am not going to start a debate about something as complex as that. You can research it yourself later, whether you succeed or fail to show me that you can imitate whatever essence you chose. Anyone have a better question?"

I was certainly not going to take another risk by raising my hand. It seemed that no one else wanted to ask anything, either.

"Two days," Leon repeated. "Now spread out."

We started to walk off as he continued to shout at us.

"If I find out any of you said even one word to another from this point on, then I don't care if you come back stronger than Gourfist himself. I never want to see you near the castle again. Don't even pick a spot where you can *see* someone else. You are to be completely alone for this."

I kept my eyes focused straight ahead and chose a route toward the nearest rocky slopes. There was no helping that some people were still walking close to one another, but everyone quickly spread out the farther they went. I was nervous to look back at Leon, curious how long he would stand and watch us go. It didn't matter. I had no plans to break a rule, and I doubted anyone else did.

Rocky hills led up to the southern mountains ahead of us. There were more than enough routes for everyone to go their separate ways, but some paths were more treacherous than others. I took the steepest one, trusting in my balance and eager to find my spot for the next two days. I needed all the time I could to learn how to cast the one spell of dvinia that I knew. It would've been impossible without the vibmtaer. It would still be difficult, but I was certain I could do it. I just needed time.

I took a steep path that twisted up the small mountain, which met the sky farther up ahead, not allowing me to see what was on the other side.

When I eventually made it, I was pleased to find a small field of mossy grass at its summit. Up this high, I could see the rest of my peers fanning out and taking other paths. Many would have to walk quite far to find a flat surface like this. I was closer to the city here as well. The nights would be the worst because I had no cover. I could keep searching for a cave, as Leon had mentioned, but I was too eager to begin. I could usually sleep anywhere, so long as it didn't rain. Fortunately, there was not a cloud in the blue sky.

It was advantageous to pick the first place, as I had done. This way I had more time to practice, and I was closer to the capital to return when we finished. I needed every advantage I could get. I was too nervous to take out my vibmtaer with everyone still walking around, but there was much I could do as I waited.

I sat down with my legs crossed. I set the ward of dteria in front of me, closed my eyes, and pushed out my mana. I couldn't feel any difference here compared to the tavern, but the quiet was refreshing. It reminded me of Bhode.

The spell I needed required me to use the note of my natural mana, uF, and the highest vibration I could reach, uuD. These two would be the easiest to practice, and I didn't need the vibmtaer to begin.

For the last five or six years of my life, I had toyed with my mana. I knew what uF felt like, and I wouldn't soon forget it. uuD was different, however. Reaching that note with my mana was like pushing my voice to its highest note. It was exhausting, but it did get a little easier as I practiced.

Eventually, I stood up and looked around. I couldn't see my peers, who I knew were somewhere south. The city wall was about a mile north, maybe farther. There was a short bridge over the river that ran south past my location. I hardly remembered crossing it on my way here. I'd had too much on my mind lately. I looked forward to being able to relax, but that wouldn't be for two days.

I took out the vibmtaer from my pocket and the rolled up color chart from my bag. I found two small stones to set on the corners of the parchment so it would stay open.

Just to ensure I was right, I tested my mana. Sure enough, I saw a light grayish purple for uF and a pale yellow for uuD. I just needed to become more comfortable casting uuD, then I could start working on the other two notes between my natural note and the highest note I could reach.

Hours passed as the sun quickly set. It somehow became harder and harder to reach uuD as time went on. It felt like my mana was being pulled lower by an outside force. It took more concentration, more of my stamina as well, to reach it again and again.

I was exhausted when night was settling in. There was just enough light in the red sky for me to see the front panel on the vibmtaer. I decided another test was in order. I tried to push out my mana at its natural frequency of uF again, but it felt off. I checked the vib-mtaer as I casted the note.

It was a pale green.

Shocked, I checked the color chart. Above the square of pale green was the note "uEm."

uEm? I hadn't been taught what "m" meant, but I could see that it was one note lower in frequency than uE. So "m" must be lower. Why didn't they just name it differently? Why "Em" instead of "D?"

There were other questions I had as I looked over the color chart. The lowest note was llC. Why did they start with C and not A for the lowest possible frequency? And why did it go from G back to A as it got higher and higher? Why not G and then H? Why not all the way up to Z?

I remembered then that Leon had mentioned that the different F notes shared similar properties. He had also told me several times that there were similarities between mana and music. This probably had something to do with how they were named.

I started pondering other questions as I tried to regain my stamina. Was mana the same thing as the magical arts? No, I reminded myself that the magical arts were ranges of mana like dvinia, wind, fire, and ordia.

Soon it was too dark and I was too tired to keep practicing. I set out my bedroll and started to drift off as my mind sifted through all the information I'd learned today.

I was so tired I must've slept all the way through the night. I woke up with my body a bit stiff but my mind refreshed. I took a little time to wake up and make myself comfortable in fresh clothing, then I was ready to get back to it.

An instinct told me to test my mana again, though, because something felt off. It was like there was mana already in the air, mana that wasn't mine.

My first thought was that I was finally beginning to feel the benefits of meditating in this area of mountains close to Curdith Forest. But the more I practiced, the more I realized that the difference to my mana was an inconvenience, not a benefit. Something was slowing my mana, lowering its vibration.

When I pushed out my natural mana, the color displayed on the vibmtaer was now light yellow. Looking at the color chart, I found out this note was uD. Last night it was one note higher, uEm. Why was my natural mana getting lower?

I picked up the ward of dteria. I looked into it deeply. I concentrated my mind on it. I even sniffed the damn thing. Was it *this* little thing that was changing the nature of my mana?

I felt a chill. Perhaps I hadn't been tricked for coin but with intentions even more detrimental to my future. Did Greda sell me something that disrupted my mana?

I took it away from my camp spot and set it down about fifty yards away. Then I returned. If it was doing something to my mana, I needed to find out.

I thought through every possibility I could imagine as I waited for its possible effects to wear off.

Perhaps it was a ward of dteria, and the nature of the ward was what altered my mana. Or Greda could've made a mistake creating the ward. Or it was intentional and this wasn't a ward at all. But why would she do something like that to me? And what could it be instead? There were other possibilities as well, but I wouldn't come to any conclusions about them until I confronted her, so I didn't see the point in wondering right now.

I tried to keep practicing, but it felt like a waste of time. I couldn't learn what a specific note felt like if that note temporarily felt different, as they all did now.

Anger consumed me. I'd had concerns about this cursed ward, but Leon was such an irritable donkey ass that I couldn't bring my concerns to his attention. I knew I was partly to blame for going against his instructions, but I didn't have the capability right then to turn my rage onto myself.

I directed it at Greda next. I understood that she was worried about her mother, but that didn't give her the right to sell me something as a ward when it most likely wasn't. If she had done it on purpose, she would pay dearly.

But why do this to me? I kept returning to the same question. I knew I'd interrupted her a few times when she was working, but that couldn't have been the reason. No one was that fickle.

The only way I could explain her behavior was that she was lashing out at me as if I was the one responsible for her mother's poor health. However, even when my father was clearly dying, I didn't take it out on anyone else. Even the monk who had failed to heal him and then recommended prayer above all else—I treated the man with respect. It wasn't his fault that he was incapable of helping. He'd tried his best.

I fumed for a while longer. Every time I tried to cast, I still felt my mana being altered by what I had come to be sure was the moonstone Greda had sold me. I was tempted to crush it or at least pick it up and throw it as far as I could, but I might need it later as evidence.

Eventually, I did notice my mana slowly returning to normal. The stone had to be too far away to make a difference anymore. I ate something from my pack of dried food and waited another whole hour for my natural mana to show as the familiar purple-gray on the vibmtaer, uF. Finally.

I was ready to practice again. It was noon. Yesterday evening and more than half of this day had been ruined. I wouldn't let it get to me right now, though. So long as I still learned the one dvinia spell I'd memorized, then I wouldn't be removed from the group and thrown out of the castle.

At least I was *almost* sure I wouldn't be removed. I supposed Leon could hold a grudge against me for going against him, but I was relying on the notion that he needed anyone who could be of use. He would have to keep me if I proved myself valuable.

I supposed it wouldn't be the end of my life if I did fail. I would find work in the city and study sorcery when I could. It would be much more difficult to accomplish anything with the magical arts without proper training, but at least I wouldn't have to put up with Leon and any risk that might come with training for the king. Should I just give up now?

The thought turned my stomach. I'd only had a taste of sorcery, but it had become more important to me than anything else left in my world. I supposed that wasn't too strange considering I had lost everything when my father passed. I had known this piece of me—my mana—was something incredibly valuable.

Pursuing it had led me this far. I wasn't going to give up now.

CHAPTER NINE

I had never sat in one place for this long in my life, but the hours flew by as I made decent progress. I barely tasted any of the food I had brought with me. I never stopped practicing and working out my mana.

Eventually it was night. The wind was freezing as if trying to bring an early winter upon us. I settled into my bedroll. My exhaustion was more powerful than the cold, and soon I fell asleep.

I was groggy in the morning, my eyes blurry. I tried to wake up with some breakfast, but it didn't quite do the trick. I decided to make a quick trip to the river where I could at least wash my face and rinse my hair.

I was ready to practice when I returned. I blissfully found out that now I could consistently cast uuD, the highest note needed for the spell, and it didn't strain my mind as much as the night before.

Tomorrow morning I would have to go back to the castle. Having only one day left, I was nervous about learning the spell in time. I still had to figure out how to cast the other two notes, which meant memorizing the feeling of the two other frequencies of mana. These were in between the natural vibration of my mana and the highest note I could reach.

The hours flew by with me making great progress, now that the stone Greda had sold me was far away. By noon, I learned how to reach both notes consistently.

That's when I stopped for lunch.

I knew it was important to take a break, at least to eat, but I was so eager to begin again that I didn't allow myself more than five minutes before I was casting once more. I altered my mana from one note to another, and then back down again.

I let out a little cheer. "Yes!" I was finally comfortable casting each of the notes necessary for the spell: uF, uG, uuC, uuD. There was still one small problem and one very big one. uG and uuC still felt a little awkward. I could push my mana to them by monitoring the color on the vibmtaer to ensure I made it to light orange and pale pink respectively, but when I tried to reach the same notes without looking at the vibmtaer, I looked later to find that I was sometimes off by a small margin because all the notes around this range still felt nearly the same to me.

I didn't have time to familiarize myself with the two middle notes as I had with the lower and higher ones, not with the big problem looming over me like my immediate expulsion from the castle. I had to figure out how to split my mana into not two...not even three...but all four of these notes to actually cast the spell.

I was excited to find out what it did, but I had to be honest with myself. There was a good chance I wasn't going to figure it out in time. Too much of my effort had been wasted because of that damn ward of dteria, or whatever it really was. I took a few deep breaths to let go of my budding anger. I had to focus.

As of right now, splitting my mana felt like splitting my voice into two different sounds. I just didn't see how it was possible. Barrett had warned me that this would take weeks. Soon I would find out if I was brilliant or laughably stupid for thinking otherwise.

I would have time to worry about being expelled... well, when I was expelled. For now, I would enjoy the challenge. I was supposed to split something that seemed to come from a single source: myself. Perhaps that was my answer. It wasn't about splitting the mana once I was holding it in the air. It was about pushing out two different forms of mana at the same time.

I took hold of the mana within me, feeling the familiar uF buzzing in my mind. It was easy to push my natural mana out of me into the air, or to cast into the air, in other words. I prepared myself to do it but stopped at the last moment, splitting my mind and the mana in half. Then I pushed.

Nothing unusual happened. It just felt like uF was buzzing in the air.

"All right," I told myself. "That's fine. It's probably just because the two forms of mana were the same note: uF. They must've merged together to become one as they left my body. Perhaps all notes of mana do that when I split it."

I started to wonder where exactly my mana was coming out of me. I could feel the energy anywhere I searched for it. I could even move it around once it was out. But where did it come from? It was a little strange and somewhat violating to think about the various possibilities.

I casted a few times as I pinpointed my mind on the mana leaving my body. I came to the conclusion that it was leaving from my hand, but it didn't have to be that way. I could push it out of my chest, my head...and that seemed to be it. I was a little glad that my other experiments with the lower half of my body didn't work.

What was bizarre was that I didn't feel the mana leaving or even traveling through my body. It was as if it was already outside my skin but still connected to me. That made me recall something Leon had mentioned when I had first met him and Reuben. He had asked if Reuben knew what a vibmtaer looked like. He didn't want Reuben bringing back something "useless like a manamtaer" by mistake.

I assumed that meant that our mana really was outside our bodies where it could be measured by a device. I imagined a manamtaer might tell someone how strong their mana was, or perhaps how much there was that could be used. That would explain how it could be useless for us, at least right now. It would be helpful at some point, however, to find out just how much mana I had compared to other sorcerers.

I set my mind back on my task. I needed to prepare two *different* notes to be used at the same time. I would have to learn to cast uF and uuD at the same time anyway, so I started with them because they were the easiest.

It was like trying to think two different thoughts at the same time. The grass is green and the rocks are gray. One after another was easy, but thinking each statement simultaneously was extremely uncomfortable. It made me shout out in frustration a few times as I continued to fail. I scratched my head vigorously like there was an itch I couldn't get rid of.

"How the hell does anyone do this?" I shouted. "And I'm supposed to do *four* at once?"

I was beginning to wish I had purchased an essence instead. It would be so much easier to match different notes already in the air. It would be like looking at the green grass and gray rocks and letting my mind think about both of them at the same time rather than closing my eyes and trying to think of one and...wait. That was it!

I didn't have to focus on each individual note at the same time. That would be like trying to picture the grass vividly, with all its green individual blades, and at the same time picture gray and speckled rocks in a separate part of my mind. Why would I do that when I could put the rocks on the grass and picture them vividly together?

I was beyond familiar by then at casting uF and uuD. I had been preparing my mana and then pushing it into the air, but I would never be able to cast two different notes that way. They had to be prepared and casted together. I groaned as I realized what that meant. There was a step I needed to learn that I had forgone.

There was no way to prepare one note at a time when two needed to be cast simultaneously. I had to learn, instead, how to cast each different note *without* thinking. It would be like trying to move my right hand and left hand in circles of different speeds and directions at the same time. There was no way to think about one and then the other while moving both. I had to move them at the same time pretty much without thinking. That would take muscle memory and complete control over my hands. The same must be done with my mana.

Now I truly understood what it meant to be a sorcerer. If I could familiarize myself with using all the notes my mana could reach, then I would be able to cast any spell within my range. But I had spent hours trying to familiarize myself with just four notes, and I felt like I needed at least another ten hours before I might barely be able to use them to cast something.

I might just make it in time if I practiced into the night. I wouldn't be able to use the vibmtaer after sunset, but hopefully that wouldn't matter. It had helped me enough already. I could sometimes cast each of the four notes from memory by now.

I had no doubt that my spell, when finally cast, would be very weak. I didn't even want to try to figure out how sorcerers could practice putting power behind their spells. There was more than enough on my plate as it was.

I practiced my highest note, uuD, over and over again. Two days ago, the high-frequency note strained my mind like a scream, but now it felt more like performing a mental push-up. I finished the last of my food as evening came and went.

Soon I realized my previous theory of needing only ten hours was vastly optimistic. If I really wanted to feel comfortable using my mana at a high frequency, I would probably need more than a hundred hours of practice. That was time I didn't have.

I convinced myself I didn't need to be that comfortable by tomorrow morning. I just had to be able to cast the spell one time in front of Leon. Just once.

I moved on to the other two notes in between the natural vibration of my mana and the highest I could force it to achieve. I practiced these notes back and forth, uG and uuC. I had to learn how they felt without checking the vibmtaer if I had any chance of casting with them. However, the note I made didn't always click in my mind quite right. It was an irritating feeling, like trying to remember a name that I knew started with a certain letter, yet another name that was close kept sprouting up in my head. It happened frequently when I tried to reach uuC. I just couldn't get my mana to settle on the exact frequency I needed no matter how hard I tried. I could probably use a break, but I didn't have time for one.

Soon the sun had almost set. The sky had a beautiful crimson hue around the eastern horizon. I wasn't high enough to see all of Curdith Forest from here, but there were many dark and tall trees that jutted out from the middle of it that I couldn't miss. The forest unsettled me, with its assortment of trees of different sizes and colors. There was an unnatural feel to it.

The few minutes I'd taken to look around was all I could afford for a break. It was time to cast the spell. My mind went blank as I tried to remember what I had figured out earlier about casting multiple notes at once. I didn't know if I'd ever been this exhausted.

I tried a few times, only to fail spectacularly, messing up even uF when I tried to single it out. I was getting worse. I needed to sleep.

I got comfortable in my bedroll. Leon said we had to be back at the castle in the morning. He didn't specify a time. I would rise early and give myself a few hours to cast the spell before I left.

I didn't know how long I'd slept, but I woke in the very early morning with the chill of night still in the air. My body urged me to lie back down and close my eyes, but I didn't have the time.

*****

I ran through the streets of Newhaven. I was hungry, dirty, and too enraged to tell if I was tired. I would be late to the castle, but there was something I had to do first. I stormed into the Enchanted Devices shop. Or I tried to. The door was locked. I beat my fist on it until I heard a response.

"We're not open yet!" Greda called.

"Greda!" I shouted. "Let me in right now!"

"Jon?"

"Yes, open the door!"

She swung it open. "I was wondering—what are you doing?"

I pushed her back and slammed the door shut behind me. She stumbled backward to get away from me as I came after her.

"Jon, what are you doing?" she asked again as she backed into the counter.

I stopped and held the moonstone up. "What the hell is this?"

She was looking down and away, her hands up to protect her face.

"What did you sell me?" I yelled. "Take it!"

The stone shouldn't alter my mana too much in the time I had it with me, but even a little alteration was not what I needed right now. I hated having to carry it back here, but I wasn't going to leave behind my only evidence of foul play.

She nervously glanced up. Her chest heaved with each breath as she reached out for the moonstone. "Where did you get this?"

"It's the one you gave me yesterday!"

"I didn't give you one yesterday," she said, sliding

along the counter to gain some distance from me.

"I don't have time for games, Greda. Don't lie!"

"Jon, I didn't see you again after I left to take care of my mother. I returned after two hours. You never came back."

"I saw you! You gave me this stone. You were rude."

"I didn't!" she yelled.

I stepped back, my head spinning. I wanted to believe her, but was I just a fool?

"But it was definitely you," I confirmed.

"I swear on my mother's life it wasn't! I didn't see you again until right now!"

"Is she all right?" I managed to ask through my enraged confusion.

"Yes. The healer believes she was poisoned. We don't know who might've done it."

I put my hand over my head and leaned against the counter. My exhaustion was catching up with me. Greda said something, but I was busy envisioning what Leon was going to tell me when I arrived and had no spell to show for all my time. I'd hoped to discover malfeasance and use it as an excuse to buy more time.

"Jon." Greda touched my arm. "Tell me what happened after I left."

I took a breath and stood. "I walked by less than an hour later and saw you had returned. I walked into the shop, and you pushed this stone toward me on the counter. I asked if your mother was all right. You nodded. You wouldn't speak to me."

"Oh no," she whispered. "I didn't say a single word?"

"No." I lowered my voice as well, unsure why we had to. "I told you I had to be certain this was a ward of dteria. You nodded and gestured for me to leave."

Greda was shaking her head as I finished.

"What?" I asked.

"That was an illusion, Jon."

"What do you mean?"

"That was *someone else* who looked like me because of an illusion!" She rushed over and locked the door. Then she drew the curtains over her large window. She went behind the counter and grabbed a dagger, then slowly crept around the small store. "They could still be here," she said, "listening to every word."

I still wondered if this could all be an act, but the simplest answer was usually the right one. Why would Greda go through all this trouble? An illusion made much more sense, not that I understood how something like that could even be possible.

I was beginning to learn that many things were possible that I had once thought to be myth, so I was inclined to believe her.

After I helped her preform a quick search, Greda deemed that no one was in the storeroom or the back office. She put her dagger back and looked at the moonstone again.

"I don't know what this is or why someone gave it to you, but it's not a ward of any kind."

I would let Leon figure it out. "Tell me more about the illusion. And hurry, I'm already late to be somewhere important."

"An illusionist specializes in ordia, like myself, but it's very different than enchanting. They have to be an extremely talented sorcerer, with access to vtalia. Are you familiar with it?"

"Very." That was uF, my natural mana.

"To create an illusion, they have to maintain the

spell during the entire time. It takes a lot of effort just to resemble the image of a person. I'm sure if you looked closely, you would've noticed differences from the illusion of me to my actual self, like the size of my hands, the width of my shoulders, and even my height. Sound is something else entirely. An illusionist can't alter their voice or silence a noise. They can only alter the perception of others."

"That's why they didn't speak."

"Yes."

If Greda was right, then casting an illusion was within my range of mana. But I was too focused on other matters to care about that right now.

Greda gasped as she seemed to realize something. "That was why my mother was poisoned! The illusionist needed to draw me away from the shop." She stared at me with horror in her eyes. "I don't know who this sorcerer is you're apprenticing for, but I don't care to find out." She took out a moonstone from behind the counter and held it out for me. "This is the one I made. It's an actual ward of dteria. Take it, and don't come back until you figure out what's going on and know it to be safe. I don't want this kind of trouble."

I nodded as I took the true ward. The false one was sitting on the counter.

"I'm going to need that back to show as evidence, but I'd rather not hold it close. It has done enough damage to me already. Do you have a case that might stop it from trifling with my mana?"

She went into the back room and returned with a thin metal box. "You can take it free of charge," she said as she handed it to me.

"I appreciate that." I put both wards in my pack.

They looked the same to me, but I had made sure the false ward was the one in the box.

"Just please don't come back unless it's safe for you to do so."

"I understand." I walked to the door, but she put herself in front of it.

"Be careful." She extended her hand.

"I will," I said as we shook.

Greda was right. The version of her who had given me the false ward was taller. I was sure of it now.

I rushed back to the castle. I wasn't sure of the time, but it was closer to noon than sunrise. I was worried I wouldn't be let inside the castle, but the two guards in front of the open drawbridge let me run by as they gave me a stern look, probably for being late.

CHAPTER TEN

Leon had everyone standing in a line in front of him, his hands on his hips. "It's about damn time, Jon!" Everyone turned toward me. Many had looks of worry, but not Reuben. He was grinning. I figured Leon had been saying some pretty nasty things about me.

Shock hit me as I realized that it looked like the king was here as well. Next to Leon were Barrett and a man wearing a crown and a regal cloak. There was a girl beside him who had to be at least a few years younger than the rest of us burgeoning sorcerers. I assumed she was the princess of the kingdom.

"I'm sorry, but there was an issue!" I called as I ran to get in line next to Michael on the end.

"I don't want to hear excuses," Leon said. "Everyone else has already gone. What essence did you choose?"

My eyes shifted to the king. He was staring impatiently with gray eyes. His silky brown hair was long for a man. He had an abundant beard that hung down a few inches from his chin. The crown was tasteful, just a gold band around his forehead. I sorely did not want to disappoint him, but it looked as if I already had for making him wait.

"I didn't choose an essence," I answered Leon. "I chose dvinia."

"You stupid tit," Leon said with a shake of his head.

"Let me guess what your excuse is. You need more time."

"Something happened. When I—"

"Yeah, something did happen. You just failed."

The king spoke in a smooth baritone. "He cannot cast anything yet?"

Surprisingly, it was Barrett who looked the most disappointed. "Allow me to explain, sire," he told the king. I let go of the hope that he would stand up for me when he eyed me as if I had embarrassed him. "Jon Oklar was told to choose an essence, but he ignored the order."

"Why did you do that?" the king asked me.

Unsure if I should bow before his majesty, I gave a small, quick one. "I knew I could learn to cast a spell of dvinia, sire, if I purchased a vibmtaer instead of an essence. That's what I did, but there was a problem."

"So you admit that you ignored a direct order from Leon."

"I told him the same thing, sire," Barrett said.

"You ignored both of their orders?" the king asked me incredulously.

"I do admit that," I said. "But—"

Worried murmurs sprang out from my peers. Except for Reuben. He laughed snidely.

"I told Leon that Jon does not belong here," Reuben boasted. "I said it."

I withdrew the moonstone from the metal box and walked toward Leon. "This is what I was given when I went to purchase a ward of dteria."

Leon looked as if I was trying and failing to amuse him as he took the moonstone from me. But then his eyes gaped as he looked at it.

"Everyone back away!" Leon ordered.

Many responded with confusion. I was the only one to hurry away from the moonstone, glad to have finally unloaded it off my person.

"Get away now!" Leon yelled.

Everyone collectively backed away.

"That's fine," Leon said when we were all about five yards away. He tossed the stone in the other direction. It landed on the ground ten yards from him. "It's going to stay there for now."

"What is it?" the king asked.

"An essence of dteria."

My heart stopped for a beat. So it was the opposite of a ward. No wonder the vibration of my mana had been slowed while that thing was near me. Dteria must be of a lower frequency.

The king spoke to me again. "You said this was given to you instead of a ward?" His tone sounded a lot more forgiving now.

"Please allow me to explain, sire."

"Yes, explain."

"I visited the shop Enchanted Devices and asked for a ward of dteria. I paid the woman behind the counter, Greda, and watched as she started to make it with a moonstone and a dog's claw."

The king looked at Barrett. He murmured something, probably telling the king that these were the correct ingredients for a ward of dteria.

"She said it would take an hour," I continued. "That's when I decided to buy a vibmtaer instead of an essence, but that's not important right now. Soon after, a guard rushed into the shop and told Greda that her mother was found unconscious on the street."

"That's really the truth?" the king asked me skeptically.

"It gets even more unbelievable, sire, but I swear this is the truth. Greda ran off but told me she would be back in an hour or two to finish the ward. So I left. I checked back at the shop in less than an hour. I saw her there already, which was a surprise. What was even more strange was that she refused to say one word to me. She hardly even looked at me. In fact, she rudely gave me that stone and tried to gesture for me to leave. I asked if her mother was all right. She nodded. I then said I needed to make sure that this was a ward of dteria. She nodded. I left. But it wasn't Greda, sire. I confirmed it later."

"Are you trying to tell me that it was an illusionist in her place?" the king asked.

"Yes."

There were more nervous murmurs from my peers.

"I didn't know such a thing was possible," I continued. "But after I returned from the mountains, I confronted Greda. She had no idea what I was talking about." I realized this was not reflecting well on Greda. The last thing I wanted was her mother's shop to be closed down while she was put in the dungeons. "I spoke with her at length about this. I really feel that it wasn't her. Somebody poisoned her mother. The healer who Greda spoke to confirmed it. Greda figured that the poisoner was working with the illusionist to trick me into taking the essence of dteria. She banned me from her shop out of fear when she pieced it together. I know this either sounds unbelievable or that it was really Greda who tricked me, but I firmly believe it was someone else. The illusionist was taller and refused to speak.

Greda explained that the perception of sound cannot be changed."

"That is true," the king said. He glanced at Leon. "And you confirm that the stone you tossed is an essence of dteria?"

"It isn't the strongest essence I've come across, but it certainly is strong enough to do some damage." Leon looked at me. "Was this with you the whole time?" There was a great weight to his question, like asking if I had symptoms of what he knew to be an incurable illness.

"It's not affecting me anymore," I told him. "However, it was with me from the first evening through the next morning, but then I realized something was wrong with my mana. I moved it far away. That's what I was trying to say when I came here. It messed with my mana severely and wasted nearly a whole day. I'm sure I would've been able to cast the spell of dvinia if this hadn't happened. I'm very close."

"I believe everything except that." Leon walked toward me. "You're going to prove that right now." He grabbed my pack and started looking around.

I took the vibmtaer out of my pocket and presented it. He snatched it.

"Go."

I took a breath to compose myself. My heart was still racing from the whole ordeal of presenting my case in front of the king. And it certainly didn't help that everyone's gaze was on me.

I started with my easiest note, uF. I let the mana disperse and quickly followed with uG. It felt right, but I couldn't be sure. My eyes drifted down to the vibmtaer as if hoping to catch a glimpse of the color displayed, but Leon pointed it away from me. I let go of uG and pushed out my mana again, this time so that it was vibrating higher, uuC.

I watched Leon's face for clues. He just stared at the vibmtaer in silence. I really couldn't be sure I was casting uuC without checking the color on the vibmtaer, but I knew I was at least close. I hoped that would be enough. The final note was easy. uuD was a comfortable strain on my mind, like doing a mental sit-up.

"So you learned the four notes," Leon said, unimpressed. "It could be weeks before you can cast them at the same time. *And even then* your spell will only be strong enough to lift a feather."

Lift? It wasn't much of a clue as to what the spell could do. Wind, fire, even water could blow a feather into the air.

"I just need one more day—the day I missed. Please give me a chance."

"You had a chance!" Leon yelled as he pointed at the great hall. "We gave you plenty of chances when we told you your range of mana was too wide to learn dvinia. At how quickly you've progressed, I have no doubt you would've learned to mimic an essence by now as the rest of them have done. But now you're even further behind them."

I would've begged if Leon seemed like the type of person who might be affected by it—someone with an ounce of empathy. I figured it was better to stay quiet and tell him with my eyes instead.

He sighed as he turned toward the king. "This is your group of idiots, sire. I could spare one more day if you want to keep Jon."

The king showed Leon a brief look of irritation, but

he said nothing. I didn't understand why his majesty put up with Leon. Wouldn't another sorcerer, any other sorcerer, be a better instructor?

The princess said something to her father that was too quiet for me to hear. But from the smile she flashed at me, I had to assume she was advocating for me to stay.

"You will have today only to show me you can cast," the king said.

Phew. I breathed a quick breath of relief. But it was short-lived. Did that mean I would have to perform the spell later tonight, or did I have until tomorrow morning? The difference could mean my expulsion.

Barrett asked the king, "Shall we postpone the contracts?"

"No, I want everyone signing them now. An enemy has already tried to corrupt Jon with dteria. There is no time to waste."

I wanted to ask if the king had any idea who this person could be. I felt that I had been personally attacked and deserved to know. I could only hope they would tell me what they'd figured out after they discussed it...if I was still around.

"You have all proven yourself enough to find out what you're doing here," the king announced.

"Even Jon, your majesty?" Reuben asked in disbelief.

The king gave him a look that smeared concern across the rich dolt's face.

"You will stop making remarks about Jon right now. If he is going to succeed or fail, it will be on his own."

"Yes, sire," Reuben muttered.

Hopefully that would shut him up for a little while.

"I'm about to tell you something that is not to be shared with anyone," the king said. "If you speak of this, you will not only be removed from the group, but you will be hanged for treason."

A chill wind whisked by.

"This is your last chance to leave now and return to what you were before this. You may say whatever you wish about this experience if you do. However, if you choose to stay, you will be compensated each week, and you will be permitted to live in the castle. You will not be charged for a single thing that you require, including but not limited to board and lodging, supplies for your training, the laundering of your clothes, and new robes for those who require them now or in the future." He politely did not look at me during the last statement.

"Everything you do will be for the good of the kingdom," the king continued. "But you will face challenges that may pose a danger to you. You eight have been chosen not because you are the strongest but because you *might* be one day."

"And because we're cheap," Michael whispered to me.

It took me a moment to realize he wasn't joking. There were other sorcerers out there like Greda and her mother, but it would be harder to take them away from their lives. People like Michael and me had nothing. We were eager to learn and would do so without much cost. But what about Reuben and Kataleya, who clearly had wealth? Perhaps their families didn't pursue coin like the rest of us did. It was political power that meant the most to them.

Did that mean we might one day hold titles or own land? It was never something I'd dreamed possible. My father had owned our house in Bhode, but he didn't own the land. The lord of Bhode did, but I'd never met him. A collector of taxes was sent in his stead.

Michael's statement brought up many questions. There was a king before this one, but he had been overthrown by the man standing in front of me, Nykal Lennox. What had happened to the coin of the previous king? How much of it did Nykal have now? Could it be that he wasn't as rich as I'd first thought? He hadn't financed the construction of this castle, after all. I knew it had been built many years ago, though I wasn't sure exactly when.

"This kingdom has enemies." Nykal paused as if to choose the right words. "I employ an army to keep the kingdom safe, but many of these men are more loyal to coin than they are to moral good. Corruption will show itself to you in more forms than just the magical arts. Your task is to find it and eliminate it."

There seemed to be more to what he wasn't saying than to what he was. Who was he trying to keep the kingdom safe from if he was paying corrupt men? I didn't imagine they were all men, either. I'd learned from my father that corruption came in all forms, like the king had said. But there seemed to be a greater threat than corruption within the kingdom, or the king would've removed these corrupt guards and sorcerers from his employment.

If he did, perhaps they would go elsewhere, where they would be paid more. Perhaps to another kingdom. I didn't know anything about the kingdom of Rohaer, south of Lycast, but I was starting to wish I did. I would let the king worry about that. Corruption right here in Lycast seemed to be the most immediate threat.

One, or even some, of my fellow young sorcerers might choose to benefit themselves at the expense of the rest of us. One of them could've already made a selfish choice. They might've been involved in tricking me into taking the essence of dteria. I didn't know how else to explain that the illusionist knew to poison Greda's mother and be at the shop at the same time I was. It was most likely someone who knew what we were doing here.

But that meant Leon could've been the culprit. He could've put on an act when I'd brought the essence back to him. Or it could've been Barrett who was working against us. Perhaps he had brought me here just to corrupt me with dteria.

I wished I knew what dteria did or how it worked. Right now it was even more mysterious than dvinia.

"All of you are to sign contracts," the king explained as Barrett handed a small piece of parchment to each of us. "Read them over. They are short and to the point."

I took a brief glance before I looked over at Michael's to ensure our contracts were the same. They were.

"I agree that I will be bound through ordia to protect Nykal Lennox against any harm to his body and stop any detriment to his health if I am capable. I will take measures to prevent his injury, sickness, and the loss of his life to the best of my ability."

There was a line to sign my name.

"For a harbinger to seal these contracts with ordia," the king explained, "you have to understand exactly what the contract is saying in its entirety. It is for this reason that they are short. I will clarify something for you. Just because you agree to these terms does not mean that your life is forfeited. However, if a situation does arise, you all will be expected to stand against any threat to my life, no matter what it is." His gaze drifted across our faces. "I'm sure many of you are wondering what would happen if you chose not to protect me after signing this contract. I will allow Leon to explain that and a little history about ordia before you sign."

"I'm sure Kataleya knows." Leon gestured for her to step forward. Reuben opened his mouth as if he wanted to volunteer, but at least he didn't speak this time.

Kataleya came out of the line as she cleared her throat. Her curly blonde hair was in disarray. Her face was caked with dirt. Like all of us, surely, she was in need of a bath. But she stood and spoke with dignity.

"When Basael gave life to Nijja, the third demi-god, her gift in exchange for life was ordia. Basael was pleased with ordia. He saw the potential it had to keep order in the chaotic world of fae, Fyrren. He let Nijja rule Fyrren with this new magic. She would keep the powerful creatures from destroying each other. Over the centuries that followed, the use of ordia in Fyrren has seeped out into the world of Imania."

Leon was waving his hand. "Enough. I didn't know you would give the doctrinal version."

"My family are Formists," she said proudly. "It is the version we see as the truth."

"Spare me," Leon said as he rolled his eyes. "God is dead and has been for a long time. You'll come to the same conclusion when you learn more about the world."

"You're Cess?" Eden asked. "I am, too."

"You don't know anything," Leon lectured her.

Eden's mouth opened to say something, but she closed it in disappointment.

"Leon," the king rebuked.

Leon raised his voice as he spoke to us. "The point I'm sure Kataleya was going to make eventually was that ordia has real power in our world depending on how it's used. If you agree to a contract bound by a harbinger, that means your soul is bound to it. You'd have an easier time forgetting who you are than trying to break the contract. Trying to let the king die after you sign this would be like trying to kill yourself. Some of you might be capable, but it's going to be the hardest thing you've ever done in your easy lives."

So it was possible.

"Why do some of you look surprised?" Leon asked. "You think ordia is stronger than your free will? There's nothing stronger than free will. You'd better remember that when it comes time to choose to do something difficult that you know is right or something easy that you know is wrong. You might have that choice soon enough. Don't disappoint me. Now it's time to sign so we can get on with our day. Kataleya, you first. Everyone line up behind her."

Kataleya stepped up to the table where a quill and a small pot of ink awaited. Barrett stood on the other side. We formed a line behind her, me at the back. We all watched as she signed her name.

"Do you agree to be bound to this contract?" Barrett asked.

"I agree."

Barrett made a face of concentration as he held up

the contract with one hand and waved his other hand around it. The contract faded to white then slowly disappeared.

"Wow," Michael said.

I was shocked as well.

When we all calmed down a bit, I asked Barrett, "Where did it go?"

"It has been turned into energy and transferred to Fyrren. The same thing happens to anything used in an enchantment."

If something like this was true, then many of the stories I'd heard growing up could have truth to them as well. The world suddenly felt wide open to me.

Barrett bound the contracts of everyone before me without delay. I was a little nervous as I stepped up. My peers were all remarking to each other how strange it felt.

"Do you agree to be bound to this contract?" Barrett asked after I signed it.

"I agree."

He moved his hand. Just like with the others, the contract went white before it started to dissolve. A tingling warmth spread down my body. It felt akin to realizing something important that could change everything, but it was over in a moment.

I didn't feel much different afterward. I thought a little test was in order. I looked at the king and thought of tackling him. Of course I didn't want to, that part was the same, but I didn't feel any additional need to refrain from hurting him. It was already the farthest thought from my mind.

I supposed I'd hoped for some internal battle against the new instinct—a sign of the power of the contract. But besides the tingling feeling that had gone down my back, everything was the same.

Leon announced, "You all have a half hour to bathe and change your clothes. Lunch will be served in the great hall."

A few people whooped, but I was too eager to finish learning the spell to worry about bathing or eating. I asked Leon, "Can I have the vibmtaer back? I'm going to start right now."

"Have a bath, Jon, and eat. The vibmtaer will be in your room when you're done."

"Can I bring my food to my room?"

"You know what?"

I cringed as I prepared for him to yell.

"I actually admire your dedication," he said to my surprise. "You might just pull this off. Your lunch will be waiting for you in your room, along with the vibmtaer."

"Thank you." I wanted to sprint away, but there was one last important thing. "Leon, sir, none of this was Greda's fault. Is the king going to do anything to her shop?"

He glared at me. "Jon, did you tell Greda you're involved with the king?"

"No, I would never. I made up the lie that I was an apprentice for a sorcerer."

"Good. Don't worry about her. The king isn't going to do anything for two reasons. One, she's innocent. Two, it would be clear that your involvement with sorcery has to do with him."

"I see. Thank you." I ran off. I was the first one into the apartments. I knew my peers wouldn't judge me for rushing past them. They had all proven themselves already while I had not. I made my way up the stairs and down the hall to my room.

I found that the clothes I'd left in my laundry bag were clean and folded on my bed. There were a number of towels provided to me as well. It made me feel, just for a moment, like I was important to the king.

The bathing room for men was on the ground floor, on the opposite side of the building as the women's. I was still in a rush, like the last time I'd been in here, but I decided to take a small moment to appreciate the luxury available to me, otherwise there was little point to all of this. There were a number of wooden tubs with steaming water, a circular curtain around each for privacy. I stripped down and climbed into the closest one. There was a little table for my soap and towel. It was the nicest bath I could remember, given that preparing the bath had been taken care of by someone else, and draining the water would be as well.

I was almost done scrubbing myself clean by the time I heard the other young men entering the bathing room. They were chatting amongst themselves.

"Jon?" Michael asked.

"Yeah, it's me." I could hear each of them preparing to enter their tubs. "Congratulations to all of you for passing."

"Thank you," Charlie called out.

"I sincerely hope you will as well," Michael said. "I wish you luck."

"Thank you."

"Good luck," Charlie echoed.

I thanked him as well. Reuben hadn't said one word to me, but I wasn't about to start caring what he thought anytime soon.

Soon I was clean, dry, and back in my room. I was eager to start training, barely noticing the large plate of food on my desk.

My appetite came back ferociously after I took the first bite of buttered fish. It was cooked perfectly and still warm like the porridge on the side of the plate. I was surprised at the seasoned flavor of the porridge. Even though it did not look appetizing, it was. There was a long carrot on the other side of the plate, cooked as well and sweet to the taste.

The bones of the fish made it difficult to eat quickly, but I managed to chow down everything in about five minutes. Finally, it was time to cast again. Not only was I eager to find out what the spell did, but I enjoyed practicing. It reminded me of sword fighting lessons with my father. After his valuable instruction, I was often able to train on my own. Much of sword fighting was footwork. An imaginary opponent could be just as valuable as a real one when shifting stances and practicing my swing.

I took the vibmtaer from the mantle over the hearth and put it on my bed. Although there were many hours left in the day, I still didn't feel comfortable with the time I had. I wasn't going to stop until I could cast the spell.

CHAPTER ELEVEN

It was late in the evening when there was a knock at my door. I muttered a curse. If this was the king coming to see my spell, then this would be the last time I would be able to enjoy this room.

"Come in," I said dubiously.

The princess opened my door. She was carrying a plate of food. I still had the old plate on my desk, fish bones sitting on top of it. I had no idea why she was giving me food, but I didn't feel comfortable having the young princess enter my room.

"I noticed you didn't eat with the others," she said. "I figured you would be hungry so I had a plate made for you."

"That's kind of you," I said indifferently as I took the plate from her hands. Food was the last thing on my mind, but I didn't want to insult her.

"You're Jon Oklar of Bhode, right?"

"Yes." Was it rude to ask her name? I knew nothing about etiquette with royalty. "I saw you on the court-yard earlier, but I never learned your name."

She put her hand over her mouth as she giggled. "You're supposed to bow. I am a princess. Did you not know?"

"I'm sorry." I bowed deeply. "Bhode is a small town. There were no princesses there."

She laughed for a long while as I stood there holding my dinner, not knowing what to do with it.

"Of course there weren't. And you just bowed with a plate of food!" she complained. "You are very funny."

I tried not to show how eager I was for her to leave. "Forgive me." I set the plate on the mantle above the hearth and bowed again.

"That's better," she said. "My name is Callie."

"A pleasure to meet you." It wasn't. I had to get back to trying to cast this spell. I didn't even have time to eat the food she had brought, though the pork was starting to smell good.

"Here," she said as she walked past me. "It looks like you need me to show you what to do, Jon of Bhode." She picked up my plate with the fish bones on it and carried it back across the room. "If you eat in your quarters, you set your plate in the hall when you are done and you cover it with your napkin. That way the servants will take care of it." She spoke like my ignorance amused her.

Callie's brown hair fell all the way down to her waist. She had hazel eyes and round cheeks. It was her elegant blue dress that spoke of her royalty, that and her snooty lilt.

"Thank you for showing me." I put my hand on the door, ready to close it. "And thank you for bringing me supper. I appreciate that."

"You're trying to learn dvinia?" she asked with a cock of her head.

"I am."

"That's impressive. My father doesn't know any wizards. I'm sure you will be in his good graces very soon."

"Not if I don't learn the spell before he tests me. Unfortunately, I still must practice it. Thank you so much for your help, princess. It was a pleasure meeting you." I bowed again.

She seemed a little perturbed as she gave a curtsy, then turned to make her way down the hall.

It was a relief to finally close the door. I tried to get back to practicing, but the smell of pork was starting to drive me mad. I finished it in a matter of minutes, then started stuffing chunks of bread into my mouth as I went back to practicing.

I was so close. I could almost feel the spell working every time I tried it. I could cast three of the four notes consistently. It was just adding the highest one, uuD, that was the hardest. I had progressed past using the vibmtaer because when casting these three notes at the same time, the colors were spliced into a pinkish green that meant nothing to me.

I failed to make any progress for an hour straight, and frustration was soon getting the better of me. A look out the window showed the sun setting. There was another knock at my door. I halted in dread.

I figured the king would be announced, instead of asking to enter a room with a simple knock, but I hurried to open the door just in case I was wrong. I almost let out an exasperated breath when I saw the princess there again.

"Callie." I gave a quick bow. "Unfortunately, I need a little more time."

"That's why I'm here," she said softly. She motioned for me to lean close to her. I stepped up to her, and she went up on her toes to whisper in my ear. "I brought something for you."

I stepped back and waited for her to give it to me.

She forced me back as she practically walked into me while entering the room. Then she closed the door after her.

"I couldn't possibly accept anything from you."

Please get out, I wanted to tell her. *I don't care what you brought me.* I also thought it unwise to have the princess in my room with the door closed.

"It will be a secret between us." She pulled a scroll out from her sleeve and handed it to me. But I didn't accept it.

"If Leon or your father wouldn't want me to have it, then I can't take it."

"You don't have to take it, then. I'll read it to you." She unrolled the scroll. "Expel: Upper F, Upper G, Up-Upper C, Up-Upper D."

I knew the notes, but I hadn't heard the name of the spell before. Expel. I might've found it interesting if I wasn't in such a panic to get back to practicing.

"This is the core of dvinia," she continued to read. "The chord has no third, which makes dvinia most similar to ordia. This raises the question as to what other possible spells can be created when combining the core of dvinia with additional notes, like enchanting is done by using ordia."

This was fascinating, but it was clear by now that it wasn't going to help me with my immediate problem.

"Is there anything else about Expel?" I asked.

Her eyes moved rapidly down the scroll. "No."

"Right now, that's all I'm trying to cast. I just need a little more time alone, if you don't mind."

"Remember what I told you about your plate?" she teased as she walked over to my desk and grabbed it. "I'll get it for you, don't worry!" She winked and gave a sassy toss of her hair.

"I appreciate all of your help," I said as I opened the door. To my shock, the king was about one step away from the doorway.

No. I just needed a little more time!

"Sire." I bowed, glad for the excuse to look away from his glaring gaze as he noticed his daughter behind me.

"Father," Callie said with shock. "I was just trying to help Jon learn the spell...then I noticed his plate." She handed it to me as if embarrassed to be holding it. But now I didn't know what to do with it. At least she wasn't trying to hide the scroll in her hands, which I was certain the king had already noticed.

"Did Jon ask you for help?" he questioned.

"No. I promise."

"So you showed up at his room without invitation?"

"I, uh. I knew he must be hungry. I took a plate to him earlier. I didn't see it in the hall later so I thought..."

I was too nervous that the king had come here to witness my spell to think of something that might alleviate the situation.

"Wait in your chambers, Callie. I will speak with you later."

She rushed out with her head down.

The king folded his arms in front of me. I didn't want to set the plate on the bed or the fancy mantle above the hearth, which were the only two surfaces in my immediate vicinity. But I felt even worse holding it, as the king seemed to be waiting for me.

"Sire?" I asked.

"Do you not realize how inappropriate it is to have my daughter in this room with you, and the door closed!"

Fear took my voice away for a moment. "I'm sorry, sire. I honestly didn't want her in here, but she walked in and closed the door after her."

"Then you tell her to leave!"

"I feared that I shouldn't tell the princess to do anything."

"She is a fourteen-year-old girl. She needs to be told what to do if she is acting inappropriately."

It was a shock to hear the king speak about his daughter like this, but a refreshing one. "I promise I will do that in the future."

"Give me that damn plate." He took it out of my hand and set it down against the wall in the hallway. "All right, Jon. It's time to show me the spell."

"May I have one more hour? Please, sire. I'm very close."

The king let out a sigh. "It is late, and I have a busy day tomorrow. I'm about to retire to my bedchamber."

No, I wanted to shout. The king was a tall man, broad of shoulder. He stared at me and made no attempt to hide that he was deliberating whether to force me out of the castle right now.

I put my hands together in a plea. "Please give me until the morning, sire. I can meet you anywhere you require. I would just need a moment to show you the spell."

He put his hand over his chin. "Fine. At sunrise tomorrow I will be stopping by your room here. I really hope you have not wasted all of our time. Good night, Jon."

"Thank you for the chance, sire. Good night."

I shut the door behind him and breathed a huge sigh of relief.

I practiced far into the night, extremely thankful the king had given me more than an hour. I would've failed if he hadn't.

If I had taken an essence, I was certain I would've been able to cast a spell by now. But after feeling what the essence of dteria had done to my mana, I was glad that I'd refused to let one of them interfere.

With exhaustion nearly forcing my eyes shut, I eventually was able to split my mind four ways and cast the spell. The only problem now was that I was too tired to put any force behind it. The chord just puttered out of my body like drool. I tried again and again. I knew each note was perfect. The spell should be working. I even felt a new sensation of my mana clicking into place like turning a mental key into a lock, but still, nothing happened.

The bed was calling to me. Maybe if I just shut my eyes for a moment.

*****

I awoke to someone shaking my shoulder. "Jon, get up."

I gasped, sucking in the drool that was running down my face. I had fallen asleep facedown, strewn across my bed. The king was standing in front of me with Barrett behind him. I wasn't sure who'd shaken me awake, but it was the king who spoke again.

"Cast, Jon."

My mind snapped back to what I'd been doing just before collapsing on the bed. With adrenaline pumping through me, I pushed out my hand and forced my mana out in the form of four calculated vibrations over my bed. Something clicked again as the spell came to fruition, but this time I felt my mana transform as it left me. It was like shooting the perfect arrow, knowing your posture and draw was spot on.

"Whoa," I said in amazement as my heavy quilt was tossed into the far wall.

I had done it! I wanted to throw my arms in the air in triumph, but I restrained myself to a wide smile. So wizards were capable of creating a physical force out of the energy made by mana. I was already drooling at the possibilities. No wait, that was just some leftover drool from my slumber I'd failed to wipe away.

The king looked at me for a long while, his hard stare eventually dissolving my grin.

"Be honest, Jon. Have you been up all night practicing, and this is the first time it's worked?"

"Yes," I admitted fearfully.

The king shared a look with Barrett. The councilman shrugged ever so slightly.

"Promise me something," the king told me. "You will keep up this dedication to improving yourself no matter how easy spell casting becomes."

"It's how I've always lived my life, sire, and I wouldn't change it whether I promised you or not."

"Good. That's what I want to hear. One more thing. You will not, under any circumstance, touch my daughter or even give her the faintest idea you are interested."

"Sire, I am not interested in girls her age. I would never touch her no matter who she was. And because she is your daughter, sire, I will even deny her friendship if that's what you wish." It was the easiest way out of this problem.

"Are you saying you cannot treat my daughter with respect without acting flirtatious?"

I realized my mistake with a lowered head. "I can do that, sire."

"That's what I expect." He put his hands together. "Very well. I'm leaving now. Because you were up most of the night, and certainly look the part, I will give you until the early afternoon. Sleep, bathe, eat—take care of whatever you need. I expect you to put your best foot forward when I return because I have a task for you."

"I look forward to it."

"I'm glad."

I escorted them out and shut the door after them. I was ready to pass out again, but first I had to see the spell work one more time. I set my quilt back onto my bed. It still took a few moments to prepare my mind, but it was glorious when I casted Expel once more and the quilt flew across the room.

I sleepily retrieved it and set it on my bed. I almost couldn't wait to show Leon and the others. I had done right believing in myself, something I wouldn't soon forget.

Finally, and with great satisfaction, I made myself comfortable and promptly fell asleep with a smile on my face.

CHAPTER TWELVE

Still immensely proud of myself, I now ate, alone, in the great hall as I wondered whether my peers thought I had been given special treatment. It would be even worse if they'd heard the princess had tried to help me. I could do nothing about that right now, though, so I would try to enjoy my meal.

I got to see another room in the great hall. The dining room on the ground floor had to be the single largest room I'd ever been in. There were three long tables of tanned oak with benches on both sides. On the far end of the room was a dais, where a smaller table of dark wood looked fit for the king and his family.

Although the room was marvelous, the size of it just made me feel lonelier. It seemed that the others were training when I'd crossed through the courtyard briefly. I might have a few moments to join them before I was sent off for the king's task.

My food was delicious again, this time poached eggs and thick bread. I'd never eaten this well before. I'd better find time to work it off, or I might soon become fat.

I was just finishing when someone called for me.

"Jon!"

I looked up to find the king at the entrance to the enormous room. I left my plate and rushed over.

"You have proven that you are determined," the

king said. "Now is your chance to show me that you can be useful as well."

I was eager. "What can I do?"

"Go to the stockades," the king said as he handed me a scroll.

I had no idea where they were, but he was still talking after I took the scroll.

"Show that to them there. You are going to be escorting a krepp back here."

What's a krepp? I wondered.

"The people of Newhaven are likely to be a little alarmed by the creature's presence. You will smile and show them that there is no reason to be afraid. No one is to hurt or threaten the krepp, and try to keep him from killing anyone on the way here. If you insult him by accident, he might show aggression toward you. You are not to defend yourself unless your life is at risk."

"Um." This was not the kind of task I was expecting.

"What questions do you have?"

So many. "I should admit that I don't know where the stockades are. I just arrived here a few days ago and have only been to one place, the Enchanted Devices shop. Is it near there?"

"No. How's your memory?"

"Very good."

"The Stockades is in The Docks, which is on the eastern side of the city, over the bridge. Take any street eastward to get there. After you cross the bridge, go north. You can't miss the Stockades. The krepp is to be treated with honor no matter what he asks of you. A message came this morning that he arrived by boat and will only speak to me. If I'm not here when you return, you are to entertain him until I come back. This is an easy task, Jon. I'm choosing you because you are courteous and strong. If something happens, I expect you to restrain the aggressor or use dvinia to make them back off. Do not take a weapon."

It was an honor. "I will make sure he gets here without incident."

"That is the right answer. Hurry over there. I've made him wait long enough."

I gave a quick bow, then darted around the king.

"Jon."

I spun around.

"Like any task that you are given, you are not to speak about it to anyone outside this castle unless absolutely necessary."

"I understand."

I ran through the courtyard. Everyone was training separately but near enough that they could speak to each other, and many were sharing words. Leon seemed to be going around to each of them to offer instruction. I looked forward to showing him what I could do and hearing his advice on how best to quickly improve.

"Where you off to?" Michael asked as I passed him.

"Picking up a krepp from the Stockades," I answered.

"Did you say a krepp?"

I was too far away to answer without shouting back. He would find out soon enough, anyway. I wished I had time to ask him if he knew what a krepp was, but the king might've been watching. I wouldn't delay.

I exited the castle through the open drawbridge. It pointed me west, so I had to run all the way around the huge outer wall to head east. I jogged down King

Street through much of the city and eventually saw the bridge. It was arched so that standing at the middle of it afforded me a view of the entire docks. They were a large district separated from the rest of the city by the wide river. There were many smaller homes packed together, along with a number of tiny buildings that seemed to be shops without any names displayed.

The Stockades had a tall fence surrounding it. A field of grass enclosed a stone structure with a lookout tower on one end. The whole thing looked like a relaxed prison to me. I was startled when I saw something, or better yet someone, who was not a man or a woman. He definitely was a humanoid, however, standing upright on two legs, but he was larger than any person I had seen.

The scaly face of the krepp resembled that of a lizard. He had a snout with a long mouth that split it in half. The folds of his face gave him the appearance of having eyebrows even though there was no hair to be seen across his bald head. I spotted no ears, but there were probably holes hidden somewhere in the spikey flesh that sprouted out around the back of the creature's head. I figured his ears probably looked similar to the two holes that made up the krepp's nose at the end of his snout.

It was his eyes that were the most bizarre. They were yellow with a black line down the middle. I had plenty of time to focus on them because the creature was looking right at me as he approached. He had just finished a duel with a swordsman, disarming the man with a powerful swing and then tossing him aside as if he were rubbish.

"You take me to king?" the krepp asked me. He

must've known someone was coming for him. His voice was deep and coarse, like a massive man who'd taken to the pipe for many years. When he spoke, I couldn't help but notice his sharp teeth.

"I will," I informed the creature. I looked past him at the guards of the Stockades helping up their fellow swordsman. "I have a decree here," I called out to them as I unrolled the scroll.

They barely glanced over before they were gesturing for me to leave, clearly eager to get rid of the krepp.

The accent of the creature made me wonder just how much he knew of our language. Did he even know the difference between polite and rude? I spoke to him gently just in case.

"Are you ready to meet the king?" I asked.

"Yes. I tire of wait."

I started toward the gated part of the fence between us, but the krepp ran at the barricade and jumped right over it. For such a large creature, I was amazed at the height he could reach as he cleared the pickets that came up to my shoulders.

I half expected the earth to shake as he landed near me, he was so heavy. He had muscles everywhere, most bulging from his chest and arms. He might've been more than a little taller than me, but he didn't stand up straight as we walked. Instead, he hunched over slightly as if he could tilt down and start running on all fours at any moment.

"My name is Jon," I said as we started back the way I'd come. I didn't know what would happen when we encountered other people. I felt that the king had undersold how alarming this creature looked.

"I am Grufaeragar," said the krepp proudly. "I am

strongest for common tongue and for sword. You have great honor meet me. Do I have honor meet you?"

"The honor is mine to meet you," I answered humbly. "I hope one day you will have honor for meeting me, Grufaeragar." I had to practice his name so I didn't butcher it later.

"I understand, Jon." He seemed pleased. "You not like other humans I see." He squeezed my shoulder. His hands were remarkably similar to that of a man except for the claws at the end of his fingertips. That and the gray scales, of course.

His claws dug into me like the talons of a hawk. I was concerned he would make holes in one of the few good shirts I had left, but he let go after just a moment.

"You strong, as human. You fight well?"

"Yes, but not as well as a krepp," I replied, continuing to play humble. I had a feeling my words were true nonetheless.

He smiled wider, his fangs showing.

We crossed over the bridge and made our way back onto King's Street. I was nervous as I saw a few people in our path. A small group of men stopped to stare from far away, but they only gawked for a moment before they quickly cleared the street.

"Humans afraid to krepps," Grufaeragar boasted. "Those humans smart."

"Should I be afraid?" I asked.

"If we fight, yes."

"I don't wish to fight you."

"You human smart too."

We continued down the street. Anyone who looked as if they might cross by us stopped and stared, then chose a different route.

"Was it a long trip from your home?" I asked.

"One week for ship."

A ship—no wonder I hadn't heard of a krepp before. I wished I had seen a map of the surrounding islands around Dorrinthal. My father had taught me about the locations of towns and cities in the kingdom of Lycast, but the krepps didn't seem to live on this continent.

"Where do you come from?" I asked.

"All krepps live Hammashar. No humans."

Did that mean no humans were allowed or they just didn't live there?

Unfortunately, the street became busier the closer we came to the castle. The only road that was usually clear of people was the road that ran parallel to the castle wall, appropriately named Longwall Street. We wouldn't be turning onto that street for a while.

Everyone made room for us as we took the center path on the wide road. Some of the tougher-looking men appeared as if they wanted to challenge the krepp, their eyes tight with anger as they faced him.

Grufaeragar saw one of the larger men glaring at him and stopped. "*Ru hyash?*" the krepp asked the man.

"Ignore them," I said as I motioned for him to follow me.

But Grufaeragar puffed up his chest and repeated the same thing.

"*Ru hyash,* human?"

With his gaze never leaving the krepp, the large man asked me, "What is he doing here?"

Many had stopped to listen.

"He's here peacefully," I replied. "Turn away."

"Yes," Grufaeragar agreed. "Turn away, small human."

There was no way the man could be considered small, even through a krepp's eyes.

"Krepps killed my father," the man said.

"Your father stupid," Grufaeragar replied.

Rage sparked in the man's eyes.

I cursed as I mentally prepared Expel. "This is not one of the krepps that killed anyone. Grufaeragar is here peacefully!" I announced louder this time, noticing a few more men encircling us. "To attack him is a crime. He is a guest in our city."

I could feel them wondering who I was. A young man representing the laws, yet he wore common clothing. I knew why the king had chosen me, though. I didn't appear like someone a man with common sense would pick a fight against. I was worried that common sense was gone here, however, as one man seemed interested in killing an innocent krepp to avenge the death of his father.

"I no kill human," Grufaeragar said. "No make me."

Many were shouting questions, a few asking why he was here. There was no point in staying in this spot any longer.

"Let's go," I told Grufaeragar as I finally got him to keep up with me again. It was a good thing no one followed us.

He was still breathing hard when we eventually turned onto Longwall Street. It looked as if he was pressing his teeth together within his lipless mouth. I had many more questions for him, but he was nearly aflame with aggression. I wasn't going to risk igniting his temper. I tried to calm him instead.

"That man was afraid of you, strong krepp. That is why he tried to stand up to you."

"Afraid and stupid?"

"Yes, afraid and stupid. He did not run like smart humans."

"I understand."

The two guards in front of the drawbridge must've known the krepp was coming. They showed little surprise as they let us through. Grufaeragar's mood quickly changed as he finally seemed to notice where we were. He looked up at the tall walls on either side of us as we waited for the portcullis to rise.

"This is castle?"

"It is."

He pointed at the barred gate of the portcullis lifting in front of us. "Magic?"

"Not magic." I guided him through and showed him the wheel on the other side, held by a burly man with a sheen of sweat on his face. But Grufaeragar no longer seemed interested. He was too busy taking in the sight of the courtyard, the keep, and all the buildings surrounding us. His yellow eyes were wide, his mouth agape.

"*Karudar!*" he muttered. "Man build this or demigod?"

It was a shock to hear him mention a demigod and not "a god." I wondered under what circumstance he had learned this word.

"This was built by men many years ago," I told him. I watched as my peers noticed me with the krepp. One by one they stopped what they were doing and stared openly across the courtyard. The king came out of the keep behind them, Barrett at his side and two armored guards right behind them. Nykal gestured for us to come to him.

The king met us halfway across the courtyard, with Leon and my peers soon surrounding us. I noticed the princess watching from the entrance of the keep. Even a number of servants peeked from the windows of the apartments.

"Grufaeragar," I said, "this is the king of Lycast."

"Him?" Grufaeragar asked as he pointed.

"Yes," I confirmed.

Grufaeragar drew his sword from the sheath on his belt. "I come to challenge human king for duel!" he announced.

"Wait." I stepped in front of Grufaeragar with my hands up, but he kept speaking around me.

"If king no accept duel of honor, then I fight to death. I fight anyone try stop me!"

The creature was clearly not as bright as most men, to think he would be able to come here and duel against the king. It reflected on his intelligence even more that he thought he could fight all of us and possibly win. But I admired his honor. There were many people I'd dealt with who I'd wished had more honor than intelligence.

"Grufaeragar, put down the sword," I urged him.

Michael flanked me. "No one here wants to fight you."

"It's all right, Jon," the king said. "Let me speak with him."

I hesitantly moved out of the way, as did Michael, but we stayed close just in case. I noticed then that I had been more than just normally compelled to protect the king. There had been a need, an instinct, to preserve his life that extended beyond our early relationship. It had to be the contract I'd signed. I might've been bothered by this nearly unwinnable urge, but the king seemed like a man worth protecting, at least so far.

"Your name is Grufaeragar?" Nykal asked.

"Yes. What is your name?"

"My name is Nykal Lennox. I believe you have mistaken me for Oquin Calloum."

The krepp let the tip of his sword rest on the grass. Deep lines formed across his lizard forehead.

"You no Oquin Calloum?"

"No, I despised him. He was a terrible king. We killed him. Now I am king."

"You defeated him in duel?" Grufaeragar asked.

"No. He was hanged for his crimes."

"Hanged?" Grufaeragar choked himself. "Like this?"

"Yes."

The krepp looked even more confused. "He hanged after lost duel against you?"

"No one dueled him," Nykal explained. "That is not how we decide matters in this kingdom."

"Yes. Humans afraid duel." The krepp spoke as if remembering a lesson. "Why are you king?"

"I led the rebellion against him. The people of Lycast follow me because I know what is best for them."

The krepp finally put away his sword. "I understand. Leaders know best. You must be good leader for all humans follow you. If no duel, I tell you important thing. Is one reason krepps no come here, no destroy every human. You know reason?"

I feared this would be the moment when the king would take the krepp inside to remove us from the conversation, but he did not, to my surprise.

"I don't," Nykal admitted.

It was a pleasure to see that he trusted us not

only to keep him safe but to find out what this krepp wanted.

"Only because Souriff," the krepp said.

The name was incredibly familiar. Many people reacted with shock, including Nykal.

"Do you mean Souriff the demigod?" he asked.

"Yes. Demigod Souriff."

The king put up his hand to quiet our murmuring. "How did you hear of Souriff?"

"Hear of Souriff?" Grufaeragar asked. He lowered his long neck, though he kept his yellow eyes on Nykal. "With her voice," he answered as if the king was stupid.

Nykal leaned forward and appeared even more interested. "You spoke with a woman who called herself Souriff?"

"Yes. She tell us, no...*gaa*..." He scratched his ass through his leather pants, which seemed to help him think of the right word. "She convince us try peace. Try speak king. You. We say we challenge king duel. She say he no duel. He make peace. You make peace?"

"Yes," Nykal answered. "I wish for peace with the krepps. We will trade and both benefit."

"Trade, yes. She say we trade. Humans have many things."

"Where did you speak with her?" Nykal asked.

"Hammashar. My home. She come as we prepare war. She tell us: Wait!"

The king narrowed his eyes. "This must've been after the krepps attacked Newhaven by boat."

"We no attack!" Grufaeragar said as he took hold of the hilt of his sword. "We need *vantikar*!" At seeing everyone's confusion, he added, "I know no word in your language. Word is when we are wrong so we kill krepp, or man, who made wrong."

"Revenge," the king specified.

"Almost same but *vantikar* more need. Krepps take boat to trade for humans, but all krepps *killed!*"

Grufaeragar had a way of almost shouting just about every word without actually shouting.

The king was nodding. "The last king expected krepps to attack later and was surprised when you didn't. It was he who ordered the attack on your krepps who came here to trade with us. He was still king when more krepps came later for *vantikar*. He prepared for war against krepps and Rohaer—the kingdom of humans south of here. We killed this king because we do not want war against krepps or Rohaer. Do you understand?"

"Yes. You smart. Last king...stupid!"

Many chuckled, but it startled the krepp, who took out his sword and looked around for a threat.

"No no," the king said. "They were just laughing in agreement with you. Laughing: ha ha ha. The last king stupid. Funny. Understand?"

"Laugh. Funny. Yes. I make mistake." He put away his sword again.

"You were saying that Souriff came to Hammashar and stopped krepps from starting war," Nykal continued. "This must've been longer than a year ago."

"Yes. She say, 'No war yet. Give humans one chance more. Humans no wish kill krepps.' They scare when krepps come. Krepps big. Krepps scary! We are. We understand."

"She told you all of this in your language. Kreppen, is it called?"

"Kreppen, yes. She give many books. Krepps learn

common tongue for books. It is me, Grufaeragar, learn best. Now I go here. I learn what humans give krepps and krepps give humans. Souriff say: We get rich!"

Nykal smiled warmly. "Do you know what a feast is, Grufaeragar?"

"Yes! I like feast."

"Tell me what you like to eat."

"*Krablark* and *kupota*, cooked. I want much."

"I don't think we have those dishes here," the king said. "You will be given seared lamb and roasted potatoes, seasoned with salt and herbs. I think you'll like them."

The krepp wiped his nose on his arm. "They valuable items?"

"Very valuable," the king said.

"Then I agree!"

"Follow these men inside. They will see that you are comfortable as you wait for the feast." He gestured for the guards to take the krepp away.

"I like that," Grufaeragar said as he walked into the great hall after the guards, a swagger to his step.

As soon as the krepp was gone, the king murmured to Barrett, "Is it possible that a woman learned Kreppen and sailed to Hammashar on behalf of Lycast without any of the nobles knowing?"

"I don't see how."

All of us were inching closer as we eavesdropped openly. Kataleya even spoke up.

"It could really be Souriff. It would make sense that she's watching over Lycast without making herself known, because Gourfist would find her if she used more of her power."

"Kataleya," Leon chastised. "The demigods are not

real, and the king doesn't want to hear your Formist chaff. Keep it to yourself." Leon glanced at the king. "I believe someone must've visited the krepps, but a woman wouldn't go alone. How this woman could've learned Kreppen, I'm not sure, but she probably found books on the language."

"The only known interaction between humans and krepps was here in Newhaven," Nykal replied. "You know how that ended."

"There must've been prior interactions. It's the only explanation."

"No matter what the truth is, it's important we find this woman who claims to be Souriff." The king turned to address the rest of us as we stood in a disorganized cluster. "All of you have proven yourselves useful so far. Many of you will be sent on tasks that are designed to improve your abilities or make use of them. For example, I sent Jon to retrieve the krepp who was waiting for an audience with me. Did anything happen on the way back?" he asked me.

"One man confronted the krepp because his father was killed by the creatures. It escalated somewhat, but nothing came of it."

"Did you have to use Expel?" the king asked.

I noticed Michael, along with a few others, showing me a surprised look. Apparently, they didn't know I had finally learned it.

"No. A crowd had formed by then. I explained that this krepp was innocent and here as a guest. Attacking him would be a crime. They backed down."

"I expect all of you to behave the way Jon did," the king said. "Until you are stronger, you are to de-escalate and report back. I want all of you keeping an eye out for crime and corruption no matter what task you're on."

Leon let out a huff as he noticed Charlie raising his hand. The king pointed at the blond young man. "Yes?"

"I don't understand. Are we the same as city guards?"

The king put his hand over his chin. I heard Barrett murmur to him, "They can find out later."

"No, it's time they know what they're training for." Nykal kept his gaze on us. "You were brought here because all of you have different strengths. I need sorcerers for several reasons, the most important being that there are none who are absolutely loyal to me. They are loyal to coin. The same can be said about the most capable fighters in Lycast."

He paused and looked a little less sure about speaking as he glanced at us. I was glad he continued, though.

"There is an army gathering in Rohaer. I have sent delegates to meet with Frederick Garlin, who many of you know as the king to the south."

Everyone was nodding, except me. All I'd known was that there was a king.

"King Frederick claims that he is arming his peasants to protect against the sorcerers spreading dteria across his land," Nykal continued. "We believe this to be a lie. It is most likely that he is building an army in an attempt to take Lycast for himself. It is just like what Oquin attempted here, except he'd planned to take Rohaer. We hope that the nobles in Rohaer will organize the peasants and stand against Frederick as we stood against Oquin.

"Time will tell. Winter is just beginning. The road between the kingdoms is blocked by Curdith Forest, mountains, or snow. There is no way for an army to reach us if he does send his men north. With nothing to forage or to feed their animals, they would likely starve during the journey here. However, the snow will melt when winter ends."

"I'm not here to fight," Charlie blurted out before I could even gather my thoughts.

"No, Charlie," the king replied. "You are here because of your skill with mtalia. Many of you are here to support the kingdom in other ways than fighting our enemies directly."

Panic took my breath away. But I *was* one of the people brought here to fight. I would be one of the fools risking his life for a kingdom that in no part belonged to me.

I hadn't agreed to that, I reminded myself. I had only agreed to protect the king from direct threats. I could leave at any point. I let out my breath. Doing so would be the most embarrassing act of my life, but at least I seemed to have the option. I could see the same fear and wonder on the faces of the others who were now realizing the same thing.

Remi, the shy woman who'd mentioned her specialty of fire, was staring at the ground with circular eyes. Michael was looking at me and shaking his head. Aliana, the ranger, had her fingertips pressed against her forehead with a downward gaze as her mouth hung open. Eden put her hand on Aliana's back and whispered something, but it appeared to do nothing to help.

I didn't understand why Reuben didn't look afraid like the rest of us. Could it be that he was braver than I was? No. He was just stupid. He thought that because he specialized in ordia, a magical art that had no place on the battlefield, he wouldn't be put to the sword when the time came. He was somewhat tall like Michael and myself, and he was young and capable. Of course he might be put to a sword. Even Charlie, who the king agreed was not here to fight, was white with terror.

This was why Leon said we only had a few months. It was also why he was so frustrated with our failures. We were the group the king had chosen. But why us?

Either there was no one better than us, or he couldn't afford the people who were. As much as Leon's attitude bothered me, I was starting to understand his frustration.

The king made a placating gesture. "I can see that all of you are envisioning a great battle. This is likely not going to happen. Ever. There are many ways to stop a war before it begins."

The king slammed his fist down onto his palm, snapping me out of my fearful line of thoughts. "That's why all of you are here. Some of you might need to fight enemies of the kingdom, but this will be a different kind of fighting. You are not to charge into throngs of armored soldiers. I have hordes of sellswords if that time comes. Your encounters will be planned. They will be designed to prevent violence and hardship, not cause it.

"You have not come here to sacrifice yourselves. You have come here to help me *maintain* peace. Now if you don't believe that's something worth training for, then you are free to leave whenever you want. I only ask that you don't speak of this to anyone. My enemies aren't just in Rohaer. They are across our kingdom, in all shapes and forms. They are sorcerers of dteria who are trying to spread the corruption for reasons we still don't understand. They are the guards who take my coin in exchange for protecting citizens, only to thieve and rape when they believe they can get away with it. My enemies are the people in this land who are ready to kill others to protect their own self-interests, and they are *prevalent*. If my enemies find out that I am training a group to seek out and find them, then they will not hesitate to kill you before you are strong enough to stop them."

Pride swelled in my chest at hearing the king speak about us in this way. My life had had little purpose before now. My buzzing mana was the only thing that drove me. Now there was so much more.

I still had many questions, like how could the king be aware of having so many enemies without already stopping them? How could he know there were guards who thieved and raped? Why hadn't they been hanged or thrown into the dungeons by now? But I trusted this man in front of me. I could tell he cared about the people in his kingdom.

I knew I had a lot to learn, but I was eager to begin. A thought made me pause, however. I had already been targeted. I'd figured it was someone here who had tried to poison my mana with dteria, but perhaps it was one of the many enemies the king had mentioned. They might already know of our group and have more plans to corrupt us, if not kill us outright.

My fear quickly returned.

CHAPTER THIRTEEN

Most of my peers were high in spirit when the king left. Leon had announced that everyone must go back to training, but first he took me away from the group for a word.

"So you finally managed to cast one time for the king, eh?"

"I did."

"Think you can do it again?" Leon asked, doubt in his tone.

I didn't want to brag, but whenever I've done something once, it's never been a problem to repeat it.

"I can," I told him.

"Show me." He held out his hand as a target.

Preparing my mana for the complicated spell, however, still took a good ten seconds of pure concentration. Fortunately, Leon didn't rush me as I readied my mana in the four different frequencies required.

I couldn't get over how satisfying it felt when the spell came to fruition. It was like struggling with a lock and then finally finding the right key. It was like trying to recall a memory and then finally having it emerge out of the depths of your mind. It was wondering for five long years what this buzzing energy could do and then finally seeing it for myself.

It didn't matter to me that it wasn't strong enough to spin Leon around, whipping his hand back instead. This was just the beginning of what I could do with dvinia. I didn't care what he said to diminish my accomplishment right now.

"I'm actually impressed," he said.

I smiled in shock.

"Tell me what else you can do so I know how to split your training and what tasks to send you on."

"I can use the sword and bow."

"Which are you better at?"

"The sword."

"How good with each?"

"Good," I answered.

He squinted. "Don't be modest with me."

"Extremely good," I answered more accurately.

"I figured. Did you bring these weapons with you from Bhode?"

"I did, but I sold my bow in Tryn." I hadn't imagined myself going out for a hunt once I arrived in the city, where all kinds of food could be purchased cheaply. Also, I'd needed the coin.

"You ever hunt?" Leon asked.

"I did all the time in Bhode."

"Good. I'll be teaching the other men sword once all of you get a better grasp on the spells you're specializing in. Take the rest of the day to practice Expel. Tomorrow, you will be taking Aliana and Eden into Curdith Forest."

I looked forward to that. Leon was leaving, though, and I wasn't even close to being done with him.

"I'd like to learn other spells of dvinia as well," I

called out.

"You and me both," he said in stride. "Expel is the only one any sorcerer knows." He stopped and slowly turned around. "Do you even know how strong this spell can become?"

I shook my head. "Everything I know about sorcery is what you and Barrett told me in the great hall."

"Practice at least six hours every day, with breaks. Learn how to change the shape of the spell, not only the force. You will find that there is much you can do with just Expel if you put your mind to it. I can't help you because my mana doesn't reach high enough to cast it."

"If I practice nothing but using my mana in the range of dvinia, will I lose my ability to reach lower ranges?"

"You should not be concerned about that. Dvinia will take enough of your time without you wasting effort trying to learn another art." Leon left me on my own.

I took that as a yes. No matter what he said, I didn't want to lose my wide range of mana. That meant I had to figure out my own way of training. Fortunately, I already had, with the vibmtaer in my room. I would take his advice in the beginning, however, focusing only on dvinia until the spell was powerful.

I practiced for a while. I'd always enjoyed improving techniques through repetition, challenging myself to learn as fast as I could. It was wondrously freeing to have no looming deadline. I would not be removed if I failed to impress Leon or the king, but that didn't mean that I'd let my determination dwindle.

I looked forward to being able to cast Expel without so much preparation. Then I could really focus on improving the force and precision of the spell.

I curiously watched the other sorcerers when I took a brief break. There were three others besides me whose sorcery could be used in combat, as far as I knew. Michael, with his specialty of wind, had an entire side of the large courtyard to himself. With a moonstone in one hand, he swept his other hand around as whirls of wind seemed to follow his command, picking up the dry dirt of the courtyard with each cast. His clothes were covered in a thick layer of dust. He wore a cloth mask over his mouth. I didn't envy him. For his sake, I'm sure it would've been nice if the courtyard was covered in grass, but watching Remi after him made it clear why that wouldn't work out for us.

The shy girl of light hair and narrow, determined eyes seemed to have control over a small ball of fire hovering in front of her hand. Like Michael, she held onto a moonstone, an essence that seemed required for her to cast.

That could've been me, I thought to myself. They had wanted me to learn the spell Fire. It could be incredibly useful if I learned to control it. Perhaps it would be the next thing I learned. With an essence, the element of fire sounded easier to control than the energy of dvinia.

Fire and Water would be the most valuable of any spell for the people of Bhode. When they'd spoken of sorcery, it was these elements that many had fantasized about. It was a bewildering concept to me, turning one's mana into fire or water. Expel made sense. Mana felt like energy, the same thing that Expel seemed to be. Comparing that to water, something every creature had to consume to live, didn't make sense to me. Could it really be the same water that we drink?

I watched Kataleya as she practiced without an essence. She was incredible. Kataleya could form a sphere of water and move it through the air. I edged closer as I watched with insatiable curiosity. When she stopped shifting it one way and made it hover back the other way, the water didn't slosh around as if disturbed. She had complete control, the clear water utterly still and contained. When she was done, she let it fall into the well nearby.

I made my way over as she panted for breath. I felt someone's gaze. I looked over to see Reuben glaring at me. I ignored him.

"What you're doing is nothing short of amazing," I told Kataleya.

She turned around, still catching her breath, her pale cheeks flushed. "Thank you."

"Do you mind if I ask a few questions about it?"

"Sure." There was a friendly sparkle in her ashen eyes.

"Seeing as how you're putting the water into the well after using it, am I right to assume it's the same water we drink?"

"Water made from mana is water in its purest form," she said.

"So when you're thirsty, you turn your water into mana and then drink it? I hope this doesn't sound rude, but that seems strange to me."

She gave a laugh. "It does sound strange when you put it like that. I've never drank water from my mana because I'm thirsty. It takes too much out of me. However, I have created water to store for later."

"And it tastes just like any other water?"

"Try it." She started to move her hand around, and

a sphere of water began to form between us.

"I don't know," I said as I looked around. I noticed Aliana glancing at me, but she pretended she hadn't been as soon as our eyes met. She had been shooting arrows at a target on another side of the courtyard. I'd watched her a few times. Even from afar, I could tell that she needed some assistance with her form, but I thought it would be too forward to impose myself.

Kataleya brought the sphere of water close to my mouth. "Go ahead," she said.

"This is the strangest thing anyone has ever done for me."

She giggled. "Don't make me laugh."

I put my lips against the sphere of water, then immediately recoiled. "*Ugh*, it's warm!"

She looked to be holding in laughter with a tightly pressed smile. "Did you taste anything?"

"I'm not sure I want to," I teased.

"Stop!" She laughed harder. "I'm losing concentration. Taste it so I can prove my point."

I quickly slurped some water out of the sphere. The fact that it was warm and verging on hot made the experience very uncomfortable, but I smacked my lips a few times as I tried to search for a taste. Kataleya let the sphere of water drop. I jumped back as it splashed against the ground where my feet were.

"That's your fault for making me laugh." She giggled as she searched for breath.

I chuckled with her.

"So what did it taste like?" she asked when she recovered somewhat.

"A little flat, I guess."

"Because there's nothing in it but water. You taste

very small things from rivers in other water. Even if you can't see them, they're there."

"Oh, that makes sense," I said. "How can you make it float in the air?"

"It's just like any other magical art. Whatever we create, we can control."

"I don't feel that way with dvinia. Once it leaves me, it has a mind of its own."

"You're just starting out. You will learn to control it." She leaned in. "And might I say that you teaching yourself dvinia, against the orders of our instructor *and* the councilman to the king is, as you said, nothing short of amazing."

"Thank you, Kataleya."

"You can call me Kat."

"Kat," I said with a nod. "Do you think you might find time to teach me more about water later? I would really like to learn how to cast with it."

"I would be happy to help you whenever you wish. Just let me know."

"That's very kind. Let me know if there's anything I can do for you."

"I will if I think of something."

"I'd better get back to training."

She nodded.

I could feel Reuben wanting to rip my head off as I walked away from Kat, but I didn't bother even looking at him this time. I did check on Aliana, however. She was focused on the target in front of her as she aimed, shot, then lowered her shoulders in disappointment when her arrow completely missed to the side.

It was uncomfortable for me to watch anyone suffering, especially when I felt that I could help. But it hurt even more to see Aliana frustrated with herself.

I didn't realize I was staring until she looked over. Now I was the one who quickly looked away—an instinct that I immediately regretted. I should've at least given her a smile of encouragement. I looked back, but she was turned away from me again. I hoped I hadn't embarrassed her by noticing her lack of skill, but I could almost feel her shame as her body shrank in on itself.

I noticed that both Eden and Charlie were not present in the courtyard. If I recalled correctly, Charlie specialized in mtalia. While I didn't know exactly what that meant, I was just about certain his skill had something to do with metal. He did mention that he was good at building and was a blacksmith's apprentice.

Eden had mentioned, after the test with the vibmtaer, that she would be an enchanter. From the little I'd learned about enchanting from Greda, I figured Eden was somewhere practicing with a dog's claw or another animal part right now.

Ordia seemed like a powerful magical art, from the little I knew so far. Enchanters used it, as did harbingers like Barrett and what Reuben hoped to be. And Greda had explained that casting an illusion required ordia and vtalia. Ordia would have to be something I looked into more, even if I never could use it to enchant anything.

Reuben looked to be casting like the others here in the courtyard, but there was nothing to witness. I had little idea how skilled he was with ordia. I doubted he could seal a contract, like Barrett. He was probably familiarizing himself with the notes required, as I had done with dvinia.

Eventually, we were called into the great hall for supper. I caught up and walked with Michael under the impression we would eat together, but he had to wash his hands from all the dust his casting had brought up. I waited as he used the water from the well as everyone else entered the great hall.

"The next spell I'm going to learn will be Water," he said. "Speaking of, I think just about everyone noticed you drinking Kataleya's water."

"I didn't think that would be an issue."

"How did it taste?"

"Bland. Warm."

"I figured it would taste like money."

I politely ignored his quip. "I saw her casting and wanted to know more about water. It looked too interesting for me to leave it alone, that's all."

He finished rinsing his hands. "Not sure everyone's going to think that. I know Reuben won't."

We made our way toward the great hall.

"Creating wind out of mana seems just as strange to me as water," Michael said. "Are you sure you're not interested in water just because Kat's rich and shapely?"

"It's not that."

"Mmm hmm." He clearly didn't believe me.

We were the last ones to enter the dining room. There were just two plates of food left on the serving table near the doorway. Both had a couple of meaty lamb legs and a generous portion of seasoned potatoes. It reminded me that the king had promised Grufaeragar a feast earlier. It was nice to see that we were included in the king's thoughts, even if we didn't eat at the same time as the krepp.

"Wow," Michael said. "I guess the king doesn't mind if we get fat."

"I'm sure he plans to keep us very busy."

"The busiest people are sometimes the fattest!"

"Not where I come from."

We made our way over to the others. Kataleya, Aliana, and Eden were seated together on the far end of the middle long table. Remi ate by herself at another long table close to the wall. Reuben and Charlie sat separated from everyone, as well as each other.

"This won't do at all," I commented. "We're all in this together. We should be eating together, too."

"You really want to eat with Reuben and Charlie?" Michael asked.

"I do," I told him.

He made a face of shock. "All right..."

We set our plates down near Charlie. He smiled. "You'll eat with me?"

"Of course!" Michael said a little too enthusiastically, giving me a smug look. "We wouldn't even consider sitting somewhere else!"

"That's kind," Charlie said, missing Michael's sarcasm.

I made my way over to Reuben. He glared at me.

"Would you like to sit with us?" I offered.

He looked at me as if this was some sort of trick.

"We're all on the same side here," I reminded him.

"We're not," he said. "You have no nobility, no honor. I don't want to see you flirting with Kataleya anymore. She is too far above your rank. You're embarrassing her."

I held in my anger. "I plan to learn from Kataleya

just like I will from everyone else. I even hope to learn something from you, when you let go of this grudge. I could give you sword lessons in exchange."

The idea of working with Reuben actually turned my stomach. It was my last attempt at trying to make friends with the ass, and it hurt my pride to even offer after the way he'd spoken ill about me to Leon and the king.

Reuben rolled his eyes. "You honestly think you can teach me *anything*?"

I couldn't take it anymore. "Here's something: Roll your eyes as much as you want, you won't find a brain back there."

I regretted it even before I finished speaking the words. He shot out of his chair and grabbed at me, but I jumped away. He fell onto the floor as I made some more distance. Everyone stopped eating to stare. Even the king looked over. He sat at his expensive table on the dais with his daughter and the queen, who I had never met.

Reuben quickly got to his feet and spun around to face the rest of the room. Everyone seemed to be waiting for a reaction. Unfortunately, the fool gave them one.

"He insulted me, sire! I demand he be punished."

The king looked more than irritated as he set down his napkin and slowly made his way over. The room was silent save the thud of his boots against the floor.

"What have you done?" I grumbled to Reuben.

"Everyone mind your own business!" Nykal announced, and all quickly found great interest in their plates.

The king stopped in front of us. "The two of you

need to stop acting like children. You aren't required to be friends, but you will have to work together. Is that something you can both manage, or should I look for new sorcerers who know how to act like men?"

"We can manage it," we both answered at the same time.

"There will be no more incidents. I don't care whose fault it is."

We nodded.

The king walked back to his table. Reuben had a hateful look in his eyes.

"Look," I told him. "The king's right. We're going to have to work together. If you can't even eat with me and the others, how are we expected to trust you?"

"I want you to promise that you will stay away from Kataleya."

I was so frustrated that I laughed. "I'm not interested in her that way! You must remember that I knew nothing about sorcery before coming here. I'm just trying to learn all that I can."

Reuben shook his head at me as he sat down in front of his plate. He took up his fork and said, "You complained about trusting each other, and all you do is lie to me."

"Reuben—"

"I will be eating alone. Good day."

"It wasn't a lie—"

"I said good day!"

I felt another insult ready to jump out of my mouth, but I managed to keep it to myself as I went back to Charlie and Michael, who were certainly close enough to have heard everything. I was glad the women had been too far. Hopefully, they knew I wouldn't insult Reuben unless pushed to do so, though I had no doubt that he would be acting as the victim whenever he spoke to any of them.

The most aggravating thing about Reuben, I realized then, was that none of what he did was an act. He really thought he was acting properly and that I was not.

I sat down next to Michael, Charlie across from us. "I could teach a pig to bathe itself faster than I could teach Reuben how to stop being an ass," I told them.

"Let him eat alone," Michael suggested. "If he ever does change his mind it will be because he's decided to, not because of anything we do. Many of the nobility are like that. It's something you're going to have to learn, Jon."

"Kataleya seems different," I said. "Not that I'm interested," I figured I'd add just to avoid further confusion.

"Aye, Kataleya is special. What about you, Charlie? Any of the women strike your fancy?"

He looked over, I thought for just a glance, but he stared for so long that Eden eventually turned to gaze back at him with an odd expression on her face.

"Charlie, stop staring!" Michael hissed.

"I'm trying to decide."

Eden was now setting down her fork and standing up. "What are you looking at Charlie?" she shouted across the room.

To my amazement, Charlie started shouting back. "Michael asked me—*mmnn, agh!*"

Michael practically dove across the table to throw his hand around Charlie's mouth. "Shut up, you idiot!" he whispered.

"What?" Charlie asked as he pulled away.

"You can't let them know you're talking about them if you ever want any of them to like you back." Michael stood and gave a little wave. "It's nothing!"

Fortunately, Eden was smirking. She sat back down and said something that brought out a loud laugh from Aliana and Kataleya.

"I like them all," Charlie said.

"Even Remi?" Michael asked. "She scares me."

"She scares me too," he agreed. But the way he said it, with no emotion as he took up his fork again, made me curious if he was just agreeing for the sake of it.

The rest of the meal was pleasantly uneventful. I hadn't even noticed Leon eating alone in the corner of the large room until most of us were finished and looking around wondering what to do now.

"Back into the courtyard!" Leon commanded.

Michael groaned. As we passed by Leon, Michael asked our instructor, "When will we have some time off?"

"Your cranny hunter stays in your pants from sunrise to sunset every day. You will either be training or taking care of some business. Get used to it."

"We'll never have a day off?" Michael complained.

"You will when you earn it."

We separated from Leon and slowly made our way back out onto the courtyard.

"This godforsaken wind," Michael muttered. "I can't train with it every hour of every goddamn day."

I felt his pain. Wind seemed like a rough force to deal with. "Maybe it won't be so bad once you have more control," I suggested. "What will you be able to do with it eventually?"

"Well, let's see. I could mess up someone's hair. I could force dirt into someone's eyes. Oh, I could blow up women's dresses. That would be nice if it wasn't sure to land me in the dungeons. Hmm, what else?"

"What can you really do?" I prodded.

He looked at me seriously. "I've been told that wind will never be strong enough to throw a man from his horse, but it could startle the beast. It'll never be strong enough to throw open a latched door, but it could close one. My point is that wind is useless, Jon, until I learn fire or water to go with it."

"That's not true at all," Charlie said from right behind us.

"God!" Michael jumped. "You have to say something if you're sneaking up on someone."

"Sorry," Charlie said. "But there's much more you can do with wind."

"I know I can make objects hover and other useless things that aren't worth mentioning. Without casting Fire at the same time as Wind, it will never save me from a foolish decision, or even a smart one."

"You can do a lot more than that," Charlie insisted. "Well *you* can't, but stronger sorcerers can."

"Thanks."

"They can create wind shields and even tornados, at least in theory."

"Tornadoes?" Michael asked.

"Yes," Charlie confirmed. "It's too bad we don't live in Rohaer. They have many more readings on sorcery. It is a whole business there, learning and teaching. I'm glad I won't be the one fighting when their army reaches us."

"I'm going to politely ignore most of what you just

said. How do you know so much about Rohaer?"

"I have spent years trying to find out everything about sorcery. Most of the sorcerers who know something have mentioned Rohaer, specifically the library of the magical arts. It is a place I wish I could visit."

"All right, then tell me how to cast a tornado," Michael said sarcastically.

By then, everyone else had spread out in the courtyard and had resumed their training.

"I don't know the spell Tornado," Charlie said, "but I imagine it is complicated. It probably involves a rev."

"A what?" I asked.

"A rev," Charlie repeated. "It's a fancy word for revision, when the spell is changed as its being cast."

"How does that work exactly?" I asked.

"You change one or two of the notes as they are being used to form the spell."

"That's impossible," Michael said.

I was inclined to agree. The spell formed as soon as I used my mana. There was no time to change anything.

"It takes exceptional strength and precision, but it is possible," Charlie said.

Leon yelled from the doorway to the great hall, "Why aren't you three training?"

Charlie answered, "I'm telling them about revs."

"Then you are wasting your time and theirs."

"Wait, so it is possible?" Michael called to Leon.

"Of course revs are possible. But they aren't for you."

"Why not?"

"Because you are a terrible sorcerer, like everyone else here, and you will be for a long time."

We seemed to be getting the attention of everyone

else as they stopped what they were doing to listen.

Leon lifted his arms. "All right. Everyone gather around. Maybe this will inspire some of you. Come on. Get closer. Kataleya." He motioned for her as she stayed back.

"Not if you're going to use a rev."

"You daisy. Fine. All the rest of you form a circle around me."

I knew I shouldn't be smiling. I should probably stay back with Kataleya, and Charlie, who also refused to get closer, but I was too excited to finally see some powerful sorcery.

We formed a close circle around Leon. I happened to stand beside Aliana, but she didn't look my way.

"Hold onto your clothes," Leon announced, then made two fists and leaned down with his eyes closed.

For the shortest of moments, wind whipped around the circle before it exploded outward. I ducked as it hit me, my feet sliding along the dirt.

It was over in a second. Everyone had been thrown at least a few feet, all on the ground. I walked back to help up Aliana.

"I'm fine," she said as she ignored my hand.

"Over here, Jon," Michael called as he reached out for me in feigned distress.

I pulled him up.

"You're the only one who didn't fall," he commented.

"I'm probably the heaviest."

"Still, that was...so strong. Look, it even knocked over Charlie, and he was back a lot farther."

Charlie was getting up with a huge grin. "Remarkable!" he said. "Can you do it again?"

Leon was ignoring him, looking at me with a strange look in his eyes. "Jon, what do you know about magical resistance?"

"Nothing. Why?"

"All right, two lessons for you all here. Oh, stop being daisies. I'm not going to do it again."

We all moved closer to listen.

"Ah, it's not going to make any sense to any of you if I don't write this down. Stay here." Leon rushed into the great hall. He was gone for a long while as we muttered to each other in confusion. Eventually, he returned with a small piece of paper.

"Pass this around," he said. "That is the spell I casted. It is called Windburst. Michael, you really should pay attention to this. The dash that you see written in the middle of the spell is what's called a rev. It is a change to the notes of the chord right as the chord is casted."

I reminded myself that a chord was a group of individual frequencies of mana—a group of notes. It was basically a spell, because all spells were the casting of notes together. Except for vtalia, I thought a moment later, which was a single note. Perhaps not all spells were chords, actually. I was quickly confusing myself and let it go for now.

"Revs are one of the most difficult techniques for a sorcerer," Leon explained. "They are dangerous as well. Use them wrong, you're going to hurt yourself. Fortunately, most of you will never be able to use a rev, so I don't have to worry about that. For those of you who think you can, you cannot yet. Don't experiment. You will regret it."

Michael was passed the written spell next. He held

it between us for me to look as well.

It was the first time I had seen any spell written, and it made absolutely no sense to me, at first. The longer I looked at it, the more I realized I knew what it was saying.

It was written out like another language: uC, uE, uG —3uD, 1uB.

I looked at it one note at a time. uC was Upper C. Then there was Upper E and Upper G. These were all high but still lower than most of the range needed for dvinia. I'd forgotten that wind required high vibrations.

Leon had said that the dash was the rev. It was marking the change that was to take place right after the spell was cast. Michael handed it to me as Leon continued. I had looked long enough, so I gave it to Charlie, who grabbed it eagerly.

"After the rev you will see the number three," Leon explained. "That is telling you which note of the wind scale is the first one to change. These changes occur as fast as blinks of the eye, but there is still an order to them. For this spell, Windburst, you start by casting wind on its own: C, E, G, all Upper. Then you immediately change the third note in the wind scale, which is Upper E, to Upper D. Immediately after, you change the first note from Upper C to Upper B." He snapped with one hand and then right after with the other. "That's casting and then making the revs." He snapped with both hands again, one right after the other. "Just a quick moment is needed between the spell and the revs. The revs need to be done in the time that the mana is still coming together."

I had not heard the term "wind scale" before. Pretty

much everything he'd said after it had gone over my head.

Charlie raised his hand.

"Yes?" Leon asked.

"I've always wanted to know how many spells there are."

"I don't know, Charlie. I'm sure there are many more than what I know. Any questions should be about this spell."

"I have one," Michael said. "When can I learn that?"

"Can you at least tell us all the spells you know?" Charlie interrupted.

"You can't even cast anything but mtalia!" Leon yelled at him.

Charlie looked down.

Leon then answered Michael, "You will learn it if you ever become ready."

"What about the spell Tornado?" Michael asked. "Is it really possible?"

Leon grinned and rolled up his sleeves. "You're going to want to stand back for this one."

CHAPTER FOURTEEN

I awoke the next morning excited to take a trip into the forest. Not only had I wanted to visit Curdith Forest since I had heard about it many years ago, but Aliana would be there as well.

None of us sorcerers in training ate breakfast together in the great hall. Instead, we had been told it would be delivered to our rooms at sunrise.

I still had some time, so I decided to take a bath. It made me feel a little like royalty to visit the bathing quarters and see the wooden tubs with steaming water and curtains for privacy. I wondered if this was the kind of pampering Reuben and Kataleya were used to all of their lives.

My breakfast was waiting for me in my room when I returned. It wasn't anything too extravagant, just oats and juice with a side of bread. Considering I wasn't even hungry because of the enormous dinner I had the night before, it was the perfect way to start my day.

While I ate, I reminisced about Leon's Tornado spell last evening. It hadn't been all that exciting. The tiny tornado of wind made by his spell hadn't been strong enough to lift anyone up, even if we had been close, and Leon was completely spent after he'd finished. It had been disconcerting to watch the rude and seemingly all-powerful instructor fall to his knees by the time the small whirlwind dissipated. It reminded me of seeing my father fall down just outside our home, after he'd told me he was feeling well enough to work. Leon made it back to his feet on his own, though. My father hadn't that day.

I'd asked Leon about resistance before retiring for the night. He'd admitted that he'd forgotten he was going to mention it and that I shouldn't worry about it right now. I let it out of my mind only because there were so many other things to think about. One was my new impression of Leon. Surprisingly, I was beginning to trust him. Although he wasn't the best instructor, it was clear he knew sorcery well.

When I finished my breakfast, I opened my window and stuck out my head. The day was warm, not a single breeze to be felt. The sun was bright in the clear sky. If this was how winters usually began in Newhaven, then I might be even happier here than I thought.

I took a deep breath. I was smiling by the time I finished.

"Jon?" asked a familiar voice.

Shocked, I looked to my right to see Aliana leaning out of her window with a surprised look on her face.

"How long have you been there?" I asked, a little embarrassed.

"Did you know our rooms are next to each other?" For some reason, she didn't sound too pleased about this fact.

"I had no idea."

A moment of silence passed as she glanced ahead of her.

"So, today we'll—?"

"Are you ready?" She spoke at the same time as me.

"Uh, yeah, let's go."

We met in the hall. I wondered how her tanned skin always seemed to shine. She was practically sparkling.

Her features blended together with elegance and grace. The sweep of her chin, the pout of her lips, and even her striking eyebrows, which might look a bit off on some women, just brought out her beauty even more. She had on a leather hood, the top down. It covered her shoulders down to her elbows, leaving the bottom of her arms bare. It was a reminder that she would be shooting a bow today. She had to shed any extra fabric. She wore a sleeveless tunic with a black belt tight around the top of her narrow waist to hold the tunic closed. The swell of her chest was extremely prominent on her thin frame.

"You look like a true archer," I said, careful not to stare.

"Yes, well I'd rather have the skill of a true archer than to look like one, but one of those things I can help."

We walked down the hall beside each other.

"Would you like to shoot a few arrows in the courtyard as we wait for Eden?" I asked.

"I guess," she said dubiously. "Leon did say you might teach me something."

I didn't understand her cold tone.

"But how much do you really know about archery?" she asked skeptically.

So that was it. She didn't believe I knew anything. "A little," I answered modestly.

She shrugged. "Well, a little is a little more than I

know."

I wasn't sure why I hadn't been more honest about my skill. I supposed I didn't feel like trying to prove anything to a woman who treated me like a liar. I didn't understand. Was it just because our rooms were next to each other that she distrusted me? She couldn't possibly think I had something to do with that?

We started down the stairs.

"It looks like a good bow," I said as I gestured at the weapon she held. "Have you had it for a while?"

"No. They told me to purchase one with my weekly stipend," she said dismissively.

"I think you chose well. The quality looks good to me."

"Am I right to assume that you spent your entire stipend on the vibmtaer?" There sounded to be judgement in her voice. Perhaps she thought my choice to be wrong.

"Just about." I didn't mind admitting the truth. I was proud of myself for what I had accomplished.

A silence passed.

I was growing more irritated. She hadn't been this cold toward me when we'd first met, and I hadn't seen her behave like this toward anyone else. What had I done to piss her off?

After a tense walk, we arrived at the target. Surprisingly, she held her bow up to me as she barely glanced in my direction.

"Why don't you shoot first to show me?"

It was tempting, especially because Aliana sounded like she didn't trust that I knew anything about archery, but we were about to go into the forest. Time would be better spent helping her.

"Actually, I'd like to see how you shoot."

"Fine."

She set herself into position and drew back the string. She completely lacked confidence in her stance, understandably. At least she didn't hold the string back too long, which was a common mistake that beginners made, letting go soon after the string was back. The arrow sailed over the target and into the stacks of hay behind.

She looked at me without really looking at me as she waited for my answer. Ignoring her attitude, I'd noticed a few issues just from that one loose.

I hummed as I tried to determine where to begin. "Has Leon given you lessons yet?"

Her hands fisted around the bow. "Do you mean screaming at me to stop missing?"

"That's not at all what I mean," I said. My tone was starting to match hers as much as I tried to remain friendly.

"Then no, he hasn't. He did shoot one arrow to demonstrate for me, but he missed over the target and mumbled something about how sorcery was better so he hasn't needed to learn the bow."

I could picture that quite clearly.

"He told me later that you might help me learn," she said as she eyed me suspiciously.

I forced myself to sound more positive about this than I felt. "And learn you shall. Can I ask something first?"

Aliana set down the corner of the bow. "Go ahead."

"Can you tell me more about being a ranger?"

"Why?"

"It's just that I don't know anything about it. Some

information might help me instruct you, if it relates to the bow."

She rolled her eyes. "I don't know much myself. It was my writing tutor I first spoke to about the mana I felt, though I didn't know what it was."

"I had the same experience of not knowing what I felt." *Except I didn't have a tutor.*

Could it be that Aliana was another young sorcerer from a wealthy family? She didn't have the lilt, but it might explain her attitude if she saw me as less than her, as Reuben did.

"Yes, I'd heard that about you." Her tone implied there were other things she may have heard as well, not that I knew what. "My tutor asked if she could set up a meeting with a sorcerer. I was happy for the opportunity, though it was a surprise when the king's councilman showed up instead."

It really was similar to my experience. "So you had no idea what this mana did?"

"No, but I'd felt it for years."

"I was under the impression that everyone else had trained for a long time before coming here."

"I think most of the others have, but I haven't. I still don't know exactly what being a ranger entails. I'm a little scared to ask Leon because he's..."

"Because he's Leon." I finished the statement for her.

She nodded. "He told me to channel my mana and listen to what it tells me. He has no personal experience with Low-Lower B. He says it's up to me to figure it out. Was it similar with your mana?"

I was glad to see her open up a bit. "Actually, that's where we're different. I knew exactly what I wanted to do with my mana after coming here. Then it was just a matter of forcing myself to learn it."

"I see," she said disappointedly.

"What do you feel when you focus on Low-Lower B? My mana can't go that low."

"It's an odd sensation," she said, finally looking into my eyes when she spoke to me. "It's like I can tell where things are going without hearing them or feeling them. I'd had hints of it growing up, but ever since our trip to the mountains it has become strong enough for me to be sure. I don't really know what to do with it."

"Are you saying you can feel movement on the ground?"

"Something like that. It's difficult to describe because it's still relatively new."

"So if I go over here..." I went about five yards away. "And I jump, you can tell?"

"I don't know." She faced away from me. "Try it, but don't tell me when."

I waited a few breaths, then I jumped and landed.

"Now," she called out. "I'm sure."

I returned to her side. "I didn't know something like this was possible." I might've complimented her if she hadn't been so cold toward me earlier.

"I haven't gotten used to the feeling. It's like a voice inside my head that isn't mine." She shuddered.

"I'm sure that discomfort will pass. I felt the same way trying to cast with four different notes."

"You can actually cast with dvinia now?" Aliana's tone made it clear she didn't believe I could.

"I can."

She looked away with an expression that told me her thoughts.

"You don't believe me." I said.

"I think you can cast some semblance of a spell that doesn't do much."

"Hold out your hand," I told her.

She stuck out her palm and didn't appear the least bit afraid of me accidentally hurting her. Of course I wouldn't, but it would've been a little nice, at least, to see her worry a bit about my strength.

I prepared my mana, aimed, then pushed her hand back with a wide force of energy. She stumbled back.

"Whoa, that was strong." Aliana looked surprised. "I really didn't think you could do much."

"I could tell."

"Was that the hardest you can cast it?"

"No."

"Show me the hardest."

"There's no way I would do that to you."

"Really? It's *that* strong already?"

I didn't want to sound like a braggart, but I was more worried about injuring her. "Yes, I might be able to pick you up with it if I tried."

"You really had never used dvinia before coming here?"

"I hadn't. I never knew mana, like I said."

She looked into my eyes pointedly. "It's just very hard to believe."

"I'm not sure what to tell you. It's the truth."

I didn't appreciate being called a liar, even indirectly as she had done. It made me less inclined to help her, but we had come this far.

"Why don't you shoot another arrow?" I suggested.

"If you say so." She started to ready an arrow but paused. "Any tips first?"

"Not yet."

Aliana drew back and shot another just like the first. It sailed over the top of the target about fifteen yards away. I thought she was standing a little too far away for someone of her skill level, but she had chosen this spot on her own and was somewhat close to hitting the target.

"It really doesn't look like it's too high when I'm aiming," she said.

"That's the first thing to keep in mind. Your eyes are always going to be higher than the arrow you're aiming. You're actually tilting the bow upward, probably without realizing. It's a common mistake. Just aim a little lower than you think."

"That's all?" she asked skeptically.

"The other changes will make it easier to hit the target once you have the angle right, so they can wait."

She shot another arrow. This one struck the top of the target.

This didn't seem to satisfy her very much as she looked at me. "I'm ready to hear the other changes."

I went through everything with her one problem at a time. First, she had all her fingers holding back the string. She should only use three. Second, she pulled the string too far away from her face as if scared of it hurting her, which she admitted she was when I asked. I told her she had to hold it very close to her face for better control and aim. Third, she held the string too tightly, which caused her knuckles to pinch the arrow. Ironically, this made the arrow fall off the bow rather than hold it steady. She had to grasp the string more loosely.

These were all mistakes my father had helped me through when I was a boy.

By the time Eden was walking across the courtyard toward us, Aliana was shooting much more comfortably. She was drawing the string back with confidence, bringing it up right up to her cheek and chin. She was also hitting the target every time. Her callous demeanor had disappeared as well, a great relief to me. I was sure that it was in part because she finally realized I wasn't a liar, but I still wondered if there had been another reason she had been so cold toward me.

She struck the bullseye as Eden arrived. Aliana gaped at me if something was wrong.

"What?" I asked.

"That's the first time I hit the center."

"Congratulations," I said with a smile and was happy to see her smile back.

Eden walked up to us. "Looks like you're ready to kill something!"

"If it doesn't move," Aliana answered. "And if I have five tries. Jon's actually a good teacher." She wore an expression that held a bit of surprise.

"Really? How long have you used the bow?" Eden asked me.

"Probably...ten years, it's been." I was somewhat shocked by my answer. It hadn't felt like that long.

"You said you only knew a little!" Aliana complained.

I shrugged.

"Let's see you hit the middle," Eden challenged.

"From here?" I asked incredulously.

Eden looked at the target again. Then she squinted at me. "I can't tell if you're saying it's too easy or too difficult."

Aliana handed me the bow.

I knew that no one liked a showoff, but I just couldn't help myself. I walked back until I was about thirty yards out. Without heavy wind, this was a shot I could make consistently. But just then, Michael was walking up to us. He stopped somewhat near the soon-to-be trajectory of my arrow. I stared at him.

"Go ahead!" he called to me.

"I know what you're going to do," I told him.

He muttered something as he walked off, or pretended to walk off. When I tested him by raising the bow, he spun around and lifted his hand.

I set down the bow again.

"Fine, I won't do it," he said.

I didn't believe him. So in one quick motion, I drew the string as I aimed the bow and then let go, something I had practiced many times. Michael still tried to blow my arrow off course with wind, but he was caught off guard by my speed.

I was pleased to see my arrow strike the center of the target. The three of them started whooping in surprise.

"Damn that was fast!" Michael said.

"Had to get it past you," I told him.

Eden and Aliana had their mouths open as I tried to hand Aliana the bow.

"No way. You keep it."

"It's yours."

"But I'll never be that good!"

"Ali, you're a ranger. One day you're going to be better than me, because I will help you get there."

She seemed surprised by my words. "Why?"

"We're all in this together now, no matter what happens. It's what I was trying to tell Reuben at dinner yesterday when I asked him to sit with us."

Aliana took back her bow as she smiled at me. "Thank you."

Eden asked me, "Is that the insult he claimed you made against him?"

"No...the insult is not worth repeating. I shouldn't have said it."

"Yes, you should've," Michael said quickly.

"What does Leon have you doing today?" I asked Michael in hopes of changing the subject.

"I'll just be training today with the rest of the people who still need their essence. Leon says we can have them until tomorrow, then he's hiding them from us. What about you three?"

Eden answered, "We're going hunting. I need animal parts to work on my enchanting skill. Aliana has to practice her ranger skills. And I suppose Jon is here to practice his babysitting skills, because he obviously doesn't need to train more with the bow."

"Have any of you been in the forest before?" Michael asked.

"We have," Eden answered for her and Aliana. "Separately, not together. We didn't know each other before coming here."

"You had me fooled," Michael said. "So Eden, are you a full-fledged enchantress?"

"*Hmm*, some might say so," she said with a wink at him.

Michael looked a little confused. "Does that mean you can enchant Aliana's bow?" he asked.

"Oh, you mean an *enchanter*," she said. "An enchantress is just a whore of mythical proportions."

"Oh.... Oh!" Michael laughed. "I see," he said with a

wide smile at Eden.

"Calm your britches, it was a joke," she said with a flirtatious grin. "I probably could enchant Ali's bow with enough tries, but it wouldn't help her aim."

I asked, "What happens if you fail an enchantment?"

"It could weaken the structure of the bow."

"What I wouldn't give to understand everything about ordia," I said. "Shall we go?" I prompted, quite eager to leave. We could chat on the way.

"We shall," Aliana said.

"Just be careful," Michael told us, "even if you've been to that forest before. It's not that I don't trust Leon to not send all of you into danger, it's...wait, did that make sense? Too many nots."

"It did," I said.

"Not," Eden countered.

"Ah, I just mean it could be dangerous," Michael said. "I wouldn't go too far."

"How far is too far?" I asked.

"What did Leon say?" he asked in return.

"Nothing." I looked at Aliana.

"Nothing to us, either," she said.

"Then I guess it should be fine," Michael said. "You're coming back before night, right?"

"Yes," I said. "We have until the evening to return."

"Maybe you can't go far enough to get into trouble, but I'd be cautious anyway."

"We will," I assured him.

We said our goodbyes. Then I took the lead and set a quick pace.

"You seem to be in a rush," Eden commented. It appeared to be hard for her to keep up, given her short legs.

"If we don't hurry, then it's going to be time for lunch when we finish buying the food we need."

"Leon made me purchase food for this trip yesterday." She gestured at her backpack. "With my own coin, by the way."

"Oh, thank you," I said. "How much was it? I can pay you back after our next stipend."

"No, it's fine." Eden paused. "You don't mind stale bread, right?"

"Very funny," Aliana said.

After some time, I asked, "What else did Leon mention to the two of you about this trip?"

Eden mimicked his deep voice. "Eden, have you been to Curdith Forest? Good. You're going there tomorrow. Have Aliana kill something that will be useful to you. Don't get killed yourself. Stay behind Jon."

"That's about what he told me as well," Aliana said. "I never saw you show him you could shoot, Jon. Did he just take your word for it?"

"Pretty much. He asked what weapons I could use, then if I'd ever hunted before, and that was that."

"He's certainly a believer of letting his students teach themselves," Aliana remarked.

It didn't take us long to leave the city. The edge of Curdith Forest was only a mile out, just past the river. There was a short bridge where the river was wide.

"What have you heard about the forest so far, Jon?" Aliana asked. She seemed like a completely different person than the one I'd met outside my room.

"That it's full of massive trees and exotic animals."

"I wouldn't call them exotic," Eden said. "More like vicious."

Aliana said, "Kat strongly believes Gourfist is sleeping at the center of the forest and the dteria created by him is what gives life to all the creatures."

I'd heard of Gourfist only once before, when Leon made a comment about it. I enjoyed stories, but I wasn't interested in one right now if it wasn't based on facts. There were too many other concerns to discuss.

I brought up a number of dangerous situations that we could find ourselves in while hunting and how I expected us to handle them. The mood quickly changed. The chatter died down.

Soon we had crossed over the river and were entering the forest. I had the impression that neither Aliana nor Eden had found herself in a precarious position before. It reminded me of what I was like when I was younger, when I thought that there was nothing in the woods of Bhode that could kill me. Seeing a bear close enough to notice each individual hair of its fur immediately robbed me of that pleasant notion.

Stepping into the tree line drenched us in shade. The thick trees leaned east, toward the river as if trying to reach over it. Most had thick trunks that separated into halves or thirds. Strong branches sprouted up around the trunks and split off into sprigs sparsely covered by leaves. It was the tops of the trees that were the densest, creating a green canopy overhead.

As we ventured deeper into the forest, the air became clouded by an eerily warm fog. We were silent for a long while. I stayed ahead of the two young women, my eyes sharp.

"Wait," Aliana whispered.

We stopped and looked at her as she shut her eyes.

"I feel something." She opened her eyes and pointed

north.

We crept through the woods. We came to a fallen tree. Aliana gestured for us to stop. We crouched down and looked over the snag.

Though somewhat large for a rabbit, that's all it was. I was surprised she'd felt something so small from more than ten yards away.

"We could use it," Eden whispered.

Aliana tapped me on my shoulder. She presented me with her bow.

I shook my head. "You need to practice."

"I'm too nervous."

"It's all right. No one expects you to hit your marks today. Just work on your form. Remember to aim lower. Three fingers. Draw back to your face."

Aliana loaded an arrow, then slowly stood up. She wore a worried expression as she drew back and fired. Her pose looked good, though.

I had been too busy watching her to see the arrow. When I turned back, the rabbit was gone and I didn't see the arrow anywhere.

"You shot well," I told her. "Just correct your aim next time."

She nodded. We eventually retrieved her arrow and ventured deeper into the forest.

We came across a few other small creatures, all useful to Eden. Aliana missed all of them, but this was her first hunt. I assured her it was normal.

I thought of all the times I'd gone hunting with my father. Sometimes we'd search or follow tracks for the better part of the day, just to come back empty-handed. However, with Aliana's ranger skill it was almost too easy to find animals. It seemed that she could sense them from even thirty yards away, and she'd only get stronger as she practiced.

We couldn't speak much out of fear of scaring the critters away, but we did stop eventually for lunch when we found a good place to sit on a cluster of rocks. Eden had purchased us bread after all, fresh, not stale. She also brought out a pouch of nuts and berries. We chatted and joked, the hunt on pause. It was a relief for Aliana to treat me with the same respect she did Eden, though I was still a little bothered by her initial attitude.

Eventually, I started to realize that there was something different about my mana in this forest. I felt better connected to it, my mind sharp.

"Do the two of you mind if I test something that is likely to scare away any animal in a wide radius?"

"Sure," Aliana said. "I can't hit any of them anyway."

"You will eventually."

I picked up a rock about the size of my palm. I pointed my fingers on my other hand as I prepared my spell.

Eden hopped to her feet. "So you feel it also?"

"Yes, what is it?" I stopped to ask.

"I wish I knew," Eden replied. "Don't ask Kat unless you want to hear all about the demigods and Basael."

"Who else might know?" I asked.

We all seemed to realize at the same time, though I said it first.

"Leon."

"I'd rather not know than ask him," Aliana said.

"I might bring it up," I admitted. "I'm too curious to let it go."

I tossed the rock into the air and cast Expel with

as much pinpointed force as I could manage. The rock shot into the air, arcing just below the canopy high above. It struck the top of a distant tree and bounced off out of sight.

"God above," Eden said. "Soon we're not even going to need a bow. We'll just carry a sack of rocks."

It was a joke, like many of the things she said. I would never match the accuracy of shooting an arrow. Besides, a sack of rocks sounded heavy. But I appreciated the compliment anyway.

We walked farther into the forest. We stuck to one direction, west, to ensure it would be easy to return. Aliana sensed a few more creatures, but she missed each one when it came time to shoot.

I could sense her discouragement as the hours passed. Soon we would have to turn around to make it back before supper was served at the castle.

"Whoa," Aliana said to herself as she stopped. "I think there's something large ahead of us."

"How large?" I asked.

Her eyes squinted and she glanced down. "I can't say. Should we see what it is?"

"We shouldn't risk it," I said. "I think it's time we turn back. We've gone far."

"I agree with Jon," Eden added. "Let's head back."

"Wait." Aliana put up her hand. Her eyes widened. "It's coming toward us."

A tense moment passed.

"It's getting close." She looked at me. "It's bigger than I first thought."

"Hide."

We scurried over behind the nearest tree, the trunk wide enough to hide all of us from view. Aliana took small looks out as Eden and I stayed still.

Aliana gasped as she put her back against the tree beside me again. "It's a huge cat of some kind."

"I swear, Ali," Eden said, "if this is a joke—"

"It's not. I think we should get out of here. Jon?"

I wasn't quite as nervous as the two of them. Even animals as large as bears had never chased me and my father if we were far enough away. "You saw where it's coming from. Lead the way as silently as you can. Try to keep trees between us and it."

Aliana walked briskly back east, the way we'd come. Eden was just behind her, with me last.

A few minutes went by before Aliana hid behind another tree and motioned for us to join her. I looked back quickly but didn't see anything.

When we were all behind the tree, Aliana said something that sent fear into my veins.

"It's tracking us. I can feel it always behind. I say we speed up." She handed me her bow and an arrow.

I pulled a second arrow out of her quiver, just in case. "Go. I'll be at the back."

Aliana and Eden jogged out, each flashing glances behind. We moved quickly like that for a short time.

Eventually, I saw something darting between the trees that made me curse under my breath. The creature was catlike in appearance, but it was bigger than any cat I'd ever seen. It was closer to the size of a bear but black as night.

It spotted us and started dashing at me.

"Run!" I told the girls with my heart in my throat.

Eden shrieked as we all started sprinting. I could've passed them, but I needed to stay in the back. Aliana broke out ahead. She looked back. I watched her face and was horrified to see the dread of her expression.

"Hurry!" Aliana yelled.

Eden tried to keep up, but she wasn't very fast. I looked back.

The beast was bounding toward me, quickly catching up. We weren't going to outrun it. I had to convince it that we were not a meal worth fighting for.

"Keep going!"

"Jon!" Aliana yelled.

"Just keep going!" I repeated as I took aim with her bow.

The massive cat was speeding toward me as fast as a charging horse, now close enough for me to see its fangs as well as the long claws at the ends of its galloping paws.

I pulled back the string, the bow creaking in complaint from my strength. The head of the beast was bouncing up and down. Its back and shoulders rolled above and below the top of its head. I couldn't wait a moment longer to time my shot. I released.

The arrow struck the cat in its chest, the small space below its head. The beast roared but kept on running as if the arrow was a minor inconvenience. I cursed as I readied another arrow.

There wasn't much time to aim. I let go. This one stuck the cat in its cheek and managed to knock it off stride.

It let out a horrible hissing sound as it twitched its head around and skidded across the ground. The arrow broke off. A moment later it was up again and leaping toward me.

I blasted the animal with Expel. My mana clashed with the face of the beast in midair and flipped the giant cat backward. I took out my sword, the cat quickly twisting and hopping to get off its back. It leapt at me again.

I let out a cry of aggression as I swung hard to meet its mouth with steel. I felt the sword connect, but I couldn't see what happened as I was pushed down on my back.

I figured my life was over as the heavy beast landed on top of me and felt to be crushing my chest, but I hadn't given up yet. I prepared Expel as fast as I could.

My sword was stuck in its maw, I saw, the cat's blood splattering my face as it tried to bite me. The blade propped open the animal's mouth, shredding the cat's snout and drenching me with even more blood as the animal cut itself trying to bite me.

Eventually, the sword fell onto me. It was at that same moment that I blasted the huge cat under its chin with dvinia.

My powerful spell flipped the beast off me. I got up and grabbed my fallen sword, then almost fell backward as the creature chomped at my reaching hand with its bloody maw. I found my balance and almost decided to attack, but there wasn't time. It thrashed out its claw at me as I leapt away. I could feel the wind from its attack. It was practically on top of me again.

With just a small bit of distance, I had to strike now or I wouldn't have another chance. I swung my sword from my hip all the way over my shoulder and brought it down with the strength of a heavy mallet as I screamed. The cat jumped at my face as I swung.

I was pushed backward into a stumble, the sword pulled out of my hands, but the mammoth cat wasn't on top of me this time.

The beast finally lay flat and motionless before my feet, my weapon buried deep in the animal's skull. With adrenaline surging through me still, I wasn't sure if it was over. I rushed over and tried to get my sword out, but it wouldn't budge. I used the bottom of my boot to push the animal's head away until eventually I could pull my blade free.

I waited, poised, for the massive cat to get up again. But of course it didn't. This had been over for a while now. I checked around for other dangers. Only Aliana and Eden were in sight. They had not run very far but stood with their eyes wide in shock.

CHAPTER FIFTEEN

They seemed stunned as I approached. "Help me wash the blood off," I said as I put out my hands.

They didn't move or speak as they stared at me.

"Come on," I said, "so we can get back." I didn't want to encounter anything else like that animal.

Aliana blinked a few times, then took out the water skin from her pouch and poured a thin stream over my bloody hands. I rubbed them clean as best I could.

"Now my face," I said.

She poured as I rubbed my face and neck until I didn't feel the animal's wet blood bothering me anymore.

"You..." Aliana pointed at my face. "You missed some."

I was busy drinking the last of my water, droplets falling down the light beard of my chin. "It's fine," I said when I was done. "I'll wash better when we get back."

I started east, expecting them to follow me, but I didn't hear any footsteps.

I looked back. They hadn't moved.

"Come on," I said in anger.

Eden broke out of her trance first. "Wait, we could use the claws from that animal." She pointed at it nervously, as if it might get back up.

"We shouldn't be here any longer than we need to be," I said. "It was a mistake going this far."

"Just one paw. I can do it." Eden rushed over as she pulled a hatchet out of her bag. To my surprise, she started hacking away. It took five painfully slow strikes for her to separate the paw as she made a face of disgust.

Her expression worsened as she picked up the now loose paw of the large cat. It dripped blood as she held it by one of its claws. She ran back to us.

"How long is it going to bleed?" she asked me.

"Not long."

We walked quickly, all of us more than eager to leave Curdith Forest for probably a very long time.

"Jon, that was..." Aliana's voice fell. "I don't know what to say. I'm sorry," she muttered.

"It's all right."

She didn't reply. I glanced back to see her looking down and pitifully sad. I stopped.

"Hey."

She looked up at me.

"Really, none of us is to blame. If it's anyone's fault, it's Leon's for not warning us to stay near the perimeter of the forest. I had no idea we could encounter an animal like that. Did either of you?"

They shook their heads.

"Then don't blame yourselves."

"But we should've done more to help," Aliana said.

"Leon put me in charge, and I told you to run. If I'd gotten hurt, it would've been because of my choice, not yours."

She didn't look as if she agreed, but she didn't say anything, either.

"Come on," I urged them as I started up again.

They walked behind me, a little distance back. They were close enough that I would be able to hear anything they said, but they were silent.

Eventually, the paw stopped bleeding. Eden put it in a pouch with a tie, then stuck that in her pack.

I asked, "What was that animal?"

"I'm not sure," Eden said.

"So then how do you know you can use it for an enchantment?"

"Because all enchantments are done with the same types of animals. It looks like a cat, so it would probably be categorized as a Felidae. All Felidae claws do the same thing, but the size and strength of the animal changes the strength of the enchantment. The claws of that beast will probably prove to be a very strong enchantment."

"What exactly can Felidae claws be used for?" Aliana asked.

"Many things, I assume. I only know of one right now. It's actually a little humorous."

"I'm not sure we're in the mood for humor," Aliana said.

I glanced over to see her eyes on me. "I'm fine, Aliana, really."

She stopped. "Are you really? You do seem to be, but I don't understand how."

"I am," I said. "Trust me. Everything's fine." It was the truth. I might relive the scuffle with the beast later, but as of now I didn't want to think about it. I just wanted to get out of this forest and possibly learn something about enchanting.

"We never thanked you," Eden said.

"Oh, it's—"

"Thank you," she interrupted. "Seriously. We owe you."

"We do," Aliana added. "Thank you."

"I'd do it again if I needed to. Now what's humorous about cat claws?"

"Well, you first have to understand that a ward against any magical art does exist and they all require a moonstone," Eden explained. "It's the second ingredient, the animal part, that determines what the ward will do, as well as its strength. Do either of you want to guess what Felidae claws ward against? Think about what a cat hates."

"Fire?" I guessed.

"Everything hates fire! What does a cat specifically hate that others do not."

"Oh, water," I said.

"Yes. I found that to be a little humorous when I first found out."

"But how does a ward of water even work?" I asked. "Does it repel it?"

"Actually yes, to an extent."

"That must look quite unnatural," I said.

"I've never actually seen it, but I hope to soon with Kat's help after I finish the enchantment...and I'm just now hearing how that sounds. I'm going to call her Kataleya for a while."

The word "cat" didn't bother me. Speaking about enchantments reminded me of my visit to Enchanted Devices and watching Greda work.

"Oh!" I said as I realized something. "A dog's claw is what makes a ward against dteria."

"Yes!" Eden said as she pointed. "You know why?"

"Because they are so good-natured," I answered.

"Exactly."

We spoke about enchantments as we walked for a

little while, but soon all of us were out of water. Perhaps I shouldn't have asked them to use as much as they did to wash off the blood. I didn't speak of it, though. I didn't want to hear them tell me it was fine.

My thirst was starting to get to me when Aliana stopped us again.

"Can we go this way?" she asked as she pointed north.

"Why?" Eden asked.

"Because I think I can sense a small lake. I was just thinking about water as I used my mana, then my senses picked up on it. I want to see if it's really the case."

We turned north. I asked, "Have you sensed water before?"

"No."

"I think it's because of the time we've spent in this forest," I suggested. "I've noticed a change with my mana as well."

"So Leon was actually right about that," Eden commented. "I feel a little stronger, too."

Soon enough, I noticed the glimmer of water ahead. I was about to comment that Aliana was right when I noticed someone cloaked walking toward the small pond. We collectively stopped and watched in silence. The person's back was to us.

"I didn't feel someone earlier," Aliana whispered. "And I still don't."

A sense of danger prickled the back of my neck. I could've called out to let the person know we were here, but it seemed better just to leave. I was about to suggest that when the person lifted their hand. To my astonishment, all of the water rose out of the pond—a massive dense cloud of liquid just hovering there.

"Oh god," Aliana murmured.

They swept their hand to the side, guiding the water out of the now completely empty pond, where they let it drop to splash loudly against the ground.

I was too astonished to turn away.

They reached out both their hands, and a sphere of water grew from nothing to the size of the small pond. They dropped it in, but they still weren't done. They bent down to put the tips of their fingers into the now perfectly clear water of the pond. They crouched there for a little while until eventually steam rose out of the water.

"A master mage of fire and water!" Eden whispered.

Then they stood and dropped their cloak. I gasped. The woman was stark naked underneath it.

Suddenly Aliana was angrily pulling me toward the nearest tree, and I realized I had been staring.

I could count on one hand the number of times I had seen the posterior of a woman, but this by far was the loveliest one I had ever seen. What was surprising, though, was that Aliana and Eden appeared even more excited about the sight of it than I was. Eden was shaking Aliana's shoulder as she spoke.

"Did you see that?"

"I know!" Aliana whispered back. "I can't believe it."

"Wait," I whispered. "Why do the two of you sound so amazed?"

"Didn't you see her ears?" Aliana asked.

"She had *ears*?" I jested.

Aliana's mouth went flat while Eden slapped my arm with the back of her hand.

"Ow," I muttered. "What is it about her ears?"

But Aliana made a face of fear as she put her finger over her lips. We fell silent. I heard the sloshing sound of footsteps coming toward us.

I told Aliana and Eden, "Stay behind me."

They positioned themselves back defensively.

I came out from behind the tree expecting to see the woman, but there was no one there. I listened but heard nothing. I looked at where she should be given the sound of her footsteps earlier. The image of the forest blurred where she had to be standing. I could even make out tiny water droplets dripping around the illusion.

I wanted to draw my sword, but I knew that would be a mistake. The sorcerer was obviously powerful enough to beat me even with my best weapon out. Instead I showed her my open hands.

"We don't mean any harm," I spoke to the nearly invisible woman. "We just happened by. We shouldn't have stopped to look, but we were curious. We didn't know you would disrobe, and we certainly didn't know you were wearing nothing underneath the robe."

My eyes were starting to get used to the illusion. I could see the outline of her body against the blurred backdrop of the forest around her. She still seemed to be naked, with generous curves around her chest and hips.

A female voice emerged from the illusion. "Turn around."

I turned and showed my back to her, now facing the backs of Aliana and Eden who had turned as well.

"We can leave," I said.

"You will wait right there," she commanded in a

thick accent that added a melodic sound to her firm voice.

I could hear her walking back toward the pond. I started to see Eden look back over her shoulder, but I aggressively gestured for her to keep her head forward.

"Don't be afraid," the woman said. "If I was going to kill you, I would've done it by now. You can turn around."

She had her robe on again, but her hood was down. She had long, pointed ears, the tips of which sprouted out from her hair. I had known elves existed, but they lived a thousand miles away. At least that was what my father had told me.

Her hair was not a color I had seen on any human head. It was nearly white but blushed faintly pink, like rosy white cheeks painted crimson from a rush of blood. It was difficult to determine her age. She was certainly older than me, wisdom evident in her large green eyes. But there was not a wrinkle across her creamy skin. She had a narrow face, with slender cheeks and a tightly pressed mouth. She was beautiful, but she also looked as if she was capable of great fury.

I was struck with fear as she walked up to me and wiped her finger across my forehead. It came back a little red. She smelled the blood close to her nose.

"Were you hunting a cantar, or was it hunting you?"

"Hunting us," I said.

"I see." She stepped close to my face. She was about Aliana's height, considerably shorter than me, but I would be a fool not to be frightened. She took hold of my chin with one hand as she studied my face, turning it from one side to the other. Then she walked over to Aliana and studied her in the same way before finally checking Eden last. She came back to face me, then gestured at the two women behind.

"Stand here," she demanded.

Aliana came up to my right side, Eden on my left.

"Who are you and what are you doing here?" she asked. "I sense some magical ability from all of you, but it is weak."

The king's rule still applied. We weren't supposed to tell anyone who we were, especially not a sorcerer who was powerful enough to end our lives with hardly any effort.

"Tell us who you are first." Eden spoke with what I felt to be an insulting amount of confidence.

The elf lowered her eyelids as she glanced at Eden. "Don't test my patience. Tell me exactly why you are here."

"We came into the forest to hunt small game," I said.

"What else?"

No one answered her.

"What is your name?" she asked me.

"Jon."

"I need to know more about the three of you, Jon, and you are going to tell me. Why else did you go into the forest?"

I couldn't think of a lie that might protect us better than the truth. "To practice."

The elf pointed at Aliana. "For you to practice earth and bow." It didn't sound like a question.

Aliana nodded.

The elf gestured at Eden. "For you to practice ordia."

Eden nodded.

"And you..." She looked at me for a long while. "I'm not as sure about you. What I do know is that by practicing all of you must wish for more power, but what do you hope to do with more power?"

I didn't know how I could keep from divulging the truth without a lie, but that was not something I wanted to do. For all I knew, a sorcerer strong enough to turn nearly invisible might be able to sense it somehow.

"Speak!" she shouted, startling us. "Or I will make you answer me against your will."

"With more power, we want to help people," I said.

"What kinds of people?" she tested.

"The people who need help the most."

"And who are they?"

"Anyone who is treated unjustly."

She looked into my eyes from so close that our lips were nearly touching.

"I think you know more about Lycast than you let on," she said as she stepped back, to my relief. "I think you know what's happening here...and in Rohaer. I think you swore to someone that you would not speak about it. And I think you are right not to say more."

She paused. It was difficult not to nod in agreement as she looked so closely at me, but I managed to refrain.

She continued, "I will not force you to break your oath so long as I am given the same respect and trust. Do the three of you agree?"

We all agreed rather quickly.

"My name is Eslenda. When you are strong enough to face a cantar without risk, you will enter this forest again. I will make myself known to you. Only then can we discuss our goals."

"All right!" Eden said dismissively as she tossed her hands up and started walking away. "But I don't think we'll be seeing each other again. I'm sorry we disturbed your bath. Come on, Ali and Jon."

"Wait." I didn't understand Eden's tone. Was it that she didn't believe anything the elf had said? It wasn't that I trusted Eslenda completely either, but she obviously knew more about sorcery and this forest than we did. There was still so much she could teach us.

"I want to understand something," I tried.

"I will not speak about myself because it might endanger all of you," the elf told us. "That is why you will come back only when you are stronger, when you can face the same danger I do."

I was beginning to realize she might be talking about people, not creatures. Perhaps she spoke about the same people who had tried to alter my mana with an essence of dteria, but I couldn't ask anything about that without opening myself up more than I wanted to.

"At least tell me something about this forest," I persisted. "I have hunted in the woods many times, but I've never seen an animal behave like the cantar. I shot it with two arrows, and it still charged me. I buried my sword in its face, and it did not back off."

"The closer you walk to the center of the forest, the more the creatures are corrupted by dteria. They do not feel fear or pain. They seek only one thing: more power."

"Why is that?" I asked. "Is there something at the center of the forest?"

"There is Gourfist. He sleeps for a hundred years."

"All right!" Eden said. "Now we've definitely been here too long." She took my hand and pulled.

I held my ground. "Wait. We feel stronger in the forest. Is that dteria corrupting us?"

"No. There is dteria in the forest, but the dvinia here is stronger. Dvinia of the land strengthens mana. It is strongest where it needs to be. Closer to the center."

I knew I was pushing my luck asking yet another question, but I had to try. "If dteria is coming from Gourfist, then where is dvinia coming from?"

She shook her head. "You do not understand sorcery enough yet for these answers to matter. Train and stay clear of dteria. Return here later if you have not given up. I cannot help you if you speak of me to anyone. Now leave. I wish to bathe."

I was the last to turn and go. I was starting to see that magic wasn't only something that could be used by people. It also seemed to shape the land around Newhaven. She was probably right that I had to know more about sorcery for the answers to my questions to actually be useful. Leon, another powerful sorcerer, never seemed to indulge anyone's curiosity either. But I couldn't let go of mine. I had a wide range of mana. I wanted to know everything about sorcery before spending more time training.

Eslenda spoke about sorcery the other way around. She implied I had to train more before I could really understand sorcery. At least she'd made one thing clear. Dvinia was the reason the forest made it easier to train. But she'd specifically called it dvinia of the land. It seemed to be different than the dvinia I used. I tried to feel for dvinia around us, but I couldn't sense anything.

We were silent for a long while as we walked. Eventually, Eden spoke first.

"Jon, you really shouldn't trust anything she says.

Elves are not known for wanting to help humans."

"Yes, I know what supposedly happened after the Day of Death. The elves traveled south and made a home away from humans."

"Do you know why, though?" she asked.

"No," I admitted.

"Because of the war," Eden explained. "They lived here in Curdith Forest before hairy and dirty humans started migrating from the north. The elves worshiped a god at the center of the forest, most likely Basael, who told them to welcome humans and allow them to live around the forest. The elves did at first, but soon the human population rose to be above the elven population. They started infiltrating the forest to hunt and kill many of the animals that the elves relied upon. It didn't take long for them to start fighting each other. This was before the Day of Death. Elves believe it was Basael who caused a star to fall, the resulting explosion killing almost all humans and elves. They believe he had been enraged by the actions of the two races."

The tale sounded very familiar. I was certain I had heard it when I was young, probably from the same neighbors who'd told me about demigods.

"The surviving elves left Curdith Forest," Eden continued, "because the demigods went to war with each other and were using humans to fight. The elves still believe humans are weak-willed, selfish, and other things, I'm sure. Eslenda could be trying to use us. It's best to forget about her."

"You can't be sure that all elves still think that way," I said. "But even if they do, Eslenda is clearly a powerful sorcerer. She understands magic and mana better than we do. I thought I might take advantage of that with a few questions. I don't think of her answers as facts. Her information was just something I'd like to keep in mind."

"I agree with Jon," Aliana said. "It's like listening to Kat...aleya speak about the demigods. It's interesting and might be true, but I'm not going to take it as fact."

"All right." Eden shrugged. "I do agree that she had *some* good advice we should heed. There's no reason to speak about her to anyone, just in case her warnings are true. She could have enemies, people who would hurt us for information about her, and we have no idea who those people might be."

"Agreed," I said.

"It will be our secret," Aliana grinned. "A naked elf in the forest told us not to speak about her, or we would be in danger."

"Yeah, I'm hearing how that sounds," I said. "We wouldn't be believed anyway."

Eden added, "Now the incident with the cantar, that I can't wait to tell everyone. Do you mind, Jon?" She tilted her head as she looked at me.

"I'd like to speak about it with Leon first. I need to know if he was aware how dangerous this forest could've been for us."

"I want to hear his answer as well," Aliana agreed.

"Do you mind if I speak to him alone at first?" I requested. I didn't want Aliana, or anyone else, to see me angry, and I wasn't sure I would be able to stop myself depending on what Leon said.

"All right," she said.

CHAPTER SIXTEEN

We rushed back and made it before supper. Everyone seemed to be training in the courtyard like the day before, except Leon was laying in the dirt, supine, his arms and legs spread. He might've looked like he was dead, but I saw many people glance over and they were not alarmed.

I approached Michael as the two girls went over to greet Kataleya. Michael was practicing the spell Wind, no essence in hand. He gawked at me.

"What the hell happened?"

I knew he must be referring to the blood all over my shirt, with some probably still on my face. "I'll tell you in a little bit. What's going on with Leon?"

"You ever get dragged somewhere as a child and get so bored that you have to lie down or you might scream? I think that's what's happening here."

"I see. Well, I need to speak with him."

"Good luck."

Leon didn't bother sitting up as I walked over.

"Leon," I said.

His eyes remained closed. Could he actually be asleep?

"Leon," I tried, a little louder this time.

He groggily opened his eyes. He put his hand over them to block out the sun as he looked up at me.

"Is that blood?"

"Yes, from a giant, black cat."

"Airinold's taint, how far did you go? Are the two women all right?" He sat up and looked around frantically, then relaxed as he saw them with Kataleya.

"Why didn't you warn us to stay near the perimeter?" I asked angrily.

"First of all, take a step back and change your tone." I eased off him a bit.

"Did you seriously slay a cantar?" Leon asked as he stood up.

"I did, but the whole exchange could've gone differently."

"Nijja's tit, I ask again, how far did you go?" He sounded perturbed, which angered me even more. This was not my fault.

I threw my hands up. "We just walked half the day before we encountered it!"

"No beast as large as a cantar is within a day of walking."

"It was. Aliana sensed it ahead of us. We decided to turn around before we saw it, but it must've picked up our scent. It chased after us. We couldn't outrun it, so I had to fight it."

Leon looked at me as if I might be lying. "Are you sure it was a large black cat?"

"Yes, I'm sure! It nearly bit my face off!"

His eyes held shock. Eslenda hadn't seemed too surprised about us finding a cantar, though, which did make me think of something.

"When was the last time you were in the forest?" I wasn't sure if I would be able to hold in my rage depending on how he answered.

He rubbed his cheek. "One year, no...god. Has it

really been that long?"

"Longer than one year?" I was almost shouting. "You sent us in there without going yourself in longer than a year? How many years are we talking about?"

"Jon, I'm warning you. Your tone."

"The three of us could've been killed! I'm *sorry* if I'm going to sound a little *pissed off* about it!"

I realized the courtyard had gone silent, everyone staring. They had all heard.

"Get inside, now!" he yelled as he pointed at the apartments.

I stormed into the building with him right behind.

"Sit!" He pointed at the stairs.

I huffed as I took a seat. He stood in front of me and looked like he was going to yell, but he stopped himself.

Leon looked down for a little while as he seemed to be in thought. When he glanced up at me again, he actually looked somewhat sorry, if Leon was even capable.

"I have never known the forest to be dangerous within ten miles, Jon. I only expected you to encounter rabbits, maybe a small fox, nothing over a hundred pounds for sure." He paced a little. Then he turned to me again. "I don't know if you somehow encountered the only cantar that has ever been that close to the perimeter, or if something about the forest is changing, but I do take responsibility for this."

I stared, surprised that I might receive an apology from Leon Purage.

"I should've gone with the three of you, but I'm on a tight schedule. I couldn't afford to leave everyone else to train on their own."

"It didn't look like you were helping much when I

arrived."

"After so many hours of instruction, I needed a break before I killed somebody. You're just going to have to trust me. I'm doing the best I can."

My temper was still hot, but then I realized something truly sad. Disappointment came over me as I told it to Leon. "That's the problem. I don't know how I'm supposed to trust you when you act like you've never taught anyone anything."

He shook his head as he looked away from me. Then he peered at me pointedly. "Well I trusted you, Jon. I trusted you to protect those two ladies and yourself. And guess what? I was right. I don't see a wound on your body."

I had no response to that.

"You've proven that you can handle the unexpected. Even the king sees that already. Now I'm going to visit the forest as soon as I can. I may even take you and the others with me because there's no better place to strengthen your mana." He looked to be in pain as he put up his hands. "I will say it. Just give me a moment." He cringed as he had a breath and folded his arms tightly.

"I made a mistake. Here's what I'm going to do for you," he continued quickly. "I will let your insubordination go without punishment this one time. But I swear to all that is holy, if you raise your voice at me again—"

"I won't." I didn't want to hear the threat. "I'm sorry I yelled. That was wrong." I stood up and offered my hand. "You were right to trust me to keep us safe. I can see that now. And I suppose I do trust you as well. We all make mistakes. The difference between people is who will admit to them and what they will do to amend them."

He shook my hand with a slow nod. "That's actually well said."

"Thanks," I muttered.

I still had no idea why the king had chosen Leon over another instructor, but if I was to thrive here, I had to believe that the king knew better than I did. I felt stronger and more capable than I ever had in my life. I could now cast my spell with confidence. It was like I had trained a week, just from this single day.

"So you're not scared of Curdith Forest yet?" Leon asked with a hinting tone.

"I look forward to returning to the forest with you whenever we can." I also secretly hoped to see Eslenda again, and not just because the image of her naked backside was vivid in my memory. I knew I shouldn't trust someone I'd just met, but I had a good feeling about her.

"Glad to hear it," Leon said. "Now wash up before supper. I can't have the king seeing you like this."

"Are you—?"

He put up his hand to silence me. "I will tell him what happened, if he hasn't heard it already by the time the food is served. I'm sure all the daisies out there are gossiping." He started to head toward the open door to the courtyard.

"Are there baths ready?" I asked.

"Yes, but they're cold."

"Will you heat one up for me?"

He laughed. Without turning around he replied, "I'd rather stick my own foot up my ass. Get Remi to do it."

"I can't ask a girl to enter the boys' bathing quarters!" I called as he was almost gone.

"Then take a cold bath. It'll put hair on your chest."

"I think killing a cantar with a sword should prove enough that...ah." I didn't bother finishing my sentence. He'd walked into the courtyard and turned out of sight.

Perhaps if Aliana or Eden, or even Kataleya knew fire I would ask one of them. But I hardly felt as if I'd really met Remi yet. I couldn't possibly ask her to enter the boys' bathing quarters just to heat my bath.

I'd have to make do with cold water.

*****

Supper had started without me. I was starving and clean, and more excited to eat than perhaps I had been for any other meal in my life. It was unfortunate to see that Reuben was still not sitting with Michael and Charlie, but at least Remi had joined the other three girls farther down the table from the boys. They sat closer to the king, who ate with the princess and the queen as they faced all us, our long table running perpendicular to the royal table. The girls were far enough away that the king usually wouldn't be able to overhear their conversation, but they were being quite loud right now. I could even hear my name from the other side of the large dining hall.

Leon must've already spoken with the king. Our instructor was sitting alone in the far corner of the room. I wondered if he wasn't just bored but could even be lonely.

What had he been doing before coming here? Did he have any family? I would've been surprised if he even had a single friend, given how rough he was around the edges. Shockingly, I felt bad for him.

I also pitied Reuben. The rich dolt glared at me with even more anger now that my heroic tale was spreading. I didn't avert my gaze. Instead, I showed him I was disappointed with a slow shake of a head. He sat alone between the groups of boys and girls, his focus returning to his plate.

I sat beside Michael. Charlie stopped eating to stare at me from the other side of the table. I thought he was going to say something, but he just looked at me...for a long time.

"You shouldn't stare, Charlie," I informed him as I dug into another delicious-looking meal, a hefty portion of chicken with roasted vegetables.

"Sorry," he muttered as he looked down at his plate.

"We heard you yell at Leon in the courtyard." Michael said quietly. "What happened after he took you into the apartments?"

I gave him a brief retelling of the conversation. Charlie was staring at me again by the time I finished. I didn't mention it this time.

"Well," Michael said. "You're lucky he didn't punish you."

"Because he knew my words were right, even if my tone wasn't. He should've been more cautious."

"Leon? What? Not cautious?" Michael said sarcastically. "He's the most cautious instructor there is."

"Just be careful if he sends you somewhere."

"Eh, I trust him." Michael seemed confused by his own words. "I know, I heard myself say it."

"I trust him as well now, but I can be cautious while trusting him."

Charlie spoke with a full mouth. "I'm always cautious." He pointed at me with his fork. "That's why I'm going to create something that will help us."

"What?" I asked.

"Two rings."

He didn't bother to explain as he went back to eating. I was about to ask, but I noticed the girls and then Reuben standing as the king walked by. We were about to stand as well, but the king announced, "Stay in your seats, everyone. Keep eating."

We kept her heads down as he walked past Michael and stopped beside me. I looked up at him.

"Jon, I heard what happened. I'm sorry you were put in a position where you needed to defend your life against a beast like a cantar. If a situation like that arises again, you will be more prepared. I promise." His apologetic tone was as if he blamed himself.

"Thank you, sire," I said, unsure what to add.

"Onto another matter, you boys should know that the krepp, Grufaeragar, is still with us. However, I'm having a difficult time keeping him entertained. He is to remain with us until he makes a decision as to whether our kingdom is honorable enough to trade with krepps. There is an abundance of raw, valuable material in Hammashar that is very much worth the small nuisance he might cause us by remaining here longer. He might try to engage with one or more of you. If he does, it will be your responsibility to keep him entertained while continuing your training or completing your tasks. Treat him with respect and show him that we have honor for kreppen culture. Are there any questions?"

"I have no idea what kreppen culture is," Michael

admitted.

"I don't, either," I added.

"We're all learning it. Just listen and adapt. Don't make assumptions."

I had almost forgotten about the krepp. An elf and a krepp, both involving themselves with us. It felt like what was happening here was one day going to have an impact on most of Dorrinthal, maybe even reaching Bhode.

The three of us were soon alone again as the king left the dining hall. I didn't bother to bring up the two rings Charlie had mentioned. Instead, we amused each other with absurd guesses as to what the king had been doing to keep the krepp entertained, and we laughed our way through the rest of the meal.

Because of the late supper, it was dark by the time we finished. I noticed something when we all were retiring to our rooms. All the boys' rooms were next to each other, with mine last, closest to the center of the hall on the upper floor of the apartments. Aliana's was first of the girls' rooms, next to mine. She was walking down the hall toward her room as I was about to enter mine from the other direction. I stopped and waited for her.

She traveled the last small bit of distance to meet me in front of my door.

"Hey," she said. "We saw the king speak with you."

"Yeah, he mentioned the krepp. He said we might have to entertain the creature."

She formed a grin. "That sounds fun," she said sarcastically. "Hey, um." She lost her smile as she looked down at her feet. "I wanted to thank you again for what you did." She glanced up at me. "It was really brave."

"It was no problem."

That felt wrong to say after I had yelled at Leon for putting me in that position. Should I have said "you're welcome?" That didn't seem any better.

"Can I ask you something?" I tried.

"Sure."

"Did I do something to upset you this morning?"

"Oh."

I was glad to hear her acknowledge it.

"I didn't know if I should apologize for something..." I began.

"No, that's not it." She looked at me and pursed her lips as if undecided whether to tell me.

"What is it?"

"I guess my attitude was because I might've had the wrong idea about you before we talked this morning."

I was a little shocked to hear that she had any impression about me, especially a negative one, when we'd hardly spoken.

"What was your idea of me?" I asked dubiously, not sure if I wanted to know at this point.

"Well." Aliana looked down for a breath and seemed to have trouble meeting my eyes after. She spoke quickly. "Everyone saw you flirting with Kataleya earlier, and I thought you were flirting with me." She looked up at me as if I might confirm or deny any of this, but I wasn't inclined to speak at all. It irritated me that she'd described my conversation with Kataleya as flirting. I was just trying to get to know Kat better and learn something about mana and water. I'd done the same with Aliana, attempted to learn about her and her ranger skill. Of course I'd thought she was beautiful, but that had been irrelevant to our conversation.

She took a breath. "And because your room is right next to mine, and from the way you went against orders to learn dvinia, I figured you were the type of guy who's used to getting what he wants...no matter what others might wish from him."

I did hear what she was really saying as she eyed me nervously, and it was an insult.

I tried to think about all of this from her point of view in hopes of calming myself. She had probably dealt with other young men who would say or do anything to get under her clothes. Perhaps showing these young men a cold shoulder early on was Aliana's chosen method when dealing with them, but I didn't find it fair for her to lump me together with these men.

Yes, I could be stubborn, but I was not the man she was implying me to be. It hurt to hear Aliana speak about me as if I was a self-centered philanderer.

Aliana glanced up with me with her head partially bowed. She had a flat mouth and clearly wanted me to say something now.

"I'm sorry if I was wrong," she eventually spoke somewhat cautiously.

"You still don't know?" I asked.

She looked at me if I might be trying to deceive her.

Michael's voice visibly surprised her from his room two doors down. "Most of us can hear everything, by the way! Just thought you two should know!"

She fidgeted uncomfortably, as did I.

Even with others hearing us, I hoped she would still at least assure me that her impression had changed.

"Well, I guess we'll talk later," she said with disappointment, then walked back down the hall.

I went into my room with a sour feeling in my stomach.

CHAPTER SEVENTEEN

After breakfast was served in our rooms, most of us boys coincidentally met in the bathing quarters for a quick bath, and soon I was headed out onto the courtyard. A grin made its way onto my lips as I saw Leon with training swords and protective leather tunics.

All eight of us formed a half circle in front of him. He always looked displeased, with his large green eyes that seemed incapable of expressing joy, and his strong jaw that appeared as if he was firmly pressing his teeth together behind his closed mouth. But something about the sight of us this morning really lowered his eyebrows. He was clearly not as excited as I was to begin sword training.

After a sigh, he said, "Girls, you will be on your own most of the day." He shooed them away. "Train, just keep your distance from us."

Aliana, Eden, and Kataleya seemed content to walk off, but Remi remained.

"I would like to learn the sword." She had a fragile demeanor as she held her hands together and seemed barely capable of looking high enough to make eye contact with Leon.

"You?" Leon asked incredulously.

Remi blushed, but she did straighten her back a little. "I would like to try."

"No." He pointed toward the other girls, who had stopped and turned around to watch. "Go away with the others."

Remi looked absolutely broken as she started to walk away.

"At least give her a chance," I said.

Remi stopped and looked back.

Leon glowered at me. It seemed that he expected me to lower my gaze or even apologize, but I would do neither. She deserved a chance. Why not?

Eventually, Leon blinked and turned his head toward Remi.

"Why the hell do you want to waste everyone's time, including your own, trying to learn sword? Didn't you hear me earlier when I said we don't have time to waste?"

"I think I might do well," she said shyly.

"You're doing well with fire," Leon replied. "Just stick with that."

"I'm sorry," she said, "but I want to try sword. There might be instances that I don't want to burn someone alive in order to stop them."

"So you'd rather cut them? It's no different!"

Poor Remi looked terribly uncomfortable as she had trouble meeting his eyes. "Please," she said. "Can I at least learn with the boys one day to see what I can do?"

"I have a better idea." Leon looked over at us. "Who has experience in hand-to-hand combat?"

Reuben raised his hand. "I was trained in every form of combat."

I suddenly had the urge to challenge him, but I was smart enough to know what Leon was getting at. I was glad Reuben had volunteered for this.

Leon tossed one of the wooden practice swords to Remi. She caught it with one hand, but he didn't seem impressed.

"Here are the rules of every duel," Leon announced. "When a point is scored, the duel stops. A point is scored when you make contact with your weapon, your fist, your elbow, or your knee or foot. You will only strike each other below the neck. You will not use your head or face as a weapon. The contact must be made hard enough that it would stagger or otherwise disrupt your opponent if you were using a steel blade. You can also score a point by disarming your opponent or tripping or throwing them to the ground. Best out of three. Any questions?"

Reuben started to reach for one of the three re-maining practice swords at Leon's feet, but Leon stepped in front of it.

"What are you doing?" the instructor asked.

"You want me to fight her, right?"

"Are you too scared to fight unarmed against a *girl* using a *practice* sword who has *no* experience?"

"No," he answered immediately. "I just thought—"

"That's your problem. You tried to think."

Leon seemed even more irritated today than usual.

"Go ahead," he said. "Fight."

We all quickly backed away as Reuben and Remi faced each other. Remi made the practice sword appear heavy as she held it with two hands and slowly shifted from one position to another. She couldn't seem to find a comfortable way to wield the sword. The wooden weapon was designed to be about the same weight as a real sword, but its edges and tip were dull. It could still do considerable damage in the right hands, however, and Reuben seemed well aware of this as he tested her with quick steps in and out of her range.

She stabbed at him nervously.

"Good," Leon encouraged her, to my surprise. "Stabbing is your quickest attack. Don't let him in."

She kept Reuben at bay with little prods, but she didn't commit to any attack. Instead she poked defensively, timidly.

Eventually, Reuben stopped attacking. He stepped back with a mean smile. "Come on. You're the one with the weapon," he taunted.

She very slowly made her way toward him with the smallest steps I'd ever seen. I could feel how badly she wanted a victory, her small knuckles white around the hilt of the sword. But more than that, she was scared. It was one of the worst mentalities to have in a fight, something every opponent could pick up on, man or beast.

Reuben aggressively motioned as if he might tackle her. She reeled back with a startled gasp. Reuben stopped and laughed at her.

Her demeanor changed. She let go of her fear as she ran at him. I was hoping to see shock on Reuben's face, but he appeared bored instead as he swiftly hopped to the side to avoid her predictable stab. He grabbed her hands from her side.

"No!" she yelled as she thrashed to get him off her, but he was much larger and stronger. He ripped the sword out of her grip at the same time that he tripped her over his foot.

"One point for me," Reuben said as she hit the ground.

The fury dissolved from her small brown eyes as she glanced at Leon nervously. Her wild hair was already in disarray, as if she had been fighting for a lot longer. Or perhaps her hair had already been wild with scattered curls and I just hadn't noticed it before. Remi had a way of blending in. Whether she wanted to or not, I didn't know.

Aliana helped Remi up and said something too quiet for the rest of us to hear. Remi nodded.

Reuben offered her back the sword with a look as if she shouldn't accept it. But she did with a spark in her eyes.

"Go again," Leon said.

Reuben stood still this time, opening his hands in a taunting shrug. I cringed as Remi ran at him again. She held her sword down at her hips with both hands, making her attack just as obvious as before. She could only stab from here.

Reuben was quick. He dodged to the other side this time as she thrust her weapon at him. It seemed that she was expecting him to go the other way, missing quite far now. Reuben grabbed the hilt over her hands. They started to wrestle just like before. I could see him wrap his foot around behind her, ready to push her over again.

But this time she let him take the sword as she pulled one hand free and slammed her fist into his groin.

The three of us boys watching all let out a sound of pain as Reuben squeaked and doubled over. Even Leon was gritting his teeth as if he felt it. Remi pushed him over, grabbing the sword out of his weak grip as he went down.

The girls cheered. Remi moved the strands of hair that had fallen in front of her face, revealing a small grin. Reuben got to his feet as he huffed in anger. His hands went to his hips as he stood partially doubled over.

"That was an unlawful strike!" he complained and groaned at the same time. "No point."

"He's right," Leon said. "You don't strike one of your peers in the groin, Remi."

"Aliana told me to."

Aliana had her hand over her mouth as she was trying not to grin. She forced her lips flat. "I'm sorry, but it wasn't mentioned in the rules."

"Do you think I have to tell the boys not to strike any of you girls in the chest? I didn't think it needed to be said. I'm disappointed in both of you, Aliana and Remi."

Reuben appeared rightfully pissed off as he took an aggressive stance. "I'm ready."

Remi didn't seem to have any fight left in her, however, probably guilt taking over. "I'm sorry, Reuben."

"You should give up," he replied.

Her face hardened. "I won't."

"Reuben, take it easy," I said lightly.

He ignored me, no big surprise. I looked at Leon, hoping he would say something to calm Reuben down.

"At least let them put on protective tunics," I suggested, gesturing at the garments on the ground near Leon.

"Go," Leon announced to my dismay.

Reuben was the aggressor this time. He charged at

Remi. She swung at him hard enough to bruise his arm if it hit, but Reuben stopped short and let her miss. Then he lowered his shoulder and slammed his body into her.

Remi flew back before she landed with a face of pain.

"Ow," she mumbled as she seemed to be holding in tears, her arms and shoulders tucked inward. She squirmed, the pain too much for her.

It hurt my heart to watch.

Aliana and Kataleya were quick to crouch over her to see if they could help. Eden, on the other hand, was yelling at Reuben. "What is wrong with you?"

"She's the one who broke the rules, not me!"

"You're fine, Remi," Leon said indifferently. "Get up."

She was sniffling as Aliana helped her up.

"Are you done?" Leon asked her.

She wiped her eyes. "No," she said with a shake of her head.

"Don't be foolish," he said. "Any man with a sword would've at least earned one fair point against an unarmed opponent. Now imagine if you had been allowed to use fire? Reuben wouldn't have had a chance. Just stick with what you know. You're actually good with fire. You're not with a sword."

"I really think I can learn if I just had some time."

"But we don't!" Leon yelled. "How many times do I have to say it? We don't have time!"

Remi looked furious, to my surprise. "I will get better!"

I offered, "What if she learns quicker than most men? Then we do have the time to teach her."

"I do learn very fast," she agreed.

Leon pulled his hands through his hair as he gritted his teeth and contained a scream to a loud groan. "You won't let this go, will you?"

She shook her head.

"You say you learn fast? Come here then. Bring the sword."

She jogged over to him. He turned her away from everyone else.

Leon spoke quietly but with aggressive emphasis, moving his shoulders and imitating a swing of a sword. I figured he was finally telling her how to use the weapon. Soon she was imitating him, but he shook his head and took hold of her arms to show her the proper stance.

After a long while, Reuben said, "This is ridiculous. She's just going to lose again."

"You're starting to make me want to learn to fight as well," Aliana told him.

"Kat, can you please explain to them that melee combat is for men, and all I'm trying to do is show her that? I obviously don't want to hurt a girl."

"You could have fooled me," Kataleya replied.

His eyes widened in shock. "Even *you* are with them on this?" He shook his head at her.

"Yes, even me."

"Even unarmed, I could beat the men," he boasted. "So how do you expect Remi to compete?"

"You could even beat Jon?" Eden asked.

He looked at me with a flame in his eyes, but I challenged him with a raise of my eyebrows and the flame went out.

"Anyone who isn't bigger than me. It is an easy win for someone of my skill."

THE KING'S SORCERER

"I'll fight you," Michael said as he started toward one of the swords.

"Good," Reuben replied as he stepped back.

Leon turned around. "What the hell is going on?"

"We're going to—"

"Shut up and get back," Leon interrupted Michael. "Go Remi. This is your last chance. First person to score one point wins."

She held her sword more confidently this time as she faced Reuben.

"Fine," he said with a shrug, then taunted her to come at him with a motion of his fingers.

I feared Remi might charge again, but she maintained her cool as she stepped toward him. He started to back away cautiously as he tried to figure out her attack, but she didn't make it clear as she held her sword poised to either swing or stab.

Reuben finally stopped backing away and tried to find his way in. Remi backed up as she swung defensively to keep him away. He leaned back to avoid the blunt wooden tip and started to dart toward her, but she had not swung hard enough to lose her balance. She was ready to stab.

Reuben had fast reflexes, however, jumping back to avoid it at the last moment. He seemed to lose his hubris as he backed away again, his expression determined. She picked up her speed as she walked toward him, but she jumped back when he stepped toward her.

At least Remi didn't swing a sword at his feint, but she did make it clear she was going to swing from her right side. Reuben tested her again, and this time she took the bait as she swung hard. She missed when he stopped short. It looked as if he would tackle her with his shoulder again, but she kicked quickly, striking him in the shin and causing him to stumble. Then she smacked him on his bottom, swinging the sword into him like a paddle. It knocked him flat on the ground, a puff of dirt wafting up around him.

We laughed. Reuben took a handful of dirt and threw it against the ground.

"That was lucky!" he yelled, red-faced.

"Does this mean I can learn sword?" Remi asked Leon.

"Yes, fine."

Aliana said, "I would like to as well, but I think it's better for me to practice with bow."

"As a ranger? It shouldn't even be a question," Leon said.

"I'm fine without touching a sword," Eden said. "I'll leave it to Remi and the boys, unless you want to, Kataleya?"

"No, I'm happy training with water."

Reuben went over and picked up a sword. "I challenge you to fight me fairly, Remi."

"Everyone knows you would win," she said with a roll of her eyes. "I just want to learn, that's all."

"All right, the three of you daisies should be practicing." Leon gestured for Aliana, Eden, and Kataleya to leave. "We're far enough behind as it is." He grumbled as he noticed Charlie raising his hand. "What is it?"

"Can I go?" Charlie asked.

"What do you mean can you go?"

"Can I leave?"

"What? Why?"

"I don't want to waste time learning the sword."

Leon looked bewildered, then enraged.

"Are you a coward?" he asked.

"That depends on what I'm facing," Charlie said. I knew he wasn't trying to be clever, but I wasn't sure Leon knew that.

Our instructor swiped his hands down his face with a groan, then flung them out at us. "What am I supposed to do with a bunch of daisies?" He waited for an answer. "Come on! Because if you don't know, I don't either!"

Charlie was clearly uncomfortable as he glanced at Leon sideways. "So can I go?" he asked quieter this time.

"Are you a man?" Leon yelled.

"Yes."

"Then you learn to fight with a sword! Oh, Airinold's taint. What now?"

Leon was looking over my shoulder. I glanced back to see the krepp walking across the courtyard toward us. He had a swagger as he strolled...slowly.

We all turned to him, but he didn't speak.

"Do you need something, Grufaeragar?" Leon asked. His tone wasn't exactly polite, but it was probably as close as Leon could manage right now.

The krepp slowly made his way over without answering. If I didn't know any better, I would've assumed he enjoyed the attention of us all staring as he stuck out his chest and swayed with each step. Leon was muttering something to himself that I was glad I couldn't make out.

Grufaeragar finally joined us in our half circle. The girls had remained, against Leon's wishes, as we waited for the krepp to say something.

"Who is best?" he asked, loud and proud.

"Why?" Leon replied.

B.T. NARRO

"I fight them. For *honor!*"

Eden seemed to have trouble keeping in her laugher as she held her hand over her mouth. I contained mine to a smile.

"We're not fighting for honor," Leon grumbled. "We're training."

"What is training?" Grufaeragar asked.

"Practicing," I explained. "We're learning."

The krepp's lizard face scrunched up. "I don't understand. Humans train for shouting?"

"What are you saying?" Leon sounded as if he might explode.

I understood Grufaeragar's question and gave answer, "No, we don't train by shouting. We are just trying to figure something out."

"What?" Now Grufaeragar seemed a little irritated. "Who fight me!"

"No one," Leon said. "We are *learning* to fight."

"You fight and you learn. No other way. Your strongest fight me now. He learn."

"You really want to fight someone, Grufaeragar?" Leon tested.

"Yes!"

"Fine." Leon snatched up one of the protective leather tunics next to him and started to put it on.

Grufaeragar let out a deep clucking sound that seemed to be a laugh. "What that? Child helper?"

"I don't know what a child helper is. Are you ready?"

"I am ready."

"The rules," I interjected.

Leon cursed the rules. "Just don't try to hit my head. Understand?"

243

"Yes," the krepp said, picking up a practice sword.

Leon gestured for the krepp to come at him.

Grufaeragar charged. I had a flashback to the cantar rushing me, the sheer size of both enough to intimidate even the bravest men. Leon, however, stood his ground with confidence.

The krepp swung hard and deftly around the height of Leon's shoulders. It was too powerful for Leon to hope to block, forcing him to duck under to avoid it. He tried to counter with his own stab, but the krepp was too fast. Grufaeragar swiped his weapon down to deflect the attack. He almost stabbed Leon in the shoulder as both swords came back up, but Leon pushed the wooden tip away with his weapon.

They swiped and prodded, but neither could gain the upper hand. I grew nervous at watching the force at which they attacked one another. This was not a friendly match. It would most likely end with one of them hurt.

Leon was a skilled swordsman, not quite as good as my father, but he could keep up with the stronger creature. Grufaeragar stepped back so he could put momentum into an overhead slash that seemed strong enough to give Leon a concussion if it hit. Leon fell backward to avoid it, shock in his eyes.

"I said no head strikes, you stupid beast!"

I wasn't sure if the krepp didn't understand Leon or didn't care, but he swung his blade down at Leon's midsection while he was on the ground. Leon rolled out of the way. He had to put his sword up to stop the next attack, but Grufaeragar's strength was too much, batting Leon's weapon out of his hand. The point was over, but the krepp didn't seem interested in stopping the fight.

Leon was back on his feet but without a sword. Grufaeragar charged him as Leon pushed out his hands toward the krepp. A strong gust of wind forced my eyes shut. When I opened them again, Grufaeragar was tumbling backward.

The krepp looked confused as if thinking the wind itself had knocked him over. "What is that?" he asked.

"Was it not obvious enough?" Leon teased. "Maybe you'll figure it out the second time."

He blasted the krepp with wind again, rolling him backward. Grufaeragar dropped his sword as he slid and dug the claws of his hands into the dirt to stop himself. He started crawling against the wind toward Leon, who showed no fear as he walked up to Grufaeragar.

"You smell like a swamp," Leon said. "You could use a bath."

He pushed out his hands. A large jet of water shot into the krepp's face. Grufaeragar started to scream in clear anger, but the water went into his mouth and turned the sound into gurgling. He lost his hold on the earth and rolled backward.

Leon was just pissing off the krepp more. I was too horrified to know how to de-escalate this. It never should've happened in the first place, but it was too late now.

"Stop! Stop!" the king was shouting as he ran in from behind us.

Leon's chest heaved as he put an end to his water spell. "He made someone duel him," Leon explained. "Wouldn't take no for an answer."

The krepp pushed himself up and charged Leon.

"It's over!" Leon said as he backed away and put his hands up.

The krepp jumped incredibly high and far, his enormous shadow falling over Leon before he came down on the instructor. Grufaeragar easily swept Leon's hands out of the way and wrapped his strong fingers around Leon's neck.

"You lose now, cheat!" Grufaeragar yelled with the fury of an enraged beast. I doubted he would be able to see reason at this point.

I was running over by then. The last thing I wanted was to try to force the krepp off Leon, but something had to be done.

"Grufaeragar, the duel is over!" I said.

"Grufaeragar, get off of him!" the king yelled.

Leon tried to pry the krepp's hands off of his neck, but Grufaeragar was far too strong. Leon started making a choking sound, but he looked more angry than afraid. He probably knew he could force the beast off with sorcery but didn't want to cast again unless absolutely necessary.

I tried to nudge the krepp off using my shoulder, but he swung his elbow into my stomach with startling speed. I lost the wind from my lungs as I fell back and started to gasp for breath.

Leon stopped trying to fight the krepp physically and blasted him with wind again, but all it did was sit both of them upright. The krepp's hand never left his throat. Now Leon started to panic as his face lost color.

Reuben rushed over with one of the training swords and started beating the krepp's back with it, like trying to drive in a stake to hold down a tent. If it bothered the krepp even a little, he didn't show it.

Everyone was screaming by then for Grufaeragar to get off Leon. I was still trying to breathe.

Reuben shifted and struck the krepp square in the back of his bald head. There was a *GUNK* sound, as if he had struck hollow wood.

The krepp yelled out in fury as he swiped at Reuben with the claws of his right foot. He moved so fast I hardly saw it happen. Reuben fell back with a dramatic scream, his hands over his bloodied leg with his pants torn around the gash.

The krepp then jumped on Reuben and got both hands around his neck. Reuben's face turned white as he tried to scream.

Leon sat up coughing, clearly unable to do anything. I was still having trouble finding my own breath with a severe pain in my stomach. I stumbled over in hopes of helping anyway.

I grabbed the krepp by his shoulders. "It's over, Grufaeragar!" I wheezed out as I pulled on him hard.

He swung back and elbowed me just above my right eye. The pain was immense as everything flashed white. I barely remembered falling.

Michael and Charlie were finally pulling the krepp off Reuben when I sat up. They yanked him back far enough for Reuben to scurry away from the beast.

Grufaeragar stood up and swiped at both of them, but fortunately they were each quick enough to jump back before their skin was torn. They both retreated quickly with their hands up.

The krepp started after Charlie, then Michael, then looked back at Reuben, and finally at Leon. His claws were up, his teeth showing. He looked like a threatened wolf.

"Shall I fire?" someone asked.

The feeling of a knife in my temple made it difficult

to see straight, but I gasped in horror as I noticed one of the king's guards with an arrow aimed at Grufaeragar.

The king, with a face as if a vase was falling, gestured for the man to put down his bow. I didn't think Grufaeragar saw the archer before he lowered the arrow.

"Why all…?" Grufaeragar's face twisted as he seemed to search for the right word. "Why all *kirjek leasp*?"

"What?" the king asked.

"Leon cheat in duel for honor!" Grufaeragar said. "He must die for cheat!"

"That is ridiculous. You swung at my head!" Leon fumed. "Then you disarmed me, and yet you still attacked. So I blew you back with wind."

"You cheat!" Grufaeragar looked at the king. "I ask permission to fight Leon to death."

"There will be no killing here." The king then spoke some Kreppen. "*Aken iwa. Aken iwa.*"

That must mean no killing.

"Then you dishonor me," Grufaeragar shouted. "All of you dishonor me!"

Reuben told the king, "He is more beast than man. You saw what he did to me when I tried to get him off the instructor!"

I said, "He only did that when you started beating him over the head with your wooden sword."

"*Oken!*" Grufaeragar said as he pointed at me. Then he pointed at Reuben. "*Felk kirjek ri leasp!*"

I made another mental note of the Kreppen. *Oken* must be yes. *Felk kirjek ri leasp* had to be something about Reuben attacking him. Or maybe it was "human attacked me from behind."

"Krepps don't trade with dishonorable cowards," Grufaeragar said slowly and surely.

"Grufaeragar, this was all a misunderstanding—"

But Grufaeragar interrupted the king with a mouthful of Kreppen. "*Kirjek ri leasp. Kirjek ri leasp! Krepps kirjek felk leasp.*"

The king put up his hands. "I don't understand."

I figured the krepp had to be repeating that we'd attacked him from behind. I tried to piece together what each word meant. It seemed like his last sentence was saying krepps would attack humans from behind. *Oh, "leasp" must mean attack dishonorably, not necessarily from behind.* If so, then he was saying the krepps would now attack us.

Was he declaring war?

I muttered a curse.

"*Felks aken farrio,*" Grufaeragar said.

I'd already figured out "felks" was "humans" and "aken" was "no," from when the king said "aken iwa." No kill. So the only new word was *farrio.* It seemed pretty obvious it had to be "honor," the most important thing to krepps. Grufaeragar was walking toward the portcullis as if to leave. My heart dropped.

"Wait, Grufaeragar!" the king said.

He said one last thing, his tone dismissive. "*Aken lyloll felk jiia.*"

I had only one idea what that could mean, Grufaeragar's dismissive tone my biggest hint: He wasn't going to "speak human again."

Then the krepp turned and didn't stop. I didn't see that there was anything to lose now, so I tried my best.

"*Felks aken kirjek leasp,* Grufaeragar!"

He stopped and looked back. I glanced at the king,

hoping he might take over, but he made a roll of his hand for me to keep going.

"Uh..." God this would be so much easier without this blinding headache. *"Felks aken kirjek leasp,"* I repeated, then said, *"Felks aken jiia. Aken kirjek leasp jiia."* I could only use words I had just heard and hope that my guesses were right.

Grufaeragar looked a little less angry, or perhaps there was just no way for him to show anger when his hairless brows above his eyes lifted in surprise.

"Lyloll felk?" I asked as I put my hands together and lowered my head in a plea.

"Only because you honor me, human. I speak your language one more. Swear what you say?"

"I swear it."

"Then say it again."

"Felks aken kirjek leasp." Then I said, "It was confusion, not dishonor."

"I see."

"We were scared." I gestured at everyone behind me. "Grufaeragar is very strong. Very scary."

He clucked out a deep laugh. "Yes, humans scare easily. I remember in street. The man."

"Yes," I said, glad he recalled. "We were afraid, too. We thought you wanted to kill us. We didn't mean to dishonor. We were just trying to defend our lives."

"I understand now." He walked back toward us. "You speak good Kreppen for human, Jon. You honor me. I stay longer. I watch humans. Decide later."

He confidently strutted past everyone and back toward the great hall. "I am hungry!" he called out.

The king gestured for his guards to hurry after Grufaeragar. "Make sure he gets whatever he wants."

There was a tense silence that lasted until Grufaeragar was out of view. My head was ringing like a bell.

The king looked too surprised for me to tell if he was proud of me. "What did you say to him in Kreppen?" he asked.

"Just that we won't attack him again dishonorably. Then I asked him if he could speak 'human' again. He was saying he wouldn't."

"How could you possibly know all of that?"

"I just listened to the words you and he used and guessed their meaning. I wasn't completely confident, but I figured it was better to take a chance than to let him walk out of here. If I understood him correctly, he was saying he was attacked dishonorably by humans and now the krepps were going to attack us dishonorably."

"God and demi, I'm glad you said something. You have a great ear for Kreppen."

"Sire," Reuben interrupted before I could thank the king for his compliment. "May I ask what the krepp is doing each day? Why is he still here?"

"He's still deciding if his kin will trade with us, leave us alone, or war with us. The krepps have been insulted because the last king killed a whole ship of them who had come here to trade. You all heard his story of the demigod coming to Hammashar. We still haven't been able to determine what might've actually happened, but it is important that we honor Grufaeragar's belief. He is not to be disrespected in any way. That includes by you, Leon."

"That's not going to be easy if he imposes himself on our training. It's hard enough to get anything through the thick skulls of these people without a krepp distracting us."

"He is growing bored and needs to see something that will tell him we have honor. You will find a way to include him without angering him if he shows up again, or next time he won't be stopped. Do you understand?"

"Oh, I understand." It looked as if Leon had more words, but he kept his mouth shut. I figured he wanted to tell the king that he wouldn't have trouble stopping the krepp himself if it came to that.

I noticed the princess watching from the second story of the great hall window. She waved to me when I looked. I gave a quick nod and turned my attention away. There had been an older woman standing behind her, not the queen, probably a tutor of some kind. They seemed to have interrupted the lesson to watch the excitement.

I was glad it was over. Charlie had his hand up as he faced the king.

"Yes?" Nykal's frustrated tone made it clear Charlie should not be asking anything.

"My time would be better spent learning about the magical arts and enchanted devices for the sake of everyone else. I do believe mana has more possibilities than what is currently known by Leon and yourself, sire. There could be many spells that have not yet been discovered."

"What exactly are you requesting from me?" the king asked.

"I would like to walk around the capital with the authority to demand that the people of Newhaven tell me what they know."

Nykal's eyelids lowered. "You will not demand

anything of my people."

"But I have spent years asking politely. No one ever wants to help me."

I didn't know if it was because of the awkwardness of Charlie's request or solely from Grufaeragar's elbow to my head, but I had to sit down. The throbbing pain in my head was too much.

I put my hand over it as I tried to relax on the dirt. I didn't see myself training effectively the rest of the day.

"Jon, are you all right?" the king asked. "You took quite a blow."

"I'll be fine in time."

I heard someone walking over. I squinted at Kataleya crouching in front of me.

"Let me see," she said.

I let down my hand.

She was close to my face as she looked at my brow just over my right eye.

"Excuse me," Reuben said. "I'm the one bleeding over here."

Kataleya ignored him. She had me follow her finger with my eyes, along with a few other tests as the king answered Charlie.

"Do you truly believe you might learn something about mana that Leon cannot teach you?"

"Leon only yells, sire. He teaches me nothing."

"That is a load of horse shit!" Leon yelled. "Nykal, you must see how difficult it is to get through to them? There's nothing more that I can do!"

I was surprised when the king snapped at him. "Are you giving up on our agreement?"

"What agreement?" Charlie asked.

Kataleya brushed some of my hair out of my face.

"You'll be sore for a while, but I don't think it's serious."

I had figured that much, but I thanked her anyway.

She moved just in time for me to see Leon red with rage. "I'm not giving up. I'm saying it's impossible. There's a difference." He pointed at Charlie. "Fools like Spayker here are hopeless to learn the sword when they lack the motivation. Most of the others you've chosen will fail to learn more than one spell before winter is over. You might as well send them to Curdith Forest for a week and see who comes back alive. Then I might be able to impart *some* knowledge onto the strongest of them without it overwhelming their feeble minds."

Kataleya moved over to Reuben and crouched in front of the wound on his leg. I found it a little sweet how he smiled at her when she wasn't looking at his face. If he would just shut his damn mouth every now and again, he might not be such a pain.

But it was Leon who was really pissing me off today. After hearing this speech, I was starting to agree with Charlie. What had Leon really taught us? All he did was answer questions angrily.

He wasn't a bad swordsman, but I had learned everything I thought there was to know from my father. I didn't expect Leon to be able to teach me anything.

I did wonder about the agreement between him and the king, though. I had always been curious why Leon was here and not someone else. What had the king promised him? Or what had he promised the king?

"Take a moment to think about what you're saying," Nykal lectured Leon. "Then answer me. Are you giving up?"

"I want to know about this agreement," Reuben

interrupted.

Leon walked toward Reuben with such aggression that I was worried he might punch Reuben square in the nose. Reuben quickly limped away from him.

"Stay still and shut your mouth!" Leon demanded.

Reuben stopped hopping backward, though he still held fear in his eyes.

Leon gestured at the ground. "Sit down."

Rueben sat but looked at Leon as if he might need to defend himself.

Leon crouched and pulled Reuben's leg to straighten it. "This is going to hurt. Take the pain like a man, for once in your easy life."

"What are you going to do?" he asked in a shaky voice.

Leon closed his eyes and drew a long breath. He put his hand over Reuben's torn pant leg.

Reuben winced, then grabbed at his leg for a breath. Then he took a few quick breaths through the pain as he withdrew his hands so as not to interfere.

When Leon finished, he sat down and looked physically exhausted.

Reuben glanced at his wound with curiosity. His eyes nearly bulged out of his head.

"Don't say I never did anything for you," Leon said as he slowly got up.

While his pants were, of course, still torn, the wound was just a faint line as if it'd had a few days to heal.

"Your turn, Jon," Leon said as he made his way over to me.

"How do you do it?" I asked.

"It's just a superficial healing spell. It isn't complicated. F and Upper F."

That was something I should be able to learn in a matter of hours! My immediate reaction was anger. "Why didn't you tell me about that spell earlier?"

"There are many spells like that which had no use for you until now."

"I want to learn them all."

"You'll lose your grasp on Expel faster than you'll learn a few simple spells. You have to improve first." He put his hand over my forehead, causing me to wince as it brushed against my brow. He hummed as if in thought. "You might actually be able to cast Heal with enough practice. Perhaps it *should* be the next spell you learn. Just keep practicing Expel at the same time." He looked back at the others watching. "I haven't even begun to teach all of you the true possibilities of your mana because none of you have proven you are ready."

Leon looked back at me and let out a small groan as he began. I gasped. It felt like a hundred tiny needles were weaving through my brow.

I wanted to curse the incredible pain, but there were women and royalty watching. Reuben's healing couldn't have hurt this much. There was no way.

My legs shook. I was just about to yell out, but it came to an end.

It was Leon who looked worse off after. He had his palms on the dirt as he steadied himself.

"You're welcome," he said between quick breaths.

I grumbled my thanks. But then I did start to feel better. The pain washed away like I'd rinsed off dirt.

I touched the area carefully. It was still tender but splendidly better. My head was clear. The day wouldn't go to waste anymore.

I have to learn this spell.

Charlie asked Leon, "How many spells do you know?"

"I know all the spells I can cast and a few more." He sighed. "I don't know how many that is. A lot."

"Hundreds?" Charlie asked.

"No."

"I know there must be hundreds," Charlie said.

"There are, but you're not going to find out anything by pestering the commoners in Newhaven. You have to ask the right person or you have to find books or scrolls on the magical arts. The best place, for both sorcerers and texts, is unfortunately Rohaer. I've never been, but everyone who knows anything has heard that the library in their capital is the place you want to go to truly learn."

I thought of Eslenda in Curdith Forest. She had to know many spells. The camouflage alone seemed especially useful, but I wasn't going to speak of her.

I still wondered if one of the people here could be responsible for telling the illusionist at Greda's shop that I would be picking up a ward of dteria. I wanted to trust all of my peers, but I sometimes had a habit of trusting too much. It was often difficult for me to see the dark side of someone.

"There is at least one book written about the magic arts and magical devices in Newhaven," Charlie said. "I've always wanted to search for more, but I've never had the money to even purchase the one I want. I would like to go now that I do have the coin."

"You will stay and learn the sword," Leon said.

"I watched Remi fight. She has more coordination than I do. I wouldn't want to waste everyone's time."

"You know what? Fine. We *have* wasted enough time. Take the rest of the day to search the city all you want. Be back for supper."

I was a little surprised at Leon's change of mind, but I was more concerned about something else to really care. I didn't want to waste my time here, either.

"I'd like to go with him," I ventured.

Leon looked dumbfounded. "You're not about to say that you wish to skip sword training as well?"

"Yes, but for a different reason. My time is better spent helping Charlie. I don't mean to offend you, Leon, but I don't believe there is anything you can teach me that I don't already know about sword fighting. I can practice with the others after they've caught up a little."

"Then I should also have the day off," Reuben said.

I gave him a look. He was ruining my chances.

"My ass." Leon picked up two protective tunics. "I'm tired of talking. Show me just how good the two of you are."

We slipped on the leather armor. There was nothing protecting our arms while wearing a sleeveless cuirass, but it was better this way, more mobility. We each picked up a training sword from the ground.

I could see in Reuben's eyes that he desperately wanted to prove he was better than me. Unfortunately for him, I knew that just couldn't be the case.

There was no one better.

CHAPTER EIGHTEEN

Long before I was born, my father had lived in Tryn. He was the head guard for the lord of the city, and he'd taken it upon himself to train the other guards. When he retired, my father moved to Bhode, and he and my mother had me. As soon as I was old enough to pick up a sword, my father started training me. He was never the type of man to exaggerate his son's strengths. So when he told me, a year ago, that I was the best swordsman he'd ever fought, I knew it was true.

We'd sparred every single day. It was how we both enjoyed passing the time. He knew many different fighting styles and used all of them against me. There were other men in Bhode who would sometimes join us, but none stuck around for long. They had no training and usually didn't enjoy losing against a boy.

I had always told my father I wanted to face a real opponent who wasn't him, someone truly skilled. I felt bad that Reuben would be that first skilled opponent, but I also had something to prove, not only to those watching but to myself. My time was better spent training in the magical arts and exploring the city with Charlie for information on spells.

I wished that Leon was better prepared to train us,

but I was beginning to believe that bringing all of us here had been done without much planning. It was as if the king suddenly had the idea to recruit a number of cheap, young sorcerers and train us rather than pay experienced sorcerers to defend his kingdom. While the idea did seem rash to me, I also greatly appreciated the opportunity and trust the king had afforded us. I did not want to let him down.

With everyone watching, I moved toward Reuben as if to attack. I trusted my instincts and speed. He backed away with feints, fake jabs at my chest, but I knew when a man was committing and when he was teasing. I did not flinch.

I saw his eyes change as I got too close for him to feel comfortable anymore. He stabbed at my chest, a nice clean attack that he'd surely practiced many times. With a flick of my wrist and a turn of my arm, I deflected his sword at the same time that I pushed the point of mine into his chest.

The force of my attack pushed him back a few steps. The fight stopped. He looked as if he wanted to curse me or perhaps call my move unfair, but even he knew that there was no excuse he could give.

"One point for Jon," Leon announced.

Speed was a swordsman's best friend. I had fast reflexes, especially for someone my size. I decided to show off a bit this time just to drive my point across that I did not need to be here.

I let Reuben come at me now. He was not the swordsman my father was, the last point making this clear to me, and even my father had trouble hitting me when I took on defensive maneuvers.

I figured Reuben was hesitant to stab me again because he would be ashamed to lose in the same way when I counterattacked. Sure enough, he went for a quick two-handed swing. I was already moving underneath it before the sword crossed overhead.

He quickly pulled his weapon back to prepare a defense, but my stab was a fake. My swing was a fake as well. So was another stab. I whipped my sword around into different poses, posturing and faking attacks with each one and watching Reuben react with the appropriate defense but always a blink too slow, and that's all it took to lose. But I would not win yet.

I attacked several times, but I always stopped and pulled back just before my sword tip reached him. I moved too quickly for him, as I did against my father, one of the best swordsmen of Tryn. My father might've been a lot older than Reuben, but his defense was nearly impenetrable when he was healthy, and I still managed to find ways through it. I honestly didn't know how Reuben could beat me, but trying to defend himself and hoping to take advantage of an opening was not it.

I stepped back and let it soak in for Reuben that I could have beaten him many different ways by now if I'd tried a little harder. He couldn't defend against someone as fast as I was. Leon had to have noticed. I figured even the others had seen it.

I assumed Reuben, overcome with embarrassment, would rush me furiously. To my surprise, however, he did not attack.

There was something in the way he looked at me that I had never seen in his eyes before. There was no longer the harsh judgment in his brown irises. I think he finally realized that I was better than him, at least at this one thing.

I did not smile or boast in any way. I showed him with a cold look that I was only doing what I needed to do.

I decided I should end this quickly, but with a bit of flair that would not result in his injury.

My father invented a maneuver that was difficult to pull off without many hours of practice. It was one of those things that, even if you could predict your opponent was about to use it on you, it was difficult to stop. It was also one of those things that only worked against someone who knew how to properly defend himself, as Reuben had proven.

I swung at a high angle so he had to raise his sword to block mine. Expecting Reuben to block in this way, I took my left hand off the bottom of the hilt to grab the base of my blade for quicker movements. Meanwhile, I tilted the base of my sword upward as if I might soon slide my sword downward against his blocking weapon and stab him from overhead.

Properly, Reuben lifted his sword higher to cut off my angle. It was then that I executed the maneuver. In a flash, I disengaged my sword from his and poked it through the small gap between his lifted wrists as he held up his sword with both hands. By then it was too late for him to stop me. He stepped back, predictably, to get away from the point of my sword coming at his chest. But rather than try to stab him, I hooked my sword back toward me—down across the top of his gloved wrist.

With me prying one wrist downward and his sword handle upward, there was no way he could hold onto the handle. I wrenched the weapon out of his hands and flung it hard against the ground with the tip of my sword. It fell and bounced as he backed away and put up his hands reflexively.

It had all happened so fast that I doubted Reuben, and surely not anyone watching, could really tell what I'd done. In fact, Reuben looked confused as if just now realizing he had lost.

"What happened?" Michael said. "I blinked."

"What the hell was that, Jon?" Leon asked me with a big smile.

"Just a little disarm trick." I bent down and picked up Reuben's sword and offered it to him. "No hard feelings?"

He took his weapon back and bowed. "No hard feelings. Good duel."

I bowed back, having a newfound respect for him. It wasn't easy for any man to lose graciously, especially one as proud as Reuben.

"May I go with Charlie now?" I asked Leon. I kept my tone humble.

"Yes, go ahead."

We started toward the portcullis.

"We're going to fight again one of these days, Jon!" Reuben said.

"I look forward to it," I called over my shoulder.

The portcullis was already up, and the drawbridge was down. There were usually two guards stationed outside the drawbridge, the only entrance to the castle, and now was no different. I hadn't gotten to know them yet, but neither of them looked very friendly. Or perhaps it was just their job to ignore us.

"So where are we going?" I asked Charlie as we left the castle.

"There is a place that has a book I want."

We walked in silence for a little while. A question began to bug me. "I want to ask you something, but I hope you won't take it as an insult."

"What?"

"Why do you want to learn more about mana if you can only use one note?"

"For you and the others, of course."

"Oh." That was surprisingly kind of him. Charlie wasn't a mean young man, but I had yet to see him be thoughtful, either.

"Also, the more I know about mana the easier it is for me to build devices that can be enchanted with magical ability."

That made more sense to me. "What do you know about the healing spell Leon used on Reuben and me?"

"Just what he said, that it uses uF and F together."

"You don't say Upper instead of u?"

"It's easier for me to say the letters how they are written," Charlie said. "That's what I picture in my mind when we speak about spells. I also picture the spell capitalized when it's the name of the spell and lowercase when it's the range of mana. Kataleya is learning to cast water spells, lowercase, like you are learning to cast dvinia spells. However, right now she only knows one water spell, and it's called Water, capitalized."

"I see."

We were silent again. Charlie clearly knew where he was going as he took me toward a crowded street.

"I was wrong earlier," he said.

"About what?"

"I do know more about healing. Each F at different octaves work differently, but they share properties of life."

I reminded myself that an octave was the same note at double or half the frequency, like F and uF.

Charlie continued, "uF has the strongest properties of life, hence the name vtalia."

"That's my natural mana."

He looked at me as if insulted. "I know, Jon. I know everyone's natural mana and range."

"How is that possible?"

"Because we all spoke about it after testing."

"That was one time, and it was a while ago."

He shrugged. "I remember."

I thought I had a good memory, but I would never be able to recall the ranges of all of my peers from each of them mentioning it just once.

Charlie said, "The notes of F, when used at the same time, create a new outcome than if each is used alone. It is the same as any other spell. All notes can change when used with others."

"You said you were raised by a blacksmith who wasn't your father."

"Yes."

"So how did you learn so much about mana?"

"I have been interested in mana since I started to feel it as a boy. I tried to learn everything I could about it, but there was only so much I could learn for free."

"You didn't have any coin?"

"No."

"None?" I asked incredulously. "The blacksmith never paid you?"

"He bought me what I needed with the coin we made from his business, but he didn't allow me any personal coin."

The blacksmith did not sound like a good father. I imagined the man had never wanted to raise Charlie after finding him in a barrel. He'd just made use of him.

It reminded me of the way the king seemed to be using Leon. The two men obviously didn't care about one another. They had come to some sort of agreement, the king admitting this.

I felt a sour mood coming over me the more I thought about it. Not only did the king seem too poor to pay everyone who he needed to fight against an impending attack, but Leon was clearly overwhelmed with the task of training everyone.

Not overwhelmed, I realized. *Incapable.*

That was even worse.

Did we really have a chance against a stronger army with Leon as our trusted instructor? I knew most of us had been recruited because we were desperate for a better life, but why had Reuben and Kataleya stuck around this long? They had so much to lose.

I felt a pang of fear. Could one of them be responsible for undermining my training? If so, they weren't acting alone. I knew nothing about their families. I should probably start to learn what I could.

"What do you know about the families of Reuben and Kataleya?" I asked Charlie.

"Reuben Langston is the son of a wealthy noble, but I do not know who his father is." Charlie thought for a moment. "I also know nothing about Kataleya Yorn's nobility."

He didn't ask me why I was asking, and I was glad. He didn't seem like he could keep the secret that I thought it possible that one of them had aided the illusionist who'd given me the essence of dteria.

Soon we arrived at Charlie's destination. It was a small, and frankly sad, bookshop. There was barely enough room for the three of us to stand in the middle of the shop, the walls crowded with books upon bookshelves. The owner was an old man who sat on a stool reading something. He smiled as he looked up at us.

"Charlie Spayker. I haven't seen you in a while."

"Hello," he replied indifferently as he seemed to be looking for something specific. He found it a moment later, pulling a book from one of the high shelves that required him to go onto his toes to reach.

"Careful!" the old man said, but Charlie had already pulled the book out without knocking any others over.

"I've come to buy this." He pulled out his coin purse. I politely did not check exactly how much money Charlie had left after our weekly stipend, but it seemed to be pretty full from the quick glance I allowed myself.

"Excellent," said the old man as he took Charlie's coins.

Then Charlie plopped down right there on the floor, crossed his legs, and opened the book to read. He didn't say a word. He didn't even glance up at me. It was as if I no longer existed.

The old man went back to reading as well, seemingly content with Charlie sitting on the floor of his shop.

"Um," I muttered.

Charlie looked up at me. "I'm going to be reading this for a while." His tone was irritated, as if I had interrupted him.

"What's the book about?" I asked.

He showed me a cold look, then went back to reading.

I glanced over at the old man, who stood and gestured for me to follow him out of the shop. On the street, he told me, "It's the only book about magic that my father didn't sell when he owned this shop. I never asked who sold it to him. It's quite old, no author listed. Charlie has come in wishing to purchase it for years now after I let him read the first few pages."

I was nodding. "Do you know anything about what's in it?"

"It discusses magical devices and enchantments. None of it makes much sense to me."

"Thank you for explaining. May we?" I gestured at the open door for us to go back in.

"Yes, but I don't think even a quake is going to interrupt him for a while."

I had to at least try. We walked back in.

"Charlie, give me just one moment."

"What?" he asked in exasperation as he looked up at me.

"Are you going to be reading here for a while?"

"Yes."

"How long?"

"Until I finish the book."

That was probably going to take hours. I thought about going back to the castle and having him return on his own, but I doubted I would have another chance to explore the capital anytime soon. I thought I would take advantage of the opportunity. I was hoping Charlie would help me, though, as he had grown up here.

"I thought we were going to search the city for other books as well, or for sorcerers who might know something."

"I will after I'm done with this. Let me read!"

He went back to the text.

"All right, just go back before supper. You're on your own now."

"Yes, fine," he muttered to the book.

I ventured out and decided to pick a direction at random and start walking. I didn't know exactly what I was looking for, but I had a feeling I would figure it out soon. Mostly I just needed a break from Leon. I couldn't believe he'd almost started a war with the krepps just because he couldn't contain his temper. Yes, Grufaeragar was an inconvenience and had disregarded —or never understood—the rule of no head strikes, but that was not an excuse for Leon losing control.

I found myself making my way toward Greda's magic shop and realized I should go the other way. She probably still didn't want me back, and it wasn't as if I had enough coin to buy anything anyway.

What I needed was some new clothing. I walked and asked around for a good tailor who was also cheap. I always kept my coin purse in my pocket. I felt better having it there than leaving it in my room unattended, even if it was in the castle. There were locks on the doors, but I could only lock mine from the inside. Barrett hadn't given me a key, and I didn't think it wise to ask him for one if no one else had.

I would have to purchase lunch if I didn't plan on returning to the castle, but that was all I had to buy until my next weekly stipend. I looked forward to receiving another forty buckles two days from now, especially because I wasn't required to purchase anything expensive like a vibmtaer or an essence.

A few hours later, I had a new shirt and pair of pants

waiting for me to pick up when I was ready to head back.

I ate a quick and cheap meal after a visit to a bakery, because it was all I could afford—the last of my coin now gone—but I wasn't worried about that.

After walking around town for a few more hours and finding nothing of interest, I was starting to get antsy. I knew my time would have been wasted sword training with Leon, but I felt that, although I was getting to know the city better, this wasn't helping, either. I really should be practicing my spell or learning Heal.

Eventually, I walked back to the small bookshop to check on Charlie, but he wasn't there. I asked the old man when he'd left.

"About an hour ago," he replied. "Didn't say where he was going."

I gave my thanks. I started to head back myself when I bumped shoulders with a man crossing by the other way.

"Watch it!" He shoved me hard.

I was surprised. There should be no doubt to anyone who saw me that I was strong. But not only did this man, in his dark cloak, seem like he wanted to start a fight with me, I had sensed something that sent my mana out of order.

I looked back at him as I tried to figure out what it was. He looked back at me. When he saw me staring, he stopped and turned around and spread his arms.

"The hell you looking at?"

A few people glanced over. The last thing I wanted was to be involved in an altercation.

He was probably twice my age. He couldn't quite be called large or even very strong. I was certain I could beat him fairly easily so long as he didn't have a knife hidden in his cloak, but there was no point in risking it.

I turned away from him.

"I thought so!" he taunted.

As I walked away, I realized what it was I'd felt. My mana had been pulled to a lower vibration, just like when I'd held the essence of dteria close to me.

I looked back again. He seemed to be in a hurry now, gesturing at no one as he appeared to be speaking to himself. I didn't know if I had sensed an essence of dteria on his person or if it was his mana. Either way, I knew I should follow him.

Figuring he might turn around again, I decided to loop around the street before starting to trail him. After I caught up to him again, I followed him down a few streets at a safe distance. I watched him bump into two other men on two more occasions and attempt to start a fight with each of them, but they backed down as well.

I tensed when I saw a capital guard about to cross by the dteria user the other way. They looked at each other long enough for me to realize they recognized each other, but they didn't speak. They just crossed by.

I kept my gaze fixed on the ground as the guard passed me farther down the street. When he was behind me, I found the dteria user again and hurried up a bit to make sure I wouldn't lose him as he turned onto another street.

I followed him for just a little while before he entered one of the larger inns I had seen in the city called The Pearl. I watched him through the doorway of The Pearl as I stood on the other side of the street and tried not to look conspicuous.

He went up to the reception counter and handed the worker a small pouch he'd pulled out from the inside of his cloak. It didn't look like anything was spoken between them as the worker walked off out of my view. The cloaked man started to turn around. I pretended like I was walking down the street.

When I had gone too far for him to see me anymore, I stopped and turned back. Looking into The Pearl again, I watched as the worker was handing the pouch back to the cloaked man.

I started down the street the other way as the cloaked man turned to leave. After enough time, I looked back to see him walking the opposite way. I had a choice. I could follow him to see what he did with what I assumed to be coins, or I could question the worker at The Pearl about the exchange.

Seeing as how I didn't want to make it known that I was involved with the law, as per my agreement with the king, I came to realize there was a third option. I could do nothing.

Doing nothing had always been a difficult thing for me. I decided to walk into The Pearl to better judge who was dealing with this dteria user and whether they may be innocent or guilty of a crime.

I wished Leon had taken the time to explain why dteria was illegal. The king had mentioned that dteria sorcerers—I was just beginning to realize there was probably a name for these sorcerers just like the way dvinia sorcerers were called wizards—were trying to spread "corruption" across the kingdom. But that was all he'd said about it. Did dteria change something about a caster's appearance? It did seem to change their personality, because why else would the king describe it as a corruption?

That explained the confident aggression of the cloaked man. It was a start. I could look for the same thing in the worker's demeanor.

"Hello," I said to the older man working at the reception of the inn.

"Good evening, young sir. Are you looking for a place to stay?"

It seemed plainly obvious this person was not corrupted by dteria. I gave him a serious look as I leaned closer. He raised an eyebrow as he leaned in as well.

"I don't want to say who I am." I spoke quietly. "But I might be able to help you with your problem."

He leaned back. "I'm afraid I have no idea what you're talking about." However, his tone said otherwise.

"The man who came in here just before me. He bumped into me earlier. I know what he is."

"That was a valued client. You should not speak about him as if he was some criminal."

I looked behind me thinking someone might be watching, but no, we were alone. This man really seemed scared of revealing the truth about the dteria sorcerer. Or perhaps he was putting me on and he was part of it, but that seemed unlikely. If they were to conduct nefarious business, for example, if this worker was paying the dteria user for a service, it would be at night when people couldn't see. The cloaked man had entered with hubris, barely caring to look around before accepting money from the worker of this inn. This exchange of money was something probably many people had witnessed before, but no one had done a thing about it.

"You seem like you don't want to be involved in... *whatever's happening.*" I spoke somewhat sarcastically, as if I knew exactly what was going on. "I understand you're scared of them. That's why there are some people...other people who are trying to stop them. People like me. Do you understand what I'm saying?"

He looked around at the empty reception. I seemed to be scaring him as he shook his head nervously.

"Just tell me one thing," I said. "I know he's here on someone's behalf. Who? Give me a name."

"I can't," the worker whispered.

"You can trust me. I want to help."

"Why?"

"Because some of us actually care about this city. And we need some proof, dammit." I relayed my frustration as if I had been at this for months, as I figured this man could've been suffering that long.

Finally, I seemed to get through to him as his eyes became glossy. He nodded.

"He claims it's a protective tax. We pay each week."

"What's his name?"

"He never told me."

"Who did he say he's working for?"

"I don't know if it's true."

"That's all right."

He didn't speak as he checked around again.

I didn't understand the worker's reluctance. "Just tell me whatever he told you."

He leaned in and whispered, "When he first came in, I told him I would report him to the guard for threatening us. That's when he laughed. I will never forget the look in his eyes." He gazed past me as if recalling the event. The older man then swallowed and looked at me again. "He told me it was the captain of the guard who had sent him and if I told anyone except for the manager here, then I would be killed. Please, young sir. Please tell me I'm not making a mistake telling you."

"You have done the right thing. I'm going to do everything I can, but I'll make sure they won't know you were involved in any way."

"Thank you," he whispered with tears burgeoning. "Thank you, young sir."

I nodded and left.

I felt pity for the man, who was clearly terrified. The captain of the guard working with dteria sorcerers seemed unlikely to me...at first. However, the more I recalled Nykal speaking about corruption within his own kingdom, the more I was inclined to believe it. God, Nykal might've even heard about the captain of Newhaven's guard falling to corruption before. He seemed like the type of king who wanted to know everything he could. I would be more surprised if he hadn't heard anything.

I relaxed a bit. That probably meant the captain had already been investigated. It was probably a lie told by the dteria user. He was working with someone, though. At least *some* of the city guards were on his side.

It was time to return to the castle, but not before picking up my new clothes. There was so much to do and to learn. At least I wouldn't look like a vagabond all the time now.

CHAPTER NINETEEN

When I was old enough to do so, I had helped my father prepare dinner for us every night. It was always an annoying chore for me as a child when I wanted to play outside instead, but I had gotten used to it as I aged. Now I missed it, as I did all the times I'd spent with my father before he'd fallen ill.

However, I had to admit that the feeling of entering the castle knowing a delicious meal was waiting for me in the great hall, along with the company of my friends, did a lot to alleviate my pain. I looked forward to hearing what had happened with their sword training after I'd left. I knew to wait until after we ate to speak with the king. He always ate with his family and looked as if he didn't want to be disturbed by anyone.

The courtyard was empty when I arrived, save a few workers walking across. I figured everyone was in the great hall. With a mean appetite, I walked in and found three plates left on the table near the door. Today was a red meat I assumed to be wild boar with a thick sauce that smelled a little sweet. There was buttered squash on the side.

I was pleased that Reuben and Michael were seated together, but Charlie was nowhere in sight. I expected

Leon to make a fuss that I had come back without Charlie, but I couldn't find Leon in his usual corner or anywhere else in the large room. Even the king was not present this time, his wife and daughter eating without him. It didn't sit right with me, the empty seat between them. But at least they appeared to be talking as if nothing was wrong, from what I could tell from across the long dining hall.

I took my plate and sat beside Michael. He and Reuben glanced up at me for just a moment before both looked back down at their food. It didn't appear that either had much of an appetite as they cut their meat without enthusiasm. I imagined something had happened after I left.

"Where's Charlie?" Michael asked.

"We got separated." I went on to describe his dismissal of me in the tiny bookshop and how I expected him to come back soon. Then I asked, "What happened while I was gone?"

Reuben let out his breath without looking up. If I wasn't so concerned about what they were about to tell me, I probably would've been happier about Reuben sitting with us. Perhaps he had finally let go of his attitude.

I heard someone running into the great hall. We turned to see Charlie. He had a cloth sack in one hand. He grabbed his plate with the other and hurried over to Reuben's side. He dropped the cloth sack on the table. It clinked and clattered as if many things were inside. Then he sat and started cutting into his meat in a mad rush as if he had but one minute to finish his meal.

"Uh, Charlie?" Michael prompted.

"What?" he said with a full mouth.

"Is there a fire somewhere we don't know about?"

"What?" he asked again, more confused this time.

"Why are you eating so fast?" Michael specified.

"Loths tha do," he said, his voice muffled by meat.

"Nox's blade, close your mouth, Spayker!" Reuben complained. "You're about to spit up on the dinner table!"

"Thorry."

It was hard to take my eyes off of Charlie as he cut the meat and stuffed it into his mouth so fast I feared he would choke. He ignored the sauce spread along the side of the plate. He stabbed the squash and put the whole thing up to his already full mouth, swallowing just before he inserted half of it into his mouth and bit off a gigantic end.

"My lord," Michael said. "I don't know if I've ever before been this impressed and disgusted at the same time."

"Before I forget," I interrupted. "There's a name for every type of sorcerer, right?"

"That is correct," Reuben said.

"So what is a dteria sorcerer called?"

"A warlock," Michael answered.

"That's incorrect," Reuben said. "A warlock specializes in dteria and vtalia, allowing them the ability to drain one life form for another."

I froze. "That's really true?"

"It is," he said with certainty, but I wasn't sure I believed him. Or perhaps I just didn't want to.

"What's a sorcerer who only uses dteria, then?" Michael asked.

"A coward. A weak man. A corrupt sorcerer. Or a dark mage, if you prefer." Reuben spoke with obvious hatred.

Seeing as how Reuben had never been one who could hide his true emotions, I was beginning to believe he wasn't the one working with the corrupt sorcerers.

"There are also witches," Reuben added. "They only use dteria, like a dark mage, but they specialize in curses. Dteria is like ordia. Depending on how the sorcerer uses it, it changes how their class is defined." He moved his fork around his plate. "Leon really should be teaching more about sorcery."

"He should," I said, glad to agree with Reuben for once. "What happened? Why isn't he here?"

Reuben sighed again. "I was tired. I made one mistake, but his reaction was inappropriate. I have completely lost confidence in our instructor." He spoke with such finality that I feared he might not ever change his mind.

"What did he do?"

Michael looked at me. "After you and Charlie left, I thought Leon was in a better mood. He told Reuben and me to duel. I don't know a thing about sword fighting, and I knew Reuben did. So I thought I would just swing hard and hope for the best. Well, Reuben swung pretty hard too, right?"

"I made a mistake. I was hardly paying attention."

"Anyway," Michael continued. "Our swords hit, and we both lost them. I thought it was kind of funny, so I laughed. But Leon wasn't amused. He applauded us sarcastically and said he was impressed, because never had he witnessed two people fight so badly that they both lost their weapons at the same time. Then he just walked out of the castle." Michael wasn't smiling as he usually did. "It didn't happen too long after you and Charlie left. I thought you might've seen him."

"No. He hasn't come back?"

"He did not long ago," Michael said. "He stank of ale and marched right into the keep."

"Jon, after supper will you show me the disarm trick you used?" Reuben asked me formally, or maybe it was just his lilt that made everything he said seem formal.

"I would be happy to, but I have to speak with the king about something I saw in town. There was a sorcerer with dteria. I could feel it on him, but I didn't know if it was an essence or his mana."

"There are many of them," Reuben said. "The king knows. You shouldn't bother him with something small like that."

I didn't want to divulge the rest. I did trust everyone here, but I figured I should be cautious just in case. "Well, I'd still like to bring it up with him, but I can show you the technique later."

"Very well."

Charlie finished the last bite from his plate and dropped his fork. It struck the plate loudly, causing us to look over.

He dug into the cloth sack on the table and pulled out a thin square of metal. It was silver with a hint of gold, as if it couldn't decide which metal it wanted to be.

"What are you doing with birlabright?" Reuben asked him.

Birlabright, I had heard that before. It was the metal used in a vibmtaer because it changed color depending on the frequency of the mana nearby. Barrett had told me this during the test of my mana's range. I assumed it was expensive.

"Don't ask me any questions," Charlie said.

Coming from anyone else's mouth, these words might've sounded mean, but I had a feeling that Charlie was incapable of insulting someone on purpose.

Charlie put his right hand over the square of birlabright. It melted right there on the table, to my astonishment. That wasn't to say that it turned to liquid; he just softened it so that it was in the state between solid and liquid, no doubt to make it malleable. I had never seen anything like it. Then he pulled it apart into two pieces and quickly started to shape one into what appeared to be a ring.

He finished quickly, clearly having done something like this before. Then he worked the other into the same shape of a ring.

"Give me your hand, Jon."

"Why?"

"So I can shape the ring to fit your finger."

I asked again. "Why?"

"Because I need to!" He grabbed my hand in frustration.

I felt uneasy about the whole thing, but causing him a fit would be even worse. I went along.

He slid the ring onto my middle finger. Using his thumbs and first fingers, he pinched and wiggled the ring until it seemed to be the right size. It was more than a little awkward having him hold my hand for this long of a time, especially when I glanced over to see Kataleya smirking at me from where she ate with the other girls. At least Remi was with them now. I grinned back and gave a subtle shrug.

Eventually, Charlie finished. He dropped my hand. "Hold it up," he demanded.

I lifted it in front of him. He cupped his right hand and moved it in the air over my hand. The metal hardened on my finger. Then he grabbed the ring and started to pull.

"Ouch," I complained as it caught on my knuckle.

"Make sure you can take it off," he said as he started on the next ring.

I slid it off and tried to hand it to him, but he pushed it back toward me without looking up. "Keep it."

Michael asked in a flirtatious voice, "Who's the next ring for, hmm? Is it for you, Charlie?"

"Yes," Charlie answered. "No questions. I need to…" He didn't finish his sentence as he started fitting the other ring on his finger.

I went back to eating and had finished my meal by the time he was done. I was glad, especially considering what he pulled out of the sack next.

With his bare hand, Charlie lifted a dead bat out of the bag and set it on the table.

The three of us had quite a reaction. I couldn't make out what Reuben or Michael yelled, for I was too busy yelling as well.

"What the hell, Charlie?"

Charlie leaned over the bat. He squinted as if trying to see something. Then he picked it up again and held it in front of his eyes.

The little thing stank. I wanted it away from me.

He got up and started walking around the table until he was on the side with Michael and me. I figured he was going to show us something about the bat, both of us leaning away as he approached. But he just continued on...toward the girls' side of the long table.

"Oh god," I muttered.

"Charlie!" Reuben said. "Don't show them that!"

Charlie ignored him.

"Michael, stop him!" Reuben demanded.

"Oh no," Michael said as he reached out for Charlie but purposefully missed. "Too late. I guess we'll have to watch."

We all fell silent. It was like witnessing two carriages about to collide. I couldn't take my eyes off it.

Aliana was the first to notice Charlie, but she didn't seem to realize exactly what he was holding until he was about a yard from her. She jumped back from the table with an expression of utter shock.

Kataleya, on the other side of the table, screamed, "Charlie! Get that away from here!"

But Charlie kept going, stopping in front of Eden, who was sitting next to Aliana. Eden was leaning away with a face of disgust. Charlie said something and presented the bat to her. She got up and backed away as she put out her hands. It was like watching a cat proudly present a dead rat to its owner.

Remi, surprisingly, appeared indifferent to it all as she kept on eating, sparing a few glances at Charlie. Eventually, Eden stopped backing away as Charlie seemed to be telling her something.

The four of us boys hurried over to listen.

"That's why it has to be now," Charlie was explaining. "I know you can do it. I've seen you use enchantments that are easier than this one."

"God above, fine. If it means you will stop harassing us."

Charlie nodded. He looked back and seemed glad to find me behind him.

"Come here, Jon."

He grabbed my hand at the wrist and set my hand down on the long table near the side wall, the one clear of everyone's plates. He put his hand down on the table next to mine, our two rings close.

Eden put the dead bat on the table near our hands. Then she squeezed in the space between us, her shoulders touching ours.

"Shut up and don't move while I do this," she said, even though no one was speaking.

She centered her hand over the bat and our two rings. The dead animal started to shift back and forth. Her breathing became loud. Her fingers bent and straightened.

A couple long minutes of this went by as I wondered what enchantment she was putting on the rings. More importantly, I wanted to know how long this would take. When Greda was going to enchant my ward of dteria, she said it would take an hour. I did not plan to stand here that long, no matter how much of a fit Charlie would throw.

However, after just a few minutes, Eden let down her hand. "It's done."

"That was fast," I commented. "The girl at the Enchanted Devices shop said it took her an hour."

"You mean Greda?" Eden asked me.

"Yeah, you know her?"

"I've known her for years. She's the one who first taught me about ordia. Unfortunately, she's a little slow at enchanting."

"Your enchant took minutes."

"All right, she's *very* slow. But she's my friend, and she's very smart. Oh, also I've been a lot faster ever since we came back from the forest."

"Quiet," Charlie said. "We need to test." He smiled as he looked at his ring. "How do I go about...? Oh, I know."

He made a fist and started slamming it against the table rapidly. "Hey, Jon! Hey!" He started laughing hysterically as I jumped back and looked at my hand. "I'm calling you, Jon! Hey!"

"Stop that!" The ring was shaking uncontrollably. It felt like my finger was violently spasming.

"Get it? It's a ring of calling!" Charlie was laughing hysterically for some reason. "It works! Now we just need a proper name. Ring of calling is too long. I know. Callring. I made us two callrings!"

I didn't know Charlie could get this excited.

I still didn't see why it was such a remarkable achievement as I massaged my sore finger.

"You'd better hope you don't feel that callring when Charlie is alone in his room at night," Michael teased.

Eden laughed quite hard, prompting Michael to chuckle as well.

I promptly took the ring off my finger at that. "Why did you fit it to my finger and not someone else's?" I asked Charlie.

He looked perplexed. "Oh I...um." He scratched his head. "I remember now. Because you're the most likely to be in a dangerous situation. Now we just have to figure out a signal. Put on the ring again and try tapping on it. I'm going to stand over here." Charlie ran all the way to the other side of the great hall.

Everyone had gathered around now except for the queen and the princess, who must have left during the commotion.

I was starting to see the purpose behind this as I tapped on my ring.

"Harder!" Charlie yelled. "I can barely feel it!"

I started flicking the ring with my nail.

"There!" He ran back to us. "What did you do?"

I showed him how I'd flicked it.

"This is marvelous!" Charlie said with a huge grin.

I did agree this had potential, but there was a problem...similar to the one Michael had mentioned.

"What happens if I'm using my hand to swing a sword? You're going to feel everything."

"No. It has to be violent jolts to the ring. Moving your hand won't do it. See?" He started swinging his hand around to fight with an invisible weapon.

It was true, I didn't feel anything.

This actually could be incredibly useful. *That Charlie, full of surprises.*

"How far will it reach?" I asked.

"It should work for up to ten miles."

"Ten miles?" I nearly shouted.

"Isn't it marvelous? We will have to test it later to be sure, though."

"Wow," Michael said. "That's actually very useful, Charlie."

"That's not all!" he said with a lift of his finger. "I'm also going to make two tracking rings. Tracker rings? Track rings? I'll figure out the name later. One person with one ring will be able to track the other person with their ring."

"How does any of this work?" I asked.

Eden explained, "Everything is susceptible to enchantments to some degree, but birlabright works very well for things like this. Callrings require the essence of bat. For the tracker rings, Charlie, we'll need the essence of a dog." She lowered her eyelids at him. "I hope you know I would never speak to you again if you kill a dog for this."

"Of course I wouldn't ever kill a dog! I will use one already dead from the dead animal shop in the city."

"What dead animal shop?" Eden asked.

"The one just south of here."

"You mean the fur shop?" Eden asked incredulously.

"Yes, the owner pays people for their deceased pets or other found animals before turning them into fur. Will you come with me tomorrow to enchant the birlabright there? I don't want to carry the dog all the way back here."

"*Ugh*. Fine."

"Jon, you don't have to come."

"That's good news."

"The tracker works differently than the rings," Charlie explained. "First the square of metal is enchanted before I separate it and make the rings. That way, it knows to only track itself and won't track other metal that has been enchanted in the same way."

I looked over at the bat on the table. It was gray and a little more deflated than usual. "So this is what happens after an animal's essence is used?"

"Why yes," Eden said as she brushed her hand as if presenting it. "Today's dinner was pork with a side of de-essenced bat. Thank you, Charlie, for this delightful experience that just had to happen while I was still eating."

"You're welcome!" Charlie said, utterly oblivious.

Eden sighed.

CHAPTER TWENTY

There was a guard outside the keep, but he opened the door for me. I thanked him and walked in. My breath was taken away by yet another stunning room. I guess I had expected the keep to be more of a military barricade than a place so artistically decorated, with elegant furniture and a wooden floor tinted gold. There were enormous stone pillars that reached all the way to the roof three tall stories above. Twin staircases rose to meet each level, a square balcony wrapping around each new floor. Although the floor was wood, the walls were stone. There were many doors on each floor, only a few shut. Three enormous fireplaces were built into the wall across from the entrance. All were lit. It was almost too warm within the keep.

I was honored to be let inside without a word. I figured the king had told his guards we could go anywhere we wanted within the castle. I was inclined to check out the dungeon, as I noticed a portcullis and stairs leading down, but it was already late. I needed to see the king.

I heard faintly the sounds of shouting. I followed my ear up to the second floor and peered through an open doorway into a hall. I saw Callie, the princess, with her ear next to a door in the hall. The shouting came from within.

She turned to me and put her finger over her lips

as I approached. I recognized the king's stern voice past the door, but he was too quiet for me to make out his words.

The king had specifically told me that his daughter needs to be told what to do when she acts inappropriately, but I couldn't bring myself to tell her to stop eavesdropping, especially when I wanted to know what was being said.

"What's going on?" I whispered.

"I sent the guard away so I could listen. Leon came back drunk and screaming. My father put him in the dungeon until he calmed down. I don't think it worked."

She motioned for me to put my ear against the door.

I tried to turn around and walk away, but I just couldn't overpower my curiosity. I leaned against the door near the princess.

Leon shouted, "You saw them! It's hopeless."

"Do you wish to go back into the dungeon?" the king challenged. "Is that what you're telling me?"

Leon scoffed. "You are putting a lot of faith in a man who would rather die than go back to the dungeon. The same man could easily kill you right now."

"So could many of the sorcerers you're training, and you'll never hear any of them threatening me. Think about what that says about you."

"It says I'm not an idiot like they are. Half of them are too dumb to learn more than one spell. The other half are too arrogant to realize that they still know so little."

"So *teach* them!"

"How am I supposed to do that when a *girl* knows

how to hold a sword better than two of the men?"

"Do you ever listen to yourself?" the king snapped. It was startling to hear such unrestricted anger in his tone. "*You* are the arrogant one. You told me you could teach anyone, and now you complain that it's impossible!"

"You had to have known I would say anything!"

There was a pause.

"Yes, I did know that. But I also decided to trust you just as you should trust your students." The king sounded calm again. "Leon, there's no reason for you to complain about this. We only have one option. We must fight."

"There's always another option. You can give up your kingdom to Rohaer."

"That's not an option," the king said firmly. His voice became quieter when he spoke again. "You should know something."

I pressed my ear harder against the door. I knew I was violating the king's trust by listening, but the princess was here as well. Perhaps my punishment wouldn't be quite as severe if we were caught, and this seemed too important to miss.

"Dteria is sweeping through Rohaer as many of Rohaer's people, not just sorcerers, look to arm themselves," the king said. "Normally, this would be a sure sign of a revolt. Dark mages would usually risk their lives for immediate power and fight against their own king, and the people would sooner turn on their king than be forced to march for war. However, there is no rebellion in Rohaer, not in any of the cities. It doesn't make sense except for one thing. The dark mages and the commoners must know they cannot stand against their own ruling government. The army loyal to King Frederick must be that strong. We're looking at the worst possible scenario. These dark mages and commoners might have joined with King Frederick and, when the snow clears, they will wreak havoc on all of Lycast."

Leon didn't reply for some time.

"Your scouts are telling you this?" he asked eventually.

"Yes, we just received another missive by bird. Do you see now what would happen if we let them win?"

Leon was silent for a little while. "I don't understand. Why now is dteria spreading across Rohaer? It has always been contained before."

"It doesn't matter. It needs to be stopped."

"It does matter! Finding out how or why it's spreading could help us stop it."

"You will get a different answer depending on who you ask."

"Don't tell me you believe the demigods are warring with each other," Leon said.

"You have to accept there is a possibility they exist after what Grufaeragar has reported. There is no better explanation for how a woman claiming to be Souriff made her way to Hammashar and convinced the krepps, in their own language, not to attack us."

"Sire, really—"

"Explain it!" Nykal interrupted. "Because no one else can."

"Grufaeragar could have lied about someone visiting."

"Then how else did he learn common tongue?"

It was silent for a little while.

"Just because no one can explain something doesn't mean it has to be the gods," Leon argued. "No one can explain where the sun came from. That doesn't mean it has to be the gods. No one can explain where the first man came from. That doesn't mean it has to be the gods."

"Those are very different topics than a human visiting Hammashar and teaching the krepps common tongue in order to stop a war. It doesn't require a difficult explanation. It happened. Someone did that recently. Now it was either a woman or a demigod, and I've never heard of a woman, or a man for that matter, who has learned the language of the krepps. There has been no contact between them and us until recently. And I certainly haven't heard of a single person going to Hammashar and coming back alive. You have to at least admit that the chances of this being a demigod are just as strong, if not stronger, than it being a common woman."

"I don't want to discuss this."

"No, you came here to yell, which seems to be the only thing you're good at."

"I came here to change your mind!"

"Fine. You wish to leave?" The king was shouting now, too. "You wish to give up? You win! Go ahead and leave."

It was silent for a moment.

"I will not be dragged back into the dungeon?" Leon asked.

Hold on. Why would Leon be dragged *back* into the dungeon...unless he was in the dungeon before all of this began? My heart trilled. *That would explain a lot.*

"No," the king answered. "An edict will be made.

You will have broken your agreement, but you will be free."

Another silence.

"I will stay until you find someone to replace me," Leon said.

"I'm not going to find anyone."

"There must be at least a few other sorcerers in your kingdom as strong as I am."

"Don't you realize that they would already be here if I could afford to purchase their loyalty? You were the last resort."

"Tax your people! You are the king, after all."

"The last time a king tried to tax his people so he could go to war, I organized the rebellion that led to his death. What do you think is going to happen...you know what? Never mind. I'm growing tired of this. Go to the great hall and have your free meal, then sleep in your warm bed. If you wish to leave, I expect you to do so at sunrise when the drawbridge is lifted. No one will look for you. You will be forgotten."

It was silent yet again.

"But if you choose to stay," Nykal intoned, "then I want your full commitment. You will stay with us until the end, no matter what happens."

This time, the silence lasted a long while.

"I'll make you another deal," Leon said. "I'll stay if you try to find someone you can afford to help me teach your fools out there."

"Very well. I agree to those terms."

I whispered to Callie, "Come on. We're lucky we haven't been caught so far. No reason to risk it any longer."

But she shook her head, then pressed her ear against

the door again.

"It's about over," I whispered. I gestured for her to follow me as I quickly walked away.

She listened for another breath, then looked at me and nodded. "All right."

We were just starting to walk away when a voice called out, "Hold right there!"

I looked over my shoulder at Barrett coming down the hall from the other side.

"Oh no," Callie whispered.

I swore inwardly as Barrett hurried toward us with heavy footsteps.

Leon opened the door to the throne room before Barrett made it. He spotted us standing there, frozen, and glared at me as if he was thinking about slugging me in the face. He opened the door wider and gestured for the king to look at us.

My heart dropped when I saw the ruler's disappointed face.

"How long have you been listening, Jon?" Nykal asked.

"It's my fault!" Callie said to my surprise. "I sent the guard away so I could listen. Jon just arrived recently. He told me to stop."

Leon and Nykal came out into the hall. The king glanced at his councilman. "Is what my daughter says true?"

"Father!" Callie said, insulted.

"I just arrived myself, sire," Barrett said.

"Jon, look at me," the king pointed at his eyes. "What did you hear?"

"A lot," I admitted.

I was shocked when Leon pushed me hard against

the wall and held me there.

"The hell is wrong with you?" he growled.

"Easy, Leon," Nykal warned.

Leon didn't seem to hear, his heavy arm across my chest. "Don't you know that eavesdropping on the king's private conversation can be considered treason? He could have you hanged for this!"

My eyes darted over to Nykal. "I'm sorry, sire. I wasn't planning on eavesdropping. I came here to speak to you about something that happened in the city, but I heard shouting and didn't want to interrupt. Callie is honorable for trying to cover for me, but it's my fault. I knew I shouldn't have listened, but I couldn't help it when I overheard the kind of conversation you were having." I swallowed as I prepared to say something either brave or idiotic. "I think all of us deserve to know what was said."

Leon stepped back from me. "He's too stupid to be scared. You'll need to punish him to get the message across."

I was surprised by Leon's sudden calm attitude. I could smell ale on him, but he didn't sound drunk.

Nykal took a long breath. "Jon's right," he told Leon. "Everyone deserves to know." The king glanced at me again. "Just let Leon or me be the one to tell them tomorrow, all right, Jon?"

"Yes, sire."

"And this has to be the last time you eavesdrop on me. Leon is right. It's a serious offense, even if you see my daughter doing it first."

"I understand. It won't happen again. We all appreciate how much trust you have given us. I hate to misuse that trust in any way."

"Stop kissing his ass," Leon said, to my frustration. "What did you see in the city?"

"One moment," Nykal said. "Callie, it is late."

"I just want to hear what Jon saw, then I'll go to my bedchambers."

"You have not apologized for sending the guard away and eavesdropping."

She lowered her head. "I'm sorry. I promise I won't do it again."

"I'm going to hold you to that promise, just as I will Jon. This is serious."

She nodded without looking up.

"Now go off to bed," he said.

She glanced at me as if I might have something to say in her defense. However, I thought her father was being more than fair.

She slowly walked off toward the balcony.

I told the king, Leon, and Barrett of my experience bumping into the dark mage and then following him. I was a little worried when it came time to divulge how I had questioned the worker at The Pearl, but no one interrupted to scold me, and soon I was finished.

The king spoke the moment I was done. "I believe you handled that very well."

"Thank you, sire," I said with immense relief.

"This isn't the first time I've heard of the captain of the guard's involvement with corruption, but it is the first I've heard of his connection to the dark arts." The king let out a slow breath. He had bags under his eyes.

"Sire," Barrett said. "The captain is a skilled fighter who knows how to lead men into battle, when it comes time. Not only that, he is the cousin of Kataleya's father. Whitley Yorn could be offended if we take action against the captain. It would then be Kataleya who suffers worst when she is removed in retaliation."

"Whitley will understand that we cannot keep corrupt officials in our government. That was the whole point to the rebellion, which he supported with a lot of coin. I will write to him tonight explaining that we will be removing Endell Gesh from his position because of corruption charges, and I will speak with Whitley personally tomorrow."

I was shocked. I hadn't expected any action to be taken, but this was Nykal after all. He seemed to make big decisions rather quickly.

Barrett argued, "There is no proof that this dteria sorcerer has any real connection with Endell."

Nykal gave Barrett a look. "We both know the chances of that. Besides, I've been meaning to replace Endell anyway. There have been too many reports of him breaking the law. The only issue now is finding someone I can trust to replace him."

"He may become our enemy," Barrett said. "He has followers. It is the reason we didn't replace him after your coronation."

"You don't need to remind me of what I already know, councilman." The king gave Barrett a hard stare.

"I apologize."

"I will figure out what to do about him tomorrow, with Whitley's input. He knows his cousin better than we do. Also, I have decided to send a letter to Byron Lawson. Have it written for me. He will make an excellent captain of the guard here in Newhaven. Have him arrive at the castle soon after he names his replacement in Tryn."

I knew Byron Lawson. He was the lord of Tryn. My

B.T. NARRO

father had worked for the man for many years. Byron was also the person Scarlett had mentioned when discussing her employer, when she'd met me in the tavern in Tryn. I had figured I would meet the lord of Tryn sometime after I'd arrived in the city, but I had been too busy trying to find a sorcerer to explain mana. Then Barrett showed up and took me here to the castle.

I looked forward to meeting Byron, if I could arrange an introduction. I longed to ask him about my father, who was the head guard of Tryn for many years. I imagined my father's role in Tryn had probably been the same as Endell Gesh's role in Newhaven. Did that mean the lord of Tryn was taking a demotion coming here? No matter. I wasn't going to concern myself with the politics of it all.

What I wouldn't give for my father to still be alive. He could fill in as captain of the guard instead. I was certain the king would have no problems with him. He always did the right thing, no matter how difficult.

"Jon, you may go."

I bowed to the king and hurried out of the keep, then I entered the apartments and walked up the stairs. I could hear chatter in the halls as I made it to the second floor. My peers were talking in the hallway. They quieted as I approached.

"Did you find out anything?" Michael asked.

"Everything's fine," I told everyone. "The king or Leon will make an announcement tomorrow."

I briskly entered my room. It looked as if many people had wanted to ask me something, but I didn't want to lie to them or break my promise to the king.

I knew my swift exit was rather mysterious, not on purpose of course, but still a little fun.

299

Michael followed me into my room. I could hear others still chatting in the hall and wondering what the announcement would be.

"You have to give me at least a little more than that," Michael said quietly.

"I can't."

"You can't or you won't?"

"I won't," I answered him honestly.

"All right fine, fine. You know we're getting our weekly stipends the day after tomorrow?"

"I certainly do." I actually had forgotten for a little while, but I was smiling now as he reminded me. "What are you going to do with it?" I asked.

"I have big plans, actually. I'm headed straight to the brothel. I'll go so many times they'll have to change my class."

I knew this had to be a jest. "Oh yeah?"

"Yeah. From wind mage to whoremaster."

His smile disappeared as someone made a comment from the hall.

"What?" he asked as he leaned out of my room.

I could hear someone asking him something. It sounded to be Eden.

"It was just a joke," he told her seriously.

I couldn't quite hear her response, but her tone was dismissive.

"Yes, it was," Michael confirmed.

"Suuuuuure!" she said sarcastically.

Michael left my room. I couldn't make out what he said to Eden, but there was no mistaking his teasing cadence, as it was one I had become very familiar with.

I went to my door to close it for the night, but I looked down the hall first. Most everyone was going toward their rooms as Eden argued that a brothel wouldn't even allow Michael to enter, while he argued that they would refuse his payment because it would be their honor to service him.

I went into my room and prepared for bed.

CHAPTER TWENTY-ONE

Leon was late to the courtyard the next morning. It didn't matter much to me because, as I'd said to Michael the night before, I knew everything was fine. Yes, the king had mentioned some dire news about Rohaer, but he had also told us earlier that we wouldn't be fighting in any battles for which we were ill-prepared. We would only engage in opportunistic fights, and I still believed that. We were valuable to him. He wouldn't risk our lives as he would easily the sell-swords at his disposal, who were paid only to fight and little more.

The meeting between him and Leon brightened my mood because I assumed Leon would finally be committed to actually teaching us something. It did concern me a little that he'd apparently been in the dungeon before all this began, but I wasn't going to let it bother me unless it became more relevant to us.

I could see that everyone else was nervous, however, as we kept to ourselves and practiced. There was nothing I could do about that.

I toyed with my mana as I used it to cast Expel hundreds of times. It was important to experiment when learning something new. Like with the sword, I used to think of new and creative ways to win a duel against my father. I'd tried tossing the sword up and catching it by its blade to attack with its hilt. I'd tried hiding my hand with my sleeve and using surprise attacks so he couldn't accurately defend himself. I'd even tried gripping it incorrectly, holding the sword down instead of up and swinging it backhanded with flicks of my wrist. Of course, none of these techniques worked, but they did help me become more comfortable with the weapon.

Dvinia seemed to be a weapon of its own. Once the spell was cast, I found that I could hold it in the air. It was about as difficult as holding something heavy completely still, but I knew it would get easier with time.

The fact that I could hold it brought up a few questions. After speaking with Michael a bit while we were practicing, I eventually figured out the difference between dvinia and wind.

When my mana formed Expel, I could still control my mana. The energy was difficult to see, a rippling translucent entity, similar in appearance to the camouflage illusion Eslenda had casted on herself, but it was there hovering in front of me. I could move it around the same way Kataleya had moved her sphere of water or Remi could move a ball of floating fire. Like the erto mages, I could hold the spell still with one part of my mind and push it forward with the other. It was like getting ready to snap my fingers. When I let go, it shot in the direction of my choosing too fast for me to see it move.

Apparently, wind did not behave in the same way, which I thought to be odd considering it was erto just like fire and water. Michael said he could not control the wind much after turning his mana into it. The force of his spell was determined by the effort he put into forming it. The same happened to my spell: I could tell the mana to leave my body with more or less force, but I could still grab hold of it after it left me. Michael claimed he couldn't really "grab" the wind at all.

I didn't want to insult Michael, but I had to suggest the possibility that given more practice, he might learn to control the wind after casting it.

"No," he said. "I've asked Leon about it. The spell Wind cannot be controlled after our mana is used."

"But isn't it strange that fire and water can?"

"They can't always," Michael corrected me. "It depends on the spell they're used for. Fire and Water can be controlled, but more complicated spells give the elements a mind of their own."

"So maybe there's a wind spell that will allow you to control it after you cast."

"I..." A thought stopped him. "Actually, you may be right."

Leon came out of the apartments. A hush fell over the courtyard as everyone stopped what they were doing. He walked toward the center. We all trailed after him like curious kittens following their mother.

I sensed movement and looked at the great hall. Grufaeragar was standing in the doorway, leaning against it as if bored. When Leon noticed the krepp, he grumbled something but did not let his gaze stay on the creature for long.

Leon turned and gestured for us to stop.

"Yesterday, I let my anger get the better of me," Leon told us.

No one gave a reply, but I could see in most of their

expressions that they appreciated the acknowledgement.

Not Reuben. "What is the agreement between you and the king?" he asked.

"Will you let that go so we can discuss more important things?"

"I won't," Reuben replied. "I demand to know—"

"You need to stop demanding things and start asking," Leon told him angrily. "You're not living in your father's estate anymore. We're not your servants."

A heavy silence followed.

Reuben had a loud breath. "*Please* tell me what the agreement is between you and the king."

"It's nothing. I agreed to help all of you. In exchange for that, I'm to receive a little payment and…" He halted for just a quick moment. "I will be free when this is done."

"Free?" Eden asked. "Free from what?"

"From not spending my life in the dungeon, all right? Now let's get on to important business."

"Wait," Eden said. "You were in the dungeon before this?"

"Yes, all right! Now what I'm going to tell you has nothing to do with me. Pay attention. There's a growing army of dark mages and armed commoners in Rohaer who seem intent on taking over Newhaven and possibly all of Lycast."

"Wait, wait, wait!" Eden interrupted again. "What did you do to be put in the dungeon?"

Leon was shaking his head. "Eden, be quiet. This is not a discussion about me. I'm talking about your lives here."

"I'm sorry," she said. "But I think we deserve to

know if our instructor is a criminal."

"The king decided not to tell you, and he's pretty much told you everything else so far. Now what does that say about this information?"

Eden didn't answer.

"Tell me!" Leon insisted.

"I guess that we don't need to know it."

"That is correct. I'm not a criminal anymore. That's all you need to know about me."

Reuben said, "But it doesn't sound like your sentence was completed."

Leon put his hands over his face as he groaned. "The next person who speaks is taking Grufaeragar around Newhaven to entertain him for the entire day!"

At hearing his name, the krepp started walking toward us.

"Humans do what?" he asked.

Leon cursed under his breath. "We are talking about our enemies, our *dishonorable* enemies. Would you like to listen quietly?"

The krepp strutted over and eventually stopped right beside me. He put his hand on my shoulder and pressed his claws into my skin. "I listen with humans!" he announced loudly and proudly.

I tried not to wince as I gave him a polite smile and stepped away. Grufaeragar had an odor to him as well. He smelled like dirt, like the earth, but pungent. I figured he hadn't taken a bath in a long time. Or maybe krepps never bathed.

"King Frederick Garlin in Rohaer is our enemy," Leon explained. "He's built an army out of dteria sorcerers, and now he's arming and training his peasants. Nykal had hoped Frederick's people would revolt against him. It is a mystery that they have not. Meanwhile, dteria continues to spread in Lycast."

"What is dteria?" Grufaeragar asked.

"Evil," Leon answered tersely. "Sorcerers with dishonor. They steal from anyone weaker than them."

"*Barshets*," Grufaeragar barked. I didn't know what it meant, but it sounded like it could be an insult. "You humans kill them?"

"That is why we train," Leon said.

"I understand now. I help you train!"

Leon's jaw tightened. "Today we're going to be training in a special way, though," he explained through gritted teeth. "We will not be fighting with swords but with our minds."

Leon tapped his head as he looked at the krepp. Grufaeragar's lizard face scrunched together in what looked to be confusion.

"Resistance," I realized.

Leon pointed at me. "Yes. We have to learn how to stand against a dark mage." Leon pulled a familiar metal box out of his pocket. It was the same box Greda had given me to block the effects of the essence of dteria the illusionist had tricked me into receiving. He opened the box.

Many of us quickly backed away. I assumed my peers felt the same thing I did, a magnet pulling my mana into an unnatural state.

"This essence is very strong," Leon said. "It'll probably take me a day to get my mana back to normal after using it, but this has to be done." He picked the essence out of the box and put the box back in his pocket. Then he closed his eyes as he cupped his hands around the essence.

He made a sinister face as he threw out his hand in Michael's direction. Michael screamed as he was picked up off the ground and hurled back about a yard. He landed on his rear end and rolled backward, his shirt riding up.

It startled Grufaeragar, who reached for his sword. Fortunately, it was not with him right now. I noticed the briefest smile on Leon's face, one of satisfaction.

"You could've given me some warning!" Michael complained as he got himself up.

Leon laughed. "Where's your sense of fun! Who's next?" Then a worried look crossed his face. He dropped the essence and walked away from it with his head down.

"Leon?" I called after him. "What is it?"

He pushed out his palm toward me. He kept his head down as he walked away from us.

Then he fell to a crouch. It almost looked like he was hurt.

Aliana started creeping toward him as if to help.

"Give me a moment!" he yelled with a strained voice, and she jumped back to where she had stood between Eden and Kataleya.

A long minute passed before he stood up and walked back to us. He looked down at the essence, just stared at it for a long time.

"If you can't control yourself," Reuben said, "you should not be conducting this resistance training."

"Then who the hell else is going to do it?"

Leon waited, but Reuben didn't give an answer.

"I can handle it just fine," Leon said. "Just give me another minute."

I asked, "Can someone please explain what's going

on?"

Kataleya spoke. "Dteria is an addictive magical art. Not only is it powerful, but it's easy to use. According to the legend, that's how it was designed."

"Kat, I don't think—" Eden began.

"Jon has never heard any of this, and I believe it to be true."

Leon walked away. He had his hands on his hips as he took deep breaths.

Eden sighed. "I guess we have time."

Kataleya turned to me. "Basael created our world and gave life to each demigod. In exchange for power and immortality, each demigod was required to give something back to the world of Imania. The more power they gave up, the more powerful the magical art they created.

"The first demigod who Basael gave life to was Valinox, the selfish firstborn son," she continued. "He created mtalia without giving up much power but would become jealous later when other demigods created magic that was much stronger and therefore gained more love from Basael. After Valinox, Basael gave life to Souriff."

"Souriff, yes," Grufaeragar interjected. "Souriff visit Hammashar."

The topic of mtalia reminded me of Charlie, who was the only one not present in the courtyard. I figured he was either learning how to craft something or actually crafting something right in this moment. After what he had done with the callrings, I was glad he was keeping himself busy.

"Yes," Kataleya agreed with the krepp. "Souriff was born much stronger than Valinox, but she gave up a large portion of her power to create dvinia. Basael was very pleased with Souriff's creation and sacrifice, but of course Valinox was jealous. The third demigod was Nijja, another powerful sister to Valinox. She created ordia to keep the incredibly powerful creatures that lived in Fyrren, the fae world, from killing each other. Basael was so pleased with Nijja that he let her rule Fyrren with ordia. It is such a strong magical art that it has seeped into our world over the many centuries that followed."

"The Cess believe that ordia has come into our world only after Basael died," Eden explained.

"And Formists believe Basael is still alive," Kataleya countered fiercely as if ready to argue.

I felt a little embarrassed that I was the focus of this lecture. All of this sounded familiar. I was certain the neighbors of my home in Bhode had told me these tales before, but when my father found out, he had disallowed them from filling my mind with such fantasies. I didn't know what I believed right now, but it didn't hurt to listen.

"Failina came after Nijja," Kataleya went on. "Each demigod who Basael gave life to was stronger than the last, and Failina was no exception. But like the other sisters before her, she gave up much of her power to create another powerful magical art, erto."

"All right," Leon said as he walked back to us. "I think I'm finally ready."

"I'm just about done," Kataleya pleaded. "Please, one minute?"

"Make it fast."

She looked at me. "The last demigod, you can probably guess."

"Dteria."

"Yes. Airinold came into this world stronger than any demigod before him. He saw how the others had given up much of their power and how pleased Basael was with their sacrifice. However, he decided to trick Basael. He sacrificed nearly all of his strength to create dteria. But he created it in a way that was different than the other magical arts. When anyone used dteria, their soul changed in a very, very small way." She pinched her fingers together. "But the more they used dteria, the more their soul was changed." She moved her hands apart and eventually spread her arms.

"The more dteria they used before they died," she said, "the greater portion of their soul would be returned to Airinold. So as you can see, he created dteria like an investment. Basael was pleased when he first saw dteria, but he changed his mind when he realized what was happening to those who used it. Dteria gives the caster a feeling of euphoric power and confidence. It makes them want to use it more and more, but the more they use it, the more they develop an immunity to its effects. It's a terrible addiction that can change not only someone's personality, but their soul as well. It must be stopped."

She went on, "Basael eventually figured this out. However, by then Airinold had become the most powerful demigod, and dteria was sweeping through Dorrinthal. Basael imprisoned Airinold as punishment and told the other demigods to do everything they could to stop the spread of dteria. While most of the demigods couldn't do much to help, it was Souriff who found the most success with her control over dvinia. It seemed to be a natural resistance to dteria. But everything changed after The Day of Death. Cess, like Eden and Leon, believe Basael died that day. As a Formist, I believe he ascended to the heavens but did lose much of his power."

Kataleya glanced at Eden. "I think everyone agrees as to what happened to Airinold afterward."

"Yes, Airinold broke out of the prison Basael had created for him," Eden said.

Kataleya continued, "Then, he waged war against all the other demigods. He was too strong by then. All the demigods went into hiding. Most people in Dorrinthal had been killed by the incredible explosion in Curdith Forest, but demigods managed to hide many of the good-natured people who had never accepted dteria.

"For many years, Airinold searched for the demigods. To aid him in his search, he transformed himself into Gourfist, an enormous flying creature. But the other demigods could change their appearances as well. They knew that Airinold would not be able to find them so long as they didn't use much of their power, because this was the only way he could sense them. Airinold, as Gourfist, would search for weeks straight. He would exhaust himself so greatly that he had to sleep for years to recover, because he could never die. This continued for centuries. He searched longer and slept even longer. Eventually, he lost his mind to the exhaustive search. Now Gourfist, the creature, has consumed Airinold. It continues to search for the demigods, sensing powerful sorcery, but it no longer understands why."

"I will say that Gourfist is real," Leon said with a nod of his head. "I have met a man who has seen him, a man I believe."

"Yes, sightings of Gourfist have been recorded in history," Kataleya agreed. "He seems to sleep in the center of Curdith Forest."

"So he's the cause of dteria in the forest?" I asked.

"There are many theories to that," Kataleya said. "Some believe he still has a hold over dteria, even though he doesn't have the mind to know what he's doing with it anymore. Others say that he's lost control of dteria but the dark magic still clings to him like a blind dog knows its master. Then there are people who say that one of the other demigods could now have control of dteria. Valinox, the firstborn son of Basael and the most jealous of all the demigods, seems the most likely to have taken control. But it's also safe to say that Souriff is doing everything she can to combat dteria. That is why there is natural dvinia in the forest, and more of it closer to the center. It's this natural dvinia that empowers our mana over time."

"Why don't the demigods kill Gourfist?" I asked.

"I imagine they separated from each other many years ago and they don't know where the others are. None of them are strong enough to kill Gourfist alone, and even using a portion of their power will allow Gourfist to sense them and kill them."

"What about Nijja?" I asked. "If she's the ruler of Fyrren, don't the other demigods know exactly where she is and can work with her?"

"Well," Kataleya said, "I think the entrance to the fae world is closely guarded by Gourfist for that very reason. It's probably near the center of the forest. Also, Valinox tried to enter Fyrren to escape Airinold when Airinold first transformed into Gourfist and started searching for everyone. But Nijja didn't allow Valinox

to stay."

"All right," Leon concluded. "Now we're moving *very* far from anything factual. The only thing all of you should take away from that story is the danger of dteria, which is certainly real. A little bit more about dteria that we *know* is this: The frequency of dteria is near the middle of the spectrum. Some of you with a high natural frequency, like Jon, will feel your mana being pulled to a lower vibration when you're close to someone who's powerful with dteria or who has an essence. The others of you with lower natural frequency, like Aliana, are going to feel your vibration of your mana increasing. The spell is this: Lower B, E min, F. It's a nasty chord that, once you understand mana better, you will realize how unnatural it is.

"The only reason I tell you the spell is so you can figure out for yourself if your mana is lower or higher so you know what to expect. You are never to cast that spell. I want all of you to agree right now. Say, 'If I cast this spell, I agree that Leon can burn me alive.'"

We all muttered the agreement tensely. I'm sure I wasn't the only one visualizing what Leon had described. Only Grufaeragar was quiet. I wasn't sure he was understanding any of this, but at least he didn't seem too bored.

"Dteria is strong, unfortunately," Leon said. "I demonstrated its power earlier with Michael, and I'm not even trained to use it. Now imagine what a powerful sorcerer could do after spending years of his or her life working on that skill."

I raised my hand.

"Yes?"

"The energy of dteria seems similar to dvinia."

"Yes, there are many similarities. Both dvinia and dteria can turn the caster's mana into a physical force. Both can be controlled. The most basic spell of dvinia, Expel, and the most basic spell of dteria, Dislodge, have almost the same effect, except dteria is a hell of a lot easier to use. Dteria is like dvinia with the power of ordia. It has many functions depending on how a spell is cast. Not only can Lower B, E min, and F dislodge someone, but the same chord can create curses. Think of an enchantment gone horribly wrong. It is a terrible, disgusting form of magic."

"Is it true that dteria and vtalia can be used by warlocks?" I asked, remembering what Reuben had said.

"Dteria can do many things. I'm not about to go through all of them."

I took that to mean warlocks really did exist.

"You're here today to learn how to resist dteria," Leon said. "As with most things, the more you deal with something—depending on your will—the better you will be at resisting it. This is also true of any magical art. Even if I burn your skin with fire, so long as it's fire created from mana and you have some control over your own mana, your mana will eventually learn to resist it. That's not to say I'm going to burn any of you. Fire does far too much damage for anyone to have hope of resisting it before it burns all their skin off, but dteria is obviously different.

"The more control you have over your mana, the easier it's going to be to resist anything. Our mana can act as an invisible shield. But keep in mind that it is very similar to a physical shield. If you're holding a metal barrier in front of you and I swing a hammer at that barrier, who do you think is going to have an easier time? Me swinging or you blocking?"

"You swinging," we echoed.

"Exactly, but now imagine I have a little dagger. I'm just going to waste my stamina trying to get through a strong shield, and it won't take much effort for you to hold it up. What I'm trying to say is that the difficulty in blocking a spell mostly has to do with the spell itself. But where this fails to work as an analogy is that you—through your mana—can become accustomed to blocking *specific* magical arts so that it's easier for you to resist them later. The great thing about resistance is that once you learn how to resist dteria, you can resist it in all forms, such as Dislodge, Curse, and even Drain Life, which, yes, Jon, does exist, but you really shouldn't worry about it. I've met one warlock in my life, and it was right before he was hanged. They are not as scary as you might think."

My face must've given my thoughts away earlier. I nodded.

"Now the actual act of resisting is going to take some practice," Leon asserted. "Think of it like absorbing a punch, but instead of flexing your muscles and bending your body, you're doing the same to your mana. Who wants to try first?"

I raised my hand.

CHAPTER TWENTY-TWO

Leon warned me, "Just because you can cast with dvinia doesn't mean you will resist dteria any easier than anyone else. What we create with our mana is different than what can be found naturally. Don't ask me how it's different, because no one knows. It's just—"

He whipped his hand at me, no doubt trying to catch me off guard. My reflexes kicked in. I steeled my mana, hardening it around my midsection where he seemed to be aiming. The dteria struck me nearly at the same time.

It felt like a large barrier of sorts, bigger than my chest, slamming into my torso. But unlike a punch or a slap, it kept pushing me up and away as it hit.

It all happened almost too fast to think. There was a brief moment of struggle as I pushed back with my own mana in a wrestling match that began and ended less than a breath apart. The momentum from the spell still had me searching for footing as I was pushed backward, even after it was over. I stumbled and waved my arms for balance, but then I came to a rest.

I wasn't exactly proud that I stayed on my feet because I had been mostly ready for the spell, and Leon had admitted that he wasn't as strong as a real dark mage. It was no wonder the arrogant ass who'd bumped into my shoulder had so much confidence. He probably *could* beat me in a fight. It was a disconcerting thought.

Now that I had at least partially resisted a spell, I realized that I had in fact somewhat resisted the wind spell Leon had casted a little while ago. I had tensed my mana when I'd braced for the impact. My reflexes seemed to know what to do, and that part I was proud of.

Leon glared, as if me staying on my feet was an insult. "You're lucky I'm not trying harder." Then he shook his head and held up his hand. "Wait, shut up."

He muttered to himself for a while. Then he let out a little shout and seemed more in control after. "Who's next?"

I was concerned, but Kataleya had mentioned that the more someone used dteria, the more dteria was required for them to feel euphoria. Hopefully, this would become easier for Leon soon.

"Wait, where's Spayker?" Leon asked in annoyance.

I found it odd and a little worrisome that he hadn't noticed Charlie missing until now.

"He's crafting something," Eden said.

"What is he making?"

"First he made some callrings. Now he's making trackers."

"Then he's a good lad. We'll leave him be. Eden, you're next."

"Um. All right…" she said nervously with a pinched expression.

Everyone moved away from her. There was no denying that it would be easier to throw a lighter person off her feet. Eden and Remi were the two smallest of the group, but Eden was an inch or two shorter. Not only that, the span of her shoulders was narrow and her arms were quite thin. Remi appeared to have more physical strength. I figured Leon would take it easy on Eden.

I was wrong. Letting out a sharp scream, Eden suddenly flew through the air.

Leon laughed like a madman, but he quickly cut himself short.

He cleared his throat. "Are you all right, Eden?"

"Yeah..." she grumbled as she got herself up, her dark hair a mess.

"You should go again," Leon said. "I hardly felt any resistance from you."

"Isn't it harder for enchanters?"

"Actually." He pointed at her with a flick of his wrist. "You're right. This horrible stuff is messing with my head. But you still should go again."

Why is it harder for enchanters? More importantly, how was Eden able to figure this out? I put my mind to the task as Leon tossed Eden backward a few more times.

The answer started to become clear to me later when I saw who had an easier time resisting and who didn't. Reuben struggled, like Eden, though he wasn't lifted off the ground nearly as far. Michael, when he was ready for the spell, managed to keep his feet planted as he slid backward, akin to what happened to me.

Remi was picked up off the ground, but she wasn't tossed far and didn't fall over like Reuben had when she landed. Considering she was much lighter than him, this was what really told me the answer I was looking for. Aliana's attempt at resistance confirmed it for me.

She was picked up and thrown quite far, but she had the agility and grace to land on her feet.

It seemed that our ability to resist depended on the strength of our mana. Sorcerers who weren't required to put so much force behind their spells had more trouble resisting, such as Reuben and Eden, who focused on ordia. Reuben had mentioned a while ago that he would be a harbinger, like Barrett. I took that to mean he would, or perhaps already did, know how to create binding contracts like the ones we'd signed to protect the king. I wondered how exactly he trained. I usually saw him keeping to himself in the courtyard, focused on his thoughts.

The other sorcerers, like Remi and Michael, who used a lot more force with their spells, had an easier time resisting. It seemed that the strength of someone's mana might be measured by their ability to resist. But there was more to it than that. There was technique, like wrestling. The more Leon cast dteria on me, the easier time I had resisting, even though my mana wasn't becoming stronger from one attempt to another.

We trained for hours. At one point, I asked Michael, "Are the effects of dteria reversible?"

"I believe so. Leon's natural mana will always go back to how it was, given time, and the effects of dteria on his mind shouldn't last more than a day, if he stops using it sooner rather than later."

"What about his soul?"

"Oh, I'm sure Leon's soul is doomed already anyway."

We chuckled without humor.

"No one can really answer that for sure," Michael

said. "It's pretty clear that he doesn't believe in it."

I agreed, though I worried for him as I watched him cast over and over.

Eventually Grufaeragar wanted to start participating. Even with him being as large as he was, he was thrown just as far as Eden was during her first few attempts.

It didn't take long to see that, unfortunately, the krepp didn't seem to have a way of improving his resistance. He was thrown the same distance every time. Leon explained to Grufaeragar that he probably didn't have mana, which was required to resist the spell. That seemed to piss off the krepp, who demanded that Leon continue to use the "human magic" against him until he learned how to defend against it.

For the better part of an hour, Leon tossed Grufaeragar away from him. Grufaeragar got up and walked back to his spot. Then Leon tossed him again. Leon didn't seem to have a reaction to the dteria anymore, or perhaps he was just growing too tired for it to show. His eyelids hung each time he blinked. He drew breath slow and deep. Nonetheless, he kept on throwing us. Fortunately, Grufaeragar soon stopped demanding to repeat his turn and seemed content to learn from the rest of us.

Eventually I was able to keep from even being pushed backward, but that changed when Leon started mixing up who he would target. He didn't announce it beforehand anymore, whipping the dark energy at us as we stood in a circle around him. I was taken off my feet not the first time, when I forced myself to be ready, but the second when he hadn't targeted me in a while and I wasn't as vigilant.

That led to a question. "Will we ever be better at

resisting when we're not ready for it?" I asked Leon.

"Yes, because you will master the techniques required to quickly resist as soon as the spell reaches you. It's just like feeling someone trying to trip or push you. After enough practices, your reflexes will improve even if you're not ready to defend yourself."

I changed my defensive strategy after that. I no longer prepared my mana to defend against the spell. I wanted to wait until he was casting at me to put up any defense, to better practice when I might be caught off guard.

The next few times I was targeted, I flew back at least a few feet. After the third one, Leon asked, "Why doesn't it seem like you're ready anymore?"

"Because I want to learn to defend without being ready."

"Fine."

He started targeting me much more frequently after that.

We trained for hours more. By the time we were called for lunch, I was able to resist his spell almost completely without being ready, but fatigue had clearly weakened him.

Charlie was already in the dining hall when we arrived. He was holding another set of rings, these painted dark blue.

I sat beside Michael. Charlie was across for me with Reuben at his side. As usual, the girls sat farther down the long table. I did not see the king, the princess, or the queen. I imagined the king was very busy today dealing with the removal of the captain of the guard. He could be meeting with Kataleya's father, though I hadn't seen anyone come in through the courtyard. Even the draw-

B.T. NARRO

bridge was closed. I wondered if there was another entrance into the castle, or if the king was out for the day.

"I finished the trackers." Charlie handed one dark ring to me.

"Shouldn't we ask Leon who should have the call rings and trackers?" I wondered.

"I want you to have one."

"Why?" I asked.

"Because I had you in mind when I made them."

That wasn't really an explanation. "You should at least ask Leon."

"I will later," he said, though I wasn't sure I believed him.

I supposed it was a little bit of an honor that Charlie thought of me over anyone else to keep the two helpful rings. But even if it upset Charlie, I would transfer them to someone else's hand if it made more sense at a later point.

"How does it work?" I asked as I held the ring up in front of my eye. It just looked like a normal ring.

"An ordia sorcerer needs to cast Identify on the ring. It's the same spell used to decipher the enchantment on any enchanted item. Once they identify it, it should give them a general sense and direction of the other piece of metal, which has been shaped into the other ring."

"Interesting."

"I know, right?"

It seemed like we would be practicing resistance the rest of the day, but there was something else I wanted to do. I finished my meal quickly and went to my room in the apartments while everyone else was still eating.

323

The spell for Heal was a simple one, just uF and F, and I already had uF mastered. I figured I should be able to learn the spell in a day or two, but only if I found time to put in the hours. I'd wanted to learn Water next because it seemed invaluable to be able to create one's own water, but the spell was much more complicated for me than Heal. And frankly, being able to heal at this stage in training seemed more important than being able to create water.

I put the vibmtaer on my bed and spread the color chart beside it. The entire bottom row of the chart consisted only of F's and B's, from uuB on the bottom left corner to llF on the bottom right. I hadn't looked at the color chart for a while. I wondered if it could be telling me anything about crafting other spells. Why else were F's and B's on the bottom row unless they went together in some way? I thought of Expel and checked the notes on the chart.

uF, uG, uuC, uuD. They were spread across three rows and three columns. Looking at the chart, it didn't seem like there were any similarities to them. I wish I knew at least a few other spells, but I hadn't yet bothered to ask any of my peers how they cast their erto spells. I hadn't wanted to overwhelm my mind. It had been difficult enough to cast a single spell.

Now I truly understood why having a wide range of mana made it difficult to memorize the complex feeling and casting of a spell. It was akin to memorizing a step-by-step routine and then having to learn another one on top of it.

I pushed out my mana that I knew by now was uF. The color on the vibmtaer was the same I'd seen many times before, a light purple-gray. Looking at the color chart, I saw that F one octave below uF was the same grayish purple color but a little darker.

I slowed the vibration of my mana until it reached that color. I found it much easier this time, partially because I had practiced changing the frequency of my mana for many, many hours, but also because F was closer to the middle of my range, where it didn't put such a strain on my mind.

I had to memorize the feeling of F, but I didn't want to forget how the higher frequencies felt as well, or I would lose my ability to cast Expel without practicing it again. So I toyed with my mana, shifting it higher and lower in frequency and then checking the vibmtaer only after I guessed it was at the right notes.

Every time I tried to reach the higher vibrations, I could do so. But when I tried to find F again, I quickly became lost.

I had secretly hoped I might be able to learn this quickly enough to finish before resistance training resumed. I knew it would impress not only Leon but everyone else as well, but I could tell now that it would take hours to memorize the feeling of F. And that was the easy part. Afterward, I had to find a way to cast F and uF at the same time. If I recalled correctly with dvinia, it had taken just as long to cast the four notes at the same time as it did to memorize the feeling of the four notes individually. Heal was very different, however. This spell only had two notes.

"What are you doing?" Callie asked from my doorway.

What are you doing? I wanted to ask in return. "Trying to learn something."

"Another spell?" she asked as she entered my room

without my invitation.

"Yes."

"How is it going?"

"I just started. It's going to take a while."

She glanced at the vibmtaer on my bed. Then she stiffly walked over to it, coming up to my side. She seemed incredibly interested in it, but I had a feeling she was just pretending as she thought of something to say.

She wore an elegant dress with long sleeves. She was a small girl with wavy hair that framed her young face. I figured she had to be cold, as there was a chill to the air these days, so I did not know why she didn't put on something heavier.

"How did you end up in the apartments?" I asked.

"I saw you enter. I wanted to see what you were doing. Do you need help with your spell? I could look for scrolls in our library."

That was right—she had brought me a scroll of dvinia I had forgotten about. It hadn't helped, but perhaps there was something there that could.

"Where's the library?" I asked.

She gave a tiny smile. "None of you are allowed in it, but I'm sure I could bring you something. It's not a big library. It's in the keep, near my room on the third floor...if you ever would like to call upon me." She batted her long eyelashes at me in a way that had to be practiced.

Even if she were closer to my age, this whole thing would still be terribly uncomfortable. I didn't appreciate being courted by someone who clearly was used to getting everything she wanted. I figured Kataleya must feel the same way when Reuben plainly showed interest in her with a strong waft of expectation attached to each interaction.

But Callie seemed to pick up on my reluctance. She stepped back. "As a friend, of course," she added.

"I do appreciate your friendship," I agreed.

Her smile seemed disingenuous. "Can I fetch something from the library for you? What spell are you working on?"

"Oh, I wouldn't want to take a princess away from her studies." My eyes went toward the door. "I'm sure there are many important things you are learning each day."

She made a noise that, shockingly, sounded to be a snort. "Right." She looked at me. "Oh, are you serious?"

Surprised by her reaction, I let out a small laugh. "I was."

"Jon, you must have no idea how boring my days are. In between my studies of math, geography, and writing, I have to learn all the history of each noble family. I'm lectured many hours of every day. There is very little time for me to learn what I actually want to learn."

"What's that?"

"Magic, of course. That's why I'm so interested in what you're doing. Oh, dear. I hope you didn't have the impression that I wanted to be courted by you?" She laughed snidely. "I said earlier I could marry *any* man I wanted so long as my father approved." She reached out and touched my arm. "I don't mean to offend, but you do not have wealth or land. I'm sorry. I hope I didn't hurt your feelings just now. We can be friends, yes?"

"Yes," I said with a smile. "We can be friends." I wasn't bothered by her statement, even if it was the truth.

"So you will call upon me one of these days?" she asked. "As a friend?"

"When I have some time off from training, I will." It was an empty promise, but what else could I say to her right now? "I do appreciate your offer to retrieve something from the library for me, but I have to return to training in the courtyard soon."

"At least tell me what you're working on so I can drop something off later."

I supposed I didn't see the harm if she was just going to be dropping off a scroll. I didn't imagine the king could really be angry for me trying to improve myself and taking up his daughter's unromantic offer to help.

"I'm interested in learning Heal, which Leon used on me the other day. I actually think I might be close, but if you find any scrolls about healing I would be happy to read them."

"Of course! I will look later. Now I should return to my *very important* studies." She gave a curtsy.

I bowed.

She ran to my doorway, but stopped to flash a smile over her shoulder. Then I heard her scamper down the hall.

I looked out my window down at the courtyard. Everyone had returned, Charlie included this time. They had begun without me, Leon tossing Charlie out of the circle and a few people chuckling at the surprised face he made as he landed on his ass, his mop of blonde hair bouncing.

I shut the door to my room. I was already pretty good at resisting dteria. I didn't think I was going to improve much more today from Leon's effort. Perhaps if a true dark mage was down there. I decided to give my-self at least an hour to see what progress I could make with the healing spell. Hopefully, Leon wouldn't mind.

CHAPTER TWENTY-THREE

I got a little too involved with trying to learn the spell. I kept telling myself just another half hour, then just one more after that half hour had passed. This had gone on four times now. I had challenged myself to change my mana into the note of F three times in a row without making a mistake. Unfortunately, I had been at it for the last two hours, and this was after I had already given myself two hours to get to this point.

Everyone was still in the courtyard. Even Grufaeragar remained part of the circle, though Leon rarely targeted him anymore as it seemed to be a waste of time. I hoped our training was showing the krepp that humans were honorable enough to trade with his kind. Just in case it was doing nothing, however, I wondered if I should challenge the krepp to a friendly duel at some point. I wanted to show him just how capable some of us were with the sword.

But after seeing how he had almost smashed Leon's head in, I was more than a little hesitant. I wasn't willing to bet my life on Grufaeragar understanding rules.

Someone slipped something under my door. Callie, I realized, as I noticed the scroll rolling back up. She must've flattened it to fit it in the small space under my door.

I stood still and held my breath.

"Jon?"

Damn.

"I'm here," I said.

She didn't reply. Would it be terribly rude if I didn't open the door?

Yes, unfortunately.

I picked up the scroll and opened the door. "Thank you," I said with a bow.

She curtsied.

I had my hand on the door as I looked at her. She still had on her ridiculously elegant dress with wide, flowing sleeves. It was probably difficult for her to do anything with her hands considering all the extra fabric around her wrists.

"I can stay and help if you have any questions after you read it," she suggested.

I cursed inwardly. I had stayed here too long. I was desperate to finish the challenge I had set for myself and return to the courtyard before Leon had a fit that I'd missed most of the afternoon and evening.

"I should be going back to the courtyard soon," I said.

"That's all right. I can help you until then."

She walked in and sat on my bed.

I let her be and took up the scroll, hoping it wouldn't be a complete waste of time.

"*Heal: F, uF.*

Vtalia, uF, is the basis of all spells of life. Healing is similar..."

I stopped myself as I realized that I couldn't trust any of this if I didn't know who had written it.

"What do you know about these scrolls in your father's library?" I asked the princess. "For example, do you know who made them?"

She shook her head. "They were here when we took the castle. Barrett looked over all of them and burned the ones that were inaccurate or had something about dteria. All the ones left can be trusted."

"How does Barrett know so much about magic?" I wondered.

The question stumped her. "I never asked," she said after a moment. "I'm not sure."

"What do you know about him?"

She laughed as she asked me, "Why are you so interested in him?"

I wouldn't tell her that I thought anyone at this point could be responsible for trying to corrupt me. Could even Callie be a suspect?

Now I really felt like I was overreaching. Nothing had happened in a while, and it didn't seem as if my life had ever really been in danger. Someone had tried to get me to accept an essence of dteria during a pivotal point of my training, but it wasn't as if I'd been attacked in my sleep or anything like that. Perhaps I should relax a little.

"I was just curious," I lied, then I continued reading.

"Healing is similar to using earth (llB). Healing relies on the use of octaves rather than a variety of notes to alter the energy of mana. By decreasing the vibration by half or doubling it, a healer relies on the power of mana alone to mend cuts and bruises. The force of the spell increases the healing, but a considerable amount of mana is required to heal even superficial wounds."

I stopped there. Of course. Why did I not remember

that an octave, like the difference between F and uF, was just twice the amount of vibrations? Other than that, they were the same. I handed the scroll to Callie.

"I need to try something."

I closed my eyes and readied F to be casted. That alone was a complicated process, but I had done it enough times for it to be second nature. My mana was an aura. I didn't grab all of it, only a small portion. My mana was normally uF, an octave above F. If I focused hard, I should be able to feel when a portion of my mana was vibrating in the same way as my natural mana, only at half the speed.

I fiddled with it for a little while as I strained my mind to feel for dissonance. It reminded me of how my father and I sometimes sang with a few musicians in my town. I wasn't very good, but I did have experience trying to match the sound of a single note with my voice. The closer I was, the more tension I felt, until suddenly it matched and the tension was gone.

There it was, F. I felt a tingle down my back. I was certain I had it when I felt the tension disappear between it and my natural mana of uF.

I knew how to find it now. It was different than memorizing the other notes, which all felt subtly different but also similar in that they were all strange. This one was almost my natural mana. The only difference was that it was lower. When I was close, there was a great tension. It was an easy sign to look for when finding F over and over again.

I was certain I had it as I casted it a few times in front of me. I didn't have to check the vibmtaer, but I did anyway as I pushed out my hand toward where it sat on my bed, near the princess.

Callie looked with me. Then she checked the color chart. "You got it!"

"Yeah, I figured it out now," I said with a triumphant smile.

She jumped off the bed. "Because of the scroll I brought?"

"Yes. That helped a lot."

"I'm so glad!" She hugged the base of my torso, pressing her cheek against my shoulder.

I put one arm around her in my attempt to politely return the embrace without encouraging her. Soon it was over and she went back to sitting on my bed.

I heard footsteps coming soon after I resumed practicing. Aliana appeared in the doorway. She looked upset at the sight of the princess on my bed. "Jon," she scolded, "you haven't been in the courtyard for a while. What are you doing?"

Yet again she chose to assume the worst of me. Her dark eyes, her lush hair, and the subtle curve of her jawline were put together in a way that was always striking—beautiful when she showed warmth or agonizing when she twisted her features into the cold expressions that seemed to be only reserved for me. I didn't understand why I had to deal with this side of her. I had little patience for it anymore.

She had taken off her coat and now wore a white shirt, her hairline a little damp from the effort of her training. She had slender, delicate shoulders with a prominent collarbone displayed where her tunic was open at the top. A line of cleavage found its way up past Aliana's shirt even though the linen rose up quite high on her chest. I knew she was beautiful, but I just couldn't see it right now.

"I figured this would be a good time to learn Heal," I explained as I politely contained my frustration in front of Callie. "The princess saw me entering the apartments earlier and decided to bring me a scroll to help."

Callie climbed down from my bed. She walked over to Aliana and curtsied. "I don't believe we've met. I am Princess Callie Lennox. You are Aliana Forrester, right?"

"I am." Aliana curtsied elegantly and confidently. "It's a pleasure to meet you, princess. I have seen you many times at the dining hall, but I have been too intimidated to introduce myself. I'm glad for this opportunity to finally meet."

Her words were so perfect I wondered if they had been rehearsed. She could've seen the princess enter the apartments and prepared something.

Callie beamed with a huge smile. "Oh, you don't need to be scared." She took Aliana's hand. "You are so pretty, by the way!"

Aliana's cheeks blushed a bit. "That is very kind of you to say, princess, especially coming from a young woman incredibly beautiful as yourself. I'm sure you have many suitors already. May I ask how old you are?"

Aliana's tone was so convincing that I had to look at Callie again. She was a cute girl, but it was her dress that seemed incredibly beautiful to me. I figured Aliana was just trying to get in the princess's good graces, which I had earned undeservedly and didn't feel the least bit right about it.

"I'm going to be fifteen soon. Yes, I do have many, but I don't like any of them," she said. "I must be going. I was just trying to help Jon in the little spare time I had." She walked past Aliana as Aliana curtsied, but the princess stopped in the hall and turned around. "I will speak to my father about allowing all of you access to the library. I think it is past time. Don't you agree?"

"That would be very helpful," Aliana said. "It was so nice to meet you, finally."

"It was my pleasure!"

She walked off. Aliana watched her go, then she turned and raised an eyebrow at me.

"What are you doing with the princess in your room?" she asked with heavy judgement.

I wasn't sure I would be able to keep my emotions under control much longer. Hadn't she just heard the reason?

"I would never do anything," I told her firmly. "She sometimes shows up without invitation like she did earlier, but I'm respectful with her and never lead her on."

"Is that *really* the truth?" Aliana asked incredulously. "I can never tell when you're lying."

"What did I do for you to speak to me like this?" I answered with anger coloring my tone. "I have been nothing but respectful toward you and the other women here. If you don't trust me, feel free to leave me alone from now on!"

Aliana looked shocked for a long while. Then her shoulders started to relax as she let her head down.

It was not the reaction I expected. "What are you doing?" I snarled, almost hoping she would yell at me so I could yell back.

"I think I'm realizing something," she told me nervously. "I'm sorry. Do you mind if I close this?" She took hold of the door and glanced at me.

"Uh, all right," I muttered, a little surprised.

She closed it and then turned around. She interlocked her fingers as she looked up me. "I think my distrust might be my fault."

I folded my arms. "That's a good start."

"All right, it *is* my fault," she corrected. "I'm sorry, Jon. It's obvious now that you weren't ever flirting with me. It's also clear that you were practicing just now before I showed up, not acting inappropriately." She paused, a twinkle in her eyes. "I actually really admire your dedication to improve."

I felt a great weight lift off my shoulders, my anger draining.

"I hope you'll forgive me," she said.

"I forgive you," I said somewhat indifferently, still not quite trusting.

She showed me a nervous smile. "Can we maybe start again?"

"I'd like that," I said, my tone a touch friendlier.

She offered her hand. "That's kind of you."

I shook it as she melted more of my anger away with a charming smile.

I was going to ask why she had acted this way toward me, but it didn't seem like the best way to start over. Besides, there was something else I wanted to know more.

"Is Leon angry I haven't been there?" I asked.

"No, I'm not sure he even noticed. I'm worried about what the dteria is doing to him."

I nodded. "I wish there was a better way to learn how to resist."

"And I wish I was as good as you are. How is it that you are so good at everything?" Her compliment felt forced. She probably just wanted to resolve the last of the tension between us.

"I'm just good with sword and bow. That's all. My father taught me most of my life, so it would be a little embarrassing if I wasn't."

"Your father's still in Bhode?"

"He passed, unfortunately."

"Oh, I'm sorry. Was it a while ago?"

I took in a shaky breath as I remembered him collapsing. Damn, now my eyes were watering. I wished she hadn't asked.

"Just a year ago," I managed to get out.

"I'm sorry," she said gently.

I blinked back tears and cleared my throat to compose myself. "It's fine. What about your family?" I asked to move the conversation away from me.

"I never knew my father, actually. My mother raised me."

"I see."

The conversation came to a rest. I hoped she would leave now. I was eager to get back to learning Heal.

"You know, Eden has a theory about all of this...I'm not sure if you're in the mood to hear it, though," Aliana said.

"A theory about what?" I asked hesitantly.

"About why we were chosen."

"Oh. I do want to hear that," I told her in all honesty.

"She assumes that, except for Kataleya and Reuben, all of us were desperate for a new life. Could it be...that you were as well?" Aliana asked cautiously.

"Definitely," I said confidently to let her know she shouldn't worry about offending me because of my past. "Michael and I have talked about this, actually. He suggested the king wanted us because we would be cheap, but I could see how it might be because we needed a new life."

Aliana looked at the door as if to ensure it was fully closed. She leaned toward me slightly.

"I don't know if the king would want us talking about this, but even Kataleya agrees with Eden. It seems like he has more plans for us than he's letting us know. There are four boys and four girls. None of us are married or even in a relationship, unless you...?"

"I'm not," I told her.

"We're all around the same age," Aliana continued. "And most of us are desperate not only to learn magic but to earn coin as well. I'm sure there are other people in Lycast who are stronger with earth than I am, but they probably don't have a life that could be disrupted like mine could."

Everything she was saying made a scary amount of sense. I had trusted that the king was not hiding anything from us anymore, but that seemed to be wrong. I had thought boys and girls of our age were probably just starting to develop their mana, so it was a likely coincidence that we were all close to each other in age. I supposed I figured it was also a coincidence that there were four of each gender. All wrong.

"I'm starting to agree with this theory," I said.

"Yeah, I can't stop thinking about it now. Kataleya believes the king is trying to create a dynasty of powerful sorcerers who will remain loyal to him no matter what he can pay us."

Although this made sense, something had to be said. "Even if that's true, everything he's done for us has been with a good heart."

She nodded enthusiastically. "Of course. I'm not

saying we have anything against the king, even if all of this is true. In fact, I'm extremely thankful for the opportunity he gave me. I wouldn't do anything to jeopardize it, and I would protect him as best I could no matter what we find out."

"I completely agree."

"So if this theory is right, then his tactic is working very well," she said with a light laugh.

I forced a smile, but I was more interested in something else she had mentioned. She had implied that she was one of the people desperate for a new life as well. So she wasn't rich.

"Do you mind telling me what you were doing before this?" I asked.

She lost her smile. "I, uh, was in a difficult situation."

"Do you want to talk about it?"

"Perhaps I should." Aliana looked tired as she walked over to my bed as if to sit on it, but she stopped short as she glanced around my room.

I brought over the one chair available from my desk.

"Thank you," she said as she took the chair.

I nodded as I sat on the bed and faced her. I was a little surprised she had chosen to remain in my room with the door closed, but I wasn't going to ask her to leave. Her past intrigued me. It might explain some of her behavior.

"My mother was a healer and midwife with no magical ability," she said. "I helped her when I was old enough. We worked out of our home." Her eyes took on a distant look. "But not too long ago, our house was set on fire by someone during the night."

"Do you know who?" I asked.

She shook her head. "I think it was one of the men who made romantic appeals to my mother. She never took another husband even though she is beautiful and had many suitors."

I was glad Aliana hadn't said her mother *was* beautiful. She was still alive.

"She kept many things from me, especially about my father. Yet there were some things she couldn't keep from me as I got older. One lie I eventually figured out was that she couldn't possibly be paying my tutor for all these years. Someone else had to be helping her financially. Eventually I got her to admit it was my father, a man she's refused to tell me anything about."

"You think he's someone well-known?" It was the only explanation I could think of as to why he wouldn't want Aliana to know who he was while he still assisted her financially. She could hurt his reputation.

"I do. I think Barrett knows him as well because Barrett recruited me recently, and I had never met the councilman before then."

"And still your mother doesn't tell you anything?"

"She says it's better if I don't know."

"Better for whom?"

"Exactly," Aliana said, picking up on my meaning. "I am glad to have him as my father, though, even if he's ashamed of me. He's helped me and my mother through some hardship."

"Like after the fire?" I asked.

She shook her head. "Not so much then. I wanted my father to look into who did it and punish the culprit. My mother and I almost didn't make it out in time." She spoke softly as she watched the fire in the hearth. "I still feel nervous around Remi when I see her practicing."

I didn't know what to say.

Aliana looked into my eyes and seemed more herself again. "My mother told me my father had done enough for us already. He wasn't going to have the crime investigated. I tried going to the guards about it, but no one seemed interested in trying to find out who burned down my home. It was probably too small for anyone to care."

"I'm so sorry, Ali. How long ago was this?"

"A year ago, maybe." Her eyes took on the same distant look for a long while. A moment of fear spread across her face. "We couldn't get out through the front because the door was on fire. Someone wanted us to die in there." She shook her head and looked at me. "I try not to think about it."

It sounded terrifying.

"We lost everything in the fire," she continued. "Even our coin we had stored under the mattress. I hoped my father would finally reveal himself and take us in, but he only gave my mother enough money for us to rent a room at an inn. We had to find work quickly. I beca..." She stammered. "I worked as a serving girl at Red's Tavern for a long time. It was the only job I could find."

"There's no shame in that."

"I know," she told the ground as she tugged the top of her shirt higher on her chest, only for it to slide back to where it had been. "But it isn't something I'm ever going to do again."

"Did something happen?" I asked hesitantly.

"Nothing the guards would do anything about.

Let's just say I dealt with a lot of harassment by not just the patrons but the other workers as well." Her eyes glistened. "No one was on my side. No one."

She wouldn't look up. So I was right earlier that she had dealt with many men making advances, but it sounded much worse than I had imagined.

It frustrated me that not even the other workers helped her. The owner especially should've done something.

"No one should have to go through that. Ali, I'm sorry."

"Many of these men were twice my age and grabby when they drank." Her tone was of anger, but then her expression showed utter defeat as she let out her breath. "I guess I just have to work out some of this."

I stood from the bed. "You shouldn't have to. None of what happened is your fault."

"And it isn't yours, either." She stood and looked strong and sure of herself, a different woman from just a moment ago. "I really am sorry, Jon. I know you're not any of these men."

"I forgive you, of course."

We shared a long hug.

"I'm glad I was able to tell you," she said.

"I am as well."

She wiped her eyes quickly. "It's about time for supper. I'm just going to grab something from my room. Do you want to return to the courtyard with me?"

"You go ahead," I said, as much as I wanted to walk with her. "I'm onto something with this spell." I picked up the scroll Callie had given me.

"I bet you would train every hour of every day if you could," she said.

"Most definitely."

"Well then, I really feel bad asking, but I was hoping we might go into the forest another day." Aliana put up her hands. "Only if you have some time and you think it would be safe."

I thought about it for a bit. It would be wise to return given how much stronger I'd felt after the last trip. Surprisingly, I had no residual fear from the cantar encounter. I just didn't want to ever see another one, if I could help it.

"We can do that," I said. "But I'm hoping to learn Heal first so I could work on it during our time in the forest."

"Right. I'll leave you to it."

"Thank you."

She opened the door to my room, turned and grinned, then closed the door after herself. I heard her opening the door to her room, but soon after she was closing it and running down the hall toward the stairs. I watched from my window as she left the apartments and rejoined the circle of our peers around Leon. She wore a tunic over her shirt, reminding me to put on something heavier when I was finally done here. It was going to be a cold night, but for once, my heart was finally warm after an interaction with Aliana.

Grufaeragar had left, most likely to entertain himself in some other way. I wondered how much longer he would be staying. And where was the king? Was he even here in the castle today? I should've asked Callie. I was always so eager to convince her to leave that I never took the time to think about how valuable she could be. She *had* given me this scroll. I was sure there was much more she could do.

The thought made me feel a little icky. First and foremost, I had to make sure I never took advantage of her friendship. It would only be if she wanted to help.

There was much more to the scroll. I continued reading where I'd left off.

"By decreasing the vibration by half or doubling it, a healer relies on the power of mana alone to mend cuts and bruises. The force of the spell increases the healing, but a considerable amount of mana is required to heal even superficial wounds. The healing can be exponentially amplified by adding a third note to the spell. The most obvious choice is lF. It is also the safest choice, but there hasn't been a recorded sorcerer who has been able to cast the chord lF, F, uF. It is too wide a range for most."

My heart skipped in my chest. The lowest note I could reach was lC, *below* lF. That meant it was possible for me to cast a healing spell using the three different octaves of F. If this author was correct, then I might be looking at the ability to heal grave wounds. I kept reading.

"Sorcerers have tested an attempt to heal a cut by casting lF, F. However, the resulting spell is completely ineffective. It is through such tests that sorcerers have discovered that uF is the basis for all vtalia spells, not F or lF. It is from this conclusion that comes the theory that all types of life-giving spells require uF, an unfortunately high frequency that is difficult if not impossible for most sorcerers to reach.

"A warning: Do not attempt to conduct your own experiments with uF and other notes. Especially be cautious when casting with uF and F at the same time. Just as multiple notes exponentially amplify the effect of the energy of mana, they will also exponentially amplify an errant spell that might be detrimental to your health."

I cursed. It reminded me of the warning Leon had given us about using revs. How sad would it be if I snuck off to learn a spell on my own and they found me dead in my room the next day? Not only sad, incredibly embarrassing.

I felt like this scroll had given me my first real lesson in sorcery. I longed to speak to the author. He sounded like a much better instructor than Leon. Why couldn't the king have found someone like the author of this scroll to instruct us?

I stopped myself right there. This kind of thinking was a magnet for negativity. It was important to be grateful for what I had, not to long for what I didn't have. I was lucky to be here, and I did appreciate Leon for what he could do for us. How could I not when he was suffering through the effects of dteria just to help us train? Perhaps I hadn't given him enough credit until now.

I checked on everyone in the courtyard. They were gone. There was still plenty of daylight left. Could they have gone to supper early?

I wished I had more time to at least attempt Heal a few times now that I could reliably change my mana into the note of F. It would still be hours, most likely, before I could even cast the spell one time effectively. Maybe I could practice after I ate if I hurried.

I put on one of my new woolen shirts with long sleeves, amazed it did not itch. I really enjoyed living in a city where I could purchase quality clothing like this. Our weekly stipend was coming tomorrow. Even though I didn't think I needed anymore clothing right now, it sure would be good to have more money.

CHAPTER TWENTY-FOUR

Leon started shouting at me as soon as I walked into the dining hall. "Jon! Get over here."

I figured he would calm down after an explanation. I left the last plate on the table near the door for now and jogged over to him as he sat alone in his usual, sad corner.

"The hell were you?"

"I'm sorry. I went—"

"Are you actually sorry?"

I thought for a moment. "No."

"Then don't apologize. Tell me like a man. Are you chasing the king's daughter around the castle?"

"No! Oh god, no!" I was horrified Leon had assumed this. Did that mean others assumed it as well?

"So you realize how inappropriate that would be?"

"Yes, a thousand times yes."

"I'm glad to hear you say that. Because everybody saw her coming out of the apartments, twice. I know you were in there."

"I wasn't trying to hide where I was."

"Then what the hell were you doing?"

"I should've asked first, and for that I am actually sorry. I ate lunch quickly to give myself time to practice the healing spell you used, but I got a little too—"

"Ohhh," he interrupted. "All right, I understand."

"You don't need me to explain?"

He stuffed his mouth as he answered. "I know you, Jon. You don't need to explain when you're working on a new spell. Just tell me beforehand next time."

"Thank you."

"And eat quickly," he said as I was leaving. "We're going to spend the night in the forest. We have to arrive before sundown."

"Did Aliana request that?"

"What?"

"Never mind." I guessed it was a coincidence that she'd mentioned going into the forest earlier.

I grabbed my plate and sat beside Michael. It seemed that we each had our own spots now, with Charlie across from me and Reuben beside him. I was glad for it. I appreciated routine. It helped me focus on the things that actually mattered.

Michael bombarded me with questions about where I was and what I was doing with the princess. I gave him the same answers I had Leon, with the same horror about his assumptions. Next time I would be very clear beforehand that I was going to my room to practice.

"How close are you to being able to heal me...if I fall down and hurt meself?" Michael asked, his tone imitating a toddler.

"I think I should be able to tomorrow if the forest will help me progress as much as it did the last time I was there."

"The last time you went so deep you almost got yourself killed," he retorted. "I wouldn't expect us to be walking that far."

"You never know with Leon."

"True," Michael answered.

"But I'm glad he's putting so much effort into this now. I don't think many other instructors would poison themselves with dteria just to help us learn to resist."

Charlie seemed stunned as he looked up from his plate at me. "You're right! Does that mean Leon is actually a good instructor?"

"No. It's the least he can do," Reuben replied. "After nearly starting a war with the krepps."

"You've got a point," Michael agreed.

"Do you know where the king went?" I asked Reuben. Just the princess and the queen were at the royal table, the king's empty seat between them.

"The king's business is not yours," Reuben lectured me.

"It is if he could be in danger," I replied. "Remember the contract."

"I wouldn't forget something like that." Reuben sounded insulted.

"I'll take that to mean you don't know where the king is."

"Here's an idea." He folded his arms and leaned on the table. "Why don't you go over to the queen and ask her where he is? Or better yet, ask the princess. You've been spending an inappropriate amount of time with her already. A little question isn't going to make it worse."

"All right, I got the point," I said, not wanting to argue.

Hell, did *everyone* think I had been spending an inappropriate amount of time with the princess? Perhaps I would be better off telling her to leave me alone the next time she showed up at my room, but I wasn't sure I had the stomach for that.

"What…?" Michael noticed something toward the entrance to the dining hall.

One of the guards who usually stood outside the castle was walking over to speak with Leon. He handed Leon something, possibly a letter, and said a few words. We were too far away to hear.

Leon looked at the letter for just a moment before he bolted out of his chair.

"That's not good," Michael said.

Leon started toward our table near the center of the dining hall.

"Better finish up quickly," Michael advised. "Looks like something's about to happen."

But I lost my appetite as I saw Leon's expression. I wasn't sure I had ever seen him this worried, even after I had returned from the forest with blood on my clothes.

"Ladies, bring your food over here," Leon said, "and hurry up about it."

The girls picked up their plates and moved down to us.

"Eat while I talk. There isn't a lot of time," Leon said. "I have to figure out which of you I'm going to send to Koluk."

Everyone suddenly looked down at their plates, hoping not to be noticed.

My father had told me a little about Koluk. It was a haven for criminals. There was no wall around the city, and it was close to the northern side of Curdith Forest.

A murderer could flee from another town and hide in Koluk for years.

"What's going on?" Reuben asked.

Leon shook the small note in his hand. "A friend needs help."

"You have a friend?" Michael teased.

"Shut up. I don't imagine any of you city daisies know how to ride a horse except Reuben and Kataleya. Am I right?" He seemed to be asking Kataleya.

"I do," she said.

"So do I," Reuben confirmed.

"Who else?"

I sighed. "I do as well."

Many people ate with their heads down. Leon waited for others to answer. I figured they all had too much honor to withhold the truth about something that seemed important. Still, I was a little surprised that so few of my peers knew how to ride a horse.

They had all grown up in Newhaven, I reminded myself. There was no need for them to learn. But more than that, many of them never had the money for a horse.

"Yes, this might work with just the three of you, if Jon's going," Leon said.

I could feel Reuben's jealousy as he scoffed.

"Have any of you been to Koluk before?" Leon asked.

"Once," Kataleya said.

"When? Would you be recognized by anyone if you go at night?"

"It was a few years ago. I don't think I would be."

"This will work after all." Leon sounded a little relieved. "All the three of you have to do is find a way into the city without being seen. Wanted men do it all the time. It isn't hard. Leave your horses in the forest when you're close and walk the rest of the way. Go to the Groovewater Tavern. You know where it is, Kataleya?"

She gave a nervous laugh as if overwhelmed. "I don't have a clue!"

Leon groaned. "I will draw you a map before you leave."

"Aren't you coming with us?" Reuben asked.

"No, I might be recognized."

"What's the harm in that?" Reuben asked. "You haven't explained anything."

Leon made a fist in his hair and pulled. "This dteria is messing everything up. What have I said so far?"

"Just to go to Groovewater Tavern without being seen," I reiterated. "Why are we going?"

"There is a woman there who needs our help. She has been fighting against corruption in Koluk for many years because the lord of the city is useless. *More* than useless. He's probably working against us. Cason Clay is the man really in charge, a dteria spreader who has come out of hiding because he's no longer scared of capture. Most guards in Koluk just watch over the people in the most cursory ways, like arresting obvious criminals to keep some semblance of peace, or putting on a show of searching for others. They take coin from wherever they can get it, sometimes from innocent people. Other times they're expected to be paid by the citizens for a service. Some have retired, while others have quietly joined Cason. There aren't many others."

I wondered why the king hadn't done anything about this. It couldn't be that he didn't care. It seemed more likely that there wasn't much he could do. It wasn't like he could burn the city to the ground, but didn't he have troops to take control of this city? Perhaps he did, but it would fall into anarchy afterward. No matter what the answer was, it seemed like a difficult place for the people who lived there.

"This shouldn't be dangerous," Leon said. "I trust that my friend wouldn't invite you into a situation where you're likely to get caught. Just don't be stupid about it."

"What would happen if we were caught?" Reuben asked.

"If Cason's men find out you're trying to aid someone who's spying on him, then you're likely to be tortured."

"What?" Reuben stopped eating. He looked around as if hoping someone else would speak up, but we all waited for him to continue. "Shouldn't you send word to the king about this before we commit to anything?"

Leon's lips went white as he pressed them together. "I will leave a message for when the king returns. He will know where all of you are going and what you'll be doing. I'm taking the rest of you into the forest. We are still going to spend the night there. All of us will meet back here in the morning."

"I think I should stay in the castle," Charlie said. "I've already mastered mtalia. Time in the forest will do me no good."

"You can remain here, Spayker."

Kataleya asked, "Why was a letter delivered from your friend if she needs our help? Why didn't she just come here?"

"Kataleya, I expect more from you. She obviously cannot come herself because she's involved in something."

Kataleya's mouth twisted. "I don't know how I'm expected to know that. You still haven't told us much."

"Because I keep getting interrupted!"

Kataleya looked as if she was holding in words.

Leon put down his head and shook it. "Forgive me. The dteria..." He had a breath. "All I can think about is throwing this damn table across the room. What questions do you have?"

I asked, "What does your friend look like so we can find her?"

"I don't know. I haven't seen Jennava in a long time. Just go to the basement of the Groovewater Tavern. She will be hidden somewhere in the cellar throughout the night. The time you arrive doesn't matter, but try to be there just after nightfall. The passcode is 'white willow.' Say it once you are there and she will show herself. I have no way of getting a message back to her. Apparently, a dirty child was the one who delivered the letter to one of the guards outside. I imagine Jennava and a few others are probably on someone's list and could only send an unsuspected boy. Bring your swords, conceal them in a cloak. Kataleya, you're taking a dagger, but none of you should be seen on the street with visible weapons, not in Newhaven or Koluk."

Leon held his hand over his forehead as if he had a sharp pain there. "What else? Oh, try to convince her to return with you. We want her here, trust me. Go get ready to leave. If I think of something else, I'll tell you."

"The map," Kataleya said as we stood.

"Right." Leon rushed over to the royal table, most likely to request parchment and ink.

Everyone stood. There was still food on many

plates.

"I guess we'll see all of you tomorrow," I said.

It was a tense goodbye as many of us shared looks and a few words. I really hoped Leon was right that this wasn't a dangerous task.

I went back to the apartments with Kataleya and Reuben.

"I really don't know Koluk very well," Kataleya said as we walked. "The map needs to be clear or we'll never find the tavern."

A strong gust of wind caused all of us to hunch our shoulders. Gray clouds hovered ominously in the sky.

We each went to our own rooms to don our cloaks, and Reuben and I our swords. Soon we were meeting back in the hall.

"How well do you know how to ride?" Reuben asked me. He seemed more worried than trying to insinuate anything.

"Very well," I told him.

"Good."

We met Leon in the courtyard. He handed Kataleya a paper. I looked over her shoulder as Leon explained how to get to the tavern. It was close to the southeastern side of the city, the direction we would be coming from, surely planned by this woman to make it easier for us to arrive safely. All in all, it didn't seem too dangerous. We were just sneaking into a city that was easy to sneak into and speaking with a woman. It was what happened afterward that might prove risky.

"Don't do anything stupid," Leon repeated when it was time to leave. "Just listen to what Jennava tells you, and do it. I would trust her with my life, so you can too. Three horses are waiting for you outside the castle. If a decision needs to be made, Jon you're in charge."

"Why him?" Reuben asked.

"Because unlike you, he'll actually listen to other opinions."

Reuben didn't argue against that.

Leon handed Kataleya a dagger.

"I have nowhere to put it," she said nervously.

As he took off his belt, Leon grumbled something about how Kataleya really should've purchased a holster earlier. "Let's hope this fits you." He took the dagger back from her hand so she would have both free.

Kataleya secured Leon's belt around her narrow waist using the last punch hole. There was a small sheath for the dagger on her left hip.

"Shouldn't it be on the other side?" she asked as she gestured at it.

"You reach across and pull out the dagger by the handle. That way it will be in your right hand at the correct angle. Airinold's taint, you've never even used a dagger before?"

She shook her head.

"Tell me you can at least cast Fire? It's only one note lower at the third."

"I know," Kataleya said. "But I haven't practiced it."

"God, all right." He crouched down a little to meet her eye level. "Just..." He couldn't seem to find the right words. "Just stay back if something happens."

"I can fight," she said proudly.

"You just said you can't."

"With Water."

He straightened his back. "We're practicing Fire as soon as you get back."

Kataleya didn't appear pleased about that.

*****

There was maybe an hour of daylight left by the time we were trotting through Newhaven. Any three people going through the capital on horseback would draw many looks, but it seemed to be especially true for the three of us. I assumed because of our ages.

I let Reuben take the lead. I was still learning my way around the city. This would be the first time I'd left Newhaven since arriving about a week ago. It was just starting to feel like my home.

I was warm enough in my cloak, but I was stronger than most men. Reuben was tall as well, with some girth to his arms and body. Kataleya was much smaller, her shoulders hunched.

By the time Newhaven's wall was behind us, Kataleya looked as if she was holding back shivers. Her wavy blonde hair was tied in a tail behind her. I tried to get a read on her emotions, wondering how much I might need to assist her if a fight did break out.

She caught me staring and lifted her eyebrows at me. I thought of a question that had been bugging me a little.

"Isn't it strange that Leon said he hasn't seen this woman in so long that he can't even describe her anymore?"

"Very," she said.

"I mean how old can Leon be?" I wondered.

Reuben was riding ahead of us. He looked back. "He's probably been blessed with life. You should be, too. You don't even know it, do you?"

In the back of my mind, I had wondered about that

many times after Leon and Barrett had tested my range of mana. They'd claimed that I was stronger and didn't have to eat as much because of my natural affinity with uF. Barrett had even said that I may live longer. Leon had replied that it was a curse. I might've been engrossed in finding out more if Barrett hadn't said there was little science behind it.

"You're talking about the effects of uF on me," I said to Reuben.

"So you do know something."

"Barrett brought it up when I was first tested, but he made it sound as if there were only theories about how it worked."

"Theories or facts, I don't know," Rueben said, "but I will say this. I bet Leon is decades older than he looks. That explains why he's so strong when he doesn't appear a year over thirty. I've recently asked my father to find out what he can about a sorcerer with Leon's name and description, a sorcerer having been arrested by the late king. I expect us to find out more shortly."

Reuben was prying into business that wasn't his own, but I was too curious to try to talk him out of it. Not that I could.

"So you're saying I'm going to live longer?" I asked, sloppily changing the subject back to myself. I wouldn't take anything Reuben said as fact, as I doubted he knew more than Barrett, but it would still be interesting to hear his opinion.

"You could, I suppose" was all he said before falling silent.

Kataleya shrugged when I glanced at her. "I don't know much about uF, either. It's rare for sorcerers to reach it with their mana and even more rare for them to reach as high as uuD."

She was referring to my highest frequency, the final note required to cast Expel. I asked, "Do either of you know anything more about dvinia than the one spell?"

"I don't," Kataleya said while Reuben shook his head.

"What was Leon saying to you about Fire being one note lower at the third?" I asked.

Kataleya tilted her head. "You don't know what a third is?"

Reuben added, "He doesn't even know how close Fire and Water are. I'm sure he doesn't know about a third."

"A third was mentioned in a scroll I read about dvinia," I told them. "It said that Expel is the core of dvinia and it has no third, but I couldn't figure out what that meant. There are more than three notes to Expel, so there seems to be a third to me."

"Are you talking about a scroll the *princess* gave you?" Reuben asked pointedly.

"What is going on with you and her?" Kataleya asked as well.

"Absolutely nothing."

"Are you sure?" she prodded.

"Yes. She wants to be my friend. I have no idea why."

"Oh, I have some idea," Kataleya said as she smirked at me.

Reuben interjected, "Can we please focus on what we need to do."

"It's going to take a couple hours to reach Koluk, Reuben," Kataleya informed him. "There's no need to be snippy. To answer your question, Jon, I can see how it can be confusing. Expel does technically have a third

—a third note, but that's not what Leon was referring to when he mentioned lowering a third of Water. The third note of Expel is not very important. Same with ordia spells. But with most erto spells, altering the third determines how the spell functions. It's a lot like music. Do you know anything about that?"

"That's the second time I've heard that. No, unfortunately I don't."

"You don't have to. It just would make it easier to explain, but understanding music doesn't change how you use mana." She paused as she seemed to be in thought. "I think I can best explain this with an example. Take the spell Water. It's cast with C, E, and G."

"No Uppers or Lowers?" I asked.

"No, the spell is right in the middle range. The note of E, which *un*-coincidentally is also the name of a note in music, is the third of the spell. Changing E by just a little bit *completely* alters the spell. It can even change Water into Fire."

"How?" I asked.

"You really don't know anything," Reuben complained.

"Be quiet," Kataleya snapped at him.

"I'm just saying he should have already learned this!" Reuben told her over his shoulder.

"He's learning now. Ignore him, Jon."

I felt pity for Reuben considering how obvious his feelings were for Kataleya, but he wasn't exactly putting me in a position where I could defend him.

"You asked how it works," Kataleya continued. "The vibration of mana converts energy into something else. Different vibrations convert energy into different things, and when mana is combined in specific ways, the energy behaves differently as well. Take the spell of Water, for example. If I was to change the third from E to E min, which is one note lower in frequency, then I would be casting Fire instead of Water."

"I understand."

"What's most fascinating to me is that the spell for Water is almost the same as for Air and Ice. The only difference is that they are octaves apart. Do you know what an octave means?"

"Yes, C and 1C are octaves, for example. Oh!" I practically yelled as I realized exactly what she was saying. "That makes complete sense. So the spell for Ice is the same as Water but all notes are one octave lower. So Ice is Lower C, Lower E, and Lower G?"

"Exactly," she said.

"And Air is Upper C, Upper E, Upper G?"

"Yes! And all of them have a third, actually the same third but at different octaves—E."

"What happens if you lower the third of Ice like you did to change Water into Fire?"

"Are you ready for this?" she asked excitedly.

"I am."

"Absolutely nothing!" she said with a laugh.

I chuckled. "But why?"

"Because that spell is too unstable, *but*! And I'm serious this time. Something incredible happens if you use a rev to lower the third while already casting Ice."

"So you're saying you cast the spell and then change it to an unstable state by using a rev to lower the third?"

"Exactly. Imagine I'm casting Ice." She gestured with one hand. "A block of frozen water is just starting to appear in front of me. It quickly forms into the size and shape I desire it to be when suddenly I use a rev. Lower E becomes Lower E min. Now I told you the spell is too unstable to cast. What do you think happens if I make this change while it's already being cast?"

"The ice shatters."

"Yes! The ice shatters violently. Dangerously violently, actually."

"Oh, I've been wondering how a sorcerer might injure themselves with their own spell."

"There are many ways," she said with a laugh. "But I think dvinia is different because it, like ordia, uses four notes instead of three. Altering one isn't going to cause as much of a reaction."

"Even with that explanation, I still don't understand why altering the third of Expel doesn't have the same effect."

"Because of how the spell is composed. Spell structuring is extremely complicated and something I don't completely understand myself. I think Leon knows a lot about it, though. I was hoping he would teach some to us, but it doesn't seem like we're ready yet. Once someone understands spell structuring and mana better, they can compose their own spells."

I was just starting to imagine the possibilities when I felt a violent spasm on my finger.

What the hell? It shook with such ferocity that it scared me. I was a little embarrassed at the scream that came out of my mouth as it started to become painful.

I stopped my horse and jumped off. I clutched my hand against my body, trying to stop it.

"What's wrong?" Kataleya asked as she jumped off her horse and rushed toward me.

My whole hand was shaking uncontrollably now

from the force of my finger twitching.

"I don't know! It just started—" Then I noticed the metal ring on the finger that had begun this whole thing. "Damn Charlie! He's shaking the callring like it's a matter of life or death!"

But as I heard the words come out of my own mouth, my personal panic faded and a completely new panic took its place. I cursed as I met Kataleya's wide eyes with my gaze.

Reuben had turned his horse around but had not gotten off. "What is it now?" he asked snidely.

Kataleya ignored him. "What are the odds Charlie's just fooling around?" she asked me.

"Extremely slim."

"What?" Reuben asked, deadpan now. "It's Spayker's ring?"

I lifted my hand toward Reuben to show him my finger shaking uncontrollably. His eyes nearly bulged out of his head.

"Shit."

CHAPTER TWENTY-FIVE

We raced back to Newhaven. The guards were just closing the gate in between the city walls, a common occurrence at nightfall, when we came galloping toward them.

One man jumped into our path and put up his hands. "Stop!"

"Move or be trampled!" I yelled. "The king is in danger!"

He dove out of the way. The other city guards started running after us but soon gave up.

Fortunately, the streets were just about empty. The few people who were still out quickly cleared as we charged all the way to the castle.

The drawbridge was up when we arrived, which puzzled me. My adrenaline started to drain. Was this all Charlie having a laugh? That didn't seem like him. Something Michael had told me suddenly popped into my head. Could this have all been Charlie's mistake? He'd forgotten to take the ring off when—?

"Look!" Reuben said as he pointed at where the wall turned north. "A ladder."

We rode over to the tall ladder. There was a dead armored guard slumped against the wall beside it. The ladder had hooks on its top, clearly designed to attach to the parapets at the top of the castle wall.

Charlie had not summoned us by mistake.

"Kataleya, you stay here," I said as I practically jumped onto the ladder from my horse.

"Like hell I will."

"I might not be able to protect you!" I said as I climbed. "There's no telling what awaits us."

"He's right, Kataleya," agreed Reuben, who sounded to be just below me. "Stay here."

I didn't look down to check if she was coming or not as I neared the top of the wall. I halted briefly to draw my sword, then peered across each direction of the battlement. I saw no one.

"Get out of my way!" Reuben snarled.

"Quiet." I listened for sounds of enemies. "Surprise might be the only thing we have on them."

I heard a shout deep within the castle.

I climbed over the parapets and planted my feet on the merlon. I sprinted to the ramp and rushed down it. Soon I was in the courtyard, my breath loud as my heart raced. I could hear them ahead, a banging of some kind, then shouting.

I could see that the door to the keep was broken in. Where was the guard? Then I saw his body at least ten yards away as if he'd been thrown from his post. *Dteria.*

I ran into the lavish ground floor of the keep. Some of the tables and chairs had been turned over. The three fires in the enormous hearth raged. I felt as if I was being cooked, so I unfastened my cloak and tossed it off me as I made it up the stairs to the second floor where the banging was coming from.

I started past one hall, barely giving it a glance, for

I had heard nothing coming from it. But as I crossed, there was a woman with red hair who threw out her hand in my direction.

I braced myself. Dteria slammed into me.

It picked me up—it felt like I was flying—as I lost my breath.

I started to sail high and realized I was going over the damn balcony! I dropped my sword to grab the railings, catching myself firmly with both hands.

I dangled there as my weapon fell far to the ground floor. I contemplated letting go before the dark mage reached me, as she was coming at me with a knife drawn, but I would probably break an ankle or maybe worse.

"Jon!" Reuben yelled from below.

"Grab my sword!" I said as I climbed up the railings.

Suddenly I recognized the dark mage about to reach me.

"Scarlett!?"

She stopped a few yards short. "Jon Oklar? You're not supposed to be here!"

She was the very first sorcerer I had ever met. When I'd arrived in Tryn after leaving my home in Bhode, I'd asked around in hope that someone might be able to explain magic to me. She was the one who'd met me briefly in the tavern before Barrett arrived and scared her off. She'd flirted. She was older, but I had thought her to be beautiful. I almost couldn't believe she was here.

"What the hell are you doing?" I tried to step back from her, now with my feet on the floor, but she rounded on me slowly, matching my stride.

"Starting a war, of course. Why are you here?"

I ignored her question. "Why start a war? What benefit do you get out of it?"

I backed away from her faster. I could see Reuben coming up the stairs holding his sword and mine. He might be able to ambush Scarlet if she kept her attention on me, but I wasn't sure I could condone the death of this woman until I figured out exactly what was going on.

"It's not too late to join us," she said, her dagger poised to stab me.

Still backing away from her, I crossed by the hallway where the pounding ensued. A quick look to my left showed me that a large man with an ax was about to break down a door. There was a smaller man with dark hair beside him.

"Scarlett?" the man called out when he saw me.

"I have it under control," she said.

Reuben was closing in on her. The sound of his footsteps was masked by the axman slamming his weapon into the splintering wood of the door and then yanking it free.

None of this made sense. Why was the king here on the second floor instead of in a more secure room on the third? And where were the rest of his guards? I had only seen two bodies. Where was Barrett? Where was Charlie?

"I'm going to give you one chance, Jon," Scarlett said. "You don't have to die here tonight."

Reuben closed in on her and lifted his sword. Scarlet spun around and threw him back with dteria. He landed and slid along the floor. Scarlett spun back to me before I had a chance to reach her.

"Sit in the corner and let this happen, and you will

be spared." She pointed behind me.

"I can't do that," I said.

"Pity."

She suddenly lunged at me with her dagger.

I sidestepped the attack and grabbed her hand, but she pushed her other hand at me and blasted me with dteria.

The power of this woman was fearsome. I flew upward away from her.

My back slammed into a hanging painting, which came down on top of me.

I grabbed the heavy canvas and held it up as Scarlett thrusted. The blade of the dagger poked through and stopped just before my eyes.

She pulled it free. I could see her manic aggression to kill me through the small hole in the painting. I tried to get up in hopes of rushing her and possibly throwing her over the railing behind her, but another blast of dteria scooped me up and pinned me against the wall.

I had not been ready for this one and completely failed to resist. My feet dangled as I tried to make myself drop, but she was too strong. She tried to get close to stab me but I kicked her attacking hand back. She stumbled backward as her spell ended.

I landed on my feet and charged her while holding the wide painting in front of me. There was a flash of light as a stream of fire shot out at me. I held up my makeshift shield, the fire licking around the edges, and slammed it into her, lifting her up against the railing.

I couldn't get her high enough to get her over the railing. She had stopped casting, but it was too late. The painting was now on fire. I had to drop it and back away.

She had a look of malice as she panted for breath,

the tips of her red hair singed black. Then she lifted her hand and shot another stream of fire at me. I darted around her in a wide half circle. I knew that if I just kept moving quickly I wouldn't be burned too badly.

Soon she had exhausted herself, her arms hanging as she struggled for breath. She held up her dagger defensively. Reuben appeared at my side and handed me my sword.

I wished I had some way of detaining her, but it seemed like the only way to defend ourselves against her magic would be slaying her. She turned and ran the opposite way along the balcony. We chased after her, with me ahead of Reuben.

I was just about to catch up and stab my sword into her leg when she turned and swiped wildly with her dagger. I leaned back to avoid it and then started my counterattack, but she jumped over the railing as my sword bounced off the wooden barrier where she'd just been.

Reuben and I watched her fall face down, her arms spread as if hoping she could soar like a bird. Right before she hit the ground, however, her momentum shifted. Her body was scooped upward as she turned in the air and landed miraculously on her feet.

Dteria, I realized. She had used it on herself to stop the fall in a way that was surely practiced. She started running toward the stairs, her dagger still in hand.

"I will deal with her," said Reuben, his bravery coming as a shock. "Stop the other two."

"All right. Be careful."

We rushed back toward the stairs, but I stopped and turned down the hall. The axman was putting his strength into a final swing that collapsed enough of the door for him to fit through.

He and the dark-haired man jumped back as a sword jabbed out from the room and nearly caught one of them. The hand holding the weapon was not human.

Grufaeragar! I realized. The king probably wasn't even here. They had come to kill the krepp! The war they were trying to start was between us and the krepps.

I watched the dark-haired man fling his hand through the air, and I heard Grufaeragar shriek. I couldn't see into the room from here, but I heard him crash into something. The axman and the sorcerer entered the room as I charged down the hall.

The krepp's quarters, I soon found, were similar to mine in the apartments. There was considerable space to walk around, but our two enemies already had Grufaeragar—and Charlie, I saw—cornered on the opposite side as the entrance.

Grufaeragar dodged a slow and lethal strike from the axman. He was about to stab the large bearded man in retaliation, but the sorcerer tossed the krepp against the wall.

"Hey!" I yelled as the axman was about to strike the pinned krepp. Both enemies turned toward me. I got low and turned my shoulder as I prepared to resist the sorcerer. He cast at me.

The blow was devastating even considering how well I had been prepared. I was thrown back as if I were weightless, sliding nearly the entire distance of the room.

Dteria wasn't as hard as brick. The dark energy was even somewhat cushiony. It felt like a carpeted floor had been turned sideways and slammed into me, but that didn't make it any easier to overcome.

Charlie jumped on the back of the axman, but the much larger man threw him off easily. As I was getting up and charging again, the axman was lifting his blade to kill Grufaeragar.

The dark mage held the krepp against the wall with the invisible energy. Grufaeragar's arms were spread, trapped, as he spat and kicked, but he couldn't reach the axman. I wasn't going to get there in time!

"No!" I yelled as the axman struck the krepp.

However, the ax head slipped off the handle. Only the wood hit the creature in his strong chest.

"The hell?" the axman muttered as he looked at his headless weapon, the metal head partially melted at his feet.

"Metal mage!" the sorcerer yelled. He aimed his hand in Charlie's direction.

Charlie collapsed to the floor under the barrier of invisible dteria. He squirmed but couldn't get out. The sorcerer was about to drive his dagger down into Charlie's chest. I assumed the dark mage would have to let the dteria disperse first, but Charlie still had no way of defending himself in time.

I blasted the sorcerer with a huge force of dvinia against his rear end. He staggered forward, then started to fall. The krepp caught the sorcerer with his blade, the other end of it coming out through the man's back.

Grufaeragar kicked the dying man off his weapon and slammed his feet with each step toward the axman, who now only had a stick as a weapon.

The axman tried to turn and run. I was prepared to stop him. We could detain and question him because he didn't appear to be a fire mage, but Grufaeragar leapt incredibly far and landed on the man's back.

"Wait!" I yelled, as Grufaeragar stepped off him and lifted his blade.

He ignored me. I had to jump back to make sure I wasn't hit as the krepp struck, taking off the man's head by his neck.

I was stunned by the gruesome sight. Was all this over now?

"Reuben!" I yelled as I remembered. I darted out of the room.

I saw him slumped against the wall near the top of the stairs. There was a puddle of blood around him, but he was alive as he held his hands over his leg. Kataleya crouched over him. Scarlett was nowhere in sight.

I ran to them. "What happened?"

"She's running through the courtyard!" Reuben said. "Don't let her escape!"

I rushed down the stairs and passed into the courtyard. I could see her climbing the ramp to the battlements. She was far ahead, but I might be able to catch up. I sprinted as fast as I could. I wasn't even sure I could win a match against her on my own, but I couldn't let her escape freely.

She passed by where the ladder had been and kept running. Soon she jumped off the wall and fell out of my view. I was still a ways behind. Where was the damn ladder? I must've missed it. I went back.

Then I realized what had happened. I looked over the edge and could faintly see it against the dark ground in the night. She had pushed it off so that I could not use it.

She was gone.

I started back toward the courtyard, but an image

was making its way from my memory into my fore-thoughts. There had been a considerable amount of blood around Reuben.

I cursed as I sprinted back. "Healer!" I yelled. "We need a healer!" There had to be one in the castle, right? What was protocol for a serious injury on the castle grounds? Why hadn't any of this been covered? Leon was a terrible instructor! Even the king seemed woefully unprepared. If it was ignorance that led to Reuben's death, I would...I would...I didn't know what I would do.

"Healer!" I yelled again across the empty courtyard.

Kataleya was yelling to me as I entered the keep.

"Jon! I can't stop his bleeding!"

"Where are the bandages?" I screamed as I ran up the stairs.

"Oh god," Reuben was muttering fearfully. "*Please*, Kat. Don't let me die."

"I don't know what to do!" Kataleya yelled.

There was so much blood around Reuben, his pants completely red. Charlie and Grufaeragar were watching, doing absolutely nothing.

He was going to die unless I did something. Kat was in my damn way.

"Get back!" I snarled as I pushed her. She fell away from me as I crouched in front of Reuben's leg.

Kataleya screamed at Charlie, "Where is the cloth I told you to get, you stupid fool!"

"I...I..." Charlie seemed to be in complete shock. Kataleya ran off with a curse.

"Where's the wound?" I asked Reuben. There was just so much blood.

"Here." He pointed at his left thigh.

I found the deep gash in his leg, blood flowing out.

I closed my eyes and shut out the world. I found F quickly, and I already had uF at my disposal. I knew I just had to use them at the same time. It was like casting Expel, but with only two notes. F was the tricky one. I had never combined it with anything, but I could use uF so easily that it was like throwing a ball. All I had to do now was manipulate my mana into uF and F at the same time, then cast. It was like throwing two balls at once, and the one with my left hand was the one I actually had to aim.

I put my hand over Reuben's wound. I could tell people were talking to me, but I paid no attention. I mentally prepared the spell like preparing to do a flip, something I had never done before, though I knew exactly how it should work. Eventually, I was ready.

I pushed out F and uF at the same time. I felt something click within my mind, like coming to a realization even though no thoughts were present.

The spell was an incredible force, a beast that wanted to be released from my grasp as soon as I began to use it. I could feel the healing energy coming out from my mana, directed by my hand over Reuben's wound. I gasped from the strain. It felt as if someone had just dumped a boulder onto my chest and I was trying to hold it up.

I gave it everything I had as Reuben screamed in agony right in my ear. I wanted to tell him to shut the hell up, but a single word would break my concentration.

The strain was too much. I couldn't breathe. My vision blurred. Why the hell was this spell so demanding?

Was I doing it wrong? No, it felt right.

I knew I would pass out at any moment, but I still kept pushing. The worst pain was somehow in my jaw. My teeth, I realized, and tried to tell myself to relax before I broke a tooth. Everything was dimming.

I had completely lost control, the spell finally coming to an end. I tried to take a breath, but it seemed that I didn't even have the strength to breathe.

CHAPTER TWENTY-SIX

I awoke with a startle. It didn't feel as if much time had passed, but I was not in the same place.

I was sitting up in the arms of someone with extraordinarily uncomfortable bulging muscles. The balcony slowly came into focus. I realized I was leaning against Grufaeragar's chest as he sat on the ground. I was still panting for breath. Reuben was about five yards ahead of me, still sitting in a pool of his own blood, but some color had returned to his face.

Kataleya was crouched over him holding his wrist, checking his pulse. I leaned off the krepp.

"You good, Jon?" Grufaeragar asked.

"I am."

"I catch you when fall. I bring you here. No blood on nice shirt. Only pants."

"Thank you." I got to my unsteady feet.

Charlie was where I'd last seen him, standing and staring at Reuben and Kataleya. I doubted he had uttered a word even after I'd passed out.

I crouched near Reuben. "Are you all right?"

"I think so. My leg's not bleeding anymore."

"You still lost a lot of blood," Kataleya said. "You should lie down. Can we help you to your bed in the apartments?"

"Use mine," Grufaeragar said. "It close."

Reuben nodded. We helped him up carefully and supported him as he walked down the hall.

"I'm sorry," Charlie said. "I'm sorry, Kataleya. I'm sorry, Reuben. I'm sorry!" He sounded as if he might cry.

"It's all right, Spayker," Reuben said. "I'm going to be fine."

Charlie took a few breaths and seemed mostly better.

I was starting to realize what I had done. I almost couldn't believe it. The thought of needing to cast that spell again terrified me. I had never felt a strain like that. I didn't even want to practice it, but I knew I would change my mind eventually.

I figured that I wouldn't have been able to heal Reuben if his injury had been anything worse than a cut. I was sure I hadn't even fully repaired his leg, perhaps just closed the wound. He might still have a slow recovery ahead of him, unless Leon or I helped him heal later, if such a thing was possible. There was still a lot to learn.

"How does your leg feel?" I asked.

"Stings somewhat." His voice was quiet as he held a look of shock.

"Tell us what happened, Charlie," I said.

"The princess allowed me to visit the library, so I was already here in the keep. Then I heard a man's scream from outside the castle. I became nervous so I looked out the window. I saw three people make their way onto the battlement, presumably from a ladder. That's when I knew there was going to be an attack. I started calling Jon using the callring."

"I felt it. What about Leon or the king? Where are they?"

"Leon left with the others shortly after the three of you rode out. The princess told me her father was not expected to return today. He and Barrett have been meeting with nobles all day about the replacement of the captain of the guard. When I saw the invaders, I yelled, 'There's an attack! There's an attack!' However, it was too late for the guard outside the keep. He was asleep during his duty. It was the death of him.

"He awoke to me shouting and tried to get in the keep. I'm sure he would've barred the door, but he was tossed away from it with dteria because the sorcerers were close by then. They killed him quickly. I assumed the princess was upstairs in the most fortified room and her guards are still there now. I wasn't sure I would make it there in time, and I wasn't sure they would let me in if I did. So I entered Grufaeragar's room instead."

"Grufaeragar!" the krepp echoed, though I had no idea why. Perhaps he was just excited to hear his name as part of the story.

"Uh, yes. We barricaded ourselves in the room," Charlie continued. "I hoped the princess's guards would take care of the sorcerers, but then they started chopping down our door, and that's when I realized they had come here for him." Charlie inclined his head in Grufaeragar's direction.

"Why they want kill me?" the krepp asked.

I answered, "They wanted to start a war between your krepps and us. If you died here in the castle, you would never return to your krepps to tell them we have honor. Your krepps would assume that we were responsible for your death and would attack us."

"*Karudar! Barshets!*" He spit on the floor. I hadn't understood either word, but I imagined they were pretty bad. "Who are they humans?"

"You saw they were using dteria, the cursed magic?"

"Yes, dteria! Cheat magic." He spat again. "I win with no dteria! *Barshets!*"

"I knew one of them," I told the others.

"The red-haired woman?" Reuben asked. He was standing weakly with his arm around Kataleya as she supported him.

"Yeah, when I first visited Tryn I was asking everyone I met if they knew a sorcerer who could help me understand magic. She was the first person who was going to speak with me, but Barrett arrived soon after. He scolded her as if she had done wrong not informing him about a recruit, but I had barely shared a few words before he came. I didn't know anything about her. To see her here, trying to start a war with the krepps, makes me wonder who exactly she's loyal to. I hope it's not the lord of Tryn, who I thought had an idea about all the sorcerers in his town."

I didn't add that the lord of Tryn was the same man who my father was allegiant to for so many years, the same man Scarlett had said she was working for. It had to have been a lie.

"What happened in the fight between you two?" I asked Reuben.

"I almost had her, but then her dteria pinned me. She cut my leg while she held me down. Kataleya showed up and struck her with water and knocked her over. By then, we could hear the men dying who had come with her. It was clear she was alone then, and she fled."

"Your water is strong enough to knock someone over?" I asked.

"Yes," Kataleya said. "I should've come earlier."

"It's fine," Reuben said.

"No," she said with a rigid stare into his eyes. "It's not."

Charlie said, "I bet that woman is working with King Frederick of Rohaer. If the krepps went to war against us, then Rohaer would barely have to lift a finger to take the kingdom after the fighting was over."

"That would make sense," I said. "Except that she has been in Tryn for a while, I believe."

"Who else could she be loyal to if not Rohaer's king?" Charlie asked.

"What about Cason Clay in Koluk? We were supposed to be meeting Leon's friend. Perhaps she has information about this kind of corrupt betrayal. You know, we could still make it before sunrise if we leave now. I know you can't, Reuben," I said as he started to open his mouth. "And I'm just realizing that Kataleya, you should stay with him. I could go alone, though."

It was silent.

"It's decided then," I said. "That means I should be leaving now."

I hoped our horses were still outside the wall and hadn't wandered off. That made me realize something.

"I'm not sure how I can get down off the castle wall, though. I'm not about to go open the drawbridge, even if I knew how."

"I know of some rope in the keep," Charlie said. "I can pull the rope back up after you're finished."

"Let's do that. Go get the rope."

He darted off.

"Are you sure, Jon?" Kataleya asked. "You've never been to the city before."

"I saw the map. It won't be hard to find the tavern." I paused as I really thought through it. Yes, I could do this. "I don't want to miss this opportunity."

"We go fight enemies?" Grufaeragar asked.

"No, I go find friend. That friend will help us fight later."

"I understand. Need Grufaeragar?"

"Thank you, but it's easier alone." I couldn't imagine going unnoticed when taking a krepp into the city.

Charlie ran back with a long rope. "Ready?" he asked.

I didn't feel like leaving again so soon, but time was against me. "Yeah."

We started jogging down the hall.

"Jon," Reuben said weakly.

I stopped and turned around.

"Thank you. Really. Thank you."

"Of course," I called back.

"Wait, Jon," Kataleya said. "Change your pants and boots. You have blood all over you."

Normally I wouldn't care in a time like this, but I was trying to remain inconspicuous. "I don't have another pair of boots."

"Take one of mine," Reuben said. "I have a few pairs by the hearth in my room."

"Are you sure?"

"Yes, go."

Leaving the keep, I grabbed the cloak I'd thrown off earlier. The apartment building was right next door, but the guard's body was in my path. I felt like apologizing to him even though I knew it was foolish.

"I'm sorry," I muttered. "We couldn't get here any earlier."

Soon I found that the door to the apartments was locked. "Hey!" I shouted. "The fight's over. It's Jon Oklar. I need to get inside."

I wasn't sure if any of them knew me by name, but they should recognize me if they looked.

A woman opened the curtains of her room near the door. She was someone I had seen many times. She hurried over and opened the door for me.

"What happened?" she asked. But then she gasped as she saw the guard's body.

"Tell everyone to go into the keep. One of my friends will explain. I have to get somewhere." I took off my boots as I spoke to her. I would be changing them anyway and didn't see the point in leaving bloody footprints all across the floor.

Upstairs, I set them down outside my room hoping they would be cleaned. I did the same with my pants, undressing right there in the empty hall without a care of anyone seeing. I could hear voices and movement downstairs as the castle workers were probably leaving to find out what had happened.

I checked my hands before putting on another pair of pants. There was no blood.

When I was finished dressing, I entered Reuben's room. It looked just like mine except his clothing was everywhere.

"Someone's used to having a maid."

There were two pairs of boots near the hearth. Two were turned over and the other two lay on their sides as if Reuben had a habit of kicking off his boots from his bed. They looked to be about the same size as my shoes. I tried on the brown ones that seemed a little less assuming of wealth, though they were probably worth more than all my clothing combined. They fit a little snugly, but they would suffice.

I rushed out of Reuben's room and bumped into Charlie with a startled gasp.

"Ah! You scared me," I complained as I found my breath again.

"Ready?" The heavy rope was looped around his shoulder.

"Let's go."

I figured someone would tell the princess and the queen, if she was here, that the threat was over and let them know what had happened. Leon and the king would find out when they returned later. I'm sure they would be happy we had saved Grufaeragar, but it would be dampened when they eventually realized the same thing I was just now starting to realize.

Scarlet's words echoed in my mind: "You weren't supposed to be here." It wasn't as if she had merely seen us leaving, it was that she had known that no one was supposed to be here who could defend Grufaeragar. Someone had told her, someone who knew.

I couldn't see any other possibility besides someone in the castle was working against us. It could've been a guard, a worker, or even one of my peers.

It also meant that there was no need to hide the fact that we were training in the castle anymore, our enemies already aware of us. One of us might be the target next time.

What did that mean? Would we need constant protection as we were training? Would it be unsafe for us to leave the castle?

I reminded myself that this attack had changed nothing. Someone had already been aware of us and had relayed this information to our enemies. This didn't mean we were more endangered now than before. It meant we had always been in danger.

Now I was certain of it: The king and Leon were both in over their heads, and all of us were as well. Things had better start to change soon, or we were not going to win...whatever this was. Hell, we didn't even know who exactly we were fighting against. Hopefully a visit with Leon's friend would clear some things up, if I made it there before she left.

*****

It was a dark and cold night. I worried about what might happen to the two horses I'd left outside the castle wall as I'd taken mine and galloped down the dark street. I had worse concerns, however. The gate would certainly be closed by now.

I rode to it quickly and was glad to see a guard sitting by. Fortunately, it was easy to convince him to open it for me, probably because there were no rules about keeping citizens in the city during the night. I didn't even have to explain who I was or how important it was that I leave immediately, as I had been prepared to do.

My horse seemed to know to follow the road west with little influence from me. There was just enough light for me to see the shapes of trees and the path ahead.

Leon had referred to his friend as Jennava. I hoped she was a lot more patient than he was, because I was going to be very late to this meeting.

CHAPTER TWENTY-SEVEN

The more I thought about what happened, the more it vexed me. What about the guards in front of the princess's room? They must've heard the sounds of combat on the floor below them, and yet they didn't come. I imagine they had some elaborate defensive setup on the third floor, but defending a single room didn't matter if the sorcerers could go about the rest of the castle freely.

What if the sorcerers had wanted to kill the princess and the queen tonight? Would they have achieved it if we hadn't returned? I was certain they would've killed Grufaeragar if we hadn't taken Scarlett out of the picture. The krepp and Charlie would've had to face all three enemies on their own. The guards from upstairs should've come to help, but something told me they wouldn't have done much good if they weren't sorcerers trained to resist dteria.

Where were the rest of the troops loyal to the king? I was beginning to believe he had no army, just a number of sellswords ready for the call as long as the coin was good. Of course that didn't include the guards he employed to keep the cities in check. But in Koluk, for example, the guards might as well not exist, from what Leon had said.

Even if the king had troops ready to defend the krepp, there seemed to be no method to call them to the castle to defend against a surprise attack. I liked Nykal Lennox, but the more I learned, the more it seemed like he wasn't the capable leader I had hoped he was.

What happened to the army of the last king? They still existed...but they needed coin for their service, I reminded myself. Coin that Nykal did not have.

It was also likely that much of the army loyal to the last king was killed in the uprising led by Nykal. Many probably died on both sides. No one was eager to take up arms again. That was why Nykal could not tax his citizens immediately, as he had mentioned to Leon while I was eavesdropping. They would sooner rise up against him than pay to fund another battle.

So what had Nykal done in this predicament? He could've promised coin that he did not have and gathered an army that was just as likely to turn against him later as it was to defend Lycast. No, instead he found us, eight sorcerers. He entrusted Leon to train us, and then entrusted us to defend his kingdom.

It was no wonder he had no way of calling for help if the castle came under attack. It was us he expected to defend it. Us and Leon. But we had left this night, all of us but Charlie. We were the guards who were supposed to protect the castle and Grufaeragar.

This was Leon's fault, after all. He should've taken us out of the castle in groups while some of us stayed to defend it in case of an attack.

Could I really blame him for this ignorance, though? Any one of us could've suggested that a few stay behind just in case. I didn't know why I held Leon to a higher standard than myself. He was an incredible sorcerer, but that didn't make him a strategist. In fact, he had proven himself to be much the opposite.

That would change from now on. I would take it upon myself to ensure that not only the king and his family were protected but my peers were as well. I'd almost lost Reuben tonight. I wasn't going to lose anyone else.

First, I would meet this friend of Leon's and figure out what else we were dealing with.

*****

The city of Koluk was larger than all of Bhode but still smaller than Newhaven. I had gotten a decent glimpse of it when I came out of the forest after leaving my horse tied to one of the trees. I strongly hoped the animal would be safe so close to the perimeter of the forest.

There were two reasons I'd been able to see Koluk decently from Curdith Forest. One, the trees were close to the southern edge of the city. The forest and city were so close, in fact, that I wondered if some sorcerers might've benefited from the natural dvinia of the forest. Or did dark mages not benefit from it like the rest of us did?

Secondly, many lamps within homes were lit even at this ungodly hour of night, providing a decent view of the buildings and streets. I didn't know if the people were awake or the light just served as a deterrent to criminals, but I was glad that I could see.

It had been a long and cold ride through the night. I really hoped Leon's friend was still where she said she would be.

I noticed only one guard watching the southern side of the city. There was no wall. It was easy to get into the city without his detection. Soon I was on one of Koluk's streets headed toward Groovewater Tavern. From the little I saw—beaten-down doors, cracked walls, and one man either sleeping or dead in the street —the city, and probably many people in it, were in need of some serious repair.

Groovewater Tavern was different. It was the largest establishment I'd come across so far along the few streets I'd traveled. It wasn't a tall building, however, but stout and wide. There was a sign outside with its name painted in blue.

The tavern seemed to be closed for business, no lights on. I was careful to make sure no one saw me as I approached the door. I tried it expecting it to be locked, but it opened.

I heard movement to my side as soon as I shut the door behind me. I tried to turn toward the person, but they grabbed my hair and pushed my head against the wall with a dagger to my throat.

"White willow," I said.

"Say what?" It was a woman's voice.

"White willow!" I repeated.

"Get over here." She pulled on my shirt then pushed me by my back, causing me to stumble along through the entrance room. "Don't turn around," she said as she dropped her hand. "Just keep walking casually."

She directed me through the tavern. "There, the stairs. Go down."

I made my way down the steps. There was a door.

"Open it."

I did.

Dim light barely found us down here. I heard her follow me into the cellar and shut the door after us. It was pitch black.

A sudden bright sphere of orange light made me shield my eyes. I couldn't see the woman behind it. She walked over to a table and grabbed a lamp, then she directed the sphere of light into the lamp and soon it was lit.

I didn't know a sorcerer could make light without fire. It was good to know.

I was given my first view of her. She had gray hair that was a little curly and a lot wild, but she didn't look like an old woman. The wrinkles to her face were shallow. There were bags under her blue eyes, but I imagined my features carried the same groggy weight. It had been a long night. She might've had a pleasant face if she wasn't scowling at me.

"Took you long enough. Now who are you?"

"I'm sorry about that. My name is Jon Oklar. Leon sent me, along with two others. We were on our way when—have you heard of a callring?"

Her brow furrowed.

"Never mind," I continued. "We heard that the castle was under attack, so we had to go back. One of us got hurt. Another stayed with him, so I came here alone."

The lines across her forehead deepened. "Who attacked?"

"Tell me who you are first."

"I'm Jennava Wesher. I sent the boy who gave a note to Leon. You can trust me, Jon."

I didn't have much choice now that I was here. "Are we in danger right now?"

"Not unless we are seen by the wrong person speaking to each other." She pulled a chair out from the table and had a seat.

I took out the other chair across from her and sat forward.

"I've been here many years," she said. "Cason Clay thinks I'm loyal to him. You know who he is?"

"Leon explained that he just about runs the city rather than the lord here. He's spreading dteria?

She groaned. "I hate that term. No one spreads dteria. It is not a disease. It's time to answer my earlier question. Who attacked the castle tonight? Was it dark mages?"

"Two of them, and a large man with an ax," I confirmed. "How did you know?"

"Because dark mages like them are the reason I told Leon to send someone here."

"Why didn't you come to us?" I wondered.

"I can't be seen leaving Koluk without making my enemies aware of my allegiance to the king."

"So you're aware of his fight against dteria and corruption?"

"Of course. Everyone who matters is aware of what King Nykal is trying to do."

"Does everyone know about the sorcerers he's training?" I asked.

"Some are quickly finding out."

"How? Who is telling them?"

"I'm glad you're not dimwitted," Jennava said. "When did you find out someone is betraying you?"

"Almost as soon as I arrived over a week ago. Someone gave me an essence of dteria when I thought I was purchasing a ward."

"Did you find out who?"

"No."

"I wish I could tell you who it was. All I know is Cason is getting information about you and the other sorcerers. He's been working with the king of Rohaer."

"Why?" I asked.

"Cason would say it's because of what all dark mages want, riches and power, but I think there's something more behind his motive. We don't have a lot of time before sunrise, Jon. You must leave before then to reduce the chances of being seen. Let me tell you what you need to know—and what the king needs to know."

"Go ahead."

"Cason Clay has been organizing a small army in hopes of taking Newhaven by surprise. I assume, from what you told me about this attack, they expected the castle to have been taken tonight while the king was away. Their plan was probably to kill the guards and then let in a whole mess of others to gain control of the castle. I assume they would then use the princess and the other innocents in the castle as ransom in some way."

It was a relief we'd stopped that.

"There is a group of us here in Koluk who are not loyal to Cason," she continued, "though he believes us to be. We are fighters, but we need a place where we can be safe after our betrayal to him. That time is coming soon."

"When he plans to take Newhaven by surprise," I realized.

"Yes, but I can't say exactly when or how that will happen. I do know that a group of enemies to King Nykal have been on their way here from Rohaer for quite a while. They should arrive the day after tomorrow."

"I thought the only route between the kingdoms was snowed in?"

"The main road is, yes, but much of Curdith Forest is still an option for travel, especially when many of these troops are sorcerers who can defend themselves."

"How large a group of enemies?"

"Only Cason knows for sure, but I have a good guess. It has to be small enough that they won't be seen by Nykal's scouts but large enough to be able to take Newhaven with the rest of the men loyal to Cason here in Koluk. There are probably fifty to a hundred of them."

"Not too many."

"Yes, and that's what concerns me the most about all of this. There don't seem to be enough troops, even with all of them combined, to take Newhaven. There has to be something else to the plan, but I can't find out what it is without arousing too much suspicion. I'm supposed to be part of the team that attacks Newhaven after the group of sorcerers and soldiers arrive from Rohaer. I'm glad you stopped them from taking the castle, but there's going to be a larger battle soon."

"I don't understand something," I admitted. "Aren't there enough people in Koluk to do something when this group arrives from Rohaer? There must be others outside of your group, even if you don't know who they are."

She nodded solemnly. "And Cason knows that, so he will kill every able man or woman who can stand against him and his allies. It will be brutal."

"Kill them all?" I asked incredulously.

"Yes. All."

"That can't be true."

"It is!" she said with gritted teeth. "That's why I took the risk to notify Leon. The king *has* to do something." She spoke as if there wasn't an option.

"I don't understand why Cason wouldn't just imprison the people who could stand against him?"

"Why would he worry about that when he could kill them?"

"He can't be that callous."

"He is!" Jennava made a fist on the table. "He has lost all empathy for humankind. It's something that happens to all dark mages after long enough, and there are plenty of them here."

Could that really be accurate? Cason would really murder all these innocent people when they hadn't even stood against him?

"Jon, this mass murder will scar probably all of Lycast. That's why the king must strike first. He should gather what troops he can and take Koluk by force before the others arrive. He will have allies here to aid him once the battle begins. There will still be many innocents who'll suffer from the takeover, but it won't be as bad. By decimating Cason's army before he gains the powerful sorcerers from Rohaer, it will be easy to face Rohaer's sorcerers if they still finish their journey, but I think they might go back when they find out."

"How many people does Cason have?" I asked.

"Are you sure you can remember all of this?"

"I can remember."

She looked into my eyes for a breath, then gave a nod.

"Cason has many more people ready to fight for him

than the group coming from Rohaer. I don't know exact numbers, but many of Cason's people are mostly amateur sorcerers with a smattering of dteria and a strong taste for the power it gives them. They could be dealt with easily if they weren't intermixed with all the citizens of Koluk. The battle will be messy. Many are going to die, including innocent citizens, but it will be better than letting Cason massacre them all."

"If all of this is true—"

"It is." She slammed her fist into the table. "Doesn't Leon trust me?"

I nodded. "He does. That's why I'm here."

"Good, because many people are going to die if we do this wrong."

I knew the difference between a liar's false frustration and that of a genuine soul with a lot to lose. I had little doubt Jennava meant everything she'd said. It was my trust of Leon, who trusted her, that boosted my confidence.

But there was another option she hadn't brought up. "It's the small group from Rohaer that we should attack, not Cason," I said. "We'll intercept them as they come through the forest. We'll kill them before they reach Koluk and join with Cason. Then he won't be strong enough to take over Koluk."

"I've thought of that. The issue is that we might not find them."

"It's better to take the chance than to bring about so much death and destruction to the people of Koluk."

"Only if it works," she answered. "If you fail to find them and let them merge with Cason, there are going to be many innocents who die no matter what strategy is taken by then." I could hear in her tone that she didn't actually want to disagree, but someone had to lay out the risks.

I pushed it. "But if we do find them, then none of the townspeople of Koluk would be hurt—none of their property damaged, either." I put up my hand as she opened her mouth. "I know we might not find them, but it's clearly the best option. I'm sure you agree."

"Not entirely. If you send a large army into the forest," she lectured, "your quarry will run. They will drag you deep into the forest. They will elude you. If the chase goes on very long, then your provisions will run out before theirs. A smaller group can always last longer than a larger one."

I was stumped at that. I cursed inwardly.

"Except," she continued, "my group could come from the north and yours from the south. We could close around them."

I eyed her with a tilt of my head. "They could still run west, deeper into the forest."

"So have Nykal's troops enclose them from the southwest, mine from the northwest. They will have nowhere to go except out of the forest, where they would easily be followed. I'm sure they would rather stand and fight then lose many trying to run. We would beat them easily."

"That's only if we find them." Now I was the one reminding her of the risks. "It could all be wasted, and then Cason would know someone told Nykal about his plans."

"I'm not concerned about that. He's going to find out about my betrayal soon anyway. Finding these sorcerers in the forest is the only issue with going after them."

We both stopped to think.

"Like I said earlier," she continued, "it seems clear to me that they won't be at the edge of the forest. They won't be too deep in the forest, either, to avoid confrontations with creatures. I imagine there's only a two-mile radius of their possible route."

"That's still a big radius."

"Yes, that's the problem."

We fell silent for a long while. I wished I could use a callring to send her a message after I spoke with the king. The number of shakes could signify different decisions. But Koluk was well over the distance of ten miles that Charlie had mentioned as the limit the rings would work. We would have to decide right now.

"What do you want to do?" I asked. "You know the situation better than I do."

"I want to find the bastards in the forest and stop them before they turn Koluk into a bloodbath, but I'm only vouching for that if you think the king would agree. If you return and find out he disagrees with this plan, my people aren't going to find out in time. We will be in the forest, vulnerable."

I tried to put myself in Nykal's position. He was likely to be angry that I made any plan without his permission, but these circumstances called for one.

"He is a good king. He will do the right thing."

"How sure are you?"

"I can't be completely sure. It is only my best guess." I paused. "What do you want to do?"

She stood. "I'm taking my men into the forest. If you and Leon cannot convince the king to join us, then we will be on our own. We are likely to die without support, but we are going to fight no matter what. Make sure he and Leon know this."

"You got it."

We shook hands.

CHAPTER
TWENTY-EIGHT

I was fighting sleep during the ride back. I was glad my
horse knew the path, allowing me to rest my eyes a bit
as I rode. The sun was up by the time I arrived at the castle. I had never stayed up throughout the night before
and was glad to find out that I still felt like myself, just
tired. I wondered if uF had something to do with it, or
perhaps it was because I had been eating and sleeping so
well recently.

The drawbridge was down. There were at least ten
guards in full armor blocking the path. I recognized
one of them, not that we had ever spoken, and he recognized me as well. He made room for me as I rode
past him. Then I dropped off the horse at the stables
between the outer and inner walls and made my way
through the courtyard.

The quiet walk gave me the sense that my peers had
not returned yet from the forest with Leon. The guard's
body was no longer there, just a bloodstain on the
dirt near the apartments. I asked a worker if she knew
where the king was. She told me he was in the keep.

There were another two guards standing in front of
the door to the stone tower. I didn't recognize either of
them. They held swords and shields but no armor like

the guards outside.

They let me pass after I gave my name. I figured the king had alerted them I would be returning.

The ground floor of the keep was no longer in disarray, all tables and chairs returned to their places. There was a small crack in the floor, however, were my sword had fallen from the second floor and struck it. I had checked my sword earlier. There were no marks on the blade, just a small scuff on the handle. It reminded me that we'd had a bit of luck last night. Our enemies had not anticipated Charlie would use callrings to summon us.

I imagined we could keep our luck going by taking out the sorcerers coming through the forest today, but a fear was rolling around in my head that the king might think of something Jennava and I had not, and it would be impossible to tell her to stop the attack.

The king was at the top floor in the throne room with more guards stationed outside. I gave my name and asked to see the king, and they opened the door for me.

There was a small army of troops in the room. The king seemed to be meeting with two men who were not armed. I assumed they were nobility by the look of their fine clothing. Barrett was there as well, the king's councilman the first to notice me and point me out to Nykal. The king said something as he left the group and approached me near the door of the throne room.

I wondered why it was called the throne room when there was no throne. There was just a long table with cushioned chairs, a hearth, and a few narrow windows in the stone wall with the shutters closed. There was a dais on the other side of the room, but it was empty. I wondered if Nykal had ordered the throne to be removed, or possibly had it broken down and its parts sold.

I smiled, genuinely relieved to see him, and lowered my head in deference.

"Sire, I'm glad you're back."

"Thank you, Jon. Kataleya told us what happened. I'm very happy to hear all of you were able to save Grufaeragar from injury, or worse. Then you saved Reuben's life, I was told by Reuben himself, so I know it must not be an exaggeration. Barrett chose well by recruiting you."

"Thank you. It means a lot to hear that from you."

Nykal smiled warmly. "Now, what news from Koluk? This was Leon's idea. I'm not familiar with the woman you were to meet. He left a note for me before taking the others into the forest, but I know little."

I had a quick glance over his shoulder. Barrett and the two nobles seemed involved in their own business, too far to hear anything we said. I was a little suspicious of just about everyone now, except the king himself.

I quietly yet quickly described Jennava and the scene at the tavern, then I told the king what she had said to me about Cason Clay in Koluk and the sorcerers coming from Rohaer. I went on to describe the options we went through, and then the conclusion we came to. It didn't take long for the king to lose his smile.

"You overstep yourself to finalize a plan without speaking with me first," he scolded.

"I'm sorry, sire. I wanted to return and speak with you, but it wouldn't have been possible to return to Jennava in Koluk in time. It was mostly her idea. I do believe in it and in her, and I'm sure Leon would tell you the same. His trust in her is the reason he ordered us to go to Koluk."

Nykal let out an exasperated breath. "These kinds of things are happening all around Newhaven, Jon. This is not the first time we've heard of an attack, and this is *not* the first time we have heard of sorcerers coming from Rohaer. I have dealt with these matters before you arrived here. It is not Leon's place to make a decision on who we help, and it's yours even less. You have created a mess out of this. I expected more from you."

The anger in his voice felt like a needle in my heart. I hung my head.

"You have nothing to say for yourself?" Nykal asked.

"I respect you too much to apologize for something that I don't believe is wrong."

I looked up. His eyebrows lowered. He opened his mouth as if he might scold me, but he took a couple breaths without speaking.

"I do appreciate that you have done what you believe to be right even when it's difficult," he said. "But Jon, this is not your area of expertise. You have been brought here because of your skill with mana and sword. Barrett knew of your father. He assumed you would make an excellent swordsman and possibly an excellent sorcerer."

"Did he know my father personally?" I asked.

"I do believe they had met. Unfortunately, I don't have the time to speak with you about this any longer. I must come up with a plan. You will be informed when a decision is made."

"I hope I'm not overstepping myself to remind you that there isn't much time. We—"

"There is time," he interrupted calmly. "Take care of yourself. Your job is done for now. You will be called upon later."

Called upon...the phrase reminded me of the princess who wanted me to call upon her. "Is your daughter all right? I never got a chance to check on her after the attack. I had to rush out of the castle to meet with Jennava."

"Yes, I understand that. She's barely aware of what happened, and the queen and I intend to keep it that way. So you will, too."

"Yes, sire."

"You are excused."

*****

I awoke later to someone knocking on my door. "Jon?" a woman's voice asked.

"What time is it?" I grumbled, still half-asleep. "Come in."

Aliana opened the door and stood in the doorway as if she might back out any moment. "It's the early afternoon," she said. "I wanted to check on you. Are you —?"

She stopped as I sat up and the cover fell away from my bare chest.

"Oh." She blushed as she stared.

"Come in," I repeated as I got out of bed and went for my shirt in just my shorts. "Close the door."

She closed the door and turned her back, her head down. "Sorry if I'm intruding."

"It's fine." I put on my clothes.

She met my gaze again when I was done and her

cheeks returned to their normal color.

I knew not to be ashamed of my naked chest after all the positive attention it had earned me during my last relationship. I'd had a strict regimen of exercise for all of my teenage years. It wasn't so much to sculpt the muscles of my stomach, the swell of my chest, and the girth of my shoulders, though I did have pride in my appearance. It was to enhance my ability with sword, a weapon I still cherished more than mana.

"Has the king made a decision?" I asked.

"A decision? I just know he's speaking with Leon and Barrett about something. I don't know what."

"When did you get back?" I asked.

"This morning, a while ago. Kataleya told us everything that happened here. Jon, it was wonderful what you did for Grufaeragar and then for Reuben."

"I didn't do much for Grufaeragar. I was barely a distraction. It's Charlie who deserves most of the credit."

"You're always modest." She had a wry smile. "Are you hungry? You missed lunch."

Did she just show me a sign of interest? The last thing I wanted was to assume incorrectly and find myself dealing with a blizzard of icy expressions again. Besides, I didn't look at her in the same way as I once had.

"I had a heavy breakfast," I answered indifferently. "So you haven't heard anything about the king's possible plan?"

She shook her head, then moved the strands of hair that had fallen in front of her face. "We don't even know what Leon's friend told you. What plan are you talking about?"

I quickly filled in Aliana on the conversation between Jennava and myself.

"Whoa," she said when I was done. "I'm not sure I'm ready to fight in a battle."

"I know the feeling." It was a complete lie.

I was eager to face these sorcerers. I trusted Jennava's words to be true that this group was part of the same enemy army who had tried to kill Grufaeragar and start a war with the krepps. If we didn't intercept them, they would unleash hell on Koluk.

"Jon?" she asked as I lost myself to aggressive thoughts. "What is it? You can be honest with me."

I wasn't sure I could.

"Please," she added. "Trust me as I have you."

"I want to fight them," I admitted. "How dare they come here in hopes of overthrowing us? How dare they plan to kill hundreds of innocent people in Koluk? And how could the king even consider letting it happen? I do understand if you're scared to fight, but I want to. I know that sounds foolish, but—"

"It's not foolish at all." She said with a shake of her head. "I really admire your courage."

I took a breath to force myself to calm down. I didn't know what else to say. I supposed now that I was awake I would be waiting to hear from the king, but patience was not my strongest virtue.

Aliana played with her hands as her gaze fell. "I take back what I said."

"Take back what?"

"I do feel ready, so long as I can shoot our enemies from a safe distance." She looked at me from the tops of her eyes and formed a small smile. "I hit my first mark in the forest last night, then another two this morning. That's what I wanted to tell you when I came in here."

"That's wonderful. I knew you would soon."

"Yeah, I finally feel like I know what I'm doing. I owe you thanks for that."

"I—"

"I know you don't want to accept it, but I still want to tell you. I appreciate you helping me. I really appreciate it, I mean. None of this would've been the same for me if you weren't here."

"You're welcome," I said.

I had always been modest, something I learned from my father. But I'd also learned from him that it was better to accept genuine gratitude, not for your own sake, but for the sake of the other person.

Her dark eyes locked onto mine. She had a piercing gaze, her beauty a distraction as I tried to think of what to do now.

"I'm going to try to see the king," I said.

She seemed a little disappointed by that as she stepped back from me. "What are you going to say?"

"I have to see where he's at with his decision. There isn't much time left."

As we walked toward my door, Aliana asked, "Do you think...Eslenda might help if she knew what was happening?"

There had been so much going on, I had forgotten about the elf in the forest. "I bet you're right. That's one more reason we should attempt to intercept them."

"We might not find her before finding our enemies."

"Yes, but she might find us."

Aliana nodded.

"Does that mean you would be with me even if the king decides not to send others?"

Aliana stopped as she was grabbing the handle to my door. "Are you saying what I think you're saying?"

"It's not that I *want* to go against the king," I said with my hands up. "I just want to do what's right."

She pursed her lips and narrowed her eyes. "Jon, I think you're little *too* brave sometimes."

"That's the nicest way I've ever been called an idiot."

She laughed. "You know I didn't mean it like that."

"Would you be with me, though?" *And would the others?* I imagined Michael would, but I highly doubted Reuben or Charlie would put themselves in danger against the king's wishes.

Her expression stiffened. "I really can't say. I wouldn't want to go against the king, even if it's to do something I believe to be right. I don't think many would," she told me pointedly.

I nodded. She was probably right.

We left my room, and that's where we separated. She went to her room next door while I hurried off to the keep.

*****

I heard shouting as I reached the third floor. The door was open to the throne room, but the two guards in my way didn't let me in this time. Nykal and Barrett were still here, might've never left, but Leon seemed to have arrived recently.

"She is telling you the truth!" Leon was yelling as he pointed his finger aggressively at the king. Nykal and Barrett wore similar expressions of annoyance, though neither told Leon to calm down. "You have been right about everything so far, but you are wrong about this. There is one choice to make. We must go into the forest and help them!"

"Leon, sit down and listen to me."

"I will not."

"Sit down!" the king boomed.

Leon turned a chair around and sat down the opposite way on it.

"There are too many risks involved, Leon. We have to wait and see what happens in Koluk. If needed, we will take back the city by force and get rid of all of our enemies at once."

I couldn't believe it. "But you will destroy most of the city in the process," I interjected from the hall.

Leon stood and gestured at me. "Jon's right."

"This is not your place, Jon," the king told me.

The guards tensed in front of me, but I couldn't restrain myself. "Jennava and your other allies might die in the forest if we don't help them."

"Listen to the man!" Leon chimed in.

"Jon, you may enter the room and listen if you do not speak," the king said, too calmly for my taste. This was a matter of life and death.

I entered the room and took a chair near Leon, sitting on the edge of the seat.

"You both have put too much trust in this woman," Nykal chided us. "Leon, you haven't seen her for many years. There are problems you haven't considered. Cason could have realized she's working against him and he's fed her incorrect information. Do you see what I'm saying? This could be a trap."

"I know her," Leon said. "She wouldn't get us involved unless she was certain. She's not leading us into a trap."

"She could be," the king argued. "This woman

must've been using dteria all this time to convince Cason she's with him. Her mind could've been changed by the corrupt magic, again signifying this is a trap."

"Jon met the woman! A corrupted mage could not hide their true nature. Did you see any signs that she was like the dark mage you followed in the capital?"

I shook my head with a firm gaze on Nykal.

"If you just send a small group of skilled fighters on horseback," Leon continued, "then we can anticipate a trap easily and escape. If we don't find our enemies, we will return with Jennava and our new allies. All of us can then await your command in Newhaven. There is little risk."

"There is always risk sending men into the forest blindly!" the king replied. "Everything you say is based on rumors. We'll wait until we can confirm how many enemies we're facing and where they are. That is how we have always dealt with threats, and that is how we will continue to deal with them. We wait until they come out of the forest. If they take Koluk, so be it. The city seems to already be lost to us."

"But there are many in the city who will fight for you!" I said, unable to hold my tongue. "They will be *slaughtered*, along with Jennava's people—"

"Enough!"

I couldn't stop though, now standing. "I'm just saying they are people like me, sire, who are eager, no desperate, to fight against the same bastards who almost started a war with the krepps. Many of these allies will die if we don't stop the group from Rohaer today."

"Troops are ready for whatever may happen, but I am not sending them blindly into Curdith Forest! Neither of you seem like you will understand, so there is no point in discussing this further. It's over."

Leon stormed out, but not before slamming his fist into the wall. I got up and left after him before I said something I would regret. There was no changing the king's mind. I could only hurt myself by trying.

I was red-faced pissed off as I exited the room. Jennava and her people might die this very evening.

I caught up to Leon as he was going down the stairs. "Wait."

"There's nothing to discuss, Jon."

"You can't be serious."

He spun around to face me in the middle of the stone stairway as I stood two steps above. "Going against the king is treason." He spoke in a hushed tone through gritted teeth. "You will not be reminded of this after you come to a plan, do you understand? It's either nothing or *treason*. There's no discussion to be had with me or anyone else."

He stomped down the rest of the stairs as I stood there. Was there anything I could do without committing treason? Should I try to ride to Koluk and find Jennava's group as they left the city? No, it was too late already.

A different idea came to me. At first it felt just like a foolish and desperate attempt to get everything I wanted, but the more I thought about it, the more I realized it might actually work.

I stayed on the stairs between the second and third floor for quite some time as I thought through my plan. Yes, it should work. Nykal would have to send his army into the forest. He wouldn't have a choice.

If the king had become furious with me just for me speaking against him, this would surely lead to my hanging if it went awry. Even if it all went according to plan, I would probably be punished severely. I didn't think it would be considered treason, but I could still be thrown out of the castle.

I had to hold back tears at the very real chance of being forced to leave. I had grown to think of this place as my home, partially because I had been treated so well and had made good friends, but also because I had nowhere else to go.

I knew in my heart what had to be done, though. With dragging footsteps, I walked back up to the third floor. The only reason I thought I might get away with it was because I knew Nykal to be a caring leader. If the lives of his people had been spared, he would forgive any crime that transgressed leading up to it. It was the same reason I knew to trust Jennava. I had seen in her eyes that she had the same good in her as the king. It was something that couldn't be explained, only felt. Nykal would realize the same when he finally met her. I just hoped I was alive and not in the dungeons when it happened.

I walked around the third floor of the keep until I found the room I was looking for. The door to Callie's room was open with one guard outside. I was glad to see she was alone. She looked to be working on her studies, writing as she leaned over a desk, and yet she still wore an elegant green dress.

"Princess," I called from the doorway, her guard eyeing me.

She perked up at seeing me. "Jon, please come in."

I stepped inside. "I would like to speak to you about something in private if you don't mind."

She rushed over and threw the door closed, a spark

of joy in her eyes. "What is it?"

"It's of a serious nature, unfortunately."

Her brow furrowed. "Is there something wrong?"

"Yes, and I think it can only be resolved with your help, but some explanation is required first." I gestured at the large cushioned chairs nearby. We took a seat facing each other, Callie leaning forward.

I told her everything I wasn't supposed to tell her, starting with the attack last night—Rohaer's plan to start the war against the krepps. I then mentioned my trip to Koluk and Jennava's desperation for help. I concluded with her father's refusal to give that help, and Leon's resulting fury, as well as my own. I laid out all the options her father had and why the one he'd chosen would result in the death of many innocent people. I was honest and upfront.

She listened with a determined look in her eyes, and I thought by the time I was done that coming to her would not be a mistake.

"My father's only explanation when I asked him what I heard last night was that it was a disturbance among the guards," she said coldly. "I don't know why he keeps these things from me." She squeezed my hand. "I do appreciate you telling me. He doesn't have to know you did. But did you kill these men who tried to kill Grufaeragar, Jon? I want to know they are dead."

I was somewhat surprised to hear the princess speak like this, but perhaps this was another sign that I had come to right person.

"Two of them died, but one escaped." I gently pulled my hand out of her grasp. "Unfortunately, I didn't come here just to tell you about what's going on."

"That's right, you asked for my help. But what can

I do? My father would never listen to me over you or Leon."

"I have something else in mind," I said in a dark tone.

She tilted her head. "Something dangerous?"

"Only for me."

She thought for a moment. "Tell me what it is."

"First, let me warn you that your father is going to be furious at both of us if you agree."

"I have made him angry before, not on purpose."

"Not *this* angry, princess."

She leaned back as she pondered it for a moment. Then she leaned forward again.

"Tell me your plan."

I laid it out for her. She didn't smile as I explained it, but she didn't frown, either. She merely listened with no reaction until I was finished. The plan was actually quite simple, as most good plans were.

"Are you sure it's the right thing to do?" she asked.

"I am as sure as I can be in a situation like this one."

"What happens if we go through with it and you were wrong?"

"Nothing will happen to you."

"I know it won't!" she replied with anger. "I'm talking about you!"

The truth was I would probably be hanged, but that was only if I let them catch me after this failed. I would hope to flee and live in the forest. I could continue to fight for good from there, perhaps even convince Eslenda to teach me about sorcery. I imagined she would do a better job than Leon, but I would miss the castle dearly and my peers even more.

I wasn't about to tell this to the princess, though,

who might not help me if she knew. But she wasn't going to believe the lie that nothing would happen to me, either. Even if this went as planned, I would probably be punished. She had to realize this.

"Just say it, Jon," she whispered roughly. "You would be hanged."

I nodded.

"And you *still* want to do this?"

"It's that important."

She was shaking her head. "I don't know if I've ever met someone as brave as you."

"Let's hope it's bravery."

She looked confused. "What else could it be?"

"Stupidity, princess."

She shook her head. "No, this should work. I know my father. It is bravery after all."

CHAPTER
TWENTY-NINE

I rode toward the forest, alone. It was the middle of the afternoon. Once I reached the forest, I wouldn't have much time to find the small army from Rohaer, but I had done everything to get here as fast I could.

I had the callring and the tracker ring, but I only needed one of them for this to work. Many lives depended on me, and I had put much of that responsibility on the young princess.

I trusted her. I knew this was not a mistake. It was a good plan, but it might not be enough. A flawed plan could only succeed with luck, but a good one could still fail spectacularly without some.

Many experiences from last night were still appearing in my mind without my choice. One of the more pleasant memories was Charlie jumping onto the back of the axman who was about to kill Grufaeragar, and the ax head melting off the wooden handle right as the man struck the krepp. I had wanted to ask Charlie from what range he could use mtalia on metal, because it seemed that he had to be quite close, but there was no doubt that he could melt the metal quickly. I had not realized until then just how valuable his skill was. I wished it was something I could learn one day, along with many other spells.

I was still at a loss as to how I should focus my training if I lived after this. Even if I was expelled from the castle, I would never stop fighting against corruption. I had seen what the enemies of Lycast were like. They needed to be stopped whether I was being paid to do so or not.

I wished there were more spells known about dvinia. From what Kataleya had told me about Water and Ice, it seemed like varying the notes of dvinia could create a plethora of different spells. But also from what Kataleya had told me, it could be dangerous for me to experiment without more knowledge about mana.

I would hate to leave the castle after such a short time. I still hadn't gotten a chance to explore the books and scrolls in the library. Maybe there was something useful for me in there, considering my wide range of mana.

I reached the forest and stayed on course. I didn't know exactly where my enemies were, but I remembered what Jennava had said. They wouldn't be too close to the perimeter or too deep in the forest. There was about a two-mile radius of their possible route.

Much of my plan was based on a single assumption. I figured these were also enemies of Eslenda, and her chances of finding me were a lot higher than of me finding her or my enemies.

Eventually, I had ridden deep enough into the forest that it was time to turn north and begin my search. My horse had to keep a quick pace. I couldn't afford to slow until I found them, or Nykal's men might catch me first.

I had followed Callie out of the castle in a route

where we were seen by as few people as possible. After we'd snuck around the courtyard and gotten past the portcullis, she had convinced the stable hand to release two horses for us. She knew the man well. Callie had predicted accurately that he would ask where she was going without the protection of guards.

She'd played innocent, implying I had convinced her to join me on a romantic ride out of the castle. I would protect her from danger, so she didn't need guards.

"Don't tell my father," she'd added before we'd sped out of the castle, a retinue of guards watching us go with confused expressions.

There was not a single person in Newhaven who didn't stop what they were doing to look at the princess as we rode out of the city. It might not have been obvious she was a princess, but her wealth was clear from her expensive dress. Any enemy of Lycast would be happy to use her for ransom, even if they didn't recognize her, and her father had to assume this would be the case as he pictured me taking her through the forest on false pretenses of a romantic date.

Callie never actually left the city. She'd split off from me and visited a friend's mansion where she would hide out until nightfall. It was a friend she visited often, she'd told me. Her friend's guardians wouldn't think that Callie had come to hide from her father and the many men he would send after her. They wouldn't think it necessary to message the king.

Hopefully, Nykal's men were after me. They had probably been ordered to catch up to us before I took the princess deep into the forest and possibly encountered trouble.

The only way they wouldn't be was if Nykal had figured out that Callie was part of the plan, and I had not kidnapped her under false pretenses of romance. But even then, he still would likely send men into the forest just in case he was wrong. This should work so long as I found our enemies before Nykal's men found me. Then there would be no reason for all of us to turn back until we fought.

My pulse increased with each quarter of an hour that I rode through the forest without sight of our enemies. I eventually started to worry that they might be behind me, to the south, but I couldn't turn around without running into the soldiers the king had surely sent after me and his "endangered" daughter.

It would be evening soon. Jennava's brigade was to attack by then. Hopefully, she would wait for us to engage first and back off if we never did, but I couldn't be sure any of that would happen.

I looked through the spyglass Callie had given me. My gaze swept over the forest from one direction to another, a mist settling down between the trees.

Eventually, I thought I could make out movement far ahead. Were those the silhouettes of men?

I screamed and nearly fell off my horse as a giant face suddenly appeared in my spyglass.

"Relax, easy. Easy." Eslenda had her hands up not ten yards away from me, her accented voice sharp and clear.

Her sudden appearance had startled my horse as well, the animal grunting and rearing up. But Eslenda approached and said something in what sounded to be Elvish, and the animal quickly calmed.

"You have come alone?" Eslenda asked in confusion.

"Allies should be coming behind me. Can you sense anyone?"

She stepped away from my horse and squinted south. "No," she said.

I cursed.

"I don't understand how it is you are unsure." The wind blew her rosy white hair away from her pointed ears. "You should know if allies are behind you or not."

"What are you doing here?" I countered as I tried to figure out what to do now.

"Following my enemies, of course."

"The dark mages from Rohaer."

"They are not only dark mages."

I looked ahead with the spyglass. I was certain that I saw men now. The army wasn't too far ahead, the mist turning their bodies into shadows.

"Who else is with them?"

"You will explain yourself first—wait, now I sense men coming. Many of them."

I hopped down off my horse. *Thank god.*

"Tell me what's happening," Eslenda demanded.

I looked her over briefly, wondering how much I could trust her, or if I really had a choice. She was dressed in a brown robe. There was no telling what she might have concealed underneath. Even without a weapon, though, she could kill me quite easily. I could only hope my faith in her was right.

"Allies are ready to advance from the north. We are to attack from the south. The king didn't agree to this plan at first, so I had to trick him."

"Trick him? Your own king?"

I nodded. "He thinks I have lied to his daughter

and brought her out here on pretenses of romance. He thinks I am purposefully putting her in danger to force him into sending troops to protect us. She is safe, though, still in the capital. She helped me with the plan and will hide from her father and the guards until this is over."

"Oh, he must be furious, Jon."

"Yes, I know. Are you with us in this fight?"

"Of course. These are bad men from Rohaer. They have come to spread dteria and destroy everyone who opposes them."

I looked behind me but still couldn't see my allies. "How far are Nykal's troops?"

"Not far."

I wondered something. "How can you sense them yet you didn't sense us when we stumbled across you the last time?"

Her eyes narrowed as if insulted. "I had never been disturbed during a bath until then, Jon. There has been no reason to sense for nosy human gazes."

"I do apologize about that."

She hummed as she gave me an icy look.

"I need to ask you something completely inappropriate and wrong."

"More inappropriate than reminding me that you spied on me?"

"Yes."

"You test my patience. What, Jon?"

"Would you help me improve my sorcery if I stayed in the forest after this was over?"

She looked surprised at first, but then she seemed to understand as she took a breath. "Because you don't plan to return to the castle."

"Not if there's a chance I will be hanged."

"I understand. Let me see." She stepped close and moved her head around my face.

"Are you sensing for magical ability?"

"Quiet." She moved around me for a while longer. "Your mana is strong, but I am not a teacher, Jon. I—"

"Everyone can be a teacher with knowledge and patience," I interrupted.

"But I have little patience for you."

"That will change when you see how fast I learn," I replied quickly.

"Perhaps, or perhaps I will grow tired of teaching and taking care of you, as I'm sure I must if you stay here. It is not a relationship I wish for. They are close now." She stepped away from me. "It's time for the confrontation. You may speak of me, but I'm not going to show myself."

At that, she disappeared. Looking closer, I could see the blurred outline of her body, the forest fuzzy when I looked through her. Then she moved, and soon I lost track of her.

I sighed. She hadn't exactly said she *wouldn't* help me, but her lack of enthusiasm was clear. I wasn't sure what I was going to do. It depended on what happened.

I could hear horses coming from the southeast. I turned to face the men Nykal had sent as they thundered through the trees. Leon was at the front of the group. There had to be fifty troops on horseback behind him. Kataleya was the only other person I recognized who'd come with Leon. I wondered if Reuben had chosen not to come or if he was still recovering from his blood loss. My other friends didn't know how to ride a horse.

Then I noticed Barrett emerging from behind the ranks of men. It was a little strange to see him on a horse and not at the king's side. He wore the other tracker ring on his finger.

They stopped their horses just in front of us. "Where is she, Jon?" Barrett asked. His emotions were hidden behind a dutiful expression. I imagined the king had been furious enough for the both of them.

"I will tell you in a moment. Our enemies are just behind me," I quickly added. "You can see them for yourself." I held up the spyglass. "And they aren't aware we are here."

"There will be no fighting," Barrett said. "I'm not going to ask again, Jon." He hopped off his horse and walked toward me.

"Wait," Leon said. "You sure you found them, Jon?"

"I'm sure."

Leon dismounted and rushed over to me. He grabbed the spyglass from my hand.

"I see the bastards!"

"Give me that." Barrett took it from him. "That could be Jennava and her soldiers."

"I assure you they aren't." I knew because Eslenda had told me.

I didn't know the politics behind elves in this territory, but there had to be a good reason she chose to remain hidden. Still, I hoped she would support me if I couldn't convince Barrett on my own.

"These enemies *must* be stopped before they reach Koluk and join with Cason Clay," I said. "Or many innocent people in the city will die."

"I know the problem at hand," Barrett replied indifferently as he continued to look through the spyglass.

Many of the other men on horseback came closer. I recognized a few of them from the castle. Some started asking each other about who these enemies were. From the confusion in their voices, it was obvious that most of the men here had not heard of the option to strike in the forest and had only come to retrieve the princess.

"How many are there?" Leon asked Barrett.

"They are too far away to tell." He gave the spyglass to Leon.

Eslenda appeared near my side. "There are a hundred men," the elf said.

Many expressed their alarm through exclamations about where she had come from, but a few seemed more concerned that she was an elf.

"Quiet!" she snapped, silencing them all. "I am with you in this. You have a hundred enemies north of here. Half of them are dark mages without armor. The other half are swordsmen with no magical ability. I have been tracking them, expecting someone to come stop them for days now."

"What do the elves have invested in this?" Barrett asked.

"I do not speak for the elves but for the good of all souls." She pointed behind her. "These men from Rohaer have no other support. Their scouts are all ahead to the north. This is the right time to attack."

"I don't know about the rest of you," Leon said to the group, "but I'm going to fight with Jon and this elf. Stay back if you're scared. But know that if you do, and the rest of us lose here, you will probably face an army against whom your odds will be much worse."

"The king gave you orders," Barrett told Leon

harshly.

"The king did not believe we would find enemies without a trap. Unless you think this elf is part of the trap, you have to agree there isn't one."

Barrett looked at Eslenda.

"I can vouch for her," I said. "We've met before."

"When?" the councilman asked me.

"When Leon sent me into the forest with Aliana and Eden. She's not an enemy."

"That's good enough for me." Leon tied the reins of his horse to a tree. "I have friends ready to attack from the north," he told the group of soldiers. "I'm not going to keep them waiting longer than needed. They are vulnerable right now. All of us should go on foot from here on. All of us. Trust me."

A few men immediately dismounted. The rest of the fifty troops looked at each other with uncertainty as they stayed on their animals.

"Leon's right," I said. "If we don't defeat this group of sorcerers and soldiers here, with odds in our favor, it's going to be worse later. The only reason the king didn't send all of you after them is because he didn't think we would find them or it might be a trap." I gestured behind me. "They are just over there, and they have no idea we've come. This is an opportunity that cannot go to waste. The king will thank you for it."

Many looked at the councilman and waited for an answer.

He sighed. "Nykal will pay handsomely for your victory here, I'm sure."

Groups of men started dismounting, tying the reins of their horses to trees. Soon all were climbing down from their animals.

"You can tell them where you hid the princess now, Jon," Leon said. "I will take command of this group."

"She's still in the capital," I told Barrett. "She went to visit a friend."

"So you never lied to her in order to get her into the forest?"

"No. In fact, she helped me with the plan."

Barrett reeled back. "Of course. I'm sure I know which friend it is also." He shook his head at me. "You're going to be punished for this Jon, you must be aware. Even if this goes well from now on."

"I understand that." But I was too happy to worry. I almost couldn't believe this was happening. My plan had worked.

Now all I had to do was fight. My adrenaline started pumping.

CHAPTER THIRTY

Kataleya and Leon stopped in front of me. "There are others on their way," Leon said, "the dolts who can't ride a horse. We're not going to wait for them, though. Do you know if Jennava's people are up north?"

"I couldn't confirm it."

"Do you know if they're there, elf?" Leon asked Eslenda.

"I don't."

"Do our enemies have any archers or arbalesters?" Leon asked her.

"A few."

"How many of each?"

"Four bowmen," she said. "No crossbows."

"We can deal with that."

Barrett rode off without a look back. I checked out the others who had come here with Leon. There were a few archers, but all others carried sword, some with shield as well.

"Are there any other sorcerers with us?" I asked Leon.

"No, but we will manage." He started north, the spyglass in hand. "We walk after them! Stay quiet. Use the trees. We'll get as close as we can before we're spotted. Then we'll charge."

Soon I was walking beside Kataleya near the front, just Leon and Eslenda ahead of us.

"Did Reuben hear about the plan?" I asked her.

"Yes, he would've fought if he could've. At least that's what he said."

"Who else?"

"I'm not sure. They were all still deciding as I was leaving."

"So everyone knows what I did?"

"Word got around pretty quickly, but we all thought you had lied to the princess about taking her out romantically. Actually, I remember Aliana said that the princess was probably in on the plan. I was leaving in a hurry. I didn't hear much else."

I appreciated Aliana's comment.

I would worry about what my peers thought later. We moved quickly as we stalked our enemies. Leon and Eslenda spoke in hushed tones. From the little I overheard, it was all strategy.

Eventually, Eslenda split off and headed northwest. It was almost time to charge.

Leon explained to the rest of us, "The elf will block their escape to the west. Jon, I want you to charge from the east. Head that way now. Wait for my whistle when you're close to Rohaer's men, then rush them." Leon halted the group here. "You lot, the Stormeagles, go with this young man. He fights well and can resist dteria better than any of you, but he's going to need protection. The king will want to see him alive after this."

Ten of the men, all seemingly five to fifteen years older than me, split off with me. There were no archers in our group, but Leon had given me ten of the most heavily armored. Their house banner, a silver eagle, was painted onto their shields and armor. They looked like experienced soldiers. I imagined they had charged the king quite a lot for their services, and fighting in a battle would surely cost extra. But it would cost the king even more if we were defeated here.

It was the enemy archers who scared me the most as I hurried northwest with one look back at Leon and Kataleya. Leon gave me a hard stare, while Kataleya added a nod to her determined look. There was no going back now. I hoped Leon knew what he was doing.

One of the younger guards, a lightly bearded man who looked to be in his mid-twenties, flanked me.

"You're Jon?"

"Yes, what's your name?"

"Calvin. All of us sellswords here have done a fair amount of fighting. What about yourself?"

"Most of it has been in training," I admitted.

Calvin appeared concerned. "You might want to stay behind us."

"I appreciate your concern, but I just faced a couple of these dark mages last night. I know what I'm doing. You should be prepared to be thrown from range." I noticed the others coming closer to listen. "All of you should be prepared to be thrown."

"We've fought dark mages before as well," Calvin said. "Nasty sorcerers, but they ain't fire mages."

"Aye," agreed a large man with a sheathed two-handed sword at his hip.

"When did you fight them?" I asked.

"It was after Cason tried to convince us to join his army a couple weeks ago," Calvin said. "After we turned him down, he sent mages and archers after us when we were leaving Koluk. We lost two good men that night. The rest of us escaped. That's when we decided to offer our services at a discount to the king."

One of the older men told me, "It's a hell of a thing what you did to get everyone here."

"We ain't heard of anything like it," Calvin added. "Using a princess to make the king send his men after you." He chuckled. "I don't imagine his majesty is going to be too pleased."

"I'd rather not worry about that right now. Let's discuss tactics instead."

"Ain't much to discuss. We rush them and hope to catch them by surprise."

I tried to think of a better plan. However, there were just too many unknowns. Eventually, I accepted that this was going to be messy no matter what.

Soon we spotted our enemies without needing a spyglass. We separated somewhat so each of us could use trees individually for cover as we got closer and waited for Leon's signal. My heart beat like a drum.

The sorcerers wore heavy black robes not too unlike the brown one of Eslenda. I hoped they didn't have any light armor underneath.

My inner voice told me not to kill any of them, only maim, but I knew I had to refrain from showing mercy. As much as it would sicken me to drive my sword into the bodies of these men, they would do the same to us. And they would do the same to the innocent people of Koluk when they took the city by force. They had almost killed Reuben. They *had* already killed two of ours on their way into the great hall.

There was a sharp whistle to my left, just west of me. Our enemies spun around.

It was time to fight! My thoughts disappeared as adrenaline took over.

I took out my sword and charged, my aggression ripping a battle cry out of my throat. Calvin and the sellswords came at our enemies along my sides, the shouts of their deep voices matching mine. Leon and his larger group charged from the south. I watched fear fill my enemies' eyes. They didn't appear to know which way to turn as they tried to scream orders at each other.

Only one man faced me, a dark mage twice my age. He pulled an essence of dteria from the pocket of his robe. His fear washed away, a confident smirk turning his lips as I sprinted closer.

He tossed out his other hand in my direction. I was about five yards from him. I figured this was too far to be thrown off balance, but I didn't want to take any chances.

I found the four familiar notes of Expel and casted ahead of me. There was a gust of wind that took up leaves and dirt as the energies collided. I felt nothing.

I had nearly reached him, but he had time to cast again. I tried to cancel out the force of his dteria with another blast of my own dvinia, but it seemed to do nothing as I was scooped up, my momentum quickly reversing. My limbs flailed in the air as I tried to get my feet out under me.

I landed hard and fell on my ass. The mage charged me while I was down.

I got my sword up as he attacked with his dagger. I blocked his stab and swiped at him as I sat up. He jumped back and blanketed me with dteria, laying me flat against the ground. He didn't advance as he made a strained expression, and soon I saw why. An enemy swordsman was stomping toward me as he swung his sword up and around from his hip. There would be too much force behind the attack for me to block it while prone.

I reached my hand out from around the blanket of dteria against my chest, aimed it at the swordsman, and casted hard at his abdomen.

He flew backward and landed on his hands and knees, dropping his sword in the process. I could see the dark mage in front of me quickly tiring as I soon found the strength to physically push the cushiony energy off of me and sat up, but it swung back and rolled me over sideways just when I thought I was free.

I stabbed my sword into the dirt and held the handle to keep from rolling over as the energy tried to topple me. All around me I saw the Stormeagles flying backward away from the fray.

A few arrows sailed into and out of the large mass of enemies. One struck an enemy mage in his shoulder. He fell back, but two enemy swordsmen jumped in front of him to stop my allies charging in from Leon's direction.

Over their head, I saw Leon drop to the ground to purposefully fall underneath a dark mage casting at him. From the ground he whipped out his hand. A jet of fire lit the mage's robe. Soon the man was screaming as he fled, the fire spreading across his robe.

I looked over my shoulder at the swordsman I had knocked down. He was picking up his sword, and soon he would be upon me.

I blasted the dark mage in front of me with Expel. He stumbled back violently and bumped into an archer behind him who was aiming elsewhere, his bow falling. Finally free from the dteria pushing against me, I rose and blocked the overhead slash of the enemy swordsman.

I took control of the melee with a kick to his knee, dropping him to an easier level to deal with. I gave his sword hand a quick, deep cut. He tried to block my next attack, a stab into his chest, but he couldn't get his sword up in time.

He wasn't dead, but he was out of the fight as he fell back and lost hold of his weapon. The archer had picked up his bow and now had an arrow aimed at me. Meanwhile, the dteria mage looked pissed off, his fatigue hidden by his glaring eyes and red face. I hit the archer with my dvinia, knocking his bow out of his hands yet again, then I hardened my mana to resist the mage as he struck me with the dark energy.

It knocked me backward but didn't send me far.

I was more than irritated at having been pushed down again. Every time I fell, my life was at more risk. The mage tried to jump on top of me and strike me with his dagger, but I lifted my legs and kicked him sideways before he could get close enough.

I drove my blade into his body, glad to rid myself of him. Then I took the dagger out of his dying hands and threw it at the archer as he loaded another arrow. It struck him in the chest. He fell back with a scream, dropping his weapon for a third time.

I finally felt a moment of victory, but then I saw two dark mages about to cast at me. I cursed.

The force of their combined spells picked me up and tossed me back as if I were an old boot they wished to discard. However, I was used to flying backward by now. I got my feet beneath me and landed with a backward slide.

I let out a single breath of anger and ran back into

the fray.

Our enemies were gaining momentum as they were driving our men back, no, throwing our men back. I even watched Leon spin through the air as Kataleya shouted his name in worry.

I was glad she was keeping her distance, staying back near our few archers. One of them shot an arrow into the torso of a mage, taking him down. An enemy archer retaliated and shot back at our archers. Kataleya unleashed a wide jet of water, stopping the arrow dead in the air.

There were still many enemies. They seemed to outnumber us two to one, the dark mages hurling our swordsmen left and right. It looked as if half of the enemy swordsmen fought with blind aggression, while the other half wanted to flee north, a separation growing between the middle. It would just take a little more coordination from my enemies before they started to kill my allies. I was eager to finish off as many as I could before then, and keep up the chaos.

The dark mages all seemed eager for combat. They put themselves at the front lines, some snarling like wild dogs but even more laughing hysterically when they tossed my allies away.

I could see a number of mages and swordsmen eyeing me, but it looked as if Calvin needed help as he was pinned by the dark energy while also dealing with an enemy swordsman. I ran toward him and braced myself. Dteria struck my side, but the mages were too far, my resistance too strong. I kept up my stride and soon used my sword to intercept the swordsman who was about to strike Calvin.

I drove my blade deep into the enemy's side, then

kicked him off as I pulled my blade free. I ducked under another swordsman swinging high and jammed my sword up between his ribs. I nearly lifted him up as I turned him to block a third swordsman from striking me, the enemy's blade hitting his own man in the back.

We each stepped away, the dying enemy falling between us. The dark mage who was holding Calvin let go. I could see him working up a forceful spell with his eye on me now. I motioned one way and then went the other to move behind the swordsman coming at me, putting him between the black-robed mage and myself. The force of the mage's spell knocked his own man into me as I had my sword up and ready, impaling him.

I pulled my blade out and left him to die on the ground as I charged the mage. He tried to strike me with dteria, but he didn't have enough time to put any strength behind the spell. I jumped and turned my back toward him as the spell hit me. It did little to slow my momentum.

I landed and spun as I swung hard, taking his head clean off.

Calvin was just getting up by the time I finished taking out the four of them.

"Whoa." His eyes wide, he shot me a lopsided smile.

The victory was small and short-lived. I noticed a group of swordsmen rushing Kataleya and our archers. Our archers shot into the swordsmen, taking down one but failing to stop the five others. Kataleya put her whole body into her spell as she thrust out her hands. A stream of water shot into the body of another swordsman about to reach her. He toppled backward and bumped into another charging enemy, sending him off gait.

I charged at them from behind. My first target was a man about to reach an ally archer who held his dagger up nervously, lacking all confidence. I buried my sword into the enemy's neck as I slammed the heel of my boot into the hip of another, sending him soaring into a third swordsman. The other two were still recovering from Kataleya's disruption of water, their eyes now on me. I charged at them, but then I noticed a dteria mage just to my side.

I stopped short and crouched down, but the force was still too much. It spun me over and rolled my body across the leafy dirt. With the world sideways, it was difficult to figure out how I would block the two swordsmen I assumed were rushing me. I rolled backward and could only hope to get my sword up overhead, flinching as I expected to be struck, but all I felt was a surge of heat as I was blinded by a flash of fire in front of my eyes.

Soon the flames moved away from me, and I could see the two men darting off to avoid the stream of fire. Remi suddenly appeared at my side. The small fire mage with wild hair aimed her palms and shot out another spout of fire at the other swordsmen between us and Kataleya. Many ran to escape it, but one tried dropping to the ground. Remi shifted the fire to cover that man, burning him as he screamed. He managed to get up and run a safe distance away, his armor smoking and smoldering.

Remi collapsed to her hands and knees, her hair damp with sweat. I pulled her up. "You have to pace yourself," I said. It was the same reason I hadn't cast too many spells.

"That's easy for you to say," Michael's panting voice said from behind me. "You didn't just run all the way here from the castle." He was sweating profusely.

There was a brief reprieve as the line of enemies ahead cautiously approached us, many of them muttering to each other. To our side, the battle still raged. I noticed Leon out of the corner of my eye slicing his sword down the chest of a robed mage.

The men flinched as an arrow came from behind me and struck one enemy swordsman in his chest. He fell to his knees as he made a pained groan, his comrades looking at him in horror before they glared at Aliana coming up to my side.

She started to load another arrow. "Watch out!" she pointed to the side. I hadn't seen the two mages and a single swordsman coming behind us. All of us flew through the air together as a huge force of dteria struck. It spun me too quickly to figure out where the ground was. I hit hard on my back and side, barely managing to hold onto my sword without impaling myself.

I looked up to see men charging us, my allies on the ground. The two mages were coming from the other side. I recognized Scarlett as one of them.

They blasted us again as we were trying to get up, scattering us from each other like a passing whirlwind. I wished I could help Aliana and the others, but I had to fend for myself as I barely managed to get my blade up and stop a swordsman from cutting me in half while I was on the ground.

He went for an immediate follow-up attack. I jumped back as I got up, narrowly avoiding his blade, and now I was ready for his third strike.

I blocked it and instantly changed the momentum,

quickly disarming him using the same technique I had against Reuben by hooking my blade between his hands when he was trying to stop my overhead stab.

I was already looking for Aliana and the others as I was impaling him. Aliana was scampering away from a swordsman about to pounce on top of her with his weapon high. I put as much strength as I had into Expel, but he wasn't close enough for the spell to do much besides cause him to stumble. It gave me enough time to get there just as he regained his footing.

He turned and tried to take my head off with a wild swing. I ducked under it easily and drove my blade up through his body.

There were two other swordsmen nearby with their sights on me, and now I was in a bad position. I could feel stray gusts of dteria whipping my hair as Scarlett and the other powerful mage tossed my friends away from each other. I wanted to help, but both of the swordsmen rushed me, Aliana behind them as she ran for her fallen bow.

I dodged one attack as I blocked another, spinning around the man I blocked and pushing him into his comrade. As they stumbled together, I cut open the shoulder of one.

The other backed away as the injured man tried to attack me again, but I blocked him and made quick work of him. The other seemed nervous now as he faced me. I moved in and swiftly got past his defenses, stabbing him through the chest.

Aliana had retrieved her bow as she watched me. She seemed safe for now. Michael and Remi, however, were clearly in trouble.

Michael tried to engage with a swordsman, but one

of the powerful mages kept blasting him down with dteria. He was forced to continuously get to his feet and jump back to narrowly avoid being impaled.

Meanwhile, Scarlett had Remi pinned on her back. Remi tried to shoot fire up through the clear blanket of energy, but it just blackened the dark energy and escaped out down Remi's legs. She stopped as she screamed. Hopefully the fire was too short-lived to have injured her severely.

Scarlett let the spell go. I didn't know if it was my imagination, or if it was a combination of her red hair, green eyes, and the fire around us, but I swear I saw her eyes smoldering. I was almost sure she was about to burn Remi alive.

"No!" I shouted as I tried to blast her with dvinia.

She tensed and pulled in her shoulders. My spell did nothing. I ran to get there as fast as I could, but I wasn't going to make it.

Suddenly an arrow crossed right in front of me and nearly took off my nose. It impaled Scarlett in her chest. She gasped as she stumbled back, her eyes wide. She looked past me at Aliana, who loaded another arrow just in case. Scarlett collapsed and sprawled on the ground.

I sprinted to catch up to Michael, who was in a bad spot. He was held against a tree, pushed higher up the trunk as the dark mage in front of him lifted his arm up.

Michael flailed in hopes of freeing himself, but it was no use. The swordsman was approaching with his blade up, but Michael shot a stream of wind down at both of them.

The swordsman stumbled back and reflexively turned his head away as the dteria mage fell over.

Michael landed just in front of them, but there wasn't time for him to attack. He had to get his sword up, blocking a powerful swing from the swordsman. Michael's weapon was knocked away. I arrived and drove the point of my sword through the back of the enemy swordsman.

He fell into the tree, knocked his head, and was out cold. The dteria mage tried to spin and strike me with his spell, but I dropped flat to the ground as I'd seen Leon do and felt it whoosh over me.

Michael yelled out as he buried his sword into the shoulder of the mage from behind. I watched the man's face change from one of sure victory to shock and horror as he fell just in front of me.

Michael put an end to him by the time I was up. We turned to face the rest of our enemies, Remi and Aliana just in front of us. Leon fought confidently in the heart of the battle, our ally swordsmen flanking him.

Then I saw it, and my heart lifted. Charging into our enemies from behind was Jennava and at least fifty other troops.

There was a great cacophony of screams, steel, and death.

It wasn't a moment later that the battle seemed to be over, the enemies retreating to the west. But that's when I noticed Eslenda for the first time, a wave of fire taller than any man washing out from her and enveloping all the enemies.

Many tried to flee the other way, but my allies were there to intercept most of them. They didn't try to fight, only escape. It was easy to cut all of them down except for one mage who made it past us.

I chased after him. He was quick at first, but it was

clear he was a lot more fatigued than I was as he huffed for breath.

I caught up quickly. He wasn't a large man, so I dropped my blade and pounced on his back. He screamed as I pinned him down and pulled his arm to bend it behind his back. I put my knee on his other arm.

"Don't move," I said. "You will live if you don't fight."

He squirmed like a trapped animal, but he couldn't get me off his back. He twisted the fingers of the hand I had under control, pointing them up at me. I felt a small whiff of dteria that I easily resisted.

He squirmed some more, but soon he had no fight left and finally gave up as he panted.

I looked behind to see Michael, Aliana and Remi coming toward me.

"Got yourself a prisoner," Michael congratulated me.

"All of you will have to take him back without me."

I saw concerned looks on each of their faces. Kataleya came over to join us, the allied archers staying back to confer with the rest of our allies. Leon was speaking with Jennava and the others, out of earshot.

"Jon," Michael lectured, "you're not suggesting what I think you're suggesting."

"I am. I'm going to stay in the forest." I still hoped Eslenda would take me in, but I would fend for myself even if not.

"And do what?" Michael asked incredulously.

"Train and fight in my own way."

My peers looked at each other.

I told the prisoner, "These people are going to take you back to the castle for questioning. If you try to fight, you will be killed. Will you cooperate?"

"Yes."

I got off of him, but he was too tired to get up without help. Calvin and a few others were coming over.

"Good fight, Jon," Calvin said. "Want me to take him off your hands?"

"Please," I said.

Calvin and two other swordsmen took the prisoner off to the larger group.

"Are you sure you want to stay here?" Michael asked sadly.

"I don't want to, but it's the only way to make sure I'm not hanged."

Aliana stepped in front of me. "Jon, please reconsider. I really don't think the king will hang you."

I agreed the chance was low, but that didn't matter. There was still a chance I would die if I went back.

"This is my life we're talking about," I explained. "I can't risk throwing it away because of one man's decision, even if the chance is small."

She wore a frown, but I could see in her eyes that she understood.

"You can't really be leaving," Kataleya said.

"I wish I had a better option."

A long silence passed. I would miss my friends, but I had to leave soon before one of the king's soldiers might try to apprehend me.

"How about this," Michael said. "If he's going to hang you, he has to hang all of us."

"What do you mean?" I asked.

"You know what I mean. We won't let him do it unless he's prepared to kill all of us. We tell him this when we get back."

"Well put, Michael," Aliana agreed. "He'll have to hang all of us. We'll all tell him."

"I'm in," Kataleya said.

"Me, too," Remi added.

"I'm sure Eden and Charlie and Reuben...well, I can't say I'm sure about Reuben," Michael said. "But six of us should be enough. We'll walk back together and tell the king he has to hang us, too, if he wants to hang you, because we're not going to let him execute you for this." He lightened his tone. "Now a punishment short of dismemberment, I'm sure we can all agree that you can handle that alone, right everyone?"

A few of them chuckled as I thought for a little while.

With them standing with me, it most definitely would be enough to convince the king not to order the rope around my neck. They might not actually choose to die for me if all of us were wrong, but it wouldn't come to that with their support.

The king would be pissed, and my punishment perhaps even more severe because of this collective insubordination, but it would guarantee that I would live. We had won, after all. Now if we hadn't, or if something had gone terribly wrong, I surely would never show my face to him or his guardsmen again.

"All right," I concluded. "Let's go back."

"Yes," Michael said with a shake of his fist as the three others beamed at me.

I looked over at Leon and Jennava hugging in between many bodies. Eslenda seemed to be gone.

No one was celebrating. The scene was gruesome.

"Look at what they made us do," Michael said solemnly.

There was a long silence.

"Well, mostly Jon," Michael said in his usual jesting tone. "Hell man, I can't believe some of the stuff I saw you do."

"Yeah, you were incredible," Aliana said.

"You were all great as well. I think Leon has actually done a decent job after all."

"Come on, you idiots!" Leon yelled at us, not privy to our conversation. "We have to get out of this forest before we push our luck too far."

I was pleased to see that Jennava and her men were returning with us. It looked as if our enemies had just gotten a little weaker and our army a little stronger.

Aliana grinned at me as we walked beside each other. "I'm glad you're coming back."

"I'm glad, too, that is until I find out what my punishment is."

"It can't be that severe," she said. "We found them and we won. I don't think any of our forces were even killed."

She was right, I noticed as I looked back. There were a few walking injured, but it was as decisive a victory as could be.

"I don't know, Ali," Michael said. "You didn't see how pissed off the king was when he found out what Jon had done."

CHAPTER THIRTY-ONE

We had a few prisoners with us. I expected at least one of them to divulge something useful later. Spirits were high on our way back, except for mine. I couldn't bring myself to smile until I knew what the king was going to do with me. It did help, however, to hear my peers telling Leon about some of the things they'd seen me do during the fight. Even Calvin, the sellsword, spoke highly of me.

"I ain't never seen a man fight like you do, Jon. You never needed more than one strike. What did you say you did before you were recruited?" he asked.

Leon answered for me. "His father trained him. Have you heard of Gage Oklar?"

"Of course I have. That explains a lot."

"I didn't know my father was that well-known."

"Most people in Tryn have heard of him," Leon said.

"Did you know my father?" I asked him.

"I did." Leon's gaze drifted away from me. "Many years ago, he gave me some good advice that I should've followed."

Jennava was walking beside Leon with us near the front. "So you finally admit it?" she asked him.

"I just did, all right?"

"I never thought I'd hear you say the words."

"I've changed a lot since we last spoke, Jenna, even if it doesn't look like it."

She nodded seriously.

"How did you know my father?" I asked Leon.

All of my peers were nearby, and Leon seemed to be very aware of this as he glanced around at us. "The king told me not to speak of it, but I think he's going to be busy with Jon for a little while."

A needle fell down my spine. It wouldn't be long now before I had to face Nykal.

"I suppose now's as good a time as any to admit what really happened," Leon continued. "Let me just start by saying that I was a hotheaded sorcerer."

"*Were?*" Michael asked sarcastically. He seemed surprised at everyone staring at him. "I don't know why I speak sometimes. Please continue."

Leon glared at him a moment before looking ahead and seemingly losing himself to the memory. "I didn't know as much about the magical arts as I do now. I was rich, though. That was nice. Some of the things I could buy...but that was twenty years ago," he muttered to himself. "A lot has changed. One night I was listening to a beautiful singer. It might've been the plentiful ale or it could've been the ordia casted through her song. Whatever it was, I vaguely remember her leading me down an alley at night. I was jumped by three dark mages."

There was life in his green eyes again as he glanced around. "It was a different time back then. Dteria was not common. I barely knew how to fight against it. They beat me bloody and forced me to take them to my house, where they stole all the coin I'd accrued."

"How did you get so rich?" Michael asked.

"Helping people, mostly with water spells. There were not a lot of sorcerers in Tryn back then. Jenna and I were quite well-known." There was a twinkle in his eyes as he looked at her. She nodded back.

"Anyway, I was livid. The three dark mages didn't even bother hiding their faces when they attacked me. They thought they were invincible. I wanted to teach them a lesson, but I knew the right thing to do. I went to the guards first to see if they could help me find my coin. Because even if I could kill them, which I couldn't, it would do me no good if I didn't recover what I'd lost. That's when I met Jon's father, Gage. I'd heard of him before. He was a good man," Leon told me.

I already knew that, of course, but it was still nice to hear.

"Gage had a different opinion about dteria than the lord of Tryn at the time," Leon continued. "I wasn't the only victim of dark mages' aggression. He thought more needed to be done than just arresting them after catching them commit a crime. But Gage didn't have the lord's permission to do what I wanted to do to them, even if he hinted that he wanted the same."

Leon looked at me. "Your father later found out where one of them was living, to my surprise. Soon after, he gave me the locations of the other two. By then, many rumors of their crimes were spreading around Tryn, but there had been no evidence found against them. Gage told me to entice them to commit a crime publicly if I wanted to do something to stop them. Otherwise, I was to keep an eye on them. 'Do not kill them,' he'd said. 'It isn't the solution. They will make a mistake soon.' But I didn't agree. I wanted to stop them permanently before they hurt someone else. If I was going to do that, I needed some help. I convinced Jenna to work with me.

"We learned dteria just so we could practice resisting it. The following weeks were rough as we tried not to let the energy corrupt our minds, but eventually I felt strong enough to confront the thieves. By then I had given up on recovering the coin they had taken. Bastards had probably spent it all."

Leon had a long breath.

"I killed them individually, at their homes." He spoke quickly, as if the words were painful. "But I was caught by a guard after I finished off the last one. I remember contemplating running or even fighting, but Jon's father showed up and convinced me that my punishment wouldn't be severe if I cooperated with him. He would speak to the king on my behalf."

"This was the last king, Oquin Calloum?" Michael asked.

"Yes. As you might suspect, he wasn't as understanding as Nykal would've been. You see, Oquin valued those three sorcerers more than he valued me. He thought he could use dark mages to fight a war. So he put me in the dungeons. Gage visited me every so often. He told me he was doing what he could to bargain for my release. But Oquin was saving me for one thing, war, so I spent a long time in a prison cell."

Leon paused for a few breaths. "Anyway, I heard news of the war eventually. I figured I would be released on the condition that I fight, but next thing I knew, the castle was under attack and Oquin was ordering my cell to be opened. He claimed he was being betrayed by his own nobles and wanted me to kill all the men who were trying to take the castle from him. He put a sword in my hand. I didn't even think about it. I cut his leg so he couldn't run and killed the guards who chose to defend him. Many others did not, aiding me instead. It wasn't long after that I met Nykal for the first time." Leon paused. "He already knew who I was, and I had heard of him."

There was a long silence.

"I'm not proud of what I did in the dungeon," Leon said. "But I would do it again if put in the same position. I knew what kind of king Oquin was. I'd heard enough from a man I trusted, your father, Jon. That was long before the rebellion happened. He later stopped visiting after he told me he was retiring and moving to Bhode. He was disheartened to leave me in there, and to leave Tryn, but his wife was pregnant and he wanted to be far from Tryn, Newhaven, and especially far from Koluk. He had done a lot to fight against the dark mages by then, so he might've been targeted if he stayed. I wished him well and told him no hard feelings."

That made much more sense as to why he'd left and didn't want to go back. He hadn't told me any of this.

"During my time in the dungeon, I'd heard news from the prisoners who came and went," Leon continued. "Even the guards spoke to me about their concerns. Dteria was spreading across Lycast, promoted by the king himself. I later heard that he was arming his own people and was going to force them to march on Rohaer. Nykal's rebellion against Oquin was exactly what I'd hoped for, but the new king wasn't too keen on letting me, a murderer, go free. So we agreed that I would train his new sorcerers and fight for him. I'd never trained anyone except myself before then. I told him to find Jennava in Tryn, but she had moved to Koluk, unbeknownst to me, and was in deep with Cason. Nykal couldn't locate her. The other sorcerers Nykal did know of were too expensive for him, all of them rich already with no need to put their necks on the line."

Leon opened his hands in a shrug. "Notice how none of them are here. Where are the other sorcerers, Jenna? What are they doing to help us?"

"The few that I know of have continued to use their sorcery to enrich themselves. They never planned to fight. They would say they have no reason to join us. But even these sorcerers have only a specialized skill set, like myself. The king was right to choose you, Leon. I've never met someone who understands mana as well as you do."

"Don't flatter me, woman. You know I can't handle it. Besides, you're going to be joining me in teaching the youths here."

"I never agreed to that."

"Neither did I, at first. Just wait until you speak with the king. He'll convince you." Leon smiled with one corner of his mouth. "You're going to like him... so long as he doesn't do something heinous to our Jon here."

"He won't," Michael said, "if there's anything we can do about it."

Leon took a moment to ponder Michael's words. "You all are going to threaten your own king?" he asked skeptically.

"It's not exactly a threat if we direct it on ourselves," Michael retorted.

"Oh, I see. All right, I'm with all of you." Leon set his

hand firmly on my shoulder and gave it a rough shake. "No one's going to be hanged here."

"Thank you," I said.

"But I can't say his majesty won't make you suffer."

*****

It was night when we arrived at the castle. I'd enjoyed hearing about Leon's past. Nothing he'd said had surprised me, not even that he'd killed three dark mages. All the tidbits about my father were expected as well. At my request, my father had spoken at great lengths about the kind of work he did in Tryn, except there had been nothing about dark mages. I wasn't sure why he had chosen to kept that to himself. Perhaps he'd worried I would want to travel south and stop them, which turned out to be a valid concern given where I was now.

He did make it clear, however, that he hadn't always agreed with the lord's rules. It had probably been very difficult for him to leave Leon in prison for stopping three criminals from continuing their abuse on the city.

I would give anything for my father to still be here. He had a way with words. I imagined he would've not only convinced the king to attack the sorcerers in Curdith Forest today, but he would've led the charge.

There was a team of armored guards waiting for me in the courtyard. They apprehended me in the midst of all my peers and comrades. As embarrassing as it was, it would've been worse if I'd resisted as they hauled me toward the keep.

They led me downstairs and into the dungeon I had wanted to see the first time I had arrived at the castle.

Finally getting my wish, my disparaging voice grumbled in my head.

There was no fresh light, only a bright yellow burn from the sconces on the walls. The whole place smelled wet. I had never been somewhere more depressing, except possibly my quiet house in Bhode on the anniversary of my father's passing.

They brought me past many prisoners, all of whom were either sleeping or dead. I figured the former, as it was night outside, but I heard almost nothing from them. Only one man sat up as I crossed by. He didn't appear dirty, and his hair wasn't too long. That was a good sign. However, the misery on his face was as plain as day.

They led me deep through the dungeon until eventually there were no other prisoners in the cells we crossed. Finally they opened one and pushed me in. They closed the cell door and locked it with finality.

I hadn't had anything since breakfast except for an apple Calvin had graciously given me during the trip out of the forest.

"May I have something to eat?" I tried.

They left without looking back.

I had secretly hoped that supper would be waiting for us when we were returned and I might sneak a few bites of something before being dragged away.

The bed was hard and itchy wherever my skin touched it. I was too hungry to sleep, but I lay down anyway and closed my eyes.

I had never gone this long without a meal, and now there was nothing else to focus on. I slept here and there but never for more than a couple hours.

It was absolutely miserable.

Eventually, however, my hunger seemed to go away and I finally slept for a while.

I awoke later and knew that I couldn't sleep anymore. It was probably the middle of the next day. I couldn't imagine being tortured on top of this hunger. I didn't care if the king told me I would stay here for another day or even another week as long as I was fed.

Some of the most miserable hours of my life had gone by when I finally heard footsteps approaching. I grabbed hold of the bars of my cell with weak hands and looked out into the hall. It was a man holding a large bowl, thank god.

I felt like a starving dog attempting to contain his excitement while the man put the bowl through the horizontal opening. I noticed it was porridge as I grabbed the spoon and dug in.

I barely remembered eating it when I was done, a mess across my face. They had left me in the cell with some water, but I had finished it after waking. My tongue and sleeve would have to suffice.

I started to worry once more. If they fed me, did that mean I would be down here waiting for the king hours longer? Maybe even days?

Another agonizing hour passed before I heard footsteps again. It was the king, thank god. He had a number of men around him as he stopped at my cell and gave me a hard look.

"Leave me alone with him," Nykal said.

Soon we were. I was relieved to see him. I was almost beginning to believe that any punishment would be better than being stuck down here wondering when we would finally speak. But as he faced me, and I saw the spark of rage in his eyes, I wasn't so sure anymore.

"Do you know how scared I was when I thought you had deceived my daughter into going into the forest?" His voice was rough but controlled.

"I know you must've been worried, sire." It had been the plan.

"I knew you wouldn't endanger her, but even though I knew..." His tone was biting as he lifted his hand. "Even though I knew, I still couldn't stop worrying. Do you know why I was so worried even though I knew that you wouldn't do anything to harm her? Do you know, Jon?"

I shook my head nervously.

"Because of the man you are! I knew you wouldn't do anything to harm her—on purpose. But how was I supposed to remain calm when I imagined trouble finding you? I imagined ambushes and my daughter screaming...and worse! I can't even describe the scenarios I was forced to envision! Ordering your execution might be the only way to instill the same fear in you!"

I let down my head, too afraid to keep my eyes on him.

"I was even more furious when I realized that *this* was your purpose! You knew I would fear for my daughter's safety and send troops after the two of you. You knew it would nearly kill me to find out what you'd done. I had to protect her at all costs. You used her to manipulate me, your king!" He grabbed the bars of my cell. "And the gall of you convincing the others to speak on your behalf! Imagine my anger when nearly all of my sorcerers told me that I cannot hang you without hanging them as well!"

I looked up. *Nearly all?* It warmed my heart, but I did wonder who hadn't joined the others, picturing Reuben of course, or maybe Leon, if he'd changed his mind.

It was silent for a long while as the king blew out his rage in loud breaths.

"Tell me something, Jon," he said. "What would you have done if you hadn't found Rohaer's sorcerers in the forest?"

"I would've lived in the forest and tried to fight for you while avoiding capture from your troops."

Nykal didn't seem too pleased, but he didn't look angrier, either.

"What am I going to do with you?" Nykal asked eventually. It didn't sound rhetorical, but I still doubted he wanted me to answer him.

He gave a sigh and started pacing with his hand on his chin.

Eventually he spoke again. "I thought I would know the answer to this when I saw you, but I still don't. How am I supposed to trust you when you've done something like this?"

I knew if I opened my mouth I would be arguing with the king, which I'd learned was not something that was likely to go my way. But he had been wrong, and I had been right. Our victory had proven this. It took all of the strength I had not to point it out to him.

"Anyone who's shown even half of the insubordination you have has been removed from my service, or worse." The king spoke slowly as he gesticulated at me. "How am I supposed to let this pass? What kind of message is this going to send to the other sorcerers and everyone else in my service who knows you went against me? A statement *needs* to be made."

He began to pace. He did not face me when he spoke again.

"I was thinking of keeping you here for the entirety of the war."

"Please no," I grumbled.

"Yes, I know how that would make you feel, but all of your friends have made it quite clear that they will leave my service if I force you to stay here that long. Additionally, if the tales I've heard of your performance in combat are true, then I would be a foolish king who makes a decision based solely on pride and reputation—and I have promised myself I would not be that kind of king."

He held my gaze for a long while. Then he gave a raspy breath and resumed his pacing.

"At least even your peers agree that you need some sort of punishment." He faced me as if he had an idea. "Here's what I'm going to do. You have two choices, Jon."

"Yes, sire?"

"You can let me decide your punishment. I admit I have not come up with one yet, but be assured that you will hate it." He let the words sink in. "Or you can decide your own punishment. Right now, you can tell me something that you think is right. It must be public enough that everyone knows you are being punished for your insubordination against me. I will let you think of something now. If I find it fitting, then that will be your only punishment. If not, I'll decide."

I racked my mind. My first thought was food. My hunger had been torturous. To deny me meals seemed worse than anything I could think of short of dismemberment, but it wasn't very public and it would weaken me. That wasn't something either of us wanted. What if I only ate dishes that were tasteless but still nourishing? That was an option, but there had to be something more public. I needed to stop thinking about food for a moment.

Other comforts came to mind, like my room, my bed, the baths provided to me. Perhaps I could take only cold baths for two weeks. I had hated the one I was forced to take after first coming back from Curdith Forest with animal blood on me. But again, that wasn't public enough. I doubted such a punishment would satisfy the king.

I wasn't going to let him choose, though. I had to decide on something meaningful, yet also grueling.

I realized what it needed to be.

"I will spend two hours each night, sire, acting as a city guard of Newhaven. This will cut into the time I'm usually given to sleep. However, I will still continue my training at the same hours every day."

He thought for a little while. "And how long are you proposing you will do this?"

All right, a good sign so far. "I will do it for..." I tried to get an idea of the minimum I could go, but his expression was unreadable. "Five days," I said conclusively, hoping my tone might sway him if my words hadn't.

The king did not appear pleased.

"One week?" I asked.

He folded his arms. "Is that your final offer before I decide if I will issue my own punishment?"

I sighed. "Ten days, sire. I will still rise at the same time every morning for breakfast and a bath. I can lose two hours of sleep every night for ten days, but no more. Not if you want me to be capable of handling any other task or even making use of my training."

The king put his hand over his mouth as he tilted his head. He thought for a long while, and eventually he started nodding.

"Yes, that is fitting. It is decided. This punishment will be known to the others. The new captain of the guard in Newhaven will immediately be made aware. You will see him about your assigned location during these ten days, and I will make sure he gives you a difficult one."

"That sounds fair, sire. Was he the lord of Tryn before, the same man my father worked for?"

"Yes, you at least have that in common with him, but I'm going to make sure he doesn't go easy on you."

"I understand." An opportunity to meet him was part of the reason I had chosen this punishment.

The king produced a key and opened my cell door. I almost fell to my knees in joy as I walked toward him, but I kept myself up on shaky legs.

"I'm only going to say this one time, Jon, and only here where no one can hear us. You will not repeat this."

I lifted my head up.

"You were right and I was wrong. You have proven this today. I should've sent men into the forest. I do want to apologize for putting you in a position where you thought you had to do something as drastic as you did."

"And I'm sorry for doing that drastic thing. I swear to you that I will never do anything like that again."

"That's what I was hoping to hear." Nykal put his hand on my back as we walked. "The punishment is not because of my anger or pride. We will speak on future matters, and you will be heard." He dropped his hand and looked ahead as if I didn't exist. "None of this is to be repeated."

Did that mean he wouldn't hold onto his anger? I supposed I would find out the next time we spoke.

"I appreciate that very much, sire. I won't speak of it again."

"I expect you to put the same effort into keeping the city safe at night as you have with everything else you've done." He showed me a hard look. "But Jon, I want you tell me something honestly. Do you have feelings for my daughter? I'm not asking if you plan to act on these feelings, just if you have them."

I wondered if it was a trick question. If I wouldn't act on any feelings I might have for her, why would he care if I had them at all? It didn't matter. The truth would suffice.

"She's nothing more than a friend to me, but I fear she feels something more."

"Yes, she has made that quite clear to me. You've probably realized by now that my daughter needs to learn some humility, and I think you're the best one to teach it to her given her affection for you. Since she became a princess, she has received many marriage offers. Unfortunately, it has gone to her head."

"May I ask why you haven't accepted any of these offers?"

"Because they are too old, too unimportant, or she doesn't like them."

"I see, but how can I help?"

"My wife and I have spoiled her, I will admit. She thinks the heart of every man already belongs to her because so many have come forward. Just rebuke her affection as you have, but, and I'm deathly serious here, do not use her against me again, Jon, or you will regret it. Never again."

It was a threat that shook me to my core. "I swear, sire. Never again."

Eventually he led me out of the dungeon and back into the courtyard. I was pleased to see all of my peers were gathered nearby, Leon included. I even saw Grufaeragar standing behind everyone with a big smile on his lizard face.

"He's yours, instructor," the king said as he walked back into the great hall. "His punishment will commence later."

I was surprised when everyone applauded as I walked toward them. I felt my cheeks grow hot.

Many asked about my punishment right away, so I explained it to them.

"Not too bad," Michael said as he shook my hand and patted my back.

Kataleya hugged me right after.

Grufaeragar slapped me on the back as we were parting. I stumbled but caught myself before falling. "They tell Grufaeragar what happen! Great fight, human Jon! I want fight but no horse. King make me stay. I'm too important! No hurt Grufaeragar!"

"You *are* too important," I agreed with a smile. This would've been all wrong if he'd gone and been killed in the fight. I was glad the king had convinced him to stay.

"Soon I go home," Grufaeragar said. "I tell krepps that humans here have much honor. Humans in Rohaer much *dishonor!*"

"When are you leaving?" I asked.

"I not know. Soon."

"All right, just warn us before."

"I will."

"Jon." Reuben had his hand out toward me.

I shook it with pride.

"I wanted to go, however I still must recover before I can fight again." The spark of his eyes showed his desperation for me to believe him.

"I'm glad you didn't force it." He might not have told the king that he would have to be hanged as well if I was, but I appreciated that he at least had wanted to fight with me.

Remi seemed to come out of nowhere, throwing her arms around my torso for a quick hug with the side of her head pressed against my chest.

"I'm glad you're back," she said quietly.

She slipped away before I had a chance to return it.

"Thank you," I told her.

Charlie squeezed me in the exact same way right after. "I'm also glad you're back!" he said with a lot more enthusiasm.

"Thank you," I said as I patted his back.

Eden embraced me next. "How was your trip to the dungeon?" she asked sarcastically. "Meet any nice people?"

"No. And the view was terrible."

She laughed.

I saw Aliana eyeing me. She approached and opened her arms. We embraced each other, Aliana holding on tightly.

"Really glad to have you back," she said.

"Thank you, Ali. I'm glad to be back."

"All right, enough of all that," Leon announced as she let go. "We have a lot of work to do, sorcerers."

It was the first time he had called us that.

END OF BOOK 1

AUTHOR AND SERIES INFORMATION

To receive an email when the next book is released, click here and enter your email. Your email address will never be shared, and you can unsubscribe at any time.

If you're considering leaving a review, please do so! They are very important to the life of a book, especially for a self-published author like me.

If you want to discuss the book with me or just want to say hello, email me at btnarro@gmail.com or look up my Facebook page (B.T. Narro) and add me. You can also visit my website at www.btnarro.com.

For more information about my other books and series, visit my author page on Amazon and check out my "About" section.

Thank you for reading. I hope you enjoyed the book!

The next book is *Hunted Sorcery (Jon Oklar Book 2)*

Made in the USA
Middletown, DE
28 January 2021